I0589514

DEDICATION

In memory of Claire Isabel Wallace
November 27th 1925 – July 30th 2015

TOBIAS

Author's Note

This has been the most difficult book to write.

It is written essentially from Tobias' point of view and I wanted him to be able to articulate the physical and emotional aspects of being small.

I went into it knowing nothing about life for people who have achondroplasia and my first steps were to google it. In so doing I found Jenovesia Porteo – *www.dwarfaware.com* – who has been so generous with her time and information.

The modicum of evidence available from the Middle Ages is that little people were viewed from two standpoints. In the noble halls, they were admired and cosseted as pets. There were those too, who by dint of erudition and wit, could make a name for themselves and become wealthy in their own right. Then there were those within uneducated and poor communities where a little person was viewed with scepticism and most often with fear.

For my purpose, Tobias had to experience all of that with honesty, and without me, the writer, being patronising.

Tyrian purple, the infamous dye rendered from shellfish that sets Tobias and his brother on their journey, was indeed highly protected. How often supplies made their way out of Byzantium in the twelfth century has been hard to identify. Thus I used fictional licence.

Mention should also be made of the Limnos icon and its miraculous tears. They are a figment of this author's imagination. There are, however, icons in existence that inspired the beautiful icon in this narrative.

Researching twelfth century Constantinople has also been immensely difficult. Much was wantonly destroyed in the Fourth Crusade and the Ottoman Conquest and so I have taken what remains and turned the facts to my advantage where possible. The formerly Byzantine Christian churches in Istanbul were converted to mosques after the Ottoman conquest and it requires a new mindset to imagine a city without graceful minarets punctuating the skyline. There has however, been wonderful three dimensional modelling done of the city at that time (*www.byzantium1200.com*) and it has been my go-to reference on a daily basis, once the narrative had reached the city.

In respect of the Patriarchal palace in the 1190's, much time was spent studying maps and information because there is no real archaeological evidence of where the eastern orthodox patriarch's palace was, beyond a vague description 'to the south of Sancta Sophia'. My adept and intuitive friend, Simon, gave me an idea that it should be relatively close to the Augusteoin and the Great Palace and so I placed it to the close south west of Sancta Sophia.

In addition, as mentioned in the acknowledgments, my friend Jane V, who has lived in Istanbul for many years, walked Tobias' steps many times and tried very hard to find the unfindable. In the end, a fiction writer must make a call and so this I have done in respect of the recreation of twelfth century Constantinople.

Zoë Komemna is a fictional character. In the 1190's, there was no Zoë Komemna although there have been others through the Komemnoi history. I wanted a female character connected to the Komemnoi by marriage and thus Zoë was created.

It must also be mentioned that Tobias and others swear repeatedly in this novel – as one would expect tough men to do. My guide for medieval swearing has been the excellent book, *Holy Shit – a Brief History of Swearing* by Melissa Mohr.

Tobias is a minstrel and frequently compiles songs and lyrics in his head. The site *www.poetryintranslation.com/PITBR/French/FromDawnToDawn. htm#_Toc246327967* has been a superb reference for the troubadour tradition.

Amongst many beautiful poems, I chose the words from Ges quar estius by Peire Vidal (1175-1205). History claims he was an Occitan troubadour who was much favoured in Toulouse, Aragon and Montpellier. I also used his career to create the character Passebru for the short story 'Troubadour' which was illustrated and published by *www.bopressminiaturebooks.com* in 2014.

I also used the words of Peire Cardenal, another who sang for Raymond de Toulouse and spent most of his life in Montpellier. The words to describe the galley master, Ahmed, came from the piece, Vera Virgina Maria.

Tobias also reflects on his brother, Tomas, with the words from Farai Chansoneta Nueva by the father of the troubadour tradition, Guillaume IX de Poitiers (1071-1127) – most suited because he was the grandfather of Eleanor of Aquitaine and great grandfather of Tommaso's hero, King Richard I of England.

CHARACTERS

*denotes actual historical figures

Tobias Celho – dwarf minstrel and spy for the House of Gisborne
Tomas Celho – twin brother of Tobias, also a minstrel and a spy within the same house
Sir Guy of Gisborne – renegade knight of the Plantagenet court,
freelance spy and now a merchant

Lady Ysabel – wife of Sir Guy
William of Gisborne – the young son of Sir Guy
and Lady Ysabel and Tobias' friend
Guillaume of Anjou – Sir Guy's half brother

Richard I – King of England
Eleanor of Aquitaine – Mother of Richard I

Saul Ben Simon – Jewish merchant and friend of the Gisbornes
and a business partner with Sir Guy
Ariella – Saul's daughter
Mehmet al Din – physician to the Gisborne household
Ahmed – galley master of Durrah and sea captain employed by Sir Guy of Gisborne
Faisal – second in command aboard Durrah

Pietro Vigia – Genovese trader/merchant
Father Giorgios – priest from the Myrina church on Limnos
Anwar al Din – Mehmet's brother and a physician
to the minor nobles within the imperial Byzantine court
Sophia – Anwar's wife
Father Symeon – priest from Sancta Sophia, Constantinople
Zoë Komemna – wife of John Komemnos and former slave
Candida Komemna – twelve year old daughter of Zoë

Isaac II Angelos – Byzantine Emperor
George II Xiphillinus – Patriarch of the Byzantine Christian Church

'The strong man is one who controls himself when he is in a fit of rage.'

Sahih Muslim, Book 32, Hadith 6313

Chapter One

×

The fist pummelled into Tomas' jaw, his head jerking sideways, his teeth splitting his bottom lip.

'Son of an arse for a mother!' the little man shouted. 'Boiled arse of an excuse for a drunkard!' He ran between his opponent's legs, turning swiftly, balling his hands to punch up at the soft parts before the thug could turn around. As the fellow made to turn, he stumbled, fell and hit his head hard on the edge of a protruding paving stone.

'Tomas, leave it!' Tobias called in German as he grabbed his brother's fist. Around them jeers and calls goaded the small man. 'Leave it, I said.' Toby grasped his brother's arms, pushing him ahead, kicking his backside and shouting 'Move it, get going and fast if you value what's left of your face.'

Surprisingly Tomas ran as the attention transferred to the unconscious drinker, Tomas laughing and whooping all the way down the street until the two pulled into a Venetian alley of shadows, far from the ruckus.

'What in Christ's name is wrong with you, Tomas?' Toby's voice could have lit a fire.

'Ah, leave it brother. The idiot was asking for it.'

'How so? He was in his cups and could barely speak.'

'He called us freaks of nature,' Tomas dragged a corner of his ripped tunic up to his lip and patted it and then tried to see the clot of blood that resulted. 'That we should have been drowned at birth. I was insulted and defended our honour. So what?'

Tobias sighed. This was nothing new – that their dwarf-sized physique should be so disparaged. They had been insulted in similar ways since birth. But they dealt with it and moved from success to success, impressing noble halls across France, Spain and the Holy Roman Empire with their musicality. Toby had oft said that music lowered drawbridges and smoothed out wrinkled souls.

Tomas' voice dripped sarcasm as he wiped his bloodied face. 'Anyway, since when did you become so righteous? Have you not noticed how dull our lives have become of late? I did not sign up with Gisborne to be nurse to a precocious child!' He hoiked up some blood and spat.

Sir Guy of Gisborne had found the twins, one in the Capetian court, the other with the Hohenstaufens, both in interesting circumstances, and recognizing their innate talent and how he could put their identical looks to valuable use in noble courts, he signed them to spy for him.

'Secrets sell, Tobias,' he had said. 'Kings will pay a fortune for the right ones. But beware; secrets breed enemies. You will have to create a hundred identities, you and Tomas. Maybe even a hundred more.'

Tobias and Tommaso had looked at each other and grinned. They loved their music, but to colour it with such subterfuge? They shook Gisborne's hand and began the best performance of their lives. Disguised as different people, they inveigled themselves separately into courts far and wide, for dwarf-sized court-entertainers were in demand. They never sang together again of course, except within the Gisborne villa in Venezia, and to any who wondered, the Celho twins from Pigna had died in an avalanche in a mountain winter. Which made this latest fracas where they were together in the public eye, something Gisborne would never tolerate.

The fighter coughed and spat more blood.

'Jesu, Tomas,' Toby began to walk away, knowing his words would be liver bait. 'These days I barely recognise you.'

Tommaso called out, words bouncing off the alley walls. 'Recognise me? Recognise *me?* Huh! You're the one who's as softened as a pile of loose shit. Creep away then, turd.'

Toby turned back, facing his swaying brother who leered at him. Cool-headed and clear-thinking, Toby brought up a swift under-cut, knuckles connecting with a square unshaven jawline – a perfect knockout punch that sent Tomas reeling back to slide down the alley wall. Toby danced around flapping his hand and swearing at his unconscious sibling.

'Tomas,' he hissed as he grabbed the slack form. 'I swear, Tomas, if you don't straighten yourself out, I will, I will…' He grunted as he pulled at a limp arm. Anyone who knew him as a minstrel and close friend of a young child would not have credited him with the strength with which he heaved his brother over his shoulder, beginning the laborious task of finding a punt for them both. The bells of the fledgling Saint Mark's rang across Venezia, reminding the population that Vespers was upon them. The echoes pealed and finally quieted, whereupon the only sound was the sigh of a dull breeze that chivvied he and his load back to the villa.

He hated treating his brother so. He was not in truth a violent man given to excesses – not unless it was with word or melody. Not that he couldn't handle a sword, a knife or his fists and be quick about it. But by and large he preferred peace, despite that his work for Gisborne could be anything but. He told himself that espionage allowed him to observe the best and worst of human nature for his music. But knocking out his own brother was not a thing of which he was proud. Nevertheless, what he hated more was the fact that Tommaso had changed from being his mirror image to someone else entirely.

The next day, as Tobias ran down the stair to the stable, Gisborne roared from the balcony of the villa. 'Tobias, get here! Now!'

Tobias stopped and looked up. Gisborne stood motionless, a towering presence filled with barely controlled rage. Toby climbed back up, barely able to meet Gisborne's eye.

'Where's your brother?'

'I have no idea, my lord.'

In fact he did know – snoring and sleeping off the grape under a blanket on a pile of straw in the darkest corner of the stable.

'What in Christ's name did you both think to do yesternight?' Gisborne asked, his blue eyes as chilled as a mountain stream. The two men had moved into Lady Ysabel's solar, the room empty of anyone else, and when the door rattled, Gisborne yelled, 'Be gone!'

'My lord, Tomas was drunk and fighting. I sought to prevent an incident.'

'Tomas is always drunk lately. And better to let the incident happen than be seen together. You effectively ruin any likelihood of being useful in the future.'

'My lord, I wore a hooded cloak. I spoke German and I yanked him into the shadows. We were gone whilst everyone crowded round the fool who had knocked himself out.'

'In the name of all that is holy, I have only ever asked for two things from both of you. One is loyalty and the other is discretion, and yesternight…'

'Yesternight my brother erred and I tried to remedy things. If I failed on your behalf then I apologise.'

Gisborne stood so still. Sometimes Toby wished he'd walk back and forth when he was angry. The stillness was terrifying – like the silence before a torrential storm. 'I was asked about my drunk *imp*, Toby. He has incurred damages for which the authorities say I must pay. *That* is how inconspicuous he was. And I said to the authorities, *You mean my wife's fool.* Yesternight you were *both* fools. What surprises me is that whilst I expect behaviour like this from Tomas since Aquileia, I do not expect it from you. It appears you both played the role of *fool* to the hilt!'

'Then I am glad we are still good actors, sir, if nothing else.' Tobias boiled with the unfairness of it all.

Gisborne threw himself into a groaning leather-slung chair. 'Toby, I have given Tomas a long leash since his near drowning with King Richard. But many men almost die in service and have to deal with it. He must smarten up without you sweeping the ground after he has soiled it. It has to stop. I am of a mind to throw both of you back into hard work where you have to think on your feet, instead of playing nursemaid to my son.'

''Tis what Tomas said, my lord…'

'Did he indeed?'

Toby studied his master – the sharp-faced, keen-eyed man who stole secrets and made fortunes. 'You must do what is right for your enterprise, my lord, but I do swear, no one knew I was in the shadows and Tomas merely perpetuated the idea of my lady's fool. Surely all is well, is it not?'

'It is if all the witnesses were in their cups and blind with it. I gather they were not. Leave me now and I shall see you both at dinner.'

'My lord,' Toby bowed and left, furious with Tomas, angry at Gisborne and dearly wanting life to be quiet and uneventful.

The excesses of the night before barely registered with Tomas later in the day, so used to drinking had he become. As to Toby's role in the bruise on his jaw, he remarked laconically, 'Christ's fingernails, brother, I must have drunk myself insensible last light. My jaw aches as if I pitched forward onto a trestle.'

'Hard luck for you, then,' said Tobias as he concentrated on outwitting Mehmet at the chessboard. If the Arab physician had an idea that the bruise on Tommaso's jaw came from bone on bone rather than bone on wood, he did not say, merely tutted quietly as Toby moved his bishop across the board.

It had been a good meal. Bridget, the villa's cook and unofficial taskmaster, had felt sick for her long gone hearth-home and had contrived a meal to remind them all of forest and field, hedgerow and hamlet in England. They sat replete. Guillaume, Gisborne's stepbrother, rubbed at his damaged leg. Gisborne sat in his habitual position, legs stretched out and hand propped under chin as he toyed with a mug of wine. Lady Ysabel, his wife, fossicked through a basket of wools, looking for a thread to suit her embroidery. At her feet, her young son, William, lay in front of the fire with the two black pups, and Ysabel's godmother, Cecilia of Upton, sat peacefully, her eyes closed; one could be forgiven for thinking she slept. And two guests, the Jewish merchant Saul Ben Simon and his daughter, Ariella, thanked Biddy for her food. It was a convivial group, satisfied with good food and content in each other's company.

'Disappointing,' Saul said much later and they all looked up. 'I've sourced some Tyrian purple dye and I would pay the asking price without negotiation but I have no one to collect it for me.'

'Tyrian purple,' said Sir Guy, his expression sharpening with interest. 'I am not wrong I think, when I say that it is one of the rarest dyes. What do you think you could sell it for?'

'A price to frighten royal treasuries.' Saul sat beside Gisborne, folding his tunic carefully away from his toes.

'And this is disappointing?'

'Gisborne, finding such dye is tantamount to finding the Ark of the Covenant. There are people who would kill to get their hands on it.'

'Go on,' Gisborne said, his voice rumbling deep within his chest. Toby looked across at Lady Ysabel as her head lifted from her embroidery, her eyes narrowing at the tone that reminded them all of danger.

'Like rare gems or Arabic manuscripts, it is highly sought after. Sale of such dye is heavily protected by the Byzantines.'

'Meaning this is outside the legal markets.'

Saul scrunched his face up. 'Yes…'

'Just like secrets,' Gisborne said. 'So what is the problem?'

'I would collect it myself, but you and I, Gisborne, have business with the Hohenstaufen court. It occurs to me that whilst there, we might just find a market for the purple. They have pretensions of grandeur. No, Ariella…'

'But…' his flame-haired daughter began.

'No. You must stay here and manage the Venetian side of business whilst I am in Germany. Besides, it is too dangerous.'

'But Guillaume could…'

'No, Guillaume could not. No offence, my friend,' said Saul, acknowledging the archer from Anjou, 'but you still limp and need to mend some more.'

Guillaume shrugged, disappointment obvious in his flattened mouth. The wound he had acquired as he defended Guy of Gisborne from his enemies had plagued him for longer than he wished.

Lady Ysabel began to stitch again, her needle shushing in and out in the momentary quiet. Mehmet moved a piece across the chessboard and Toby sighed at the sign that he could lose – yet again.

Tomas laughed. 'You toy with him, Mehmet. You tease and taunt like a fisherman with a baited hook.'

The Arab smiled and said to Guillaume, 'Saul is right. You are not fit enough yet, nor you, Sir Guy. To be honest, my lord, I am unhappy that you choose to travel north but I see I would lose such an argument.' He surveyed the chessboard and made his move. 'That said, I doubt something as sought after as Tyrian purple will wait for too long. Am I right, Saul?'

Saul's face creased with concern – the concern of the man who would make money and much of it. 'Unfortunately yes, which is why I say it is disappointing. More than disappointing.'

'Then *I* would go to collect it,' Mehmet said as he rolled an ebony knight in his hands.

'You would?' Saul's face split with delight. Or was it a form of relief,

Toby wondered.

'Of course. I have nothing to keep me in Venezia momentarily. And because these two singers do nothing just now, they could travel with me. I have heard there are those who search for a small minstrel in order to lay charges of assault and compensation. As far as I understand it, Tomas was seen by many witnesses yesternight and would stand guilty before the courts. Perhaps it is better he makes himself scarce…'

'Indeed,' said Gisborne. 'In fact I *order* them to attend you. Tomas, you are in trouble in Venezia and I don't thank you for it. Better you leave the town until things settle.'

Tobias studied Gisborne. Obviously he and Mehmet had talked and this was the convenient way out…

'But caution,' Gisborne continued. 'Disguise and immense care. You will be travelling together for the first time in an age…'

Mehmet turned to the twins. 'This is a way of avoiding the law, Tomas. You don't deserve to but I would not see a good friend in prison. Between the three of us we can collect the dye and be away from … where, Saul? Tyre?'

'No. Constantinople.'

'Ah, then I really *must* insist you allow me to collect it. My brother and his wife live in the city and I have not seen them for a long time.'

Gisborne walked to the hearth and pushed at the fire with the broken tip of a pike. 'Then the problem is solved, Saul. But Mehmet, this will be dangerous. Saul's dye is already outside the Byzantine monopoly and that alone creates tension. Should you be caught taking it from the city illegally, your life and liberty could be under threat. Be under no illusions.'

'None at all, my lord. But I am comfortable in Constantinople and do not forget I can still handle a dagger or a sword. What think you of a journey east, Tomas?'

'Well,' Tomas held his hands out. 'Let me see. Prison on the left. Constantinople on the right…' He leaned to one side as if Constantinople was weighted like heavy coins. 'No contest I think. Besides, we have nothing better to do these days and I fancy some clandestine activity. It's been a long time since my blood has rushed with excitement. Tobias, what say you?'

'Ah, well,' Toby noticed everybody in the room waiting for his reply. 'Well … I've never been to Constantinople…'

The journey was planned for the end of spring when the seas would be calmer and galleys aplenty on which to secure passage, and Saul chafed, seeing his dye disappearing to other markets, a fact he noted to Toby until the minstrel quite tired of hearing it. But then Gisborne returned from the docks before a sennight had passed to say Ahmed was in port and would provide immediate passage. As long as Gisborne and Saul agreed to him filling the hold with good cargo from which he, Ahmed, could make money.

'Ahmed? The Arab galley master? You trust him?' Tomas scoffed. 'Jesu…'

Gisborne's face became impassive, a sign of danger. 'I trust *you*, Tomas and you have stretched that trust thin of late. Tell me why I should not trust Ahmed?'

Tomas humphed, not at all put out by Gisborne standing over him. 'Then what about the sea, my lord? It will be taciturn at this time.' He coughed, a legacy of the Lionheart's sinking off Aquileia.

'You need have no fear. Ahmed is a skilled mariner and knows the waters between Venezia, Al Mahgreb and Constantinople as well as the lines on his palm. But harking back to your question, I *do* trust him and have done since long before your time. Keep that in mind.'

Toby slapped Tomas on the back. 'Come, brother, surely this is the adventure you wanted us to have.' Privately he hoped this would be a chance for Tomas to rid the Devil off his back and return to being the good brother of yore.

A farewell meal was had during which time young William of Gisborne became tearful. 'Everyone alwayth leaveth me behind,' he wailed as Toby hugged him. Toby's heartstrings stretched a little. He loved the boy like his own and had spent far more time than Tomas with the child. William's pain had always sliced into his sensibilities.

'That is because there will be no minstrel in the house and someone will have to sing for the family so you must take the place of Tomas and I. Besides, what would happen to the pups if you left them? It would be very sad if they forgot you. Tell me, how goes your sword training with Guillaume? Do you progress?'

'Yeth…' William wiped his hand under his nose and then transferred the thin trail to his tunic.

'Well then, Tomas and I need a knight to guard our *vielles*. They are as valuable to us, William, as a sword is to a knight, or a ransom is to a king. When we return, we need to know that they have been protected and that they are in good health. Are you able to do that for us?'

'Mm…' William's eyes had brightened.

'Then we can travel content that the *vielles* are in good hands, and I will bring you back a gift. What would you like?'

The child sat stroking one of the black pup coats. 'Don't know,' he said.

'Oh come now! Every young knight must want for something from far-off lands. A chess-set? A pipe?'

'Knightth don't play pipeth,' he responded scathingly. 'I would like a bow, a tharathen bow.' He sprang to his feet. 'Thank you, Toby.' He hugged the minstrel and said. 'I'll mith you and Tomath.'

And then he and the pups were gone.

Mehmet, Tobias and Tomas checked their packing, buckling swords and making sure they had forgotten nothing. Their *vielles* sat in the corner of the chamber – almost sulking, Toby felt, at being left behind.

'How long shall we be gone think you, Mehmet?' he asked.

'If all goes to plan, we shall be back within a three month. Ahmed plans a fast turnaround. Having the purple in our possession is not a thing worth dallying over in Byzantine lands.'

The chamber door was wrenched open and heads were raised as Saul rushed in, hair flying.

'Oh, the heavens be praised that you have not left for the docks, I need to talk to you privately. Mehmet, I have just received word from Constantinople from the trader who sourced the dye…'

'And?' Tomas pinched his finger on a buckle and sucked at it. 'There is something wrong?'

'Yes. Oh my, yes. Things have become awkward…' he waved a wad of parchment at them and sighed. 'These are messages from Constantinople… all delayed and months old. It seems that someone told the authorities that a smuggling operation might happen and so noses are very close to the ground. Too close. The messages tell me that the Byzantines know exactly how much dye is rendered and how much is used and made available for sale…'

'Well, that's surely the end of our little jaunt,' Toby piped up.

'No.' Saul sat and dropped the parchment wad at his feet. 'My trader contact says he has managed to avoid being caught and …'

'Then we are going?' Toby found Saul's ability to perambulate the long way round an issue quite tiresome, for all that he respected the man and had affection for him. He fixed an expression of patience on his face and waited.

'Yes…'

As he spoke, William of Gisborne could be heard in the courtyard, calling the two pups. A tick-tack of racing claws sounded on the stone cobbles as they raced after William and then a heavily pregnant silence descended in their wake.

'Tell and be done, my friend,' said Mehmet.

Saul shifted in his chair. 'The trader was hunted, Mehmet, and injured. He could be dead by now for all I know. Oh woe!' The Jew lapsed into silence, gnawing at his bottom lip.

The nub of it is coming…

'Is purple dye worth this trouble, Saul?' Mehmet asked.

'Oh yes. By the Prophets yes. And may I say sadly so.'

'What say you?' Toby asked. Evidence of real danger was not something he wanted to hear if truth were known. The last few months of placid canal living had soothed his own soul and to enter another surreptitious hunt was *almost* a little too soon.

'I paid a fortune in advance for the dye,' Saul said. 'I thought that by offering it to any of the royal courts, I suspected even a tiny scoop of the dried powder would recoup the original investment and more, simply because the dye is so rare.'

Mehmet sat with hands lying on his lap. 'What you are not saying, Saul, methinks, is that you staked almost your entire fortune on this purple.'

Saul didn't answer but his eyes told a story that made Toby shudder. 'Saul! You are a wise man with money – it's your trade. How *could*…' The words blurted out.

'Traders trade in hope, Tobias, in possibilities, in a better future,' Saul said with tangible sorrow. 'Sometimes they need to know when to stop. You ask how could I? Quite simple really – I would say base greed.'

'Does Ariella know?'

'No and she must not.'

'And Gisborne? What of his investment?'

Again Saul did not answer, but equally he did not drop his eyes from scrutiny. A brave man, thought Toby. 'Jesu,' he whispered. 'His money as well?'

'Christ,' hissed Tomas. 'Remind me not to do business with *you*...'

'Enough, I think, Tomas,' Mehmet ordered. 'Saul is well aware of the outcome if we cannot secure the dye.'

'No pressure, then,' muttered Toby.

'None at all,' grumped Tomas. 'Just the knowledge that if we fail, our employer won't be able to pay us.'

'Don't forget Saul's family will suffer too,' added Toby.

'I'm hardly likely to forget,' Tomas growled. '*Our* lives for their financial security. Excuse me.' He stalked to the door and slammed it shut behind him.

For the moment there was nothing but the sound of the villa living around them – laughter from the kitchen, singing from a chamber, the guards' banter in the courtyard – and the ever-present William and the pups.

'Forgive my brother, Saul,' Toby finally said. 'He is liverish these days.'

''Tis no matter. I deserve his disapprobation, Tobias. I...' Saul raked fingers through his iron-grey hair. The hem of his long woollen tunic had a streak of mud on its edge and his boots were caked, dried clumps falling upon the floor as he shifted his legs.

'Christ's nosehairs,' Toby said. 'This dye must be breathtaking.'

'It is,' Saul said. 'And I rue the day.'

''Tis done now,' chided Mehmet. 'And our job is all the more necessary. It is no different to other times when we have led covert operations to recover something of value to us.' The allusion to William of Gisborne's recent abduction was like an icy wind on a spring day. 'Tell us as much as you are able, Saul.'

'It appears that my friend, a man I have known forever and indeed whom I would trust *with* my life, has been set upon by some of the Varangian Guard who have been ordered to seek out the smugglers of Tyrian purple. They have been questioning the fishermen who catch the sea snails. They interrogate the renderers of the dye, the dyers, the fabric-sellers, tailors... Everyone...'

'The Varangian Guard? This dye is *that* important to the Byzantines?' Toby shuddered as he recalled tales of the axe-armed men from the far north of Europe who were legendary for their barbarism and their loyalty to the

Byzantine rulers. He couldn't imagine himself running from a Varangian Guard and living to tell the tale.

'The Byzantine Court wants it to remain under their control,' Saul continued. 'It's almost as if they measure themselves by this dye – it *is* the colour of emperors. Michael … oh, did I mention his name? Michael Sarapion was betrayed – perhaps by a fisherman or a dyemaker. Money speaks so who knows? The Varangian Guard hunted him down and he was injured but miraculously he got away with the powdered dye. His last message said that he was vanishing along the Mar Maggior coast and that he may double back to Constantinople where he can hide amongst the crowds.'

For someone like Saul who ran a vastly profitable trading enterprise, it was inconceivable that such disorganisation and disaster should eventuate but then, thought Toby, anything illegal was rarely straightforward.

Saul picked up the pile of bent parchments. 'To be honest and under the circumstances, it is a wonder he has managed to find our couriers at all. It surely proves he is a man of integrity.'

'He used *our* couriers?' Toby could barely imagine Gisborne's fury at such a thing.

'Yes. Michael is a Gisborne man like you, Tobias. It is he who has furnished so much of the information on the loosening of power within the Byzantine court, even within the Byzantine empire.'

'I'm sorry. I did not know Gisborne had a man in Constantinople, nor that the empire had problems.'

'Why should you? These last few months have been trying for everyone and you are entitled to retreat and regird. But the truth is that the Byzantines are losing traction in the Balkans and have become increasingly sensitive about anything that threatens their power base. It is not an easy place in which to sojourn these days.'

'Saul,' Mehmet said, 'do you have a location for Michael? Will we be able to find him readily?'

'No, I have no knowledge of where he is, or, as I said, if he is still alive. But I can give you the name of a woman. She is an embroiderer. She will know.'

The mission had changed in an instant, Toby thought. What might have been dangerous before was now a given.

'Saul,' he said. 'Correct me if I am wrong, but my lord Gisborne doesn't know of any of this, does he?'

'No,' the Jew replied, sagging like an emptying sack of barley. His sorrow was palpable and Toby felt a certain amount of compassion for him. He had never before been a profligate speculator who threatened friends and family.

'Then you must tell him. He is your good friend and a business partner.'

'You tell me nothing I have not been thinking since the messages arrived, Tobias. I dread his dismay.'

Mehmet stood and grasped Saul's arm, Jew and Saracen, of a height and age, learned and with mutual respect and affection. 'Honesty is the only way forward, my friend. You know this and besides, there have been many occasions through the years when Gisborne has surprised me. This might be one of those times. Seek him out whilst we convey our luggage to the yard.'

The family lined the docks to farewell their companions. Ahmed waited aboard, head tilted to the spar where the lateen sail sat tightly furled. Gisborne took the three aside, drawing them into his circle, sliding into the role of commander of a troupe of men.

'My friends, Saul has told me of his unwise actions and I will say to you that he thought quite legitimately that no harm would come to our investment. I claim that this is one of those unforeseen moments that occur in business and in life. And let us be honest. We are used to this sort of event – it is something that underlies espionage. What Saul and I would both say is that nothing is worth your lives, least of all some dye or the money that we have invested.'

Saul was speaking to a fellow merchant on shore and Toby could read much in his upright stance – a manner of calm assurance, nothing to indicate any turmoil – anything to further mercantile interest and to keep his business afloat.

'I mean it,' Gisborne emphasized, following Toby's gaze. 'Take no risks. If it looks at all as if walls might tumble and sword points await, I would prefer to sell an extra secret than lose my close friends. Including you, Tomas!'

'We heed you, Sir Guy,' said Mehmet. 'No risks.'

'Exactly so. And Tomas – I speak directly to you when I say control *your* excesses. You almost ruined your place in the network the other night and you are on notice. We want you to return to us in one piece. Not with an arm missing where you jabbed it unkindly between the legs of a Varangian guard.'

'Me?' Tomas grinned through a newly sprouted and tinted beard. 'You think I would be so careless? Why, I even have genuine papers supplying me with a name and identity. Julius…' he bowed stiffly, his accent not unlike Johannes', '… of Lübeck, disenchanted minstrel at your service, my lord.'

Gisborne scrubbed the top of Tomas' head and his mouth tilted to one side. 'Ah Tomas. You watch yourself. I mean it!' He stepped back then, a tall darkly-clad presence whose hair blew in the ocean breeze, whilst Lady Ysabel kissed each of the departing cheeks.

'Tobias,' she whispered when she reached him. 'I love you all but you have a special place in my heart. You and I have been through much. Let us continue to do so.' Her veil rippled in the seabreeze and she hugged him tight. As always, he marvelled at her growth from a tiresome free spirit into a woman worthy of respect and love. He clasped her hand and squeezed.

Finally they were aboard and the oars were pushed out with a growl of timber on timber and then an orchestrated squeak as the stroke began. The craft glided through the water of the harbour into the ocean end of the lagoon as Venezia began to disappear behind them.

For some reason Toby wished he could explain, his stomach twisted and the hairs stood on his neck. But then he decided he was merely once again becoming used to the deck under his feet. And besides, he could not foresee the future and there was little point in trying to do so.

Chapter Two

×

Vomit shot in a curdled yellow stream over the larboard side of the galley and Tomas, with a dead man's face, groaned as he laid his head on the rail.

'Come on, Tomas, buck up,' said his brother. 'It's froth and bubble, do you see? You've nothing left inside now, and Mehmet said if you nibble on this,' he passed over dry bread, 'just little bites chewed well, you'll be better in a moment. Ready to collect the dye of kings.'

'Ah, cease babbling!' whispered the sick man. 'Who gives a shit in a bucket for Saul's Tyrian purple. And it wouldn't hurt Mehmet to nurse *me* instead of spending so much time with Ahmed. Every time we leave a port, I am sick. Right down the coast of the Adriatico. I wish to hell I had never said I would come on this voyage. Leave me. Just go away and take your bloody bread and your heartiness with you!'

Tobias looked at Tomas, saw a grim line of anger pressed hard into his brother's brow by ceaseless retching and gave in. 'Please yourself,' he said. 'I'll leave you to puke alone, then.'

He turned away and walked to the stern where the captain, Ahmed, steered the vessel east toward Crete and thence to Constantinople. Mehmet stood alongside, reading a chart weighted down with a worn wooden pulley.

As Toby gazed at the seething wake, he wondered how even *he* could have agreed to board a vessel again. Not renowned for being seaworthy, he remembered the last time he'd sailed – returning from Toulon to Genova after seeking the whereabouts of William of Gisborne upon the child's terrifying abduction. Despite the fact that Toby had become well acquainted with the sides of the vessel and the weathered rail over which he leaned, it had all ended well for the Gisborne family. But as ever, some of those within their ambit had fallen by the wayside.

There had been Walter, energetic and efficient guard, and Peter, blacksmith and loyal retainer – both brutally slain by the hand of Simon de Courcey upon whom vengeance was served. Gwenny, Peter's wife and Lady Ysabel's maidservant – a babe miscarried and the young girl grieving and embittered until William's return cracked her armour. Bridget, Gwenny's mother, harder and more apt to cynicism unless she had William upon her knee. Toby had thought they would leave, flee back to England, far from the convoluted tensions of the Gisborne house, but they had stayed and let time heal.

Mind you, thought Toby, Lady Ysabel had made a wise choice inviting her godmother to live with them in Venezia. Lady Cecilia and Biddy were two sides of the same coin – tart but loving, and between them they had soothed Gwen and pieced her back together again. Along with the discrete attentions of Johannes of Lübeck, one of the guards, Gwenny had begun to smile. And just before Tomas and Toby had left on this mission, she had laughed uproariously when the household had joined in to sing:

D … drunken…
Drunken, drunken, y-dronken
Drunken is Tabart ate wyne
Hay! Suster, (Johannes and John)
Ye dronke al depe
And Ichulle eke.

Toby and Tomas had changed the names in the song – Walter and Peter were not names to be mentioned lightly. But Gwenny had sung on quite blithely, her hand for once not smoothing her belly.

Stondëth allë stillë…
Stillë Stillë stillë…
Stondeth alle stillë.
Stillë as any ston.

It was as though William's disappearance and return had prompted everyone to value each moment and be grateful to God for the privilege. Gisborne had mended, along with his milkbrother, Guillaume – the two keeping company in their convalescence and planning an arm of business that was less secret than the spy trade, a bid for merchandise and markets around Europe. But then the new business was structured in such a way as to hide the spy trade within its spiced and silk-wrapped folds – plenty of money to be had with both.

Toby glanced at the seabirds flying at eyelevel as he thought of young William, tables champion, a small knight in the making who was invariably accompanied by two strange little pups called Tristan and Iseult – or as William was apt to shout, 'Trith! Ith!' which lifted hands to mouths to hide kind laughter.

But sometimes the child's eyes flattened and Toby would sense an ugly memory emerging and so would jest or sing until the memory receded and happiness returned. Ah, he thought, so much happiness across their lives now. Ariella – a partner with her astute father and Guillaume courting her, all of them alive with the thought they could dominate the marketplace with exotic imports from the east. Which, God curse it to a point, was how Toby and Tomas ended up on this galley in the first place.

Constantinople, thought Toby, sitting on the deck, back propped against the mast. He had been to the edge of the Holy Land but in his mind it had none of the enigma of that point further north which was dominated by Constantinople. Curiosity bubbled inside him and he knew it was to be controlled, if not countered. It could oft lead him to trouble.

Mehmet sat beside him, sliding easily to sit on the deck with none of the stiffness of a man of his age. Tall, upright, his hair now was pale, almost white, and partly concealed by a grey *keffiyeh* that shifted in a rising breeze. His dark eyes burned with knowledge and a depth of wisdom that Toby had only just begun to tap. He smiled at Toby, glancing across at the twin who still knelt piteously, with head lying on the wale.

'You needn't worry. He mends by the moment. He just feels sorry for himself.'

'It is the difference between us, Mehmet,' Tobias pulled a wry face. 'Tomas can indulge himself sometimes.'

'And there are no other differences?' Mehmet asked mildly.

'None that would be seen by others,' Toby replied. 'But if there *was* any single thing apart from our hairline that marks us as separate individuals, it is that I have an innate curiosity about lives and the people living them. Tomas appears to have worn his very thin or lost it entirely. In fact he can be downright disrespectful in his mad moments and it has caused problems.'

'What do you mean?'

'I mean that when his guard is down, he can be insulting toward others, causing fights and risking his own life because of it.'

'I have not seen that side of him.'

'No, you wouldn't, because when you joined us, he was already working elsewhere for Gisborne. Remember, we are oft interchangeable for Gisborne's purpose.'

'Then does he cope with being what he is amongst those who may mock him?'

'You mean that we are oddities? That we are small and different? That we are *"Devil"* spawn?' Toby was brutally blunt.

'If you put it that way, yes.'

'He took it on the chin for a long time, knowing that our musical talent and the noble need for unusual attractions within their courts has eased our comfort in life. But lately he gets drunk amongst common men and *then* he is not so tolerant of the banter. Whereas I…' Toby shrugged, knowing full well that he could have been punch drunk with the belittling that had come the way of he and his brother. But Toby just smiled, flicked the bow across his *vielle* and danced a step and the courts in which he existed would laugh and pronounce him an excellent fellow, a brilliant troubadour.

He would not tell Mehmet that since Tomas returned to Venezia after being rescued from King Richard's sinking galley, his brother had been crisp around the edges. And bitter. As though he enjoyed pushing himself and others by goading, harsh words rolling off his tongue. Almost, Toby thought, as if he was in a state of perpetual tension and needed to expend the energy. But then he had been ill enough to die and Richard the King had left him with monks, to be cared for until the inevitable happened. Fortunately

Gisborne was that piece of inevitability. As the knight searched for the King under Queen Eleanor's orders, he found his employee – Tomas – paying for him to be doctored by the best and then sending him back to Venezia to recuperate under Mehmet's care. Such an illness, such a scare as nearly drowning would surely change the best of men.

Wouldn't it?

Whatever the case, Toby knew it was indeed why they were on the galley with Mehmet, in pursuit of the purple. It was quite simply that Tomas had been bored and craved the excitement.

Like dancing with death.

His heart skipped beats as the words sped through his mind.

Seabirds swooped in the wake of the galley, Ahmed grinning at Toby and giving him the thumbs up, yelling that some bad weather was on the way, 'Allah the Beneficent protect us! Can you feel the sea putting up its fists?'

And indeed, Toby felt the boat slew as the wind freshened, causing the sail to empty and then fill with a crack.

'The wind and weather force Ahmed's hand,' Mehmet said. 'The wind is hard on our beam which makes poor Tomas a little more unsteady too, I think. Does it not, my friend?'

Tomas crawled toward them, his hands spread white and tense upon the deck. 'I hate this boat, hate it,' he growled.

'You must have a crust, Tomas – your belly rebels with bile,' Mehmet said gently.

'I told you,' Toby said. 'Here…'

'Oh Jesu, give me the bloody stuff and if I puke it back in your laps, 'tis justice.' Tomas snatched the crust and shoved it in his mouth, burping but beginning to chew.

'Better?' Toby asked.

'Not so as you'd notice. Oh God,' he grasped at Mehmet. 'The sea gets rougher, surely.'

'Be calm, Tomas. We are not in trouble and we are not going to sink, I swear. This is a bit of a storm that will blow itself out shortly. Trust me.' Mehmet reached across and patted Tomas' knee.

'You don't know what drowning feels like, Mehmet.' Tomas stared at the rising sea. 'You want to scream but there is just water, water filling your mouth and you choke as you breathe and…'

'But you survived.' Mehmet spoke even more gently.

'If the King's hand had not reached for me as I sank that last time, I would have died, Mehmet. All I can remember are muffled shouts and as the boat sank, an horrendous pull from underneath that dragged me with it. So much water and so cold and it filled my eyes, my ears, my nose and my mouth…'

'Hush, Tomas,' Mehmet shuffled closer to the little man. 'Look at me, Tomas. Look at me!' he ordered. 'That is better. We are not in danger.'

'By the sins of the Saints, I feel cursed by the sea…'

Mehmet stood, touching Tomas' shoulder as he moved away. 'Breathe deep and slow, my friend.'

The twins sat with heads to the freshening breeze, smelling the salt air as scuds of wind blew across the deck. Toby had not heard his brother so panicked. Ever. Nor did he know that it was the King who had saved Tomas. He longed to ask more but could see that the woes must be left well alone.

'You know,' he sighed, 'Sometimes I wonder why we don't just lead a quiet minstrel's life, brother. All this secret-seeking and sword-rattling with my lord Gisborne ages one no end. Do *you* ever wish you could just settle to creating *cansos* and be done with it?'

Tomas pursed his lips, looking off into the never-ending surrounds of the rising sea, just for a moment seeming to forget his traitorous belly. 'Once, but no more. A troubadour's life is nothing but pandering to over-wealthy and unlovely egos. It has become dull and fatuous. I crave the salt as well as the sweet.'

'You do? Even after…' but then Toby bit his tongue.

'Yes. Even after nearly drowning when the King's boat sank. Once you have seen Death, spoken to it, felt its arms encircle you, nothing is ever the same. Death is a cold friend, Toby. And one you never forget meeting.' His eyes became harder as he vented. 'Venezia is predictable, I tell you. I need to get away. And whilst the sea is not where I wish to be, I am happy to see excitement in other lands. Make of me what you may.'

The wind rose further and the brothers hiked their cloaks tight, spray blowing over them. Perhaps if they had run before the wind, Toby thought, then it might have been less terrifying. But the wind was still abeam and it threatened to tip them constantly – the short sharp waves lifting them, the wind seeming to scoop beneath, waves washing over the starboard wale, swilling angrily around them.

Suddenly the boat tipped right up, almost laying itself out for the sea to swallow.

'Christ Jesu!' exclaimed Tomas, grasping the mast tightly as the sea opened its mouth. The wind roared but somehow the boat slapped back down. 'God and the Saints…' He uttered nothing else but Toby caught sight of a tiny cross on a leather thong grasped in his hand.

The storm blew from the hard northwest for the whole morning. By the time the dull light of midday surrounded them, it had blown itself to an inconsequential sigh, the sea sloppy but easier to cross. The galley floated bedraggled and steaming, Ahmed swearing for a night sky and the stars to plot his course. He ordered the sail unfurled and shifted their course slightly more to larboard.

'Crete by nightfall, Allah willing,' he called out.

Allah willing indeed, Toby thought. 'Insh'Allah,' he called back. 'Tomas, how do you fare?' His brother had begged God repeatedly to stop the rocking during the storm but he had not puked again.

'I am a little better, I think. Maybe your stale crusts are worthy of holy relic status.'

'I wish,' said Toby. 'Just think of the coin to be had. Bread from Christ's Last Supper! Get your crusts here! Must be nice to be endowed with such wealth.'

Tomas snorted. 'You talk rubbish. Show me where you have ever stinted in your life because of lack of funds. After all, who has the most luggage amongst us? Not Mehmet nor I, that's a surety.'

'I like good clothing,' Toby replied. 'It is not a sin in my mind, although perhaps it might be in the eyes of the Church.' He glanced at his current attire – modest wool that was rimed with salt and mildew and which felt perpetually damp. He ran stubby fingers through his knotted hair.

'Huh, you think too much about yourself,' Tomas said.

And you don't? Jesu!

Toby wanted to argue but sat on his words.

So, Tomas can see into my *mind still. Then why is it I can no longer see into his? Because for sure, he is the one whose mind needs reading.*

'Do not worry yourself, brother,' Tomas elbowed him. 'I can be generous spirited enough for us both.'

How I wish…

Toby knew the truth was far different. Tomas' near-drowning had turned him inside out. Now he wrote the words and melody for a life that pleased *him* alone. Such self-indulgence when Gisborne reiterated the need for subtle behaviour time and again. Keeping low to the ground, Sir Guy had said. Ha! That should not be difficult for us, Toby thought wryly.

'That's better,' Tomas nudged him. 'A grin! Because you see it's I who should have a face as long as a list of the Pope's sins.' He chewed on some more bread, crumbs spraying as he continued. 'You think I jest? I don't, not at all. I know I …' he paused then, 'I am sometimes not what I was, what you want me to be. Whereas you? More often than not, I think you are so reliable, the epitome of a saint.' He walked away for'ard, grasping at anything to steady his way as a crewman stowed loosened ropes away from incautious feet.

Tobias was left with a feeling that once again he had misread his brother. Such a statement from Tomas made Toby wonder if there was hope yet that the minstrel of old could emerge from the puckered and sea-dunked skin of his brother.

Is it impossible?

From the mast there was a shout. One of the seamen had climbed up as far as the top edge from where his view was unobstructed.

'Land!' he called. 'Land to starboard.' Toby rushed to the starboard wale and scanned the horizon and indeed a dark mound sat almost directly in front. Leagues away yet but land nevertheless.

Ahmed stood beside him. 'Crete,' he said. 'This island is an interesting place, quite vast with high mountains and snow. Me? I'm used to Al Mahgreb where the heat fries locusts in a second. But good food and good wine is to be had in Crete. I suspect you might like the wine they have there better than anything else on the island.'

More my brother's taste than mine, thought Toby.

'An old place I think,' he replied. 'Do they not say it is the home of the legend of the Minotaur?'

'This is true, and the home of some of the Greek Gods they say. Good legends for you to make songs about, my minstrel friend. But *I* prefer that I can trade for olives than ancient stories. It is a big island and their exports are fine quality – I have never failed to make money from what they trade and I do like money.' Ahmed rubbed his thumb and forefinger together.

'You speak Greek, then?'

'I speak all the tongues of this sea,' he swept a muscular arm around, robes following in the gesture's wake, his sleeves sliding to his elbows. His fingers were calloused and his nails uneven and short. His domed head gleamed in the sun that emerged from heavy cloud. If he had been as tall as Gisborne, Toby thought, he'd have been quite an impressive man – all the more so with the scythe-like *kilij* that was suspended from a belt at his waist.

'You think you will need that?' Toby asked, pointing to the cruel curve of the weapon.

Ahmed patted the hilt. 'One never knows. It is best to be prepared. The sea is thick with *peirates.*'

'I knew of the sea-robbers but I assumed you would sail on a much frequented trading route. Safety in numbers, if you see what I mean.'

'Oh indeed, Master Tobias. But we sail before the season begins so we are like the … the…' his brow creased for a moment. 'The lamb in the lion's cave, yes?' he finished triumphantly.

'Right,' said Toby looking askance over his shoulder. 'And I've never really liked lions. Prefer small cats if I have to. But essentially I'm a dog man.'

'Dog man?' Ahmed's eyes half-closed in puzzlement.

'Dogs. I prefer dogs to cats. And in truth I much prefer dogs to lions.'

Ahmed scrutinised Toby, digesting the dry irony, and then he laughed, a single raucous expulsion of clove-scented air accompanied by a flash of white teeth. 'You are a funny man, little Tobias.' He clapped Toby hard on the back and the minstrel tripped forward a step. 'I like you.'

He departed, his knee-length robes swirling around his body like the smoke from which a *djinn* might arise, his gait the rolling seaman's step so common at sea.

'Oh good,' muttered Toby, out of hearing of the Arab sea captain. 'Methinks you just might be the kind of man it is better to have as a friend than an adversary for I believe, Ahmed, you could be a *peirate* yourself.'

They sailed under the shadow of the coastline by dusk light, furling the sail, finally dropping the anchor under a moonless sky filled with the crisp twitch of a thousand stars. A brazier was lit and flatbread deftly cooked in a pan whilst other crew cast a net in the shallows. The net broke the water and tiny flapping fish were pulled in – fresh *anchovia* glittering like slivers of iron. The fish were thrust into the pan with crushed garlic and olive oil and each person took a piece of flatbread and scooped up the fishpaste.

Toby savoured the salty flavour on his tongue, closing his eyes and thinking of Genova and the food of the Genovese way. He missed the town – the villa, the ambience of the place, despite the uniqueness of his Venetian home.

But then it's not such a large world really.

Tomas merely chewed the flatbread, excluding the fish completely.

'Belly not settled?' asked Mehmet.

'Not yet. It seethes a little. I crave something homely – a broth, some frumenty. Christ, even a wine and honey.'

Mehmet nodded. 'Give yourself a day and you will be able to eat what we all share.'

'Two days and a night is all I have before we set sail *again*,' Tomas whined, the sound of someone who might genuinely be afraid of the sea.

'Plenty of time for your belly to settle and for you to seek plain food ashore.'

'Time ashore means nothing. I have gone ashore repeatedly on this journey, Mehmet,' Tomas argued. 'And you know that I begin puking again the moment they pull on the oars.'

'It will be better this time, my friend, because you eat the dry bread and it calms the bile in your belly. You will be able to eat more and all will be well.'

'So you say…'

'I do say. I think you might be surprised when we depart this time.'

'Surprise would be welcome for sure.' Tomas looked across at the darkly silhouetted shore that rose above them. From that same tumbled coast they could hear waves breaking and their galley rose and fell gently at anchor. Somewhere above, a lone kite cried, raising images of the dead, but then there was only the murmur of voices on board, the flames of the brazier and lanterns lighting the hooked noses, angled cheekbones, beards and wrapped heads of the crew.

'Where are we?' Tomas asked.

'A little to the southwest of Chandax,' Ahmed answered. 'See that shape in the far distance off the larboard bow? It is the mount they call Stroumboulos. It broods over Chandax like an old hag.'

Toby and Tomas both turned to stare.

'It's odd,' said Toby. 'In all our journeys across the sea to Outremer for Gisborne, Crete was never visited. I tell you, even one day here will be a pleasure – if only to allow my land-legs to bend and stretch. What shall we find in Chandax, do you think?'

'Stones, my friend. Stones and more stones from the days of the Greeks – although the condition of some will be less than one would hope after the Byzantines routed the Saracens. Astonishing buildings really. Mosaics if you look hard. Much history. In its time it was a safe port for *peirates*.'

Toby looked across at Ahmed.

Nothing changes, then…

'Taverns? Women?' Tomas asked, clearly bored with times past as he pulled his damp cloak close.

'Of course, Tomas. From Spain to Outremer it is exactly the same – taverns, women and wine,' Mehmet's reasonable voice broke in. 'But a word of warning. You have eaten little. If you drink too much wine immediately you will feel as if the Minotaur has slammed into you from behind.'

'In other words be careful, Tomas,' chided Toby. 'Remember what Gisborne said.'

Tomas grunted, hunkering down in his cloak and laying his head on a pile of ropes. He looked uncomfortable and yet in moments he snored.

'Can sleep anywhere,' said Toby. 'Lucky bastard.'

'Watch him tomorrow, Tobias,' Mehmet said quietly. 'He's tinder dry in so many ways…'

'Can you give him anything to calm his mood?'

'There are many herbs but he needs his wits about him and I would not dull those.'

And from the darkness, as if the Devil's agent sat at his ear, a thought shouted from Toby's mind – so hard that he sucked in his breath.

'Is aught wrong, my friend?' Mehmet laid a hand on Toby's arm.

'It's…' But he could not bring himself to utter those three confronting words and instead said, 'Just cramp. Land legs won't come soon enough.

Good night to you, Mehmet.'

'And to you. Sleep well.'

But sleep sat on the wales and laughed at Toby as the three words went round and round in his head.

Death stalks him…

Tommaso and Tobias were born to innkeeper parents in the village of Pigna in Italy, close to the borders of Provence. The small inn sprouted from the stone, moss and grass of the surroundings and a previous generation of the brothers' family had called it *Et Lyra et Laus Mea* - such a grand Latin name for a common little inn, but the family had always been music lovers and through the years, voices could often be heard raised in song. It was a favourite haunt for travelling minstrels and jongleurs, as if the very stones had melodies to sing of times past, and indeed musicians had been heard to say that if it wasn't an inn, it should surely be a monastery, filled with Divine harmony. But in addition to its music, the place was known for more pedestrian things as well – good Ligurian wine, a full trencher at mealtimes and flea-less cots for the nights.

Their mother had oft regaled the twins with the story of their birth – how the midwife had said,

'Well, they breathe and are healthy but they will be very small in stature, Teresa. There will be some who will see them as Devil spawn and the family marked for that. For myself, I say a gift from God. They have been born thus for a good reason and He will lay His hand upon them. Of course, if you want, I can drown them in the river on my way home…'

They had been baptised unwillingly by the priest at that time and he was heard calling them seeds of the Devil, just as the wise woman had predicted. But by Divine providence, the priest had tripped, fallen, broken his arm which became grossly infected, and shortly after, had died. Village talk said God protected those He loved and punished those He didn't. And so the villagers generally treated the twins well, only a few spitting as they walked past, crossing themselves in protection and anguish.

From an early age, Tomas and Tobias displayed musicality – singing Ligurian folk songs to applause, and joining with passing troubadours to voice refrains with ease. They displayed a confidence and joy when they entertained, as if they were born to the art-form. It was then that the villagers began to whisper amongst themselves that the boys were indeed loved of God and that He had laid His hand upon them and given them the voice of angels. Subsequently it was common for the villagers to touch the twins and cross themselves, as if the twins represented a miracle and a chance of salvation. The twins of course, laughed but allowed the villagers to think such things and to go on rubbing the tops of their heads or taking their hands and kissing the fingers.

''Tis like being a bishop or a pope,' Tomas giggled as a toothless hag let his hand go and he wiped it on his tunic.

When they were young adults, and during a particularly cool winter, a minstrel from Aquitaine stayed longer than his fellows, suffering as he did from an ague. He repaid the family's hospitality and kindness by singing for his supper as soon as he was well and *Et Lyra et Laus Mea* attracted a swelling clientele, enabling the twins' family to pocket money for improvements to the establishment.

The minstrel, a man called Berenguier de Palazol, sat with his *vielle* one day and the twins gravitated to his side. As he laid his head back against the sunlit stone, he placed the instrument on the bench beside him, closing his eyes.

Tomas nodded and Toby reached for it and they crept away to sit behind a wall of the inn. Toby began to pluck a melody, having left the bow alongside the minstrel, and the two sang – a song of heroism and love that filled the air with haunting and sweet emotion, as if a zephyr had drifted down from the mountains with the smell of snow and ice and alpine flowers blooming beneath the drifts.

A head appeared around the corner and Berenguier said softly. 'You take a minstrel's soul when you take his *vielle*, my friends.'

Toby held it out and he and his brother apologised. 'It's just that it is such a beautiful instrument, *messire*,' Toby said. 'So wonderful that it sets up the hairs on our necks.'

'Where did you learn to play? In particular, who taught you to pluck a melody so well? Most would use the bow.'

'No one,' said Tomas guilelessly.

'I see.' The minstrel seemed unconcerned that they had purloined his *vielle* and moved round the corner to sit beside them. 'But you have watched others?'

'Indeed,' said Toby.

'Of course,' said Tomas. 'We watch everyone who comes to the inn, we wish to learn how their fingers dance along the strings.'

'And the song – who taught you that?'

'No one,' said Toby. 'We made it up and sang it over and over until it was scribed on our minds. Did you like it? Our hero, Claudio the Bold? He's not real of course but we just made him so.'

From then until Berenguier left for Provence a month later, he taught the twins every day until they mastered his *vielle* and could sing with him to entertain the customers at the inn.

'Your sons must go to Paris,' he said to the innkeeper and his wife one day. 'They have a gift that is too precious to languish here, no matter how much your customers love them.'

It was hard for the parents to let their sons go. Such little people in stature, such oddities, and moving into a world where they may not be tolerated, where superstition may be even stronger than in their own corner of Liguria. But they had heard of such malformed people who were in demand amongst noble houses and they felt their children, with such a talent at their disposal, deserved a chance to succeed outside the tiny village. As Tobias would often say, it was extraordinary thinking from people who had never travelled further than a league down the road. He never stopped thanking them as his life progressed, even though Tomas developed an ego that was bound to cause them both problems.

And thus it was that the next group of pilgrims returning from Rome to Paris had the twins amongst them. They carried two letters for their future – one to the Congregation of Minstrels so called, and one to a particular Brother Antoine who could accommodate the boys in a friary.

It was barely a twelve month and the twins began to tread the path of the troubadour, never looking back until their fame could almost equal the great Marcabru. The difference was that the boys, now young men, had no intention of being political or causing wrath with their poetry. Instead they enticed and charmed men and women, becoming adored by the nobility. Their music was unique – their words poignant, witty, and dramatic by turn, their melodies so entrancing that every hall from Spain to Italy demanded their presence and they were able to send money home to their parents in gratitude.

From the two little boys who finished each other's words and thoughts, they were the light and shade that complimented each other in adulthood. Until it began to unravel when Tomas, filled to the brim with an inflated idea of his own excellence, began to drink heavily.

At first Tobias let it pass, but after slipping too many bags of coins to innkeepers or disgruntled patrons for damage caused by Tommaso's ill-judged behaviour, he growled,

'Tomas, this has to stop. I cannot keep using our savings to pay for your excesses. We are almost living from hand to mouth.'

'You only live once, Toby. And life is for living,' was the not-so-innocent reply.

But the fast life took its toll and finally not quite five years ago, Sir Guy of Gisborne found the twins in separate locations – perhaps not so accidentally as it transpired. He patched them up and paid Tomas' nursing costs for the minstrel had become ill with his drunken ways in the Capetian court, and the knight also paid off Tomas' mounting debt. More importantly, he offered them both employment.

As spies.

The caveat was breathtaking. They must never appear together in public again, never sing together, indeed never be seen as brothers nor contact their family and they must be moderate in their behaviour which meant Tomas must stop drinking heavily. And until his most recent misadventure in Venezia, they had observed that caveat with steadfast loyalty. Tomas had barely misbehaved until the sinking of the Lionheart's galley.

Thenceforth, he became the erratic man of the moment.

Toby watched his brother's chest as it rose and fell in sleep and was angry.

I love you, Tomas, but I cannot keep protecting you.

The words of Genesis flared in his mind.

Am I my brother's keeper?

He tried to analyse the underlying fury that made his heart beat like the hooves of a phalanx of Saracens at Arsuf. He wished he could talk to Mehmet and rationalise everything. The guilt of his thoughts weighed upon his shoulders like a wooden yoke when he just wanted to be free. That was all. Free…

Jesu, Mary and Joseph, why should I suffer this now? Why can't I follow my own lodestar and leave Tomas to his?

He sat still, waiting for some sort of Divine answer. But there was nothing and Toby knew instinctively that God would not guide his hand any time soon.

He no longer wanted to share anything with his brother, least of all those moments when he might be himself. He wanted to be a minstrel, a troubadour and a spy, but without worrying about his brother. He wanted to play chess with Mehmet and tables with a child. If he must chase danger and secrets in the process, that was fine, he would be with the family he loved. Not that he didn't love his own parents, of course. Gisborne had visited them in Pigna, explained what he wanted of the twins and that the twins willingly wanted to be involved in his schemes. He also said money would continue to arrive for the twins' parents by virtue of their value to his network. They loved their sons, they said. And would never stand in their way.

'Besides, my lord,' said Toby's father. 'We trust you to see our sons safe, by the Grace of God.'

So Gisborne's family have become my own adoptive one, thought Toby, more acceptable to be with than my very own sibling.

Jesu, Tomas! You constantly plague me.

Even as he thought, so the fury sent a flush sweeping to his cheeks and he crunched a fist and punched his chest near where lay his heart. He thumped so hard his chest cavity hurt. That must surely be akin to the pain of losing his Gisborne family. Perhaps too, that was the pain of losing his brother … as if he cared.

As the reverberation settled, less and less until it was like a watery ripple jostling a riverbank, he knew that nothing would change. He would remain his brother's minder until his brother lost this perilous outlook.

Quite simply, he would see him safe.

He rolled onto his side, staring away from Tomas across the deck to where Ahmed stood at the tiller, head tilted to the heavenly map above. Barely noticing the Arab, he sighed, a great gush of air as if that could release the tension coiled inside him.

'Christ, I wish I was a monk,' he muttered.

Chapter Three

×

Chandax basked in a turquoise and amber glow and Stromboulos hunkered like a poisonous spider waiting to pounce. If Tobias turned toward the sea and the dock alongside which the galley was moored, the view was of never-ending placid beauty. The kind of sea that was so clear it made one shake one's head in disbelief. As if vessels floated on air, not water.

Odd ... not of this world.

And if Tobias turned the other way, it was if a threat sat waiting – the distant mountain quiet but like to explode and destroy at any moment.

'I'm off to find a tavern,' Tomas said, flicking his bleached hair back. 'Want to join me?'

'Tomas, please heed Mehmet's words. You are no so fit yet...'

'Oh come now, be honest. You think I will drink myself into a fight again?'

Toby examined his twin's face before he answered. No expression there. 'No...'

Tomas laughed. 'You are a bad liar. Don't go to Confession any time soon, will you, if you want to hide your sins.'

'Tomas, it is no joke! What does it take these days to make you see sense?'

Tomas' face hardened like a frost settling. 'Last time I looked, Tobias, it was me living my life, not you. I would that you took your sanctimonious soul and stroked it elsewhere rather than in my ambit. I think we are finished here. I shall see you anon.'

He swung away with an angry stride and was lost in the press of taller bodies very quickly.

'Christ on the bloody Cross!' Toby almost went to follow but his own perverse anger grabbed him by the collar and he swore again, turning the exact opposite way, to walk along the ancient cobbles of Chandax.

At first he was too incensed to take notice of the elderly Greek buildings or of the people that walked by him, but slowly his demeanour evened out and he breathed again. The poet's curiosity drew him out of himself.

He could have been anywhere in the Adriatico or even in Tyre or some of the alleys of Acre. The warmth of the spring sun had the promise of summer fierceness and light passed from exposed sunwhite to the deepest black of shadow, depending on which side of the street he ambled.

The people too – as much of a melange as anywhere. Men as tanned as old leather, the women hidden behind folds and veils, the elderly creased and crumpled like old clothes. A Greek priest wandered by, his dark robes faded and worn and held by a group of children who laughed with him as he tossed them grapes.

It was an unfettered scene of peasant existence and it served to soothe Toby as he drew in the sights. He tried to imagine the Greek gods of legend finding their secret way amongst the plain folk or the Minotaur pawing at the ground in fury, a little way out of the town.

In his mind he began to form a ballad that he could later set to music and which served to settle his spirit so that what Tomas might or might not be doing was of little consequence. He was walking backward staring at the fluted columns of a broken building when he collided with someone coming the other way. He was knocked sideways, banging hard against a corner of stone projecting into the street.

'*Ignosce mihi*, I am so sorry.' The stranger grabbed him and set him to rights.

Toby rubbed at his arm. 'You speak Latin, sir, and I can understand you which is as well, as my Greek is perilous poor. And please, don't trouble yourself. It is my fault. I was walking backward…'

The stranger, a young man of medium height and with smooth black hair, smiled. 'I am from Genova and I speak no Greek at all. And I confess I had my nose safe squashed within this…' he held up a small wood-covered book and waggled it, 'my bills of exchange. And I did not see you.'

'Blessings to be sure! You not only speak Latin but you read as well.

And yet you are not dressed as a priest.'

The young man's dimples sliced down his cheeks. 'Me a priest? Lord God! I take His name too often in vain to be a priest. My name is Pietro.' He dropped his head in a brief bow.

People rubbed by them, a donkey toiling past with a red blanket and a teetering load of woven baskets.

'A saintly name if ever I heard one,' said Toby. 'And I am Tobias from close by Venezia. It is a pleasure to meet a fellow traveller. Perhaps you are familiar with Chandax?'

'Sadly no, this is my first visit. I am here to trade for my family. And you? Why are you here?'

Pietro's skin was darkly olive and stained from ear to ear by the stubble of a fledgling beard.

Like a mask.

Such growth, thought Toby. It reminds me of Davey. As if the growth could hide the real man.

Don't be ridiculous! You barely know him so how can you determine if he is play-acting?

Indeed, thought Toby, in answer to his conscience voice. I don't know him, which is why I must be cautious.

'Me?' he said lightly. 'I am here but one night and then we continue on to Constantinople. Our galley reprovisions. Frankly I am glad. I was beginning to walk with a seaman's gait…' He took a couple of rolling strides with his legs apart and Pietro grinned. 'And believe me,' Toby continued. 'When one is as short as I, one needs to stand taller rather than with legs spread. Tell me, do you know anything about this building?'

They looked up at the columns of the tired structure next to them. The morning sun had bleached the surrounding stone so that it could almost have been ivory and it was pockmarked with the scars of an age of battle and occupation.

'No. It's old, it's Greek. That's all I can tell you. I am not interested in piles of stone – seems to be rather a lot in this place. Master Tobias, would you honour me with your company at a tavern on the waterfront? I have not yet broken my fast and am as empty as a drunk's costrel.'

Toby gave the building a wistful last glance. He disliked not having settled his curiosity but chatting to this Genovese trader might serve another purpose. Toby was as curious about him as he was about the building.

'I would be honoured, Master Pietro. We can swap tales with each other – me about … anything, and you about Genova.'

Pietro frowned. 'I am an uncultured man, Master Tobias. I know little and recall even less, unless of course it is to do with money and its making.'

His eyes glittered and for one very brief moment, Toby thought he should stop the conversation right there as Gisborne's voice sounded from far away – *'Caution my little friend, caution.'*

Indeed, this swarthy man from Genova was hardly a kindred spirit except that he and Toby both followed a path of trade. If vicariously in my case, thought Toby. But like most creative spirits, he shook off the cautionary ties. He had already begun to fashion a character for a *canso* out of the man before him. It just needed a little more flesh…

'I know nothing about making money,' he said. 'You may find me an uninteresting companion.'

'Travel throws unlikely folk together, Master Tobias. Come, the tavern is this way and you can tell me what you do that does not make you any money…'

The waterfront glistened in the noonday sun and to ameliorate its blinding nature, Toby and Pietro had found a trestle beneath a vine arbor and had a platter of sardines, olives, steaming bread and the salty sheeps' and goats' cheeses beloved of the Adriatico. They washed the whole down with a wine that had Toby pinching his bruised arm.

'By the Saints' noses, I am drinking nectar!'

'Not nectar,' said Pietro. 'It is wine grown and blended here on Crete. There is nothing like it across this sea. That,' he sipped, closing his eyes and kissing the tips of fingers, 'is what I am buying.'

'You must have extensive financial resources, my friend,' said Toby as the flavour lingered on his lips like a kiss from a virgin. 'I imagine this is not cheap.'

'It's true and whilst I can only buy a small shipment, it will more than repay our family's investment. My thought is that whatever we trade, it must be unique and worth much. We will never make money otherwise.'

Toby examined his companion. The man's eyes were lit from within by a fervour, not unlike Saul if truth be told, and Toby doubted the fellow had any idea how much his face revealed. This was a man who was filled to overflowing with ambition whereas perhaps Saul had already reached that comfortable place. Until recently…

Imagine if this young man knew of the purple…

'Do you load the wine and sail back to your markets?'

'No. I have to travel to Constantinople … yes, I do!' He grinned. 'We may see each other in the harbour, my friend.'

'What do you purchase there?'

'I have a consignment of rare spices and some frankincense to collect. The Church pays well for the best quality. I think to find a market in Rome.'

'I am impressed and salute you.' They drank again.

'But enough of me, Master Tobias. What about you?' Pietro reached forward and tapped Toby's chest.

'Me? Ha!' Toby scoffed. 'I am but a minstrel. Perhaps a mediocre one at that because my purse is almost empty.'

'A minstrel!' Pietro sat back, his eyes wide with excitement. 'I am in awe!'

'Don't be. I am no troubadour. Marcebru has no competition from me.'

I don't know of troubadours, let alone this Marcebru. But minstrels! Those I do know. Do you play an instrument? A pipe? A tabor?'

'The *vielle*. A stringed instrument that one plays so…' Toby held it make-believe and mimed the action. 'It is a beautiful thing.'

A vision filled Toby's mind of his *vielle* leaning against the corner of the chamber, streaming with the wine-coloured ribbons Lady Ysabel had insisted he tie to the very top of the neck. It was an affectation he rather liked – the streamers swooping and gliding as he became impassioned with his playing. It was a wonder that the pups, Tristan and Iseult, had never set to chewing them and with *that* thought came an image of William and the words, *I will mith you tho much, Toby. You're my betht friend.*

I miss you too, William. Beyond measure…

He realised Pietro was speaking and pinched himself back to reality. 'Your pardon, I missed what you were saying.'

'I said that I know stringed instruments require skill. I've heard it said by minstrels. None of *them* play such things. It's always the pipe and tabor and singing, *lots* of singing. So you must be accomplished at what you do.'

Perhaps I am, thought Toby. But in truth it had been many months since he had performed for an audience beyond the villa, perhaps not since Cyprus when he had been in disguise as the troubadour Di Dia and performing for the inexorable Halsham. Ah yes, that long ago. And he felt he had traded the artform for a sword.

Sometimes it irked him, so many words in his head and melodies in his soul – all giving way to the art of secrecy. Ah well. Adventure had a way of calling…

'Ah, mayhap I can play the instrument,' he continued. 'But I cannot play the game. Being a true troubadour requires the skill of telling lies, Pietro. At every new court, I was expected to write and sing a *canso* lauding the lady of the house. It was expected that I write of my own love for her and our unbridled joy at such a secret unfulfilled relationship. I tell you, some of those women were as puckered as a bull's backside. How could I write of love? Seriously. Don't laugh, my friend…'

But Pietro had thrown his head back and was roaring.

'At any rate,' Toby added as the Genovese quieted. 'I found I could not tell a lie and I also realised that me being me, a squat, short man, to laud love with noblewomen of great presence and height was little short of ridiculous and so I began to sing other sorts of songs. It was not appreciated and I began to lose commissions. Soon my money dwindled and I became a plain minstrel, journeying from fair to fair. I live, sir, from hand to mouth.'

Such a good story, Tobias – you should be proud. And not so far from the truth.

'A difficult story my friend,' Pietro reached for the flagon and poured. 'You know, I saw one such as you, earlier.'

One such as you!

In an instant, Tobias understood his brother's flammability, because that self-same anger coursed along his own veins like fire in a trench at the bottom of a *glacis*. One moment nothing and then a stampeding conflagration protecting castle walls from ingress. He wanted to grab the trader by the neck and squeeze, shouting,

'What am I, then? Some curious animal? A different breed?' And then as the man choked, he would reach for the misbegotten groin and punch hard, saying 'Funny, I have those too. And a brain. I'm half the height but twice the man!'

But he liked Pietro so instead he said, 'Oh yes? Did he have rope-coloured hair by chance and a reddish beard? Or at least the excuse for a beard?'

'Indeed he did. And he was with an Arab who carried a weapon that made me walk to the other side of the alley.'

Ahmed! God be praised. He will see Tomas safe.

'That would be our galley master, and the one like me would be my friend from the north – Julius. We met in Venezia, drowned our spectacular failures in good Ligurian wine and whilst drunk, wrote a list … what? I can write? Of course! All troubadours are educated. Anyway, as I was saying, we compiled a list of places we thought might appreciate our attributes. We blindfolded ourselves, took a dagger and stabbed it into the parchment. And we both stabbed the same name. Does that not spell Fate to you or perhaps the Saints watching over us? At any rate, we go to Constantinople.'

Pietro's expression was of a man who would never approach life so flippantly. 'You have plans of course? And contacts?'

'None. But minstrels are well known for tumbling down from immense heights and always, like cats, landing on their feet.' Toby sucked on an olive and spat out the stone. 'At least that is what we hope will happen…'

Pietro sat still, examining Toby with slitted eyes and Toby stared guilelessly back. Gisborne would have been proud – not a secret revealed. This was the part of subterfuge he loved. The making of an identity, the acting of a part.

'It is as I said, Master Tobias. I am in awe – of your spirit of adventure at the very least. Myself? I need to know that money will eventuate at the end. But listen, in honour of our new friendship, may I offer you some advice?'

'Of course…'

'When you reach Constantinople, do not settle for a small fee for your services. You are unique. I mean no insult. You are a … troubadour, yes? You are…' he ducked his chin and then continued, 'unusual, and you read and write *and* speak some languages I presume. These things are worth a lot and the Byzantines are wealthy, have no doubt. Make your purse clink with rich gold *hyperpyrons.* We all have things to sell and you are no different.' He opened the fat purse at his waist and counted out silver dinars to cover their extensive food and wine repast. 'Now, I must meet my wine-seller. I hope we meet again and if we do…'

'Then I shall buy *you* a meal. I enjoyed our time together, it has been a pleasure.' Toby stood and clasped the Genovese's arm and in a moment the fellow was gone, leaving a faint fragrance of sandalwood and a curiously contemplative space under the arbour.

Where did my anger come from? thought Toby. I have never felt disturbed by my differences in the past. It has always been Tomas who over-reacts, never me. Has *his* behaviour so honed my edges that I could slice a man in half for an innocuous and ill-judged comment?

He bit his teeth together hard, rubbing at the headache that had begun to throb in his temple.

Tomas, always Tomas.

He thought back over every word, every nuance of his conversation with Pietro – sifting it, examining it for weaknesses and then decided that he had protected all players – Gisborne, Mehmet, Ahmed, Saul, the purple … and Tomas.

It appeared there was nothing to reproach himself for because he had not even betrayed the fact that he had lived in Genova himself not long since. Ha! *And* delicious wine as a reward. He swallowed the last of his mug and passed Pietro's glinting silver into the innkeeper's eager palm. But he stayed seated. No one was about and he allowed the peace, the absence of his brother and the feathered energies of a golden oriole flitting through the arbour to soothe. Eventually he heard the bells of a nearby church and stirred.

The shadows had lengthened, the sun sitting much lower in the sky and Tobias decided to walk one small loop around Chandax before returning to the galley. Just one more because the innkeeper had said there were the remains of a Greek temple close by – empty of course, except for wild goats that grazed the surrounds.

'Does it have mosaics?' Toby asked.

The innkeeper nodded as he palmed Pietro's silver from one wine-stained hand to another. 'Oh yes, sir. Many mosaics. Good for you to look at, yes?'

Toby had thanked the innkeeper and wandered away feeling uplifted, whistling the stirrings of a melody that had shivered into life in his soul. Some children latched onto him for a moment, amused no doubt at what he was, but this time his equilibrium had returned and he took no umbrage, singing a dirty little Genovese street ditty to them. They had no idea of the innuendo but laughed anyway and then they were gone and he turned up a narrow street where old grandmothers sat spinning thread with drop spindles whilst a black cat sat in a doorway, its green eyes half closed as it minded Toby to keep away. It arched its back and hissed and then jumped up onto the tumbled wall across the street.

The eyes of the old wives watched the cat, watched Toby too as he came to a doorway that yawned like an old man. He looked back at those women, at their sucked in mouths and the wrinkles crosshatched over their cheeks, at the white hair fluttering like old cobwebs from beneath their heavy dark veils. With the spontaneous nature of the born performer, he leaped laughing through the entrance, disappearing after the cat into ebony nothingness.

The smell of goat and grass quieted him as he landed awkwardly amongst a pile of cracked and fallen stone. Remnant daylight still filtered into the temple through the collapsed roof. Goats watched from fallen plinths and hand-hewn stone and a black kid stamped its tiny hoof, *clack*, and bleated at him – a woeful sound like a child who'd lost its family. But then it danced in its own circle and cantered away to its nondescript mother, butting the udder and suckling greedily.

'More like your papa, I think,' Toby said as he walked across the weed and dirt-strewn floor of the temple. He scuffed the soles of his boots, feeling beneath the detritus for anything unusual. Finally he knelt and began to scrub at the muck with an edge of broken stone, scrabbling to find the *tesserae* that might indicate a mosaic.

A tiny patch of cracked tiles revealed itself in a last beam of light and Toby sucked in his breath – a muscular leg, robes falling away from a bent knee. He licked his finger and dragged it across the *tesserae* to heighten the faded colours but then the light was gone as surely as if someone had blown out a torch. For a moment he sat back on his heels, shivering at the ghosts of the past that he might have unearthed.

Not might … they are here…

He lifted his head, about to turn and something hit him a glancing blow.

Not enough to knock him out, but enough to knock him flat. He fell hard, a trail of stars dancing across his vision. Instinctively his hand reached for the haft of his knife and pounding head or not, he shot to his knees and crawled away from the next blow. It hit the *tesserae* and chips and dust flew, the goats skittering away to the far end of the temple, bleating in fear.

An indistinct twilight blurred everything between shape and shadow and Toby rolled beneath two fallen pillars, hoping he was just another form amongst many.

I should call out, he thought. The old wives, they'll hear me.

No, keep quiet. You'll be dead before they move their decrepit knees.

Footsteps sounded and he held his breath, but couldn't stop the hollow echo of his heartbeat – a tabor, a drum on the battlefield…

Who is it? Why?

And then the club cracked onto one of the pillars and he rolled swiftly into the next shadow, lifting himself, running in the dark, tripping, needing another hiding place. The stony ground, the dried grasses, the crack of old twigs – there was no chance of silence. So he pulled himself onto a block, up over another, jumping to the next, thanking the Saints for agility and speed.

His attacker stumbled and swore.

A dialect? From where? Ever alert to an audience's mood, he sensed pure fury as the fellow tripped again.

He can't find me. A point to me…

But then Toby halted in his race across tumbled stone, stopping dead, hiding behind a large block as the assailant crashed beneath him.

And stopped.

Close…

Toby bent down, his knife slashing, aiming for anything in the dark. The blade found softness – muscle, flesh – and he pushed the point in and twisted it, dragging it out again. A shriek of agony filled the dark; then a roar and the club swung upward, almost catching him. He jumped, rolled; all those jongleur moves that delighted audiences as the determined feet came after him.

He wished he could understand the words, or perhaps not, because the meaning was implicit – pain, a bag full of it. And then he had nowhere to run, his back against a drystone wall.

Sard!

He turned and crouched, pulling a mean little *misericorde* from a soft sheath in his boot and stood, a weapon in each hand, arms spread, knees flexed to jump in any direction. The attacker moved forward growling, even a chuckle – a huge man-shape, the Minotaur.

The club moved through the air and Toby jumped to the side. The club swung back, but with it a cry, a piteous howl, and the club flew off on its own trajectory, the attacker falling to his knees, then face forward near Toby.

He advanced with caution, but the man was lifeless, and in the nightlight, a pool of dark liquid spread from beneath the body toward Toby's toes.

'My little Ligurian music man,' Ahmed's voice filled the subfusc. 'Next time take a friend with you, huh?'

He laid his *kilij* on the ground in order to strike a flint and illuminate the scene. 'Who is this, my friend? Who wanted to part you from your melodies?'

Toby walked carefully around the body. 'No one that I know of.' He stashed his knives. 'But I owe you my life, it seems.'

'Allah be blessed, Tobias. I did what I must to look after my friend.'

Ahmed rolled the man over, the sight of the profane slash in the fellow's side turning Toby's gut. But as the seaman stripped off the man's hood, he bent closer, examining the face that howled in death. The skin was swarthy, perhaps from as far north as Sicily or as far south as Al Mahgreb or anywhere in between. A scar cut from temple to jaw, violently ridged so that Ahmed's flame caught the dip and rise of the puckered skin.

It was a stranger.

A chance encounter?

No, Toby thought. He entered the temple after me. He knew I was in here.

The old wives?

Toby grunted – gossips for gold. Money always speaks.

'You do not know him?'

Toby shook his head.

'Then let us leave him to the street curs. They will eat what they want.' Ahmed began to move away. 'Come. It is better we don't linger.'

As they began to walk, Toby asked if Ahmed was not worried the authorities would find the body and confine the boat and crew, and Ahmed said that Death was everywhere and it would be considered a murder over money for when was it not? And besides, the body was hardly likely to be found before they departed from port.

'Allah protect a poor unfortunate soul.'

Toby wasn't sure if Ahmed referred to his own soul or the murdered man's but God it was good walking down the alley where friendly light fell out of doorways in oblong patches on the cobbles and people could be heard laughing.

Chandax heaved gently like a ship riding at anchor in the harbour, the populace chasing wine, food and nefarious activities. The idea that such activities happened at all wouldn't normally have worried him, but his composure had been shaken and this in a man who had been used to danger from the oddest and darkest corners.

Perhaps I have become too soft minding a child as Tomas says. My wits are dulled, my brain even duller…

'You are very quiet, Toby.' Ahmed measured his pace at Toby's side.

Toby looked up at him. 'Am I?'

Ahmed smiled, the brazen face reflecting danger more than ever. He had the knack of halting a smile at the cheekbones so that the eyes could remain empty and unreadable. Consummate skill, thought Toby.

Peirate…

'Indeed! Almost as if you are wondering a little too hard about your attacker. Perhaps you think it may have been deliberate…'

Toby stopped. 'Perhaps. Who knows?'

Ahmed had walked forward a step but now turned and faced him. The light from *torchères* hit upon the edge of his *kilij* and it was just possible to see blood, a sinister reminder. 'I had thought that our trouble would be with your brother. Lord Gisborne warned me, Allah bless him and give him many sons. But it seems the quiet ones are the ones to be watched.' It was said without rancour.

They had reached the waterfront where sailors and men and those who hung on the edge of waterside life ambled along under torchlight. It had a relaxed air, nothing like the urgency of mercantile endeavour in Genova and Venezia. Here, people stopped to chat in a dozen different tongues and some sat round small braziers cooking fish and drinking the rougher wines of Crete. Occasionally a whore would lead someone into an alley, or men would roar with laughter at someone being bested at dice, but it was less frenetic. Toby found it calming after the temple.

'It was a mere vagrant, Ahmed. 'Tis all. Don't build it into an intrigue. I am sorry for your trouble and I owe you a life debt, there is no doubt, but more than anything right now, I'm tired!' He leaped from the shore to the wale, grasping at a stay, and then sprang down onto the galley's deck. Turning, he asked, 'Have you seen my brother? Was he insensible once more?'

'I was with him at an inn. He was pale and tired but not drunk. He said he would return to sleep.' He nodded toward the masthead.

'You say?' Toby followed his glance. 'Holy Christ, may the angels polish the Saints' toenails!'

Ahmed, patently bemused at the words emerging from the minstrel's mouth, shook his head and leaped aboard to move for'ard and Toby sought the shape lying covered under the shelter of the canopy.

Tomas slept like a baby, face relaxed, breathing even. Mehmet was nowhere in evidence and Toby found two empty sacks from which grain had been poured, placed them on top of each other, swaddled himself in his cloak and lay down. But as was the habit of late, sleep went elsewhere to flirt with more worthy and innocent folk. Other business crept into the vacated space, the attack going round and round in Toby's mind.

His conversation with Ahmed had been filled with untruths. He was shaken because his attacker was no vagrant; of that much he was sure. Whomever it was, they had been very deliberate – to maim if not kill.

Kill? Where was the advantage?

Toby represented nothing dead, but alive and in pain, he was a source of information that could be tortured from him.

What information?

Toby had no political secrets worthy of divulgence – none of interest to anyone currently. He had been left to enjoy a sabbatical after William's return to safety – intelligence gathering had come from further along the web, directly to Gisborne and about what Toby couldn't begin to imagine, nor did he care. He rather liked the idea that he hung like a fledgling moth, insulated in a cocoon. That is until Tomas changed…

Both he and Tomas had had more to do with Lady Ysabel than Gisborne in the last few months. Ah, *there* was someone who had emerged from a cocoon! A butterfly of great beauty, courage and soul. How Tobias loved her. He would have sung *cansos* for her until his voice disappeared. Bless her, she had insisted they all mend. Had been adamant and Gisborne had agreed. Toby wondered if it had been a meek agreement and decided that Gisborne would never be meek. Not even for Lady Ysabel.

And so his mind ran as it does in sleeplessness, here and there, but he drew it back to the event of the day.

Secrets.

But what secrets? He had none.

But then his eyes flew open. Surely not. It couldn't be…

The dye! The purple! Has someone found out what we do?

He groaned, perhaps too loudly.

'Brother?' Tomas' voice croaked out from the depths of sleep and his hand touched Toby's arm. 'Wake up. You have the night terrors. Wake up!'

'Huh?' Toby replied carefully. 'Do I?' He stretched as if he emerged from a deep and convoluted sleep.

'All is well.' Tomas patted his arm and almost immediately fell asleep again.

No it isn't, Tomas, thought Toby, but I will not tell you. I will inform Mehmet instead. Not you. Only Mehmet.

He had thought he would not sleep and yet sleep came and he woke to the gentle roll of the galley and the cry of seabirds, the sun warming his leg where his cloak had rucked up. For a moment he lay quite still allowing the motion of the vessel to cosset him and then he realised that they moved. Not just the dip and rise of a boat at moorings, but with the push and pull of the open sea and the wind. He sat up.

'You wake, my friend.' The physician sat cross-legged, holding a small densely figured book.

'We have left Crete? How long ago? How did I not wake?'

'Just as dawn broke. You slept heavily, Tobias, and if I did not know you better I'd say you slept off the grape and besides, I saw no need to wake you. The sail was raised immediately we cleared the harbour and we have had a very easy breeze for some time.'

'Sleeping off the grape sounds as though it might have been the perfect option. Especially in Crete. I drank wine there that was as smooth as a good woman's thighs – begging your pardon, Mehmet. It is living with the likes of my lately unfettered brother that makes me speak so. Anyway, what happened that urged Ahmed to leave earlier. I thought we had two days for him to collect cargo and supplies.'

Mehmet closed his book.' Ah. Well I would say that *you* happened.'

He said it so quietly it was almost a thought rather than words and Toby was grateful. He looked round quickly for Tomas and was relieved to see him sitting on the wale further to the stern. He had no wish to air this latest drama in front of his brother and gave himself up to the inevitable scrutiny of the elder before him.

'You know.'

'Indeed. Ahmed told me.'

And so the two discussed the incident, Toby finishing with,

'I would that Tomas did not find out, Mehmet. If you don't mind.'

The Arab's brows pulled together. For all that his hair was the palest silver, his eyes retained a fierce clarity that was enhanced by the blackest arch of brows with not a strand of grey anywhere. 'Well, that is your choice, Tobias, and if you so wish…'

'He is difficult at the best of times, Mehmet. You know this. And I would not jeopardise what we aim to do for Saul and Gisborne by creating further tensions. You know that such drama would be to Tomas like boiling oil to a flame.'

'No accident, then.'

'I think perhaps not.'

'Are you the reason or is it Gisborne's secrets?'

'Gods' teeth but I wish I knew. It could be any number of things. A contract on my life for past deeds?' Tobias rubbed at his lips. 'Someone may have undressed the characters I play and discovered I am just a common spy when all is said and done. Perhaps I am hunted to pay Gisborne back. Or perhaps a noblewoman or her husband feel slighted by my lyrics. It is not impossible to imagine they might have finally hunted me down. There are not so many like Tomas and I who sing for their supper through the halls and courts of Europe. We do rather stand tall for being small.' He flung off his cloak, feeling overheated and disturbed in the morning sun. 'Don't forget we already have experience of vengeful minds, Mehmet.'

'Indeed, but let us put revenge aside for the moment. Do you think your attacker might be connected to the purple?'

'But how?' Toby threw his cloak over some roped bales. 'No one knows except our enclave. It's impossible. Even more, it is unthinkable that a secret could be leaked by those we know and trust.'

'Sirs…' Toby jumped as Ahmed approached from behind. '*Insh'allah.*' The seaman touched his forehead and heart. 'Music man, do you feel revived after your long sleep?' His eyes glinted like two pieces of the purest obsidian and his mouth drew up in a smile.

Peirate…

'Revived,' agreed Toby. 'Even more so if I might break my fast.'

Ahmed passed over a knotted cloth. 'Faisal saved something for you. And there may be some fresh fruit, you will have to ask him.'

'I will, I thank you.' Toby unwrapped flatbread still warm from the pan and some cheese. 'Where do we sail to, Ahmed?'

The boat sped forward evenly in the following wind, the sea creaming smoothly behind, a lacy pattern leading back to Crete. Toby breathed a sigh as he swallowed the food, seeing the calm sea, and his brother with sealegs. The breath went part way to removing the angst that sat forever in his belly like stones these days.

Once I was at peace, I was quick-witted and funny. But now…

'I think we shall head to Limnos, perhaps rest and re-provision and thence sail on to Constantinople. We should have fair winds for some days and we loaded enough supplies in Crete to last. I anticipate no trouble…'

Well, thanks be to that, then!

The twins settled into a familiar partnership but one that had laid dormant since Tomas' near-death. They took on the work of crewmen when they could – scrubbing, cooking, coiling ropes, helping to shift cargo to better balance the vessel. They sang for the crew at night, the crew claiming they would rather have the entertainment and leave Faisal to cook, to which the twins grinned ruefully, having burned the bread the day before.

And they talked.

Of Richard the King, imprisoned in Durnstein. What might the ransom amount be? How would it be secured? Was Eleanor even now raising an army to free her son from the clutches of the Holy Roman Empire? Would England be better or worse for his return?

Tobias wondered if they should care for his fate and decided for himself that apart from hoping the man was unhurt, he really cared not one iota.

Tomas was more circumspect. Odd, mused Toby, seeing that he was so traumatised by near-death.

'No,' Tomas said. 'Whilst I *could* blame the King for running haphazardly across the Adriatico, he did save me. When the boat sank, he held me until he found some debris for me to cling to. And he paid for my care. I owe him my life.' He tipped a bucket of scraps over the wale, seabirds swooping in with strident cries, snatching the food that floated in the vessel's wash.

The wind had swung and was off their larboard beam again but there was little listing to upset Tomas' equilibrium.

'You surprise me, Tomas.'

'Why? Because I owe a man a life-debt and that man a king?'

'Not at all. You are your father's son and he taught you to repay debts. No, I meant that many men would choose to blame the King for a near-drowning. They certainly wouldn't praise him.'

'But then,' Tomas dropped the bucket on a rope into the wash to clean it and then hauled it in. 'I am not many men. You may see me as difficult on occasion, but I know a debt when I see it.'

Toby felt a small shaft of annoyance that his brother could jibe about being difficult.

Difficult? Christ!

'Perhaps you should have left Gisborne's employ, then,' he replied tartly, 'and sought the King's court where you could repay your liege in kind a hundred times over.'

'In time I may.'

Toby gasped. 'You say? Christ Jesus and Mary! Do you not think you owe Sir Guy *two* life debts for arranging for your care so long ago when he first found us, and then when the King had so kindly left you behind to live or die as the case may be...'

'I worked for Gisborne unstintingly. I paid my debts to him time and again.'

'Tomas, you were paid in coin. It doesn't cancel out the greater debt to Gisborne.'

'Pah. Things have become too quiet with Gisborne. Since the Crusade ended and William was recovered, it seems to me that you and I have settled into an oblique cosiness. And such a state does not sit well with me. It is why I said yes to this mission to the east. But when King Richard is ransomed I would seek out his court and swear my allegiance. There will be plenty to keep me occupied – he has numerous lands to keep secure for a start. Such things suit me more than the shadowed world Gisborne offers. At least I would know where I stood with the King. He is a force to be reckoned with, Toby. Such majesty…'

'You forget I saw his majesty in action in Sicily, Tomas, and his majesty was the stuff of legend in Acre…'

'Nevertheless,' Tomas' square jaw had hardened to steel and his short, thick fingers drummed on the bucket. 'It is what I want to do.' He thumped Toby on the shoulder with a tight fist. 'Come now, brother. You look as if I have just pulled a flagon of Cretan wine away from you. We are not conjoined, you know.' He walked off whistling and left Toby winded.

How dare he? Toby thought. For months now, I have cared for his fragile state and now he tells me he will up and leave our brotherhood. The ungrateful, self-serving…

But only days ago, you moaned to the Almighty about being your brother's keeper.

That the two brothers were growing apart in their ideals and aspirations was more obvious than cracks in the curtain wall of a castle. For Toby, life within the Gisborne house gave him everything – fraternity, joy, comfort, even a form of security. And with the ancillary move into trade, the world of secrets had just broadened beyond measure. How could Tomas think there would be no excitement? It was the perfect combination if that is what he wanted from life. Toby's ego loved playing diverse identities – surely an entertainer's dream. It certainly added dimension to one's life, even if writing poetry and song alone was a distant dream.

No, he could not understand Tomas at all. But then if his brother wanted something else from life, who was he to stop him?

You are not God!

He crossed himself, realising that whilst he would miss his brother, he would not miss the distress.

So be it!

But there was just a tiny part of him that wondered if Tomas loved him and would care for him as much as he had watched for his brother.

Cease this, Tobias. You are like an old nursemaid to a noblewoman.

He had been leaning against the larboard wale, staring toward the coasts that continually lined their passage. Periodically they dropped anchor and Ahmed and Faisal would go ashore and pick up the most basic provisions, but it was done quickly. They had not engaged with people for any length of time and to Toby it was almost as if Ahmed had an agenda.

'Deep in thought…' Mehmet appeared at his shoulder.

'We seem to be making good speed, Mehmet. Almost as if Ahmed must make landfall by a certain time.'

'I suspect that is exactly what he does, Tobias. Don't forget we have a man waiting in hiding for us and the longer we take, the more in danger he is.'

'Will he return with us?'

'I don't know. It may be as well for him if he does.'

They sat together and Mehmet laid out the chessboard and they played for a little while with no talk between them and then Toby said, 'I have had rather startling brotherly revelations,' and gave his friend the detail.

'I think the time has come,' said Mehmet. 'You will be happier following your own feet, albeit a blow for Gisborne, though. Having twin minstrels within his web has been a boon for gleaning information. But I can imagine Tomas will be happier with King Richard. He formed a bond with the courtiers in his time in the Holy Land and on the voyage back to Europe. In its own way it is a brotherhood, and even more so because they nearly all died. Try to understand this from Tomas' viewpoint, Tobias.'

'Christ on the Cross, Mehmet. It is all I ever do.'

'Then let him go. It won't alter the love between you. In fact it might prolong it and prevent it from degenerating into hate. Which is possible on his mad, bad days.'

'I know…'

'We must not lose our focus, Toby. We are almost at Limnos and after that, within a sennight, we shall dock in Constantinople.'

'Good. Much as this enterprise sounded as if it was just what I needed to get me working again, I would that we were well beyond the reach of the Varangian Guard and on our return.'

Mehmet began to pack the chess set. 'My friend, it is a poor game we have here. I never play without a challenge and I tell you, there is no challenge in your moves today. You worry about your attacker?'

'I am sorry to be such a bad partner, and yes, on top of Tomas, the enigma is always there. But perhaps I tilt at a phantom quintain. I was always the more imaginative of the two of us.'

Mehmet patted his shoulder and began to walk away. 'I seek some refreshment, Toby. Shall you come?' he asked over his shoulder.

CHAPTER FOUR

×

The morning they moored at Myrina on the island of Limnos was as grey as a dead man's innards, with no colour in the sea, no life, just a maudlin shade so filled with woe it might as well have been a shroud.

The colour of mourning, thought Toby.

Every now and then, a hard scud of wind would blow across the harbour from the northwest and birds would wheel away inland as if they had been sucked by the in-breath of a giant. Dampness pervaded, rain not far away. The night before, the moon had been surrounded by a misty penumbra – a sure sign of bad weather.

Clouds rolled and heaved, jostling for a position of power over Limnos. In the far-across-the-water distance, they could hear the pealing of the bells of the monastery at Mount Athos and Toby would swear it was like the tolling for a recent death.

They had wanted to stretch their sea legs, eat a meal of fresh meat in the tiny taverns overlooking the bay. But the wind and cloud cast a miserable shadow over them all. Even Ahmed complained.

'Allah the Merciful, *take* this cloud away!' He turned to Mehmet, rubbing his temples. 'I can always sense a thunderstorm approaching because my head throbs like desert drums. This one will bring cold with it, maybe even snow.'

'But it's late spring,' said Tomas.

'Here it can be anything it wants between winter and summer. Snow can whip across the waters there.' Ahmed nodded to the sea. 'We need to find shelter…'

But the taverns were small and there was no room.

'One perhaps, maybe two people. But not four. Sorry.' An innkeeper shook his head and shut the door against the wind.

'A pity there is no friary,' said Toby as his hair blew in a mad skein across his face. 'A hospice would be welcome. Perhaps we should have sailed to Mount Athos instead.'

'Huh,' grumped Ahmed. He called to a passer-by, a woman with baskets of pockmarked lemons. The smell that arose from the basket drifted around them like the promise of a summer that might never come.

The woman pointed away from the town toward a hill that appeared briefly in the low cloud. She smiled at Ahmed, revealing pink gums and few teeth.

'A pretty picture,' whispered Tomas.

'Just for you, Tomas. The kind you dream of,' Toby replied, wrapping his cloak as tight as swaddling bands round his body, and lusting for a warm bath.

The woman went on her way, giving Tobias and Tomas a look and fingering her good luck charm – an eye painted on a wooden bead and suspended on a leather strip.

'She thinks we are spawn of evil,' Tomas said. 'Just another amongst many who believe so. Ignorant hag!' he called after her.

'I don't care,' Toby replied. 'She can believe what she likes and I think it will have little effect on us. I'm more interested in what she told Ahmed.'

'She said there is a small chapel outside the town. The priest might give us shelter. If we run, we can beat the storm.'

His words were underlined by thunder as the weather bore down upon them. The thick roiling cloud split with lightning and the companions needed no goad to set them running.

'God's teeth, it's freezing. How far?' puffed Tomas, holding a hand against the stitch in his side.

'Not far,' called Ahmed over his shoulder. 'The top of the hill?'

'*That* hill? Jesus wept. My legs can't do it,' Tomas said. 'I can't keep up.'

'Then don't,' said Toby. 'I am no better. Ahmed, Mehmet!' he shouted, 'Go ahead, we shall follow as best we can. There is no point in you getting wet too.'

The rain had begun to fall in hard drops, stinging the face and warning of an impending drowning as the storm moved closer.

'Toby…' Mehmet called back.

'Go! All will be well.'

The two Arabs looked at each other and then began to run, Mehmet surprising them with the steady pace of his limbs. Toby watched them leave, feeling the pain of exertion, the ache, the need to rest and cursed the difference between his own body and theirs.

'Nothing for it, Tomas, we must keep going or risk life and limb in this. How do you fare?'

'The usual.' He tucked his cloak in tight. 'We have no choice, though. Let's go.'

They bent their heads into the wind and rain and began to toil up the hill to the unseen chapel, praying to God and Mary that the lightning would not strike.

'For what use are two dead minstrels, Lord? And small ones at that?' muttered Toby.

But the Almighty decided small ones, minstrels or not, were of more use dead than alive as a storm of biblical proportions rained down upon them.

'Shelter,' yelled Toby. 'There!' He grabbed at Tomas' arm and they ran toward a rocky overhang covered in *phrygana*, something Toby recognised as he ducked to avoid the thorns – a common plant in the windy, desolate isles that they sailed by. Close to the entrance was another plant he recognised as Spine of Christ. He'd seen it all over the Holy Land, a mean plant with outrageous thorns and an even more blasphemous reputation as the plant used for Christ's crown. But he'd tasted its fruit – an olive sized fruit that was as sweet as an apple, the kind of plant that sustained one in the inhospitable reaches of Cross and crusade.

Thunder crashed and lightning crackled sharply across the sky, illuminating a little bleached stone chapel much further up the steep incline. They flung themselves under the shelf, turning round, pushing their backs against the side walls of the overhang, gazing at water which had begun to cascade over the stone edge, splashing onto the ground sloping away in front of them, dragging pebbles in its wake.

The wind and the crack and rumble of the storm assaulted the twins without mercy, both slamming hands against ears.

'It's Zeus!' shouted Toby. 'This is no word from *our* God!'

Tomas shook his head as the thunder shook the rock under which they sheltered. He leaned forward and rubbed at his legs, pushing in circles round his knees.

'Pain?'

'Yes. You?'

'Nothing that straighter limbs wouldn't fix. I need some of Mehmet's potions.'

Tomas grimaced. 'What he offers tastes like something mixed with dust from a crypt filled with rotting corpses. Steeping the stuff in wine makes no difference to the taste. Just give me the wine – at least being drunk cures the pain. Christ Jesus it's cold! Look, it's not rain. It's wind-driven ice!' He dragged his cloak tighter round his body and pulled his hood up as Tobias moved in closer.

'Let's huddle. Shared warmth is all we have.'

Outside, the thunder and lightning had begun to move further away leaving a bitter wind in its place and the clatter of sleet on the ground.

'It's not just an overhang,' said Tomas, looking into the darkness. 'It's a cave. See? It goes further back…' He pushed himself up, grunting as his knees flexed, and felt along the wall. 'Wish I had a flame.'

Toby followed behind, eyes trying to make sense of dark shadows. 'Ow!' His foot struck something and he bent down, stretching out his hands and arms to feel blindly. 'It's wood. And a pail filled with something.'

'Don't touch it! It could be shit…'

'There's no smell, Tomas. No, it's leaves and twigs and some strips of rag…' Toby took a handful and backed up closer to the entrance of the cave. 'Strike a spark whilst I get some of the wood from the pile. I think this might be a hermit's cave.' He felt around for the fuel, finding some thick branches and hauling them back to where Tomas struck his daggers together – a sharp scrape in the muffled space. Toby thanked the Saints for weapons tucked into boots and clothing. One learns much when one spies on others.

The flame was paltry, belittled by the howling wind driven in under the overhang, but they fed it as if it were a starving babe, kneeling on their aching knees, shielding the spark with stocky hands and blowing on it tenderly.

'Christ,' muttered Tomas as he came up from the smoky fug for a breath. 'We should kiss the flames and we'd do as well.'

'Look! That last little huff of yours…' Toby broke up some twigs with crisp cracks and piled them on, the infant now well and truly awake and demanding to be fed. 'It's growing.'

Eventually they had a fire, smoke eddying to the back of the cave in the wind. Toby took one of the rags and wrapped it around a stub of branch and held it to the flame until it caught. Armed with the makeshift torch, he shuffled to the back of the cave but there was nothing of significance – a bowl and a pitcher, a cot frame. But then the flame settled on something golden and Toby stopped, drawing in his breath and bending closer.

A small icon stood propped against the wall, an abject Virgin holding a sad infant. Only the gold leaf of the piece glistened with anything that could be called hope. But it had a serenity that was beautiful – a window into the world of God. Toby's breath slid out in wonder.

'Nothing back here,' he lied to his brother. 'We'll just have to sit this one out.'

Why did I lie?

The thunder now rattled much further south, a muffled grumble, and sleet continued to pepper the ground outside, a chilling wind pushing the flames into dips and dives. Toby and Tomas could see nothing beyond the entrance – the sky a large blot of dark grey bleeding across the land.

Tomas lay down close by the fire. 'Maybe if I sleep, the pain will diminish.'

'Maybe,' agreed Toby, lying close next to his brother so the warmth of each cosseted the other. His own aches had settled but he understood his brother's discomfort. He knew the agony like one knows one's enemy – through to its very centre. Sometimes when it became viciously bad, he understood why wounded men in battle would scream, 'Cut it off, cut it off!' No one really understood the pain of life for the twins. Not even Mehmet or Lady Ysabel.

Unless they have felt it, they cannot know.

He rubbed his brother's back in sympathy and eventually a deeper breath reached Toby's ears and he let his hand fall, relieved Tomas had sunk far from the reach of the ache.

But Toby lay awake.

This journey is a mistake.

He almost woke Tomas as he jerked at the thought wandering into his mind. Why he should think so he had no idea. Because when all was said and done, he had seen places he had never been to before, had met enigmatic people from different ways of life and better than anything, such experiences were feeding his muse. A long way to the back of his mind, there hummed verse and melody – something that had lain dormant of late. He was not ready to burst into song yet, but soon… Besides, he wanted to see Constantinople, albeit without drama.

Outside, the wind tore at the surroundings in a frenzy. Gusts blew into the cave like the grasping fingers of a madman's hands. Only the fire, furiously glowing in the gale's breath, stood between the twins and death by cold. Toby sat up, reaching for more wood, piling it on, allowing the wind to ignite the blaze further, for in fire there was life. He huddled again, finding comfort in his brother's form and despite the weather outside, his eyes grew heavy.

Vaguely in the firelit shadow of the hermit's cave, he could see the glister of the icon. 'Mary Mother,' he whispered. 'Protect us and grant us a safe return.'

He wished he could discern the Virgin's face to see if she acknowledged his prayer.

'I'm a fool,' he chided himself in secret tones.

Fool, fool, fool.

And at last, he slept.

'Toby, Toby!' Tomas called in his ear. 'Wake up you lazy sod, wake up!'

Toby groaned. 'Go away, Tomas. Let me sleep…' The air around him was sharp with cold and his breath sliced at the inside of his nostrils. Beneath the hood of his cloak, he heard his brother cursing him. He heard the wind and he heard…

His eyes flew open. There *was* no wind. It had died. Dead. Gone. And as Tomas' impatient sigh bounced off the walls, the muffled silence of winter closed about them.

And yet it is almost summer.

He sat up.

The fire had reduced to sad, ineffectual coals and the cave was as cold as a mountain snowdrift. He glanced out to the entrance.

'See?' said Tomas.

Snow covered the hill, the sky had cleared and the sun pushed weak beams to the frozen ground.

'Jesu,' breathed Toby. 'It's a long time since we've seen snow, Tomas.' He shivered, remembering a childhood spent staring at the winter mountains behind Pigna. 'We need to move,' he added. 'Or we shall die in here. How a hermit can believe they are closer to God with such discomfort I do not understand.' He scuffed dirt over the remains of the fire, red coals disappearing to a grey nothingness.

'Except,' said Tomas. 'When you are on the edge of death by freezing, you know God will be waiting with warm open arms. Which way?'

'To the chapel…'

The two wrapped themselves doubly tight and strode into a white world that had already begun to melt as the sun took possession of the sky. A kestrel with a rose-coloured chest swept by, a bad tempered shriek dropping down upon them. Faintly, they heard another sound.

They looked at each other.

'Calling. Someone's calling…' Tomas put his hands to his mouth and hollered and the two headed up the steep incline, following a path through the spiny *phrygana*. At a bend, just as they prepared to grind on ever upward, a tall darkly-clad Greek priest appeared, his cloak falling in straight folds. Mehmet and Ahmed followed behind.

'Allah be praised,' Ahmed grabbed the twins and squeezed them. 'I was sure you had been struck by lightning or at the very least blown from the island into the sea. Or even frozen into little pillars of…'

'What he means,' Mehmet interrupted, 'Is that we have been more than worried for you and are relieved beyond measure.' He clasped the forearm of each and then spoke to the priest, thanking him for his kindness.

The priest turned depthless dark eyes upon them. Tobias wondered at his likeness to an icon's elongated face – a face filled with patience, compassion and humanity. His hair flowed abundantly and mingled with the curls of an equally bushy beard and the only sign that he was a priest, apart from his funereal robes, was a large wooden cross hanging on a leather thong across his chest.

Mehmet said, 'This is Father Giorgios. He is pleased that God saw fit to direct you to the cave…'

'So are we,' Tomas said as the priest continued to talk. 'We *can* speak Greek, Mehmet, so we can understand what he says.'

'Of course you can. In which case you might answer his question. Did you touch anything in the cave?'

'No, Father Giorgios,' said Tobias. 'I assume you mean the icon and it resides exactly where it should be. But we ask your forgiveness for using most of the wood supply. We were so very cold…'

The priest nodded and then passed Tomas a small bag. 'Bread, some goats' cheese, and a little wine in a costrel.'

The physician reached for the priest's hand, grasping it with both his own. Smiles were exchanged and the four companions were presently striding down the hill toward the Myrina harbour as the twins supped on the supplies in the bag. Toby looked back at the priest guarding the cave – his figure dark against the snow-covered ground.

'He is a very kind, holy man,' Mehmet said. 'Newly come from Mount Athos.'

'He seemed perturbed about the cave,' Tobias said. 'God alone knows why. Only those *in extremis* would seek it out. It is sparer than a monk's cell and if we hadn't had the fire, we would have frozen our privates to iced marbles.'

'It is a sacred place. Hermits require deprivation in order to be closer to their God.'

'But why leave an icon there. If they are closer to God just by being cold and uncomfortable, they don't need a painting…'

'That icon is as valuable as a king's ransom to the hermit and the priest together. In their view it is a window into their Heaven. Father Giorgios told me that the painting of such work is performed to a rigorous set of rules and spiritual preparation, and that painters consider the work a submission of love to their God. I find it intense and wonderful in its own way. Father Giorgios has a solemn and very beautiful collection of icons in his chapel but the one in the cave is apparently considered eminent.'

'Why have a hermit's cave so close to a chapel?'

They had reached the foot of the slope and their boots slipped in the slush, their cloaks dragging on the spiny thorns lining the path.

'The hermit's cave was there first. It was considered a remote place for priests from Mount Athos to become hermits. Until recently, the only spiritual person on Limnos was the hermit on the hill and the villagers would ask him for blessings and to intercede with God and he was kind in his turn. But he was aged and infirm and he died two winters past. Mount Athos sent

Father Giorgios with coin and he and the villagers built the little chapel and furnished it with precious icons painted at the monastery.'

'Shall there be another hermit, think you?' Toby looked back up the enormous incline.

'Fancy being a hermit, brother,' Tomas mocked. 'I can just see you dressed in rotting silks and velvets and on your knees before a woebegone Virgin.' He knocked Toby's arm and proceeded on with Ahmed, whistling a tune as he went.

By the hems of the Blessed Virgin, Tomas, I hate your hard edges.

Mehmet ignored Tomas' sarcasm, though his gaze followed the little man through slitted eyes. 'Father Giorgios did not say, but in the meantime, it seems it is his duty to keep the cave in readiness, making sure it is fit to receive another who may seek the solitary path to being at one with his God.'

Tobias thought how accepting Mehmet was of Christian practice and said so, but Mehmet merely shrugged and commented that all men are the same in the eyes of their God. As well you are not built like me, thought the little man. God shows no recognition of *us* as equals to our fellow men or He would make our path a little less stony.

And we would not have ended last night with our rears frozen to the ground.

Tomas was already aboard the galley where small mounds of snow clustered around the base of the mast and a white dump sat in the torn awning, victim of the night's high winds. The strakes shone damply in the strengthened sun and there was no part of the vessel that hadn't been touched by the weather.

The small crew rounded the corner of the street, emerging boldly from whichever whores' rooms they had taken shelter. It was as though they knew Ahmed would depart on the tide so that Toby thought the man had an invisible force of will. He imagined the Arab's thoughts drifting through the alleys like a fisherman's net, drawing in his catch, one crewman at a time. Toby couldn't help a bubble of awe, once again stacking the man equally against Gisborne. There was only one difference that Tobias could see – Ahmed laughed so much more. It was a memory Toby would carry with him forever. When Ahmed turned from the helm or wherever he stood on the galley, his eyes would seek Toby out and he would grin – that wide white smile that was so vastly different to the rotted smirks of peasants and nobles in Toby's past.

Faisal pushed a barrow loaded with a bag of flour – Limnos was well regarded for its cereal crops, and atop the flour were stacked herbs – rosemary, bay and dill. Hanging over the front of the barrow was a damp bag and as Faisal walked on, Toby sniffed the aroma of roast meat, an image of shredded goat steeped in rosemary and pepper bringing juices flowing onto his tongue.

'Banquet tonight,' Ahmed said. 'We shall feast a little before returning to fish and bread.

Tomas stepped aside as Faisal placed the haunch down upon the snow gathered near his little stove.

'Are you hungry, brother?' Toby asked.

'Hell, yes. Even it was an oliphant I would eat it.'

The coast of Limnos slid by and yet it seemed to draw them ever closer rather than allowing them to leave. But by midday, they were off the northeast tip and Toby would swear he could smell the spice and incense of Constantinople drifting on the breeze. They ate at anchor and Toby and Tomas sang again – something suited to men returned from whoring so that the chorus sank into easy memory. It was the song Toby had sung to the Cretan children and which they loved but fortunately did not understand and after the song was finished, the crew began to sing songs of the desert and Al Mahgreb, so he sat with his back against the wale and recalled his friend, the Genovese trader.

He wondered if the fellow had acquired his frankincense and what else he had sniffed out. Toby had visions of a lymer hunting down valuable prey but then he decided that Pietro was too pleasant for such a comparison, although he had a vague feeling that had Pietro known of the valuable icon, he would have pilfered it and sold it to the highest bidder with not one qualm. Not a shred of guilt emerged that Toby should think so of his new acquaintance. Instead, his neck prickled with a prescient dismay.

Shoving the feeling away, he allowed the deep chant of the crew to lull him, their small *tabla* an insistent beat. Someone had taken a *mizmar* and blew a plaintive melody and it harmonised with the men like a woman's voice. It stirred the minstrel in Toby and he took note of the tonal dips and rises, aware of the claim that his troubadour tradition owed much to Arabic instruments. But then Ahmed gave an order, the instruments were stilled and the sail unfurled.

It began to fill, rounding out like a perfect breast and the leagues began to slide beneath the galley's hull. Imvros appeared off the larboard bow and Tomas and Toby begged Ahmed for a bath and more roast meat on the island.

'Between bells, Ahmed. That is all the time we need.'

'I sail by wind and tides, not your Christian bells,' Ahmed replied.

'But Faisal says we run low on salt and that the water barrels are emptying.'

'Then perhaps Faisal should have spent less time seeking Heaven between the thighs of Limnos' virgins and more time re-provisioning. No. We will sail on while we have good weather. Because when we reach the Hellespont, we may have to wait until conditions are right for us to proceed. It is a stretch of water to respect.'

Tomas was set to argue but Tobias grabbed his arm and whispered, 'Leave it,' as Ahmed's black brows drew together in a stormy line and the mouth covering those infamous white teeth twitched like a wolf about to draw his lips back to expose its fangs.

As the day drew to a close, the sun set behind them, a stain of gold leading from the western horizon to their stern.

Solid enough to walk upon. Perhaps we could go home...

But Toby chided himself for his momentary lapse, instead, drinking in the apricot and violet hues of approaching dusk.

Almost purple. Do the Byzantines own sunset as well?

'Look Toby, there, that landmass. It is the Hellespont, surely. See how the water runs between the points of land. And Ahmed says because night approaches rapidly, we will row to anchor upstream catching the last of the incoming tide, and then we will wait until the next incoming tide and use the surge to proceed to Constantinople. It means we get to go ashore once more and I can bathe, banquet and bed a wench!'

He rubbed his hands together and Tobias found he shared some of his brother's high spirits because beyond those headlands, past the site of Troy, and on through the Hellespont was the city of dreams.

Despite that finding Michael and the dye was fraught, Toby could barely contain the anticipation of seeing the centre of the eastern universe. Even though the Byzantine Empire was beginning to lose its hold in the southern Balkan lands of the Sklábenoi and even though the emperors changed as swiftly as a new fashion, to Tobias, Constantinople was the cradle of civilisation. He had heard of trade routes beyond the city to places about which he could only dream and from where camel trains emerged with spices, silk, precious gems and metals and it was surely the stuff to stir the blood of dreamers.

The sail was furled as they approached the twin points guarding the Hellespont. The oars rattled out and hit the water and the crew braced themselves for the stroke that would be called by Ahmed at the helm.

'The tide is incoming,' said Mehmet at Tomas' shoulder. 'Although it is perhaps not long from the turn, Ahmed says. We must reach Gallipolis before then. It can be quite a bullish flow.'

The oars dipped and pulled and the jerk knocked Toby and Tomas and they grabbed at Mehmet, gaining their balance, standing one foot in front of the other.

'We would be better seated,' said the physician. 'Besides, it gives Ahmed a clearer view of anything for'ard.'

The sides of the Hellespont were as if God had cleaved a sword through the land and as the curious violet dusk began to cloak itself over water and land, casting strange elongated shadows from the stern to the stem of the galley, they rowed with the tide, to the moorings at Gallipolis.

Tomas and Mehmet had moved away and Toby gazed at just another watering place in their travels. He grabbed at his and Tomas's cloaks, reasoning the night would be cold and as he flipped them out to fold them, a solid object dropped onto the deck and Toby picked it up. It was wrapped in rags that he remembered well and his heart sank so quickly that he thought it would disappear through the strakes of the hull and onto the floor of the ocean. He unwrapped the square parcel, knowing there was really no need but he did it anyway.

The Virgin stared back at him, reproachful and sad and he felt so ashamed that his eyes filled with tears and a heated flush crept up his neck to his cheeks. He looked up and found his brother watching him but he could utter not one word of admonishment.

Tomas shrugged his shoulders. 'A hermit doesn't need something so valuable and we can sell it for an excellent price.'

'*We!*' Tobias hissed.

'Christ, you angelic little prick! Me, then! And the profits will be mine!' Tomas grabbed the icon, wrapped it in his cloak and leaped ashore before the last line had been knotted firmly.

Tobias' shame burned into anger.

Never again, Tomas. Never!

He was glad Tomas had left, because Virgin notwithstanding, he thought he might have jumped at his brother's throat and squeezed until he was dead…

'Tobias?' Mehmet's voice spoke quietly from behind.

Toby tried to clear his face of all expression as he turned, but it was pointless. 'I saw,' said Mehmet.

'What do I do?' Toby's wretchedness bled across the space between them.

'Nothing. It is done. You are not responsible.'

'And yet the sorrow I feel for Father Giorgios and for the village makes me responsible.'

'Nevertheless, there is nothing to be done. Perhaps on our homeward journey we can stop there and make reparation…'

Mehmet chivvied Toby onto the dock, whereupon he called to Ahmed, telling him they would see him anon. The galley master waved, caught up in the business of ordering his crew.

'He is so much worse than I ever imagined, Mehmet. A blasphemous, detestable person.'

'Yes.'

For a moment, Toby wished Mehmet had disagreed with him, that the physician might argue there was something dormant in his brother that might be re-awakened to the good. But it was a fruitless wish.

'Tobias, there is nothing you can do to protect him. What will be will be. Perhaps we should pray to God for him, but that is all.'

'*My* God would despair after this latest. And Tomas has the gall to want to serve a king! He wants to leave Gisborne and enter King Richard's court! 'Tis surely a joke! He has no honour.'

'Worse men have served the King. It may be his saving grace.'

Toby stood still for a moment, closing his eyes. 'I could have killed him. Killed my brother for the shame of his actions.'

'And doomed yourself to a lifetime of guilt, Tobias.' Mehmet bent and reached for Toby's shoulders, shaking him gently. 'He chooses his own path. Let yours be wiser. You serve my lord Gisborne and your God. Remember that. We have a job to do.'

Toby scoffed. 'Does it occur to you that it is entirely within Tomas' power to ruin this venture?'

'All the time, and sadly we cannot un-apprise him of what he already knows. But we must keep vigilant and tell him nothing to jeopardise what we hope to achieve. His ignorance from now on will be our success. I'm sorry, Toby, but it is the way it must be.'

Toby nodded and with a heart heavier than stones from a trebuchet's basket, the two walked on, all enjoyment at being on Byzantine land having dissolved like salt in seawater.

Tobias had long ago decided that all ports, large and small, inland and sea-based, had been moulded to a pattern. Taverns, shrieking birds, clusters of weathered travellers and crew and babbling noise. Even as night fell, it was the same everywhere and comfort could be gained from the familiarity and constancy.

This port bubbled and fussed like potted water over a fire. A fleet of craft all waited for daylight and the next incoming tide, to continue on in a motley flotilla of trading vessels, to the mother-port – Constantinople.

Voices, dialects and languages assaulted Toby's ears, but he took in little as he fumed at his brother's dishonour. At one point he looked up from examining the flame-lit way beneath his feet. 'Where do we go?' he asked Mehmet.

'To find good food in a quiet eating house away from here,' Mehmet replied. 'I think you would prefer it, would you not?'

Toby nodded.

'But Tobias, we will not talk of Tomas again. It achieves nothing.'

'Agreed,' said Toby. 'If you think so.' But some perverse part of him wanted to disembowel his brother's action, to take it apart bit by bit until it lay in all its hideous boldness across the ground in front of him. He glanced across toward the doorway of an eating-house that spilled hungry customers onto the alley and his gaze sharpened as he scanned the faces at the entrance.

'Pietro!' he shouted.

But no one took any notice and if the swarthy Genovese had been there before, he was nowhere in evidence when the knot of folk cleared.

'Toby?' Mehmet turned back.

'Sorry. I thought I saw a familiar face, but I was wrong.'

They turned up a narrow lane and found an eating-house that could barely seat six, sliding onto a trestle, Mehmet ordering food and then sitting back against a wall and picking pistachios and almonds from a small clay bowl.

He's like a solid rock in a raging river, thought Toby, but kept his eyes away from the physician because he couldn't bear to see pity writ there. The food arrived on a massive clay platter, palm sized loaves of wholemeal bread still steaming and dishes of mashed black-eyed beans in vinegar and honey with a bowl of black olives and mustard seeds. He dragged a dagger from his boot and played with the bread, pulling at it carelessly and wishing he was hungry.

'Eat, Tobias. Don't let your brother wear you down.'

Toby pierced a piece of the bread with his dagger, dipped it into the bean mash and pushed it into his mouth. Mehmet had asked for mugs of wine and he picked one up, guessing it would be a common wine of no great flavour, but his nose caught the fragrance of cinnamon, cloves, black pepper and spikenard. Tasting it, he gasped a little.

'It is called *konditon,*' said Mehmet.

'It's very … enlivening. I had thought they might be disguising bad wine, but these are not cheap spices and the wine is pleasant. In fact, this is quite exceptional food. Did you know of this place?'

'I confess I did. It is owned by a trader in herbs and spices with whom I am familiar, and I hoped it would still be here. When I lived in Constantinople, my brother and I used to purchase our medical herbs from this fellow.'

'Does he live in Gallipolis?'

'No, he has always lived in Constantinople. But his daughter married and her husband runs a small trading house here, and of course this eating house. It is a way of encouraging a market. Get people to taste the herbs and spices in simple food and they will become customers very quickly.'

Toby pushed the food around with interest, skewering pieces and chewing, tasting Constantinople, camel trains and things exotic. If he didn't know better, he would say that Mehmet had deliberately requested the uplifting food as a curative for Toby's obvious melancholia.

'Is Constantinople your home?' he asked as he licked the blade of his dagger clean. 'You have never said…'

Mehmet casually wiped away Tobias' question. 'My past is just that, Toby. And my future is in the Prophet's hands. It is only the present in which I wish to live.'

'Of course, but you have a brother. Unless he is like mine and you wish to consign him to a dark and questionable corner of Hell – *that* I can understand.' Bitterness rang across the table between them like a cracked bell.

'Not at all. Anwar is a good man who is a physician like myself. When we were young and with a world to conquer, we became much enthused with medicine and healing. We trained in the city of Rey, using the teachings of the great Ibn-Sīnā. We travelled to the Holy Land treating the sick and injured, where our skills were of greatest use during a time of crusade.' Mehmet pulled at some bread and looked into a far distance. He had settled into the telling and some part of Tobias appreciated the rhythm, knowing it took him far from his own problems.

'But then we wandered on,' Mehmet continued. 'Finally reaching Constantinople. My brother met a Byzantine woman, Sophia. And that, as you say, was that.'

'But you chose not to stay.'

'Perhaps I am more of a wanderer than my brother.'

There was a finality to the discussion and Toby knew it was pointless to push further. He respected his great friend too much and some things are best left alone.

'Enough examination of the past, Toby. It is not healthy. Tell me, you said you thought you saw a familiar face earlier.'

The faintest prickle of concern dampened Toby's armpits. 'Yes. A man – a trader I know. But I was mistaken.'

There. Washed away with the spices in my wine.

For a moment he wondered why he didn't offer more detail about Pietro and then decided it didn't matter. Not now, because Tomas represented more of a threat to their trading venture than anyone.

'The thing is, Mehmet,' he said ruefully. 'I see shapes and shadows everywhere just now. My brother makes it so.'

The physician pulled out some coins from his purse and gave them to the cook, offering fine words of praise. 'Let's walk back to the galley,' he said as they entered the lane. 'Or perhaps you might prefer to sleep ashore?'

'No. I haven't the interest to seek a clean cot at this hour. The galley suits me well enough, a home away from home…'

They moved off together, talking of mattresses and warmth, and the ropes of tension that bound Toby began to loosen as the glow of wine and calm friendship sustained him.

Only Faisal was aboard when they reached the dock, a lamp beside him as he stood with a hand on his scimitar. The lamp flame lit the folds of his muscles and he looked fearsome – exactly Ahmed's plan, thought Toby. He welcomed them aboard, telling them captain and crew were eating on land and would be back forthwith. No one was to sleep ashore.

'Ah, I think Ahmed wants to be one of the first to leave at tide's turn,' said Mehmet. 'It is a good strategy because we will get a better position for mooring in Constantinople.'

They tucked themselves into cloaks and hoods and burrowed amongst the nest of empty grain sacks. Beyond the galley, the distant chatter of foreign tongues flicked round the port and it served to lull Toby. Despite his angst, he slept, the galley rocking him like a mother's arms.

'Toby, Toby! Wake up! I need your help.'

Tobias dipped his shoulder away from the frantic prodding and growled at the familiar voice, burrowing further into his cloak and hood. 'Get off me. Piss off, thief.'

'Toby, wake up. This is important!' Tomas shook Toby into wakefulness, his urgent tones also drawing Mehmet into a rapid sitting position, Faisal watching with interest.

'What is it, Tomas?' Mehmet's voice carved up the air with an authority Toby had never heard before.

'Nothing you need to concern yourself with, Mehmet. Toby can help me.'

'It seems to me he always does,' Mehmet's soft reply stung like a bee, Tomas's eyes slitting at the tone. 'But this time you deal with us both,' the physician continued.

Tomas' mouth turned down, his eyes hooded, a petulance that was becoming second nature. 'Then listen both of you. There is a slave market happening…'

'They happen everywhere and at any time, Tomas,' said Mehmet. 'Legal or illegal, they happen.'

'You say,' Tomas retorted sourly. 'I do believe I have heard that. Christ, give me some credit, Mehmet. But I tell you, this is different and I need your help…'

'I can't imagine why. We have no role to play in such an event.'

Tomas shook his head impatiently. 'There is a woman, you see…'

'Slave markets have a habit of selling them. It is what they do. Tomas, get some sleep.'

'But you don't understand…'

'I think I do and I suggest you leave well alone.'

'No, you *don't* understand!' Tomas stamped his foot. 'I bought her…'

Tobias would have leaped on his brother if Mehmet hadn't barred the way. Instead he shouted. 'You stupid, irresponsible…'

'She would have been bought by a whore-master, a man they call the Snake and who peddles women and beats and starves them. If a woman's earnings drop, he sews them into bags with stones and throws them into the sea.'

'I'm sorry for the woman,' Toby growled. 'But it has nothing to do with us. Christ Jesus, Tomas, what do you plan to do with your whore? Set up your own business?'

Tomas swung his fist and Mehmet caught it and held it. 'Tomas, Ahmed will not have a woman on board. You will have to give the woman some money and a document of manumission. She must survive as best she can.'

Tomas glared at Mehmet and then ripped his arm from the physician's grasp. 'I will *not* leave her. She is highborn – I would stake my life on it. So if I have to leave the galley I shall. I bought her and I shall care for her.'

For a fleeting moment, Tobias wanted to say how proud he was of his brother's generosity of spirit and compassion, but instead…

'Then so be it. Thenceforth you are freed from any obligation to Sir Guy. Good luck brother, and may God watch over you.' Toby turned away from Tomas, jumping off the galley, stumbling in the dark. Swearing, he stamped away, his breath pumping in and out in ragged bursts.

So that's it. Done. A brotherhood no more.

Chapter Five

✕

He had no idea where he walked in the night, nor how far – perhaps right to the walls for all he knew. But he was lost in some deep pit of anger and disillusionment. Whilst Tomas' activities over the years had been more pointed than his own, he had always dealt with it in the guise of moral guardian and because of a deep-seated love for his twin. The speed with which this had eroded since the Lionheart's galley sank was terrifying and Tobias found he could hardly countenance that he and his brother were done with each other. There was something in Tomas' face that had said *I never want to talk to you again in my lifetime.*

He chooses a whore over me, Tobias thought and then picked up a stone, hurling it into the shadowy night.

Ahead of him, a little more than that stone's throw away, a knot of men filled a small square. The place flickered gold and black in the light from sconces and voices lifted, whistled, whispered and groaned. Hands reached for purses, scrips and sashes to count money. Lips pursed and frowned and money would then be tucked back into secure places. Above all, a single Greek voice could be heard, bouncing to the walls and back and Toby vaguely thought it was an illegal game of chance.

Despite his stripped emotions, curiosity raised itself and he was glad. With stealth, quick action and by virtue of his height or lack thereof, he tunnelled round legs and through. Sturdy Bruges-dyed woollens, smooth Byzantine silks and sumptuous eastern velvets all brushed against him. On the edge of some tunics hung borders of black or brown fur with fine leather boots underneath and he realised that this was a place where money would be spent and little pain would result from the expenditure.

Eventually he pulled up on the inner edge of the wide circle.

Before him, and barefoot in the dusty square, stood a row of men with hands chained. Olive skin and pale, black hair and fair, young and old – all stripped to sagging loincloths. Some were muscled and oiled, standing proud, arrogant stares daring anyone to touch or find fault. Some tried to cover their nakedness, hunching over themselves and looking down at their feet as if shame held them tied to the ground. Two old men, wretched in their scrawniness, leaned on each other – almost as if a wind might blow them away.

A rotund, sharp-eyed man with a leather caplet edged in fleece and a long padded gambeson called out a number, a magnificent black-skinned giant stepping forward.

Slaves…

Something shifted in Toby as he watched one after another of the men sold and led away like breeding bulls or camels. One of the old men was pushed forward and he wet himself, the sour stench solidifying the humiliation.

If he could he would have saved those two old men; bought them and sailed back to Father Giorgios, begging him for forgiveness and asking him to care for the grandfathers. He despaired as they were led away without a bid, a small stain of damp in the sand the only sign they had even been.

'It would be a pity,' said a voice in his ear. 'And a loss. The trader says they are trained herbalists from beyond the western shore of the Propontis.'

'Mehmet,' Toby said without turning. 'You followed me?'

'I am a friend, Tobias, and you were in need.'

Toby ignored the inference. 'What will happen to them?'

'The trader has in his hands a note, see? He will also have been given money. Without it, their future would have been short.'

'You have *purchased* them?' Toby squeaked.

'Not I, no.'

'Then who?'

''Tis not your concern, do not worry. Just accept that old men have a lot more to offer than many people…' he lifted his palm to indicate the surrounding wealth, 'give them credit for.'

'Like women who are offered up for sale,' Toby said bitterly.

'Tomas is here,' Mehmet replied.

'Perhaps he is better as a whoremaster than serving King Richard. Or perhaps he wants his own harem.'

'Such retort doesn't suit you, Tobias,' Mehmet scolded. 'I believe he is here to collect the woman he purchased.'

Even as Mehmet spoke, the fury crept up Toby's legs from the hard-packed earth beneath. His soul began to curl like parchment too close to a fire.

'Ahmed is here as well,' Mehmet added.

'Oh 'tis a veritable meeting of true hearts.' Toby scanned the crowd for familiar faces. 'And from where does this female paragon hail?'

'Chaldia. I can tell you nothing more.'

Toby couldn't care and merely said,' I'm leaving. There is nothing for me here.'

'Perhaps not, although if you examine yourself and your reactions during the sale of those men, I think you might understand why Tomas acted as *he* did.'

'Why do you defend him?'

'Am I?'

'So it seems to me.'

'Tobias, Tomas is what he is. At this moment and even though he managed to draw attention to himself, one could almost believe there is hope for him. I prefer to nourish the positive anyway. Besides, we have too much at stake to arouse enmity in him.'

The next row of slaves had walked out and stood lined up in the flickering torchlight and the selling began in a robust spiral, men eager to purchase muscle and might. There beat an air of sexual excitement and Mehmet said,

'You are right, we need to return to the galley and sleep. Ahmed will leave early tomorrow, I am sure of it.'

They began to walk, the physician's stride long and the minstrel's twice as fast to keep pace. Toby wondered if there really was such a need to hurry, for it seemed that Mehmet wanted to get back to the dock with speed. Spy's intuition cautioned him to listen.

There...

A step outside their own echoes.

And another and more, and Mehmet began to cover more ground.

'Quickly, Tobias…'

He didn't need to say they had company because it was a sensation that surrounded them and raised the gorge in Toby's throat.

They ran swiftly round corners and down narrow streets, over cobbles that twisted ankles and stubbed toes, past darkened doors that threatened to suck Toby's heart from his chest. His fingers had immediately sought his daggers as they ran and one sat within his small-fingered grasp like a talisman, the other hugging his leg.

Mehmet ripped off his white *keffiyeh*, throwing it away, pulling at the hood of his cloak to cover his head, holding it tight as they ran – shadow figures amongst shade.

The echo behind had increased in rhythm but no voices sounded. Toby wished Mehmet had chosen a more direct route to the dock and not the circuitous one designed to walk off his small friend's frustrations.

He began to lag, cursing calf muscles that ached and the sharp pain that cut through his side. It was inevitable for he was no marathon runner and he could almost feel the hot breath of his pursuers on his neck. Mehmet was far ahead, almost to the next corner and Toby knew he had no chance of catching up, so lurched sideways up a tiny alley, sinking into a deep-set door, sliding flat against the scored wooden panelling, heart thumping.

Rasping breath halted not far away and he put a hand over his own telltale mouth, praying to God and anyone else who might listen.

Run on…

One moment of indecision it seemed and then the feet continued on.

Count them! One-two … three-four … five-six. Three sets…

They faded into the night.

Safe?

He waited, knowing Mehmet would find his way – every man to his own. He waited for the length of a small verse, then a repetition of a chorus and still no sound so he ventured out, one step, two… Down to the main street where he had last seen Mehmet, carefully scrutinising every shadow ahead.

Nothing…

He pictured the docks somewhere to his left and continued as fleet as he was able, stepping over a supine shape – snoring separating the shape from dead to living. Around the corner into the next thoroughfare – a quiet way with an occasional flame flickering behind shutters, the murmur of a voice, the bark of a dog, a cough, the guttural grunts of a sexual encounter.

By now he could smell the docks and so he began to run, dagger in hand. Always cautious, he had learned his lessons with punches to every part of his body, bruises as purple as the Byzantine dye, a knife prick to his throat once until the assailant had been head-butted backward in the groin. Once he had been laid flat by someone eager to take a purse that contained a coded message. Flat enough to hear the bells for Compline as he went down and he would swear he heard nothing until the bells for Matins woke him. The message of course, had left his purse in the intervening period. As well it was a coded message to himself about a patron for whom he wished to write a *canso*. His insurance this time sat in his hand, as the oiled fish odour of deep water slid toward him.

Close…

But something hooked his hood, pulling it hard so that it tightened against his throat, dragging him into a lane. He drove the dagger backward swiftly, hoping to pierce a thigh or a misbegotten groin.

'Leave it, Tobias,' a familiar voice hissed in his ear as a fist clamped down like an iron cuff round his wrist.

'Mehmet! Christ's teeth! I could have pierced you!'

'Ssh!'

Tobias turned and scanned the way he had come but the street was empty.

'Nothing th…' he stopped as Mehmet's back pressed hard against him.

'To me, Toby,' his friend shouted as he stepped forward, a *kilij* swinging, moving in close to slash. The weapon scored flesh, a shocking cut that ploughed onward as Mehmet continued the arc. The wounded man screamed, blood spurting, his shoulder opened diagonally to his waist, blood pooling with speed. Toby's eyes widened as the man he knew as a healer, a physician in the style of Avicenna, swung the weapon again, hitting the sword edge of another attacker, the man grunting with the impact, the sound ringing out along the lane.

The minstrel jumped over the dying man, dragging his other dagger from his boot, armed in each hand as a further shape stood at the top of the lane. Toby sidled through shadow, bending low as a knife flew from an ugly hand, missing him and striking stone. A curse followed, grunted from deep in an Italian chest. Toby ran a few strides, slipping past the angry man who struggled to free another knife from his belt, then spinning around to heft his own blade, no aim. Just a wild throw and he prayed it would strike home.

It hit something metallic, a buckle perhaps, maybe a small shield.

Are you laughing at us, God? Do You see an amusing side to this?

Mehmet had freed the *kilij* from the lock with his opponent and had begun another swing, his robes flying out along with the folds of his cloak, his hood back, his white hair wild.

No buckle in the way, no shield…

The man screamed, clutching half an arm, spouting a black stream, backing away and crying *'Dio, no, no!'*

'Mehmet,' cried Toby. 'Turn!' The attacker upon whom he had thrown his knife was advancing swiftly but Mehmet swung himself in a circle and caught a chest puffed out in fury. A glancing blow, but Toby cast his remaining knife and the point crunched into the exposed back, deep into a dead man's spine. The fellow fell next to his accomplice, the half-armed felon sobbing, running on faltering footsteps out into the street and away.

The lane heaved with ragged breathing whilst a cat yowled in frustration and a burst of hoarse laughter poured its inappropriate way toward them.

'No one came to help us…'

'This is a port filled with aggression. It is lifeblood and common. Who would bother?' Mehmet stubbed his toe on Toby's dagger, bending to pass it over. Toby yanked the other from the dead back and wiped it on the hem of the deceased's cloak.

'The one that spoke – I swear it was a Ligurian accent.' Toby's throat burned and his voice cracked.

'Half the mercenaries of Europe are from the Italian provinces, Tobias. It means nothing.' The two men left the dead behind and walked into the broader lit thoroughfare.

'Deliberate, think you?' Toby sheathed his knives.

'Yes. Of *that* I am sure.'

Toby crossed himself and flung a glance at Mehmet as the *kilij* was wiped on a hem and sheathed with a muffled rattle. He'd never seen Mehmet with anything bigger than a knife and to see him wield a blade with such critical precision had been a shock. The man's face glistened with a fine layer of effort.

'Are you hurt?' Toby asked.

'No. For all that they meant to kill us, they missed any part of me, but I'm not as supple as I once was. And you?'

'Not a scratch. It pays to be small. Who do you think?'

'Someone who wants to stop us. They want the purple.'

A shiver passed over Toby. 'They were unlucky, then.'

Ahead, the galley rocked mildly at anchor and the dock had long since ceased seething. Lights flickered on the waters of the Hellespont, illuminating bows and sterns, galleys and dhows, flat rivercraft and barges, lights hanging from mastheads and dancing in the flirting nightbreeze.

'Would you take a drink with me, Mehmet? Just to settle our heartbeats?'

They stood in front of an empty booth, the yawning purveyor cleaning his fingernails with the end of his knife.

'No, I thank you, and to be frank, Tobias, I think you should return with me. Being alone, being an individual, is not something I countenance now. We are marked men. Even your brother I would say, although there is little we can do about him now. I will see you aboard with me.' He pushed Toby a little on the shoulder, but Toby dug firm.

'Mehmet, there is the boat,' he pointed. '*There* is Faisal. I am only a few feet away. Please. After Tomas, after the chase – I just need to restore my calm…'

'Toby, this is *not* what I recommend. Do you think to rush to the wine bottle like your brother every time we are stretched on this venture? Because stretched we will be, I can tell you.'

'Just one drink? Please? You know me well enough to know I'm a man of my word and you also, I think, know what it is to realise you may not see your brother for some time, if ever again.'

Mehmet's eyes stared right into Toby's saddened and exhausted soul, perhaps looking for something he might recognise, and then he sighed. 'One drink only and I will tell Faisal to watch you.' He touched Tobias' shoulder and turned away, crossing to the waterside and stepping aboard the galley where he spoke to Faisal.

Toby saluted as Faisal looked toward him, then walked to the stall that leaned its wood and hemp backside against the wall behind. The vendor stared down at him with wide eyes, his fingers feeling for a charm, a relic, a cross.

Something angry flickered inside Toby's soul and he said in Greek, 'Yes, I am indeed Devil's spawn and I can turn your *peos*,' he pointed to the man's groin, 'to a snake by clicking my fingers. Give me a wine. Now.'

He slapped down a coin, something with the gloss of silver but which wasn't, as wine was slopped in front of him and he drained it in one gulp.

'Don't stop,' he added. 'Snakes are on the tip of my tongue this night.' He flicked his tongue back and forth and hissed and the fellow slammed another wine in front of him, crossed himself and then pulled a hemp curtain down, closing the booth between he and Toby.

'Cruel, my friend. But amusing. And you seem to speak Greek far better than you said in Chandax. By the look of the fellow's face, you seem to have made your point.'

'Pietro! Ha! Trust me, the night warranted it. I am in an evil mood. It happens to we creative spirits when the muse deserts us.' Toby nudged the Genovese. 'But you said you didn't speak Greek and yet you understood what I said.'

'In trade, Tobias, one never reveals too much. Which,' Pietro said with charm, 'makes me wonder why *you* claimed to speak Greek badly.'

Think Toby! Dance on your toes...

'I *do* speak Greek badly, Pietro. I would not be accepted amongst Byzantine nobles for the way I spoke to the wine-seller. There are two forms of Greek – a colloquial manner and marvellous for curse-making and gutter talk. And then there is the refined style. Which sadly isn't mine.'

'Then how will you sing for your supper?'

'I am a fast learner. Already I am learning from an Arab physician who travels with us. By the time we reach Constantinople, I will be able to conduct myself in perfect Greek with great aplomb, have no fear. Now tell me, are you here in Gallipolis waiting for a tide-change?'

'Yes, and I chafed to sit anchored until I realised one can always make money!'

Toby huffed out a laugh. 'Really? Here? Not frankincense, surely.'

'You remembered. How delightful.' The Genovese touched Toby's arm. 'No. I have merely chanced across this and that which will give me a return. Would you like to see a little to whet your appetite?'

Tobias nodded. Despite himself, he was disarmed by Pietro's manner. Mayhap the fellow would be different with someone who threatened he and his merchandising, but Toby was just a minstrel…

'But before I do,' Pietro said as he sat on the trestle next to Toby, 'tell me, have you made money yet?'

'No. Although the galley cook feeds us better when we sing.'

'Tuh,' Pietro shook his head. 'Money is there to be had, my friend. I just said exactly those words to the man who sold me this.' He tapped the wrapped bundle lying before them – a cocoon of light hemp fabric with a cord tied round.

'Expensive?' Toby asked.

'A little. But I will double or triple my investment.' Pietro began to unknot the cord. He had fine hands, unused to hard work, Tobias thought, with olive skin and a course dusting of black hair across the backs. His fingernails were square and clean and the chemise sleeves that poked out of the long tunic at the wrists were as white as pristine snow. The tunic itself was finely woven wool the colour of a pomegranate and it became Pietro's swarthy colouring well. Between Chandax and Gallipolis, the merchant had become affluent.

Or so it seemed.

As the cord fell away, Pietro rolled it and laid it down neatly, the flame of the torches on the town walls catching a silver dagger handle at the belt.

Do you fight, my friend?

But the man was so filled with lazy amiability that the idea of a fighter sitting opposite failed to take root. He took an age to unroll the hemp and Toby had an intuition that was cold and hot all at once. He looked around, sure he was being watched, and caught only one man staring – a rough-cut type with round eyes and a smudge of a beard. He wore an unremarkable cloak and in the brief blink, Toby doubted he'd recognise him again, so ordinary was he. The man looked over Toby's head, touched his forehead with a finger, pushed himself from the wall against which he leaned and walked away.

So I am not your quarry, then?

He dissolved into the shadows of the docks as if he had never been but Tobias' stomach churned.

'There,' said Pietro, smoothing out the wrapping. A picture lay face down, red and blue paint showing a squeeze of colour between the boards. Toby watched as the long fingers turned the piece over and the cheap wine that he had drunk shot to his mouth in a flood tide.

'Ha!' Pietro exclaimed. 'You are speechless. So was I when I saw it. Do you know how valuable are icons like this? Since the Byzantine rulers reinstated them within the Church, it is almost impossible to find any of quality to take to our own markets. The Byzantines are very protective of things they value, Tobias.'

Tobias swallowed bile and pulled himself together. 'It is truly beautiful. Divine, I would say. Work from a true master with much love for his subject.'

'That's exactly what I thought. I am told it may have emerged from the monks at Mount Athos although I know nothing about these things. Do you?'

Toby couldn't bear to look at Pietro, taking the icon in his hands, running his fingers over the smooth gold leaf and the thicker paint on the boards. He lingered on the Virgin's mournful expression. 'Do you seek to keep it for yourself?'

'By the Saints, no. I'll take it to Genova. I can make a goodly return by selling it to a noble lady who would crave to hang it above her oratory.'

'So you have a fortune in your hands. You are very lucky.'

'Then so, may I say, is your singing friend, Julius.'

Toby's stomach sank to the dusty ground beneath his boots and he scoffed. 'Julius? Well, that *is* news. Only this day he asked me to add to an empty purse!'

'Then you will be thrilled to learn his purse was plump after doing business with me, although he may have spent it by now…'

Toby bit down on anything he might have wanted to say. Anger, disgust – even fear had rippled round his mind the moment he had seen the icon. To hell and back with the icon anyway, he thought. That his brother should be doing business with Pietro who sniffed trade like a bull sniffs the air behind a cow at the ready!

Christ's nosehairs! What price the Tyrian purple now?

'*He* owned this? Julius? He never said,' Toby pulled at anything to deflect the man from a possible trail of discovery.

'And you wonder at the depth of your friendship perhaps? Do not. We all have secrets.'

More than you can possibly imagine, Pietro from Genoa.

Concern rattled Tobias as he thought of Saul, of Gisborne – all relying on the need for secrecy in this endeavour. Within moments of seeing the icon, the air that Toby breathed had thickened like a noxious fog and his head ached because of it.

'But if it is so valuable,' Toby said, 'why then did he sell it to you? Surely he would have done better to take it to the highest bidder himself.'

Pietro smoothed his hair back from his face, slicking it down so that the swarthiness and glittering eyes stood out even more in the flickering flame light.

'I would say he needed to divest himself of something that was stolen. What say you?'

'Julius? A thief?'

'It is just a simple answer to your question, my friend. I do not mean to insult him. But he did need fast funds and I was able to help him.'

'You say?' Toby pushed sweaty palms between his knees, pressing hard.

'He wanted to bid for a slave woman from Chaldia or some such. I was dumbfounded. Do you need a woman for your performances?' Pietro asked, eyes widening with blithe interest.

'Perhaps *he* does. *I* do not.' Toby's reply was crisper than he intended and Pietro's head tipped to the side as he assessed Toby.

'I see. You have parted the ways.'

'In a manner of speaking but I don't wish to speak of him anymore. I have been sitting here, Master Pietro, compiling lines in my head for a new *canso* with which to dazzle Constantinople. Do you wish to hear?'

Pietro stood, wrapping the icon with care. 'Another time, I regret.' He looked across to a group of men who beckoned to him. 'I am coming!' he called and cast a smile down upon Tobias. 'I have a feeling we will meet again, Master Tobias, and when we do, I hope your luck will have turned. Good luck and farewell.'

As he turned away, he tucked the icon under his arm, joining his companions and laughing loudly as they walked into the darkness.

Tobias sat winded.

Some deep part of him felt that nothing about that meeting nor its content had been spontaneous. It was almost as though he had been tested by the Genovese – as if the fellow had been mining for gold. *Was* he a malicious man, probing with intent, or was he merely amusing himself at Toby's expense? Because for one moment he felt as if Pietro had got pleasure from informing on Tomas. Ah, so many knots and tangles because more than the icon and the slave woman, or money and Tomas' doubtful behaviour, had Pietro discovered the purple?

He jumped off the seat and strode across to the ship, nodding at Faisal as he swung on board. '*Salam alaykum*, Faisal,' he said. 'Has everyone returned?'

'Yes, Master Tobias. Except Ahmed who says he will stay on shore this night and Master Tomas, who has not returned.'

'He is no doubt with Ahmed,' Toby replied. 'Good night to you, Faisal. Stay safe.'

Tobias trod around the sleeping forms on deck and found Mehmet at the stern, cushioned on the fortuitous sacks and wrapped in his cloak. Above them, the Gallipolis sky hung like ebony velvet and stars sparked and spat, a sliver of ivory moon punctuating the dark sweep of the heavens. Not a single veil of cloud spoiled the clarity of that view and at other times, Tobias may have observed it long, plucking words from his lexicon to describe its magnificence and then building a melody to frame it. Instead, amongst the discordant sound of snores and farts, Toby shook Mehmet's shoulder.

The physician rolled over, a *janbiyah* in his hand, the other grabbing Toby's ankle to trip him. The moment he recognized his chess partner, he hissed, 'Toby, I could have killed you.'

'’Tis a night for it, Mehmet, and a long one at that,' Toby shook the hand from his leg. 'I need to speak with you urgently. It can't wait.'

Mehmet sheathed the knife and beckoned, the two moving as far to the stern as they were able.

'What goes?' Mehmet grabbed his hair and twisted it back out of the way.

'It's Tomas,' he said. 'No please, don't sigh like that. Listen! We may be at great risk.' He related the meeting with Pietro, explained who he was and the progressions of the hour just passed. '… so I am concerned that Tomas may have revealed the truth of our secret venture. Pietro is as sharp as a knife point, Mehmet, and if he knew the purple was hidden, he would race the Devil to get to it first.'

Mehmet surveyed the crew and then looked over Tobias' aching head. Toby swore he could have fallen asleep on his feet, so filled with exhaustion was he as he waited for the Arab to offer advice. He rubbed at his head, pushing ragged hair away from eyebrows and feeling rough stubble on his cheeks – nothing like the silky troubadour Di Dia at this moment.

'Then we must ask Tomas,' Mehmet replied. 'He approaches this moment with his lady slave and Ahmed.'

Toby whipped round.

The sky was beginning to soften, pearly light stitched along the eastern edge. Behind him, Faisal yawned and he wished they could stop the further progressions of their journey until they had sorted the issues of the moment. But difficulties would be laid bare as the crew paddled to midstream, ready to speed the galley on to Constantinople. Tomas' rope-tinted hair flopped on his forehead and his eyes flashed with the kind of bold triumph that made Toby want to cuff him. Even the bow to his legs, object of lifelong discomfort, aroused no sympathy in Toby.

Beside him walked Ahmed, stormy and grim. That expressive mouth curved down like a scimitar but Toby suspected the description would not be welcome. Between the two men, a delicate woman of no great height walked with her hands unbound, pride in the tilt of her chin. She wore a veil over her hair, but a small dark tendril had escaped, curling at her forehead, speaking of a once carefree nature, Toby thought, as his imagination raced ahead of him. She had been captured surely, near Chaldia and forced into slavery. She had lost her family, perhaps even her husband and children…

Her robes, common cotton in a faded blue, grazed over parts of her body as a small breeze blew. She was desperately thin, a fact compounded by the scythe-like angle of her cheekbones as she turned her head away.

Ahmed jumped aboard and the craft rocked a little, causing murmurs from the sleepers on deck, some shifting a hip to compensate. Faisal stood still – curious, staring, the more so when Ahmed turned and invited the woman aboard. Faisal's mouth dropped open as Tomas jumped onto the wale, holding onto the mast stay, laying his palm out for the woman to grasp as she stepped down.

Everything about her intimated grace as if she were born to it. She had a timeless face somewhere between nineteen and nine and thirty years perhaps. As she gained her balance on the deck, she looked around, her eyes meeting Toby's whereupon his heart bounced from his chest and lay beating at his feet. Her eyes told a story that frightened him with its breath.

She reminded him of the icon. In that one glance, he saw immeasurable sadness deep in her very soul and he knew he was right. She had lost much when she was sold into slavery. It seemed as though she knew the world's pain and measured it equally with her own.

Oh Blessed Virgin, here is my story, my poem, my canso. *Glory to You and my everlasting gratitude.*

But the woman's gaze had moved on as Tomas explained to her where she must sit. She said nothing, merely nodded her head once and he gave her a gentle push toward the canopy near the mast. Faisal had roused each member of the crew and as they rose to move like shadowy spectres to their posts, they cast surreptitious glances at the woman, some reaching for their good luck charms.

The oars slid out on the larboard side, the mooring lines were retrieved and with a barely audible sweep of the blades, the vessel swung out from the shore into the swirl and tug of the incoming tide.

Toby lifted a thumb to his mouth, chewing on it, in awe of this woman and her effect upon him. What shocked him was that the feeling was almost as strong as his emotions when he had first met Ysabel of Gisborne, and he had thought she was the apogee. Briefly he also wondered how Tomas had convinced Ahmed to transport a woman upon his ship – and not just a woman but a whore! Indeed, why had Tomas changed his mind and returned to the fold at all?

Well, perhaps not returning to *all* the fold, because he avoided his brother utterly, turning his back upon him or turning his head away.

Mehmet however, would appear not to be put out by any of it, because he ignored Tomas' posturing and asked directly why he had returned.

'Because I need to travel to Constantinople as swiftly as I can,' was the reply but Tobias walked away. If there was aught else to be revealed, he doubted Tomas would do it with his brother within touch. Better to allow someone subtle to secure answers to difficult questions.

Instead he walked to the canopy where the woman sat with her back against a bale of cloth. The sky had paled a little more and the light illuminated shadows under her eyes and a bruised face. Her eyelashes feathered softly onto her cheek and Tobias' heart fluttered in his chest.

It was like a bird in a cage, wings beating, searching for freedom and Tobias had long since called it his muse. It only sprang into life like this when he was truly inspired. But as well, there was something else.

He was captivated.

'Excuse me, *Kyría Mou*, can I fetch some food or wine for you?' He spoke in common Greek, wondering if she understood. She flicked her head upward, her hands crunching into tight bunches. 'I'm sorry. I didn't mean to startle you,' he continued. 'My name is Tobias and I am a passenger on the galley.'

He watched the calculation going on in her mind. Was he from the good or bad in life, because she had clearly seen both – the massive dark blue and yellow bruise on her cheek was testament.

He smiled and bowed, saying 'I am a minstrel.'

She replied so delicately he wondered if she spoke to him at all. 'I am called Zoë. I…' she bit on her lip leaving indentations. Any harder and beads of blood would have appeared. 'I need nothing. Thank you.'

'Tobias, move away. You are unwanted,' Tomas growled as he approached.

'Peace, brother.' Toby held up his hands. 'I only asked Zoë if she needs sustenance.'

'As you see, she does not. So kindly leave us.'

Tomas folded his arms across his chest, legs spread against the forward motion of the galley as the rowing continued. Astern, as the sky lightened further, agitated voices rushed across the water as other captains and crew realised Ahmed had made the break ahead of them in the race to moor in Constantinople. Within a breath, as those urgent voices filled the air, the atmosphere changed. The crew lifted their pace at the oar, Ahmed on the tiller and Faisal calling the stroke.

'As you wish,' Toby replied. 'But Tomas, we are in close quarters. Civility smells sweeter in such circumstances.' Without waiting for a reply, he hurried to the stern where Mehmet pulled at leather straps around a hemp bag, withdrawing a small jar stoppered with wax and with the tip of his knife the physician levered the wax off and smelled the contents.

'Arnica,' he said, as he pushed the wax seal back into the neck of the jar.

Her face…

'Tomas admits meeting Pietro at the slave market,' he told Tobias. 'When

Zoë appeared, they were both rather taken with her. Tomas is convinced she is of noble birth although she does not admit to this. At any rate, he did indeed buy her with money raised from the sale of the icon. As to the purple, he maintains he said nothing – that he had neither the time nor the inclination as he needed to conclude the sale of the icon and bid successfully for the woman.'

'Do you believe him?'

'Yes.'

'Then why are we being followed and attacked, Mehmet. Who has betrayed us?'

'I do not know and we will think on it anon. I must see to Zoë's face, excuse me.

'It does not concern you that you dally with a whore?'

Mehmet stopped in his tracks and swung round. 'Did it concern *you* just now? Tobias, sometimes you are as sullen as your brother. I do not remember this about you. And do not excuse yourself with the moral high ground. I said the same to your brother and told him to examine his behaviour. I suggest you examine yours.' He left the verbal crossbow bolt hovering in the air and turned away.

Toby looked up to the heavens and hissed a whisper. 'Christ Jesus, if You care at all – take Your blessed nosehairs, Your toenails and Your damned largesse and push it where there is not one beam of sunlight. Because as someone who cares and who guides, You truly have no understanding.' He gestured rudely at the sky and feeling not a speck of guilt, pulled himself up onto the wale and sat astride, watching the froth and bubble of the water cream past.

He had changed.

Of that there was no doubt.

It was as well that the water was ruffled as they swept along under the power of oars and tide because he had no wish to see a reflection of what he had become. He no longer represented di Dia or Passebru or any of the hundreds of identities he had inhabited. But equally, he was no longer Tobias, the friend of an almost four year old nor the intimate of the light of his life – Ysabel, lady wife of his master, Sir Guy of Gisborne. No, he was merely a common, judgmental peasant from Liguria.

Just like his brother.

Mary Mother!

He looked heavenward once more.

Is this how You show me the way? Send me round in circles within my head until I meet the answer coming toward me?

He and Tommaso were indeed the same. The hard point for Toby to bear, though, was that Tomas had every reason to change. Even Sir Guy had only chided him lightly for his behaviour, aware of the damage the near drowning had caused. And that was only a few months ago. What excuse did Tobias have?

None.

Except that his pretty feathers had been roughened once too often by his brother. He grimaced as a seabird flew overhead and a ribbon of birdshit slopped onto the wale, just missing his knee.

Mehmet appeared at his side. 'Tobias, I have been thinking that we were betrayed in Venezia. From the moment we left port we have been followed and unless we can unmask the traitor, we will be fighting at each other's back to the end. Unless we kill them first.'

Toby swung off the wale, making sure he lifted his leg high enough to avoid the shiny white dung. 'But who? Our household is stalwart. Especially so since William's abduction.'

'It may not be from our house. Perhaps from Saul's...'

'But apart from Phillipus there are only Saul and Ariella. Oh ... Rebekah the housekeeper and her daughter, Rachael, as well. They are all devoted to Saul. Even if they knew anything, they could be nailed to a cross before they revealed it.'

Mehmet frowned. 'Phillipus?'

Toby thought hard about Saul's clerk. He knew little of his early history except that Saul had met him in Trapezus on one of his expeditions and impressed with his language and writing skills, had offered him a position. Tobias was sure he had read the man right the first day he met him – a loyal retainer. This close devotion within the Jewish merchant's house had been one of the things that so delighted Toby – disparate people but a family nonetheless, just like the Gisborne household. Perhaps it was why the two families bonded so tightly.

'He is a good man, Mehmet.'

'But then did we not think the same of Ulric of Camden?'

It was something Tobias preferred to forget. How blind everyone had been. But he could see Mehmet's point.

'Tobias, this venture seemed so secure. I imagined any danger would occur in Constantinople, not as we island-hopped across the Adriatico. We must examine everyone in both households over and over until we find the leak and we must also complete the venture with renewed speed and secrecy. Someone is on our tails...'

He looked back to where a flotilla of vessels had begun to follow them along the strait, filling the densely flowing water between the high riverbanks. On the left was the western gateway to Tobias' history and on the right, the eastern gateway to lands of mystery and magnificence.

And potential murder...

'Is my brother with us or against?'

Mehmet picked up the hemp bag, undid the straps and placed the arnica inside. 'I do not know. I was speaking with Zoë and Tomas said nothing.'

The galley flew. As they sped toward an insipid sun and the Propontis, it was as if they followed some enchanted path – perhaps in the wake of Jason and the Argonauts. For Tobias, the venture had secured an edge beyond his imaginings. His muse was now singing in full throat and the drama and the expectation of this voyage filled his head with words:

No Greek among us
Has dealt such pain
Cruelty plain,
I would maintain,
As that I've seen:
In such misery and fear I've been...

He turned his head toward Zoë who had the face of a tragic queen from a weakened empire.

My eyes scarcely move it seems
When I see her, fear so extreme,

Sweet, gracious words lacking I mean.
Since with pleasure I'm out of tune,
And nothing can I force her to,
For I know that I'll win nothing,
Except by praising, and by loving...

Chapter Six

✕

The Propontis spread before them in a dove grey sheet, a curtain of rain sitting low ahead. A breeze sniped at the decks and grabbed spray from the larboard oars, flicking it against the passengers. Toby picked up his cloak and flung it on, cursing that his dreams and fancies were about to be washed away.

He wanted to approach the waters of Constantinople in fierce sunshine so that the dome of Sancta Sophia might glisten and so that he might see every stone of the Great Wall of Theodosius as they sailed into the harbour. But rain moved toward them, turning dove grey surfaces to darkly damascened iron.

Looking astern, he watched the following flotilla disappear as a mist enclosed the ships. Rain pattered on the deck and upon the canopy in tabor rhythm. Zoë sat wrapped in a patched cloak, hood pulled forward so that no one could tell if she were man or woman. But Toby knew and the words of his new poem ran again through his head:

My eyes scarcely move it seems
When I see her, fear so extreme,
Sweet, gracious words lacking I mean.
Since with pleasure I'm out of tune,
And nothing can I force her to,
For I know that I'll win nothing,
Except by praising, and by loving…

'It won't last!' Ahmed's shout punctuated the progress of the lyrics.

'You say?' Toby called back.

'A spring shower. It means nothing.' Ahmed's *kilij* frown had righted itself. 'We lead the race to the harbour and will be moored firmly and ashore as they all limp into port.'

Obviously the idea of a woman on board had been dealt with. The greater issue was beating his fellow seamen on the water and showing exactly who was the galley master. Tobias wished he was able to put superstitions and worries aside without a care and with such abandon. Perhaps that explained how Ahmed sailed the fine line between honest ship owner and questionable *peirate* so easily.

They were all the same – Davey, Dante and now Ahmed. Toby rather liked their curiously wild nature. It was always fuel for another poem, another ballad. After all, words of love became meaningless when repeated endlessly. He looked at Zoë.

Most of the time.

The galley swung slightly to starboard, the oars held for a beat or so.

'Why are we swinging off course? Surely we should continue in a straight line.' Toby watched their wake curl away to be lost in the petty squall that surrounded them. 'They will beat us!'

'It would be an ignorant master who sails on in a straight line, little music man. The wind strengthens, you see, as the rain diminishes. And it is a headwind, hardly suited for my oarsmen, despite their strength. But if we cut across it and raise the sail, we can fly along the edge of the southern coast here, reaching closer to Constantinople when we turn again. Like so…' He sketched a zigzag pattern on the deck with his fingers.

'I see,' said Toby when he really did not – he knew nothing of sailing the seas and had no wish to learn. Ahmed's shout to ship the oars and set the sail filled the air, whereupon the canvas bellied with a bad-tempered ruffle and then a loud flack. The galley lurched and then banked and Tobias grasped at the wale. He glanced at his brother, not unsurprised to see a pale face and he wanted to reassure him, but Tomas had knelt by Zoë's side, picking up her hand in his own and squeezing it.

Sard! She might as well be a pet dog as a whore, he thought.

'Why is speed of such great need, Ahmed?'

Does he know for sure that our murderers follow us? That they want the purple?

'There are only so many spaces to moor alongside within the seawalls. To moor close in means we can be ashore quickly and just as quickly be loaded with our cargo and gone. If we miss out on such a position and have to anchor in the harbour, we will waste time and money transporting ourselves back and forth and making ourselves vulnerable to attack. I would prefer not to give the Guard or any others anything that belongs to me.'

Indeed, an axe-fall rarely misses.

'You think we are in danger, do you not?'

'Of course, little man. Don't you?' This time Ahmed grinned as if the whole idea of theft and murder was the best thing to have come his way in a long while.

'Yes...'

Ahmed patted his *kilij* and then looked up at the sail, shifting their course slightly to fill the sail to bursting point with the fresh wind that had lifted the surface of the water to a white chop and which cut into Tobias' cloak like a honed blade.

He moved forward a little, leaving Ahmed to his sailing and slid his back down the starboard side of the galley, casting his mind back to Venezia. Person by person, he wished to examine each of the households and make sure that everyone was beyond doubt.

Lady Ysabel, Lady Cecilia, Bridget and Gwen. Beyond reproach. Johannes of Lübeck, Adam of London and Pretty Boy John, all with mouths tighter than a maiden before swiving. Guillaume, Mehmet, himself and Tomas; he had been through this list so often it read like a Domesday Book.

And within the Ben Simon house there were people of honour who had remained by Saul's side after the dreadful Jew-baiting in York and London. 'Mehmet,' he said as the elderly man sat next to him. 'I do not know Saul's guards well...'

'They have been with him since York, they are Jewish. It is a solidarity built on their Faith and on persecution.'

'As I thought. And in respect of Phillipus, I am sure he has a small share in Saul's business. If the purple comes to Venezia, he will make a small but handsome profit.'

Mehmet nodded as words continued on relentlessly through Toby's mind.

Then it must be Tomas...

But he says no…
Even so…
He has no reason…
But he is changed…
As are you…
I am loyal…
Are you?
I will not listen!
'Tobias?'

Toby looked up. His brother stood before him, pale, less ebullient. 'Yes?'

'You are right. Civility is required. For Zoë's sake.' He held out his hand and there beat a moment before Tobias took it.

'Thank you, brother,' he replied. Nothing more. He knew it was the only thing to do. The galley was a small space made up of a team of men who worked together hand in glove with not a ripple of discontent. Ahmed had shaped his crew well. Tobias and Tomas had no right to add an edge to the harmony aboard and besides, as Tomas said, there was Zoë to consider.

Zoë, the enigma.

Tobias didn't believe in love at the first glance so he discarded the notion that he was smitten. But he believed most completely in kindred spirits and whilst he and his brother no longer had that connection, something vibrated between Zoë and himself. He had no doubt she felt none of it but he felt excitement and enervation all in one.

He wondered if this fresh diplomatic stand between he and Tomas would allow him to get closer to the woman and decided that Tomas would do everything he could, short of pushing him overboard, to prevent it. An overreaction surely when all Toby wanted to do was talk, draw her out.

And gaze upon her…

They sailed along the coastline of the Propontis, mists twining amongst the pines and coastal scrubs, drawing back up the edges of low cliffs like nothing more than spectres or shrouds as the rain died. Tobias sat lost in his thoughts until he realised Mehmet was studying him and so he pulled himself back to the moment.

'All is well, my friend?'

A blush coursed across Tobias' cheeks and he could have curled up like a silkworm with embarrassment.

'Of course. My brother behaves with lately acquired maturity. And not before time,' he replied dismissively, wishing to change the subject. 'Mehmet, I cannot find anyone likely to have betrayed us. I have been through it time and again…'

'I disagree. Somewhere there is a very dangerous leak.'

'But we have examined everyone. We have only the pups and William left.'

William…

His eyes opened wide.

'*Sard!* Surely not! William? Could it be he?' he could not believe it was possible. And yet…

'William? How so?'

Tobias squirmed, rubbing his face and shaking his head – a child with innate curiosity possibly betraying them all.

'We went to the market in that sennight before we left Venezia – myself, William, Lady Ysabel and Johannes…'

The first day of spring, primo vera, *the kind of day where the earth wakes with the promise of seduction. The green is like malachite, the blue like lapis, the water as crystal clear as glass from Constantinople. I stood at the gate to the villa and my heart sang. For the first time since we had returned with William from that dreadful time at the Toulon Commanderie, I could feel the muse stretching. No one was about and so in honour of the day, I bowed to the world in my most courtly style. As if I were dressed in velvets and silks and with my hair combed and with rings on my fingers. Ah yes, the troubadour Di Dia or Passebru or a dozen others was alive again.*

'Toby, what are you doing?' William's voice spun me round and even though he was almost four years of age, I flushed with embarrassment.

The child laughed. 'You bowed. I thaw you.' He put a hand over his round belly and bent forward, sliding his leg out and looking at me through his thatch.

'Diavolo!' I called and began to chase him as he shrieked with feigned fear. It was the stuff that spring is made of – laughter, youth, hope, love.

'Mama wantth you to come to the market with uth. Will you?'

'Of course. Now?'

'Yeth. We are walking becauth the day ith perfect.'

They weren't his words but they had a charming innocence from his mouth.

We walked across the wooden bridges between the islets, under budding trees, through meadows that were filled with wild sage, clovers, loosestrife. What a name for a wildflower – its colour is a vivid purple. Strife and purple – ah, if only I had realised what a sign it was.

I walked with Johannes of Lübeck and we talked of our homes as we remembered them – of the mountains around Pigna, and the Trave that flowed through Lübeck like a ribbon. But it was easy to look at Lady Ysabel and William and say, 'There is our family. And this,*' looking at the water by our sides, 'is our home.'*

The market in the square of San Marco had been working its magic since the early hours and we had taken our time to get to the business of the day which was, apparently, to buy silk from Saul's market stall. He had taken a shipment of Byzantine silk and Lady Ysabel had heard he had lengths of blue. She had a predilection for the colour blue and it suited her. Enhanced her eyes and highlighted her fair hair. She was a queen of the northern countries when she dressed in blue silk and it was quite possible to love her all over again. You think I jest when I say such things? As if being me, I am not capable of love and lust? I know I am a small man but I tell you, I am as capable as the next of feeling my manhood rise in the presence of such feminine beauty. It sounds wrong, does it not, to say this of my lord's lady but I am a poet and a troubadour. It is my job to notice beauty and to comment upon it. It is not salacious or wrong and I would never let her know how I loved her so much more than a friend…

We found the stall, although by circuitous means as William hung off our hands wanting to see everything. The booth is always in the same place, a prime position, close to the massive wooden doors of the cathedral that forever seemed to be in a state of enlargement and construction. Even so, that square had beauty and it promises of great things to come. You are of course, well aware of the grandeur and spectacle yourself, so perhaps I preach to the converted. But, back to the stall…

Phillipus saw us coming and waved, his grey woollen tunic of fine quality and encircled by a ruby red girdle of chamois and silk. It spoke of subtle wealth, a sign that the silk merchant Saul Ben Simon sold nothing but the best. Never gaudy, always exquisite. The nobles knew and their ladies haunted the stall and

Phillipus was even then passing parcels to servants to carry away.

His walnut brown eyes softened as he gazed upon Lady Ysabel, just another like me so afflicted, and he said, 'My lady, we have the blue you wanted.'

'I did not think I wanted it until Saul beguiled me, Phillipus. Oh!'

Phillipus had flicked some of the length in front of my lady and it was the sky and the sea, sapphires and lapis and it glistened and sparkled with a fine silver border and it took very little imagination to see her coming down a stair, the garment flowing round her as if she had stepped from the ocean. Gisborne would see her and walk toward the stair and hold out his hand and she would step into his grasp and all those watching would feel the fierce attraction between the two. It would be as tangible as a fine glass goblet of the best Cretan wine.

'Of course Saul knew I would need it, didn't he?' She laughed and people turned to stare at this lovely woman with the cultured low voice that set butterflies dancing through one's very soul. 'He is such a prescient man, and an excellent merchant if I may say. Cut me a length, Phillipus, if you would be so kind. I would celebrate my lord Gisborne's name day in a gown of blue, I think.'

And just as she drew coins from her purse, William said,

'Papa liketh purple better, Mama. He'th getting purple from far away.'

For a moment I just stood, not really thinking much of what he had said. I saw a booth selling pies and I was hungry. But then I heard my lady hush William, and take him by the hand, pulling him to her and wrapping her arms around him, so that he was muffled, as though he had said something momentous…'

'I remember Phillipus looking nervous momentarily and Lady Ysabel and Johannes scanning the crowd for eavesdroppers close by.'

'Were there any?' asked Mehmet.

'I can't recall. I think we all hoped it was mere childish comment lost in the noise. For sure, we paid it no more thought at all. Until now.'

'And now, Tobias? What think you?'

'I … I don't know.' Tobias shook his head in defeat, finally sighing in unwilling exasperation. 'Yes. Someone did indeed hear. One does not suffer such pointed attacks otherwise, does one? It is as you have been saying. Someone knows and we are being targeted at every mooring we make because of it. The thing is, Mehmet, I don't think they want to kill us immediately. They want to capture us and pull the detail from us. Then, once they have it…' He drew a finger across his throat.

They sat together discussing the revelation. In truth it meant little. That William was the source of the leak was a blessing and a curse in one. A blessing that no one from the respective households had deliberately set out to betray them. A curse that they still had no face and no name to their enemy.

'Tomas!' Mehmet called to the twin, beckoning him over. He explained what they believed had happened, that a leak had occurred within the family, although through an unspoken agreement, neither mentioned William's name. Instead, they told Tomas of the attacks and asked for his opinion.

'You want my opinion now, when you did not see fit to tell me before?' That Tomas burned with misunderstanding and anger was as evident as the noses upon their own faces.

'It was my decision, Tomas. You were viciously seasick and then we had a dispute. At what point amongst all of that would I have found the right moment to tell you?'

'Anytime,' the man replied, his voice as cold as the mountain air near Pigna. 'I am your brother.'

'Then for Christ's sake act like you are!' Toby shouted.

'Cease this!' Mehmet exclaimed. 'If I had known that two people I respected would turn into such children, such liabilities,' he hissed this last, 'I would never have invited you to accompany me. Liabilities, you hear me?' The force of his fury stopped the twins' words as surely as if he had ripped out their tongues. 'I need cohesion and clear-thinking loyalty. If neither of you can give that, then in the name of my lord Gisborne, I will discharge you from his service forthwith. I will order Ahmed to halt at any place on this coast and you will be put ashore. Zoë will continue on to Constantinople without you, Tomas. I have many ways to see her safe when I disembark. I will find the purple with Ahmed's help and whatever happens to both of you will be beyond my interest. Do you understand? Now *get* from my sight. You disgust me. I wish to speak to Zoë alone and for some time.'

The air crackled around them, faces that had turned toward the heated exchange quickly turned away and Ahmed was seen to give a brief salute to Mehmet. There would be no support for the twins from him.

Tobias stood, his face more flushed than ever.

'Go!' Mehmet's cold anger crushed anything he might say.

He pushed past his brother, and headed toward the bow, Tomas glancing at Zoë and then following more slowly.

Tobias's breath came in gushes that filled his chest. Anger? Guilt? Pain? All of those. But whispering away in a more reasonable part of his mind was a recognition of the truth...

That he and Tomas, far more than William's mistake, would be the undoing of this venture. That two households would be reduced to nothing. Everything that Gisborne and Saul had built for their families would be gone. Even worse, what Toby saw as his family would be banned from his reach forever. He, Tobias, would turn from friend to foe in an instant and he knew that Gisborne had a penchant for revenge.

Something brushed his arm and he turned to see his brother standing next to him, enough space between so that no part would touch – just the fold of an errant cloak. Without meeting Tomas' eyes he spoke.

'I wronged you, Tommaso, and I owe you an apology.'

'You have no trust or faith in me.'

'With respect, brother, you have done little to inspire trust of late.'

Tomas said nothing and the harsh cry of seabirds and the flack of the sail seemed to underline the pathetic nature of the twins' conversation. But then,

'Did they really try to kill you?'

'No, although with the force of their attack you would think so. I tell you, that first time I jumped and spun and I was more acrobatic than I have ever been in my life! *And* in the dark. But I got a knife thrust in and thanked the Saints that you and I had learned to tumble with the best of them. The second time I barely did a thing. Mehmet's *kilij* was guided by his Prophet, I am sure. I threw two knives in the dark – one missed and the other scored but I think the man was already dead from a slice from the *kilij*. No, they didn't plan to kill us, they wanted to maim enough to capture and then torture so that pain revealed truths about the purple.'

'And you believe they will try again?'

'Most assuredly,' said Toby. 'But I think they will become more insidious. Especially when we reach Constantinople.'

Tomas stared out to sea as if he might spy his future. 'I am not a pleasant person anymore, Tobias,' he said carefully. 'I know it. Something dark holds me in its thrall most times. But at the slave market when I saw Zoë, it was as though I was unshackled.'

Tobias went to speak but Tomas stayed him, sitting next to him, flicking the dyed hair from his forehead and then encircling his knees with his arms. His clothes were rimed with salt and other questionable stains and his stubble had become a beard. He rubbed at it with nervous fingers. 'This will have to be removed before we sail into port. It is dark, isn't it?'

'It looks ridiculous.'

'You are quite unlovely yourself. And you smell.'

'God's eyelashes, do I?' Toby lifted his arms and sniffed his armpits, curling his lip as he breathed in the odour.

'Tobias,' Tomas spoke with difficulty as if he revealed too much of what bubbled inside. 'I haven't written music or words for a long time. I made it easy for myself by singing the work of others. But even if I wanted to write music it was impossible, because it had dried up like water in a cistern in Outremer. Thus I found it easier to drink and fight. It gave me the same excitement if not the same joy.

'I noticed.' Toby scratched at his filthy clothes, flicking his nail at something hard and crusty on his tunic. 'And to be truthful, Tomas, when I returned from Toulon with William and Lady Ysabel, a similar thing happened to me. I could compose nothing. As you say, it was easier to sing another's music.'

'What changed, then?' Tomas said, still picking his words as if he picked his way.

'Did I say it had? Huh, an odd few words here, a scrap of melody there but nothing like it used to be.' Toby would not say that whilst the sight of the icon had been like a key jiggling in a lock, it was Zoë the whore who had turned it. Mary Mother, he would have loved to tell the world what a feeling it was but discretion was needed. Even he could see that his brother struggled to build a bridge between the two of them and it was surely up to him to meet him halfway.

''Tis exactly so for me,' Tomas continued in a low voice. 'Or it was. Until I saw Zoë and then a well of emotion fountained up and I found I had words in my head again and it has become another debt I want to repay. It is why I sold the icon. I needed money to free her and help her find her family.'

'I understand, I really do.'

I wish I could tell you how her face and her soul have freed me...

'But why steal the icon in the first place, Tomas. It was so important to the village and to Father Giorgios. It was wrong.'

Tomas' eyes cooled a little. 'Perhaps. But I felt it was of greater use elsewhere. As it turned out I was right. You wouldn't have loaned me money to buy her, would you?'

Toby grunted, playing with a knot in the plank between his feet, pushing at it, feeling the grain of the wood. 'Well, all I knew was that you wanted to buy a whore, so most likely not. But still, theft is theft and theft of a religious piece...'

'No, enough moralising, brother. You have made your point.'

Toby nodded, although he would have liked to pursue the argument. But instead he took a different path, aware that every word felt as if it must be tasted before it was offered. 'So you will leave us when we dock?'

'I had thought I would but Mehmet said something that has made me change my mind.' Tomas turned toward the canopy for a sight of Zoë. Relieved, he sat back.

'Yes?'

'He said he had ways of helping Zoë and I decided that if he would do that, I would help both of you find the purple. After that, I would leave. Whilst in Gallipolis, I heard news of King Richard. I would go to England and join with his courtiers to await his return.'

'Why do you bother, Tomas? King Richard has not even learned the language of the people who are his subjects. He cares nothing for England beyond what he can wring from its coffers.'

'You know why.' Tomas' mood began to harden and Toby knew he had overstepped civility.

'I apologise,' Toby replied hastily. 'It is not my right to comment on your decision. But I *will* say that Gisborne will miss your service and the family will miss *you*. And I...'

Tomas' mouth flipped into a momentary smile and then he left, leaving a huge space behind.

Tobias moved as far for'ard as he was able, standing hard against the prow, curling his hands around the wood, the wind tearing at his hair and pulling all the sadness from him.

Or so he hoped.

Once, he had been the family's jester, making everyone laugh, easing tensions and enabling a sense of wellbeing to drift through the household. Ha! How life had changed. He leaned over the stem of the galley, watching the water split past the bow, waves fanning out like pieces of torn parchment, the wind rushing into the sail where it was caught, imprisoned – a slave to the canvas and the ship.

A slave…

Zoë had unlocked he and Tommaso, freed them from dull nothingness and surely not because she had a remarkable face. Perhaps it was her graceful bearing in the face of years of slavery. She seemed so politely mannered, if cowed. But then inspiration didn't come from manners in his experience. It must be that her face had such stillness, and a depth that waited patiently to be plumbed.

Toby shook his head.

Leave it, forget about her. There are greater things at stake…

There was a shout, feet stamped on the deck, ropes were pulled, an oar fell hard against the larboard side of the boat as the vessel slewed, shifting to a diagonal course, the empty sail filling. Toby held onto the wale as the boat settled to its course, noticing they had crept onto a more northerly passage, flying onward and gaining leagues. Looking back, he could see nothing of the trade flotilla in any direction and breathed a sigh of relief. Tomas and Mehmet sat with Ahmed who leaned with his arm over the tiller, a leg propped on a bale. The men stood around the decks or sat at their oars alert to any nuance in the sail or the sea or on the face of their sailing master. He decided to keep to himself for the moment and had never felt more alone in his life.

He must have dozed because a hand shook his shoulder and his head flew up from a very cricked neck. 'Ow, ow, ow!' He eased his head from side to side and opened his eyes. Mehmet stood tall above him, looking down, his *keffiyeh* tossed like a leaf in the hard wind. Grabbing his robes around him, he squatted down by Toby in the lee of the vessel's side.

'You have talked with Tomas?'

'You saw for yourself,' Tobias replied, feeling moody and out of sorts. 'And no doubt he has told you that we have built a temporary bridge across our differences. Does it matter?'

'Toby,' Mehmet lowered himself and sat cross-legged. 'Of course it matters. I want us to be a team until the job is done. It would have been a soul-destroying thing to have put you both off on the coast.'

But Toby had no doubt he would have done exactly that. One thing he had begun to learn was that Mehmet had a core of iron. He must have been fearsome and fearless amongst the injured upon the battlefield.

'In view of our destination approaching with speed, I am at liberty to tell you what Zoë, has revealed. It may affect how carefully we seek the purple. Tomas knows this and has vowed he will preserve our need for secrecy.'

The intrigue in that revelation had Toby sitting up straight. He could almost feel his eyes brightening and a burst of energy seizing him.

'Tomas was right,' the physician said. 'She is indeed nobility. Her real name is Zoë Komemna. Because there was much political disease between the factions within Byzantium when she was born, her own family chose to live far away across the Western Balkans before finally settling in Trapezus when she was a young girl of marriageable age. She was married to a nobleman, a man called John Komemnos, a long distant cousin. It was a diplomatic marriage and they had two children – a son and a daughter. She despairs of their lives, being Komemnoi. They all tried to escape from Trapezus to the Balkans when the Angelids came to power but their ship was attacked and she and her children were sold. Of her husband, she knows nothing and says that Isaac's court in Constantinople must not know she is alive. She believes she and her husband and children were captured at their behest as the Komemnoi held such power in the city and empire for so long.'

Toby sat back. 'Holy God!'

'Indeed.' Mehmet's response was so dry it crackled, but his mouth tipped up. 'So our task becomes even harder with her amongst us. And of course we shall return her to her fold somehow. However whilst we are in Constantinople, Ahmed has agreed to her staying on board and being guarded by the men where she will be safe. He has even told Faisal to leave if the boat and Zoë seem threatened in any way and we are still on shore.'

A shadow from the dying sun stretched along the deck as Toby digested this new information. 'I am astonished. Serendipity is an odd thing, is it not?' He pulled his hair back and tucked it into the folds of his hood. 'Did I sleep the day away? It appears to be dusk. How far are we from the city?'

'We might make the harbour before the chains go up but we need to make more speed, so Ahmed has decided to ditch anything superfluous to lighten the vessel. He will not ditch his trading cargo because it is valuable.'

Toby realised that the crew were hefting goods over the sides and that some of the objects being carried were not just kegs. 'They throw our luggage over? My clothes? Jesus wept!'

'Toby, we have our weapons and I have money. We need nothing more.'

'But I had a sheaf of notes in my roll! There were words for a new *canso*.'

'Which I am sure are in your head. Speed is paramount. The rest of the fleet will not sail into the harbour until the chains are lifted on the morrow. By then, we will be well into the city. Needs must, dear boy. Do not forget we are not the only ones who seek the purple.'

'My little *Durrah*, she is a fleet and dainty ship do you not think, minstrel man?' Ahmed had padded softly on bare feet toward them as they talked. He stood in the wind, faded robes blowing around him, a sash the colour of blood tied round his waist with a wad of rolled and tied parchment tucked in.

'She is indeed, Ahmed, and no doubt ably assisted by the disappearance of our supplies and our luggage, my clothes amongst them.'

The galley master flicked his hand as if Toby's clothes were of little consequence. 'She may be small for a galley, but she has left *dromōns* in her wake and me laughing as she did so. We are a lightweight crew and she is pared down for running swiftly if she must and you and your brother should be glad this is so, Master Tobias.'

'Oh I am, Ahmed, may you be blessed with a rare and rich fortune!' Toby bowed before the galley master as if he addressed a sultan. 'But when you infer that she may have to run fast and that we should be grateful, I become afraid and fretful. I am in essence a coward.'

'And *I*,' Ahmed tapped his own chest with a taut finger, 'think that you jest. You surely have not forgotten that I *saw* you in the temple ruins, slashing a dagger with great skill. That was no coward, that was a man who thought quickly on his feet. But, coward or not, there it is … your destination.' He swept out his arm in an arc.

'Holy God!' Toby stood next to Mehmet, Tomas and Zoë appearing at the wale beside them.

In the distance lay a rich skyline – ruby-coloured tiles and glistening domes and a defensive wall that snaked away to right and left. Vessels filled the water – *dromŏns, sanădil, caiques* and galleys, and the crews on each turned to examine *Durrah* briefly before resuming their shipboard tasks.

'We have little time to enter the Harbour of Theodosius before the chain is raised. Be seated all of you, under the canopy, and I shall deal with the officials. My Lady Zoë, do not be afraid.'

My lady? He knows…

'Mehmet, stay by my side if you will.'

Ahmed took the helm and swung the boat, the sail changed its angle, and they began the last run across the wind, reaching far higher than Toby would have thought possible, almost to the entrance of the harbour.

The city ranged up the softly moulded hills – it was so much more than Venezia or Paris and it made London laughable. It also made Toby worry as he muttered under his breath, 'So big and we must find *one* man.'

'So big, Master Tobias, and I must avoid *many* men.'

Toby and Tomas swung toward Zoë as she uttered these words softly.

'Zoë, hush…' Tomas said.

'Everyone on the ship knows I am Zoë Komemna, Tomas. If Ahmed and his crew are as trustworthy as he claims, then I have nothing to fear here. Only on land…' Zoë's eyes were like almonds and her lashes were thick and she looked at the brothers intently as she continued. 'I know I should be more circumspect, but it is the first time for many years that I have been able to feel anything like hope. To me, this little ship, this *Durrah,* feels like a haven of security.'

'I trust we will be able to get information for you, Zoë,' Tomas had rarely sounded so earnest for years. 'Perhaps even find your family.'

As they spoke, the galley had drawn closer and closer to the entrance to the harbour. Birds wheeled above in great numbers, gulls, oystercatchers and terns – all content to live off the detritus of men that lined the shores. There was a faint sound too, the noise of the city, a vibration that titillated and enticed all in one. The light had become muted as if a great hand had smeared a cloth through it and taken the last colour away from the day.

Ahmed ordered the sail furled and the oars were pushed out, the men feathering gently until Faisal and Ahmed were happy with the balance of the craft and then the command to pull was given and they slid evenly through water that had stilled to a silken swathe.

The walls of the city stood square to attack and continued out into a sea wall that was striped in bars of thick rubescent blocks, a similar shade to the skyline they had observed from the sea. A mark of rich green weed showed along the water's edge, perhaps a sign of the current that had propelled them from Gallipolis and across the Propontis. To larboard as they approached, and as was common in so many other harbours, a tower stood sentinel with space for the Watch and on the starboard side, another tower for a signal fire.

As they approached the entrance, a handsome *caique* sat blocking ingress, a voice calling for them to hold. Toby's heartbeat jumped up several notches and he dare not look at Zoë or Tomas. Here, rising above them, in hand cut blocks and bricks was the city of silk and spice. Here was the city from which they planned to steal the single greatest dye in Christendom. Here was a justice system whereby if they were caught they would first lose their hands as a punishment for stealing and then their heads for a crime against the Empire, but Tobias tried valiantly not to be cowed because this was the place of his dreams.

The voice swung aboard followed by three guards, the fourth holding their craft alongside the galley. Papers were demanded and Ahmed pulled them from his sash, handing them over with a gesture that was mannered and polite and which amused Toby. He wondered if money had been passed as well and then decided not. This venture was not worth the risk.

The official, no doubt a mere minion from the large bureaucracy that ordered Byzantium, was dressed well, if not exceptionally. The fabric was finely woven – Toby recognised good stuff when he saw it but oddly for a man in charge of a harbour, his clothing was subtle green, as if he could fade into the hills like a forest legend and never be seen again. Toby wondered why the knee-length tunic that had been pleated by a fastidious tailor was not the colour of the sea – perhaps dark blue with shades of lapis. Ah, how it calmed the nerves to think of such banal things.

But in any case, there was just this earthly green tunic with tight fitting hose and fine boots laced to the calf. The cloak however, was like wine – a rich garnet secured with a filigreed silver *fibula* at the shoulder. The fellow had sat a cap on his curling hair like a hen on a nest.

How does it not get blown off?

Toby had forgotten for a moment that the accompanying men were Varangians. But then his roving eye had caught on the hair – as fair as birch trunks. One of the men was vivid – fiercely autumnal. He reminded Toby of Adam in Venezia, whom they called Rufus occasionally – the red hair, the pale skin. These men however had plaited their long locks, or pulled long tails of hair back hard and topped them with conical helms. Glistening axes hung from their belts.

Can you swim, my friends? For sure you would sink like a stone if you fell overboard.

If Ahmed's papers were false in any way, the guards would take them all in a bloody moment and shove their remains over the wale. Toby's heart had begun to flail again, as the papers were unrolled, the leather strip that had bound them falling to the deck. The official indicated those under the canopy.

'From Venezia?'

Ahmed demurred. 'That fellow…' he pointed at Tomas. '… is from Lübeck. Julius of Lübeck, a minstrel. His papers are attached.'

'The one with the hood,' said the official, looking closely at Zoë.

'A slave. Her name is Zoë as you will see from the bill of sale. She's from Chaldia, it says. Julius, what do you want her for?'

Tomas, newly shaved and with his best accent, bowed to the official. 'She can sing. It suits me to have a fair-faced woman alongside. Does Constantinople not allow such things? Woe is me if they do not, she cost me money!'

The official waved Tomas aside. 'The others?'

'From Venezia – a physician and a troubadour. And I have merchandise to trade, as the papers say.'

The papers were thumbed and the official ran his finger down Tomas' papers again.

Why?

'It seems all is in order, but I shall keep these until you leave.'

'My boat offloads its cargo tomorrow, sir,' Ahmed maintained his decorum, 'and then proceeds to the Prosphorion Harbour to collect goods. I will need the papers to enter there, I presume.'

'You will. And I shall return these to you on the morrow as you leave.' The official swished his garnet-shaded cloak as he began to turn. 'A pity you didn't arrive before a brother merchantman from Gallipolis. One of your fellow traders beat you to the one remaining prime mooring near the colonnade…' he pointed to starboard where a graceful colonnade swept in an arc round the side of the harbour and where moorings were filled with masts and shrouds, furled sails and curved hulls, all illuminated by the weak light to the west. 'You must therefore turn to larboard inside the harbour wall and move to the last dock space. Make haste because we are in the process of preparing the chains for lifting.' A nod closed the conversation and the official preceded the Varangians over the wale. As they rowed away, they were followed by the expulsion of breaths from aboard the galley.

'Someone beat us,' Tomas whispered.

'Who?' Toby answered, flustered and anxious, 'And *how?*'

Mehmet shushed them and they all turned to Ahmed, but the galley master's face was like a thundercloud.

A man who does not like being beaten… peirate.

He barked orders at the crew to guide the galley carefully to the moorings and in moments, a rope was thrown up from the bow to helpful hands, another from the stern and *Durrah* was made fast.

Behind them, orders had been shouted from either side of the sea-entrance and the heavyweight chain attached to floating hogsheads was dragged from one side to the other and fastened off. No ship could now enter the Harbour of Theodosius until morning and the Venetian cadre should have been happy.

Instead, a mood hung heavier than the nightsky which had finally settled. Along the sea wall, braziers had been lit and guards had begun sentry duty. Stars had emerged to compliment the flickering flamelight of a vast jewelled city. Toby stood still, trying to push the thought of potential evil away, savouring the smell of land. Perhaps it should have been spice-filled but it was enough that it carried the odour of roasting meat, even the musty smell of the seaweed on the wall and of smoke from the braziers. His feet itched to climb ashore – as much to explore as to find the purple and be gone. But one was inevitably tied to the other and with a sword drawn and wits sharp.

'Tobias!'

Ahmed spoke more sharply than Toby had yet heard. 'When you are ready to endow us with your lofty presence, little music man…'

Toby blushed and hurried over to the group as they stood around the galley master. His face still raged with thunder and lightning and it would have been a brave man who demurred.

'Sorry,' said Toby. 'I was just thinking…'

'Then I hope you *think* on the dilemma we face,' said Ahmed. 'We have been bested and it galls me to say so. *Durrah* is the fastest ship I know, may Allah bless her, and I speak from experience. So – someone left before the current changed, making headway into the Propontis during the night – a foolish captain or a desperate one, or one who is very well paid and with a very powerful crew of rowers. And damn them to Scilla and Charybdis, they beat us. Given the endeavours to slow us down, I would say the ship is the one who may well seek what we seek. Over there, my friends…' Ahmed pointed to the colonnade that gleamed palely in the light of braziers, 'is the man, or men, who have set others upon us.'

'We don't even know which ship it is and where it is from,' said Toby.

'And it would make no difference if we did, Tobias,' said Mehmet. 'The point is, we can assume our enemy is come; that they wait for us and that they will dog our every move as we search for Michael. We will in fact lead them to what they want. All they need is to keep us in their sights.'

'Then how do we divert them?' Tomas asked. 'I imagine our only way is to split in different directions and lead them a dance.'

'Perhaps…' said Ahmed.

'You think of another idea?' Tomas moved along a bale, allowing Zoë to sit more comfortably.

'Perhaps,' Ahmed replied and a ray of sunshine burst through his thundercloud expression. 'Tonight we shall head off into the city to Mehmet's brother and stay close together for there is safety in numbers. The cargo will be unloaded and then *Durrah* can proceed to the Prosphorion, *Insha'Allah*. Faisal will reload the ship with a few very lightweight but valuable goods and if we have not returned in three days…'

'Three days?' blustered Tomas. 'We have three days to find Michael, or at the very least *word* of him and to try and find Zoë's family? Three days? Ahmed!'

'Three days is two and a half days more than is safe, my little friend. Do you not see that the moment you reach for the purple, your life is forfeit?'

'The purple?' Zoë exclaimed. 'You intend to steal purple dye? My friends, you are mad. You will pay with your lives!'

'We know,' said Tomas. 'Although strange to say, when we left Venezia it didn't seem so real. Now...' he shrugged his shoulders.

If I didn't love my Gisborne family so much, thought Toby, I would seek passage away from here right now...

'Enough!' Mehmet ordered. 'We knew the risks. And we contracted with my lord Gisborne to do this anyway. Zoë, are you comfortable with staying aboard for the moment?'

Zoë nodded her head. 'I think I shall be safer than you, and for a Komnenoi to utter such things here in Constantinople is food for thought, kind Mehmet. Will you not heed me when I say you must leave this venture behind you?'

''Tis too late, dear lady. We have offered our word to our master and thus we are bonded.'

'Then may God travel at your shoulder. It is all I can say.'

'Zoë, whilst we are on land,' Tomas added, 'we shall try to find word of your family and bring good news back to you.'

'I know, Tomas, and I thank you but do not put yourself in danger. I would not ask it of you.'

Dear fair Zoë, we are in danger anyway so what is a little more?

'You are very quiet, my little minstrel man.' Ahmed reached and pushed at Tobias' shoulder.

'Am I?'

'Yes, and when you are without comment, I am always sure you are *thinking* something we need to hear.'

'I see.' Toby rubbed at the peak of hair on his forehead. 'Well, firstly I wonder why the official read Tomas' papers again, and secondly, it's the purple. It's so ... *nebulosus...*'

'*Nebulosus*? Another of your Gods' and Saints' words?' Ahmed asked.

'In a manner of speaking, Ahmed. Because for sure, only God and the Saints know where is Michael.'

'Huh. You disappoint me, my friend. I thought you would have an answer to our problems.' Ahmed turned to Mehmet. 'We are invited to a meal, are we not? With your brother?'

'Indeed. Zoë, keep well concealed. For the rest of us, come...'

Chapter Seven

×

The paved streets of Constantinople were wider than Tobias had expected but perhaps not as ordered, not as linear as he thought they would be. Thus they switched and turned quite frequently as they walked away from the docks. The thoroughfares throbbed with activity, with people flooding inns and covered markets before curfew. Toby found word after word placing itself into *motets* as he observed the mixture of foreign faces and tongues, his eyes widening at the scale the of the city. The Byzantine Empire was supposedly shrinking to a pinhead, a fact marked by the density surrounding him. But he couldn't care about the Empire – he was in awe of the polished buildings around him. Unlike Venezia which grew haphazardly like an awkward but charming young adult that had inherited riches, or like Genova that watched Venezia over its shoulder, both wanting to win the race to dominate the sea and its trading potential.

London and Paris grew untidily and were too dominated by Church wealth and yet here, Byzantine Christian churches sat at every corner, pretty little gems that formed a crown of astonishing beauty. But then, as they rounded corners and crossed streets, Toby knew society was the same everywhere. The poor scavenged in the gutters, the merchant class pretended they were nobility and the nobles clustered in poisonous groups around any regal household.

'We head to the Valens Aqueduct, friends,' Mehmet said, 'and must move quickly before curfew.'

'My little minstrels,' added Ahmed, 'do not lose us, yes? Or you might never find your way or worse, you might lose your lives.'

Of course he was right. Tobias and Tommaso knew nothing of the city beyond the legend of the place and were cognisant of the danger that had most recently presented itself so they hurried to keep pace, jogging across the cobbles and dodging out of the way of horses and mules.

Vaguely Toby heard a shout and then someone pushed by him, knocking he and Tomas apart, the crowds swallowing Mehmet and Ahmed in folded shadow.

'Toby! Toby!' Tomas' voice edged between legs to where Toby lay with his head on the edge of a gutter. Water trickled past him and he sat up, shaking his wet hair and feeling a lump rising on his forehead.

His brother's voice sounded again but from a foggy distance. 'I'm here,' he shouted back and no one seemed to care, all going about their business and ignoring the small man sitting in the gutter with a bloody forehead. But then Tomas was beside him, clutching an arm from which blood dripped.

'Well that was no accident,' he said. 'How do you fare?'

'A headache with blood,' Toby dabbed at his forehead. 'And you? Punctured I see.'

'Ah, Toby, just like old times, eh?' Tomas patted his knife scratch with the hem of his tunic. 'He meant to fillet my arm I think, but I rolled so a scratch is all and lucky with it. Can you get up?'

'Of course I can,' Toby grabbed at the corner of a stone-layered building and hand over hand, levered himself to stand straight. 'The world spins a little. Let me breathe for a moment.' He shook his head gently from side to side. What had tilted like a moneylender's scales slowly righted itself.

'Mary, Mother of Jesus – that's better.' He looked around. '*Sard!* We've lost them.'

'Ahmed and Mehmet? Surely. Where were they headed? I wasn't listening.'

'The Valens Aqueduct. Exactly where it is…' Toby shrugged. 'I don't know. I shall ask…'

'Not you.' Tomas pulled Toby back. 'You're bloody and will attract attention. Let me go.' He crossed the road, a busy thoroughfare, and spoke to a group of men outside an inn. One or two reached for crosses or amulets as they looked at him, others whispered to each other.

Tomas, do not lose your temper…

But one pointed and words were politely exchanged; Toby could tell by the smile on Tomas' face and the way he bowed in thanks. He walked back to Toby who had shrunk further into shadow and dabbed at the blood, trying to clean his face. It wouldn't do to let them be seen together too often here – they were a memorable pair after all. Thank the Saints for night.

'That road,' Tomas pointed, 'is the Mese. It heads toward the Hippodrome which is attached to the Great Palace. We must follow the Mese until we come to a little church called Saint Basil the Confessor, turn left and head up steps toward the Fourth hill. The Aqueduct is there with a street running parallel. So methinks Mehmet's brother lives in that street.'

'Did you ask if they knew of the Arab physician called Anwar?'

'No. I will go back…'

'Tomas, no. It may be safer to leave things as they are.' Toby heard a gabble of familiar tongues behind and turned. 'Look,' he said. 'Pilgrims! Mary Mother, hearing French makes me quite homesick for the north. Come on, we can join them; safety in numbers.'

Toby called out to the pilgrims asking if they walked to the Mese and was told yes, to their inn before curfew. And when asked if they could fit two small men in their number were told they would be poor Christians returning from God's Holy City if they did not welcome all who wished to join them.

The pilgrims were swathed in ubiquitous *mantelets* and broad-brimmed hats, walking with metal-tipped staves and with scrips hanging from their belts, and whilst Toby and Tomas were not similarly attired, the crowd was big enough to lose the men in their midst and Toby crossed himself in gratitude. They passed statuary, large buildings and columns of immense height but nothing seemed to interest the pilgrims who talked of the simplicity of Jerusalem, of walking the way of Jesus and the Saints, of treading the Via Dolorosa and weeping.

'You felt safe?' Tobias asked, remembering Saladin and Richard and the eternal battle for the Holy Land.

'Indeed, young sir. The Templars guided us, the Hospitallers cared for us and the Arabs left us alone. It was not what we expected so close to the end of the Crusade. And now we return to our homes in Paris, renewed and refreshed with the Holy Spirit.'

They trudged quite swiftly along the Mese until Tomas grabbed Toby's arm. 'Is that it? The Church of Saint Basil?'

Toby asked one of the pilgrims but they did not know and could not read the name on the stonework above the arched doorway. Tomas stepped closer and looked up, trying to read the Greek letters so high above. 'It is … Saint Basil, see? My friends, we must leave you here. We go this way to our friends…' he indicated the steps climbing vertically between the walls of the church.

They waved the pilgrims away and turned to climb the steep stair leading up between the Third and Fourth hills. But then Toby put a hand across his brother's chest and a finger against his lips and they pressed themselves hard against the wall of the little basilica. The pilgrims' chatter had faded and instead, the soft tread of two sets of feet approached. Two shrouded men stopped, looked up the stair, whispered and the twins waited, hands on daggers. But the footsteps passed by on the path taken along the Mese by the pilgrims.

Silence fell. Almost as though when curfew had fallen, all of Constantinople had made itself safe behind locked doors. The city seemed lonely, as empty as graveyard and so Tomas and Tobias crept up the stair, carefully avoiding any noise or disturbance. Branches of an oak leaned over them at one point, but thereafter they continued on without shadow or shelter.

The city had grown on terraces carved out of the terrain, and rampant streets followed whichever way the contours lay, so calves aching and breath catching in their throats, the brothers had to stop to rest. But looking back down was merely looking into blackness and looking up was to see Purgatory in stone yet to be climbed, so a breath was all and then they continued, chests tight and throats burning.

'We'd be dead men if someone had chased us up the steps,' said Toby, his voice hoarse. 'I couldn't do it at speed. Hilly place this town, isn't it?'

They reached the top of the stair and took their bearings.

'Christ!' Tomas leaned over the stone balustrade. They looked down over the dainty cupola of Saint Basil's and across the terracotta roofline of the city and to the shining waters of the moonlit Harbour of Theodosius. The safety of *Durrah* looked leagues away. Turning, Toby murmured, 'Jesus, Mary and Joseph…'

The Aqueduct stretched east and west above them and in front of them – two levels high with a street passing through an arch that was slightly wider than the others. This thoroughfare, aptly labelled Water Street, a name that amused Toby, ran to left and right.

'This must be it, Tomas. That's the aqueduct and this is the only street close by. What a structure!'

'A bridge to Infinity,' Tomas agreed. 'I've seen aqueducts but this is monstrous. Which house do we need, do you think?'

'We'll have to knock at a door. We have no other choice.' Toby looked at the nearest entrance. 'That one.'

He walked over to the gate, legs aching, almost trembling with exhaustion, his throat still burning because Christ, that was a climb. He rapped at the aged wood, the thick dry planks resounding with a hollow thump. No one answered and so he knocked again, this time with a balled fist. They heard tentative footsteps on paving stones and then the grille in the gate slid back with a squeak. A woman's gimlet eyes looked out.

'Yes?' she said in tremulous Greek. 'What do you want?'

'Pardon lady, but we are seeking the physician, Anwar. My brother is poorly…' Tomas had hunched over and begun to cough, not so difficult since his drowning experience; he had a cough that was apt to sound wet and congested.

'Then stay away,' the woman was elderly, her voice frail. 'I do not want your sickness.'

'Lady, he near drowned not long since and he needs herbs for his chest. We were told Anwar is the best…'

'He lives down the street – the iron gate, you will see it.'

'But which way?' Toby called as the grille began to slide shut. But it was too late and he heard her slippers drag over the paving stones and an inner door slam shut with finality.

'Down the street. An iron gate. Thank you, old woman…'

Often in their convoluted lives, Tobias and Tomas had been left with a decision to be made. Invariably, rather than examining a potential outcome, they would make a quick decision by tossing a coin. Inevitably it worked. Tobias said it was because the Saint of Good Gamblers sat at their shoulder. After all, what else *was* life for people like he and Tomas but a gamble. He dragged out a coin, a lucky *bianco* from Venezia and laid it on his thumb and forefinger. Tomas winked and of a sudden, Tobias realised they had bridged a gap. That once again they were brothers in arms and he felt his heart warm.

He flipped the coin, grabbed it as it fell and slapped it on the top of his hand. 'Backs that way, fronts that way?'

'Your call…' said Tomas.

Toby lifted his hand. The front lay glinting in the moonlight. Despite the low value of the coin it had a valuable sheen and it was one of the few things that reminded them that Venezia was a part of the Byzantine Empire and extremely wealthy because of it.

'Fronts then,' Tomas said, looking up at the Valens Aqueduct, 'west we go.'

'Wait … I need to ask you something.'

'Yes…' Tomas fiddled with his belt, pulling the buckle back and forth as if he sought for it to sit comfortably at his hip.

In the night quiet, where only the occasional cricket played its wings and a nightjar called in response, and where a cat stalking along a wall hissed at them to watch their step, Toby asked, 'Were you concerned when the official thumbed your papers the second time?'

Tomas pushed at his buckle once more before answering, 'Not at all. The papers were excellent forgeries. Worth every coin Gisborne pays.'

For a long time, monks in a small scriptorium at the edge of the Venetian seaboard had forged papers for Gisborne's men in return for a decent stipend – enough to keep them comfortable in the winter months.

'Why?' continued Tomas. 'Were you worried?'

Toby looked along Water Street, searching for the iron gate. 'Well, yes. He seemed a little too interested.'

'Brother, I have always said this of you. Your imagination is too florid. You see spectres where there are none.' Tomas began to stride off to the west past gate after gate and Toby followed, twisting his lip at the glib way Tomas had spoken.

'Tomas,' he called after they had passed ten gates. 'It's not here, not to the west.'

The aqueduct disappeared into the night and Water Street accompanied it – houses and empty spaces edging the thoroughfare. Oak and linden trees grew along the street's edge and the moon cast spiky shadows through branches that whispered silkily in a night breeze. Not a soul walked the street anywhere and Tobias straightened his spine as a shiver slid down, touching and warning as it moved on.

'Let's try the other way,' he said. 'Or else we will be at the city walls before we know it.'

They jogged back to the stair and continued walking easterly underneath the aqueduct. Toby touched the stone and could easily persuade himself that he felt the slick chatter of the water passing above him to the city cisterns. It was clear, clean water from the forests far outside the walls of the city, clucking and gurgling at speed as it flowed along to finally pour out in crystalline patterns from fountains and spouts. Water, the stuff of life that covered tiled and columned spaces, that dripped and ran and flowed in echoing chambers of watery emptiness. He ran his hand over the stones, feeling the indents where mortar had worn away. The structure towered over him, so that even tilting his head he could barely see the top. It seemed like a bridge to the heavens above.

He turned away as his brother began walking, the street becoming more populated with dwellings the closer it drew toward the Hippodrome and *Sancta Sophia* and wooden gate upon wooden gate defeated them – the only difference between each was the size and shape, and then,

'There, an iron gate! Come on…'

They hurried over, both rapping the door, the iron cooling their sweaty hands. An ornamental grille slid open and a face looked out, lit by a lamp in a raised fist.

'Is there an Arab physician here? Anwar al Din by name?'

'And what if there is?' the man behind the gate asked.

'If there is,' Tomas spoke clearly, enunciating each word, a sure sign he was tired and reining himself in. 'Then we would welcome the chance to speak with him as we are in dire need. Please, let us in…'

'How do I know you're not thieves chancing your luck?'

'God's bloody chest hairs!' Tomas had had enough. 'Just get your master and be done!' He began to cough, no act, another sign of exhaustion.

'Abdul, you can let them in,' another voice spoke and the grille was closed, the bolt on the gate sliding back smoothly to reveal an upright man, very slim, his white robes falling in unapologetic straight lines to leather slippers with a subtly upturned toe. Behind this slim vision in white, the gatekeeper, a man of indeterminate age and with a *kilij* tucked in a belt, ran a disapproving eye over the new arrivals.

'Abdul,' said the more authoritative man of the two, 'shut the gate, bolt it and keep watch. Thank you.' The man touched the gatekeeper's arm and smiled at the brothers.

He wore a dark *keffiyeh* but Toby knew the hair beneath would be somewhere between pewter and ivory and so he bowed, saying, 'Anwar, I am Tobias Celho, late of the galley, *Durrah,* and formally of Venezia, friend of your brother, Mehmet al Din, and this is my brother, Tomas.'

Anwar placed his hand on his heart. 'Allah be praised, good Tobias, dear Tomas. My brother will be much relieved. How did you know it was I?'

'Your voices have the same resonance. Like a rolling stone wrapped in velvet. And now that you are close, I see that your eyes are the same.' Toby grinned. 'You could almost be twins.'

'Heaven help you, then,' said Tomas as he leaned around his brother to clasp Anwar's hand. 'Being a twin is as much curse as blessing. Is Mehmet here?'

'Indeed, he and Ahmed have been here for some time. Come, I will take you to them and you can rest.'

He led them through a simple arch and along a plain colonnade that had large tubs of lemon, bay and olive trees. Somewhere a fountain played a tune as clear and discreet as a plucked *vielle* string. They stepped into a paved room where sconces lit the space and two very familiar men sat on large cushions on the floor.

'My little music men!' Ahmed jumped up. 'Praise be to Allah, we thought you were done for and have been plotting on how to find out. And look, not a mark upon you.'

'You think? Toby asked, lifting his hair from his forehead to reveal the cut and an attendant blue bruise. 'And Tomas has a slash on his arm.'

'What happened?' Mehmet asked as he gently fingered the bruise and Anwar fetched some clean water to bathe the injuries.

'Someone separated us from you,' said Tomas, rolling up his bloody sleeve. 'And were determined to keep us separated. We joined a group of pilgrims in order to hide as they walked along the Mese but we were followed. As we began to climb the stair at Saint Basil's we hid in the shadows and watched our stalkers continue on after the pilgrims.'

Mehmet sighed. 'Someone is fully aware of us. Of that there is no doubt. This whole venture has almost become impossible.'

'I tell him he should not give up so easily.' Ahmed picked at his nails with the tip of his dagger. 'At least not until we know whether Michael is still alive. Anwar thinks he can talk to the embroiderer without drawing attention. As far as we know, after we were separated, Mehmet and I were left alone. It seems to us as if our pursuers are targeting *you*.'

'Hardly surprising,' Tomas growled. 'We are recognisable, even if in disguise. They only have to look for small people and pick them off, one by one.'

Mehmet made a clicking sound as he checked over Tomas' arm. 'And this is part of the picking off? Presumably you were quicker than they anticipated?'

'Indeed. Aren't we always?' Tomas jerked as the vinegar wash sank into the wound and then sat on the edge of his seat as Mehmet wound a clean linen strip round.

'What Anwar is proposing is to send his wife to the embroiderer in the morning and Ahmed and I shall go with them. Sophia is aware of the importance of secrecy in this endeavour'.

Secrecy? Huh. More likely the need to fade into the background until we are invisible and then to no avail...

'It is my hope that they think we will make mistakes. But they do not perhaps know that the ability to blend is a tool of trade for us.' Mehmet continued.

'How do you plan for us to blend and fade, Mehmet?' asked Toby. 'It's impossible for Tomas and myself.'

'I agree. Right now, it's best you stay hidden.'

'All very well,' said Tomas, 'but how shall I find out about the Komemnoi for Zoë? I have made a promise.'

Toby pulled a face. For just one moment he had forgotten about Zoë and what she had done to free his soul from lethargy. He chided himself because his music was everything to him – *almost* everything.

'Anwar has knowledge of such things,' said Mehmet. 'He is regarded as a favourite healer behind the palace walls.'

'I am fortunate to have such recognition and it may just help find the information you seek, Tomas.' Anwar said. 'But I have to say I have heard nothing of Komemnoi within the city or the palace. As to Trapezus...' He shrugged. 'But I shall make discrete enquiries. Have no fear.'

'How long will it take? We have so little time.' Tomas said.

'I go to the palace in the morning,' Anwar replied. 'One of the nobles has need of my assistance and she is generally filled with news, so do not worry. I would say Zoë is the least of your problems.' Anwar poured two cups of pomegranate syrup and passed them to the twins. 'So. Sophia will visit the embroiderer and I shall visit the palace. Until we have answers from those two sources I think you cannot move in any direction and thus I suggest we all retire for the night, sleep well and awake refreshed for whatever life decides to throw your way.'

The twins were led to a small alcove where there were two thick mattresses, with rolled blankets lying across the bottom. Between the two beds, a squat table sat with a brass lamp lit, flickering images leaping across the room. It seemed as if they were at a banquet and that couples danced freely in front of them. Toby decided it was companionship of the best kind, designed to enliven and gratify. He enjoyed his make-believe world sometimes. It had the capacity to provide walls between he and his problems and so he stretched out on a soft wool-filled mattress and sighed with guilty pleasure. Life aboard the damp decks of *Durrah* and being pursued rubbed him raw, and to sink onto a simple bed was like sipping poppy in wine. Within moments his mind had quieted and he fell into a deep sleep, his brother snoring next to him.

They were woken at dawn, not by anyone rudely shaking their shoulders, or the sound of a fight breaking out around them, or even the galley turning hard about, but by the gentle burble of turtle doves so that Tobias had one moment where he wondered if he had imbibed too much and that they had left him at Saul's to recover. But it was only a moment and then realisation hit him hard and he sat up, looking toward the curtain separating the alcove, seeing the fine gold light of a new day spreading through the house of Anwar and Sophia and dragging thoughts of what might be with it.

Enough. It has not happened yet. We must just bide our time.

He examined Tomas as he snored on the other mattress. The rope coloured hair seemed so odd and yet it was perfect for the alter-ego of Julius of Lübeck. Would it fool the Byzantines? Would it enable the Gisborne men to slide through the city unrecognised and able to carry out their plans without interference? The worst thing – the very worst, would be coming across someone who recognised them. Toby chewed on his thumbnail.

And what of Zoë? He owed her so much and she had no idea. Nor had she any idea of what she had done for Tomas. How odd it was that a doe-eyed slave should inspire both brothers to write music again. He stopped chewing. Perhaps it was lust that caused the shackles to fall away, he thought, because she was indeed beddable...

But no, her graciousness precluded the idea, surely. But maybe Tomas? Did he lust after her? Or if not lust, then love?

But I do not believe love comes from a first glance. Not for Tomas, not for me and not for that peasant or this king.

And yet – if Tomas had time enough, would he woo her? And what would she think of an oddity loving her? Oh – she would be kind. Toby had no doubt. But Tomas' reaction was another thing entirely. How would a tinder-dry man react to rejection?

Besides, she's married...

True.

And she is nobility...

And there was the rub – the Komemnos name. If any of the Angelid dynasty found that a Komemnoi sat in the harbour, Toby thought they would hear the Varangian Guard baying from the Great Palace. Ahmed was right, it was best to keep the galley moving.

Tomas let out a pig-snort and opened his eyes, looking around as if like Toby, he was disoriented.

'Christ's toenails, I had forgotten what a mattress felt like.' He yawned and stretched, elbows cracking as the bones straightened. 'What is the hour?'

'Dawn if you look outside. There are bells but I am unsure what hours the church keeps here. Do you think it is the same as our own?'

'Damned if I know. Does it matter? Has anyone left yet?'

'I doubt anyone else is *awake* yet.'

Tomas lay back on the mattress, scrubbing at his hair. 'I'm not happy biding my time here, Toby. Zoë relies on me.'

'Zoë relies on all of us, Tomas. But you know our purpose for being here was cast long before Zoë came into our lives and we must keep that to the forefront.'

Tomas humphed and pushed his head deeper into the pillow. 'I meant what I said – that I help with the purple only to secure help for Zoë.'

Toby unpicked Tomas' words, trying to find if there was a physical attraction at the root of all this.

Ask him…·

But he thought it was safer to leave well alone. It was though, more than disheartening that Tomas' reliability was once more at risk, because if there was a choice between Zoë and the purple, there was equally no doubt which hand Tomas would take.

And what of you, Tobias?

Indeed, thought Toby. What of me? Images rolled through his mind of his Venetian friends and family. To be replaced by a sobering view of Zoë being dragged away by the Varangian Guard.

The curtain across the alcove twitched and Mehmet's face peered round. 'Good day to you, friends, did you sleep well?' He checked Tobias' head wound and Tomas' arm and pronounced them 'superficial and lucky with it.'

'We will break our fast if you would like to join us, and then we will leave you for a short while. Ahmed and I will walk with Sophia and her maidservant to the embroiderer where we will leave them to their business and go about our own. We will then escort them back here.'

'And what shall Ahmed do? Tag behind you like a nursemaid whilst you purchase twigs and leaves?' asked Tomas. 'I cannot see that *peirate* carrying your wares.'

'He will talk with merchants and seek commodities for purchase. All legitimate. And if he should hear market gossip about families of note on the trade routes, then that is all to the good. I have no doubt he will mention that his galley possibly heads toward Trapezus. He will be blithe and offhand. He is good at what he does.'

Toby could see that Mehmet and Ahmed would put up a deliberate disguise – that they were visiting relatives, were representatives of a solid Venetian trading house and were filling the hold with marketable goods. It was politic to claim Venetian citizenship. The Venetians were allowed trading privileges beyond those endowed to other states because its naval fleet was often put at the disposal of the Byzantine empire.

'And what of Zoë?' Tomas chipped in as he washed his face in an ewer, drying it on a square of fine linen provided by Sophia.

'Anwar will be at the palace. He cannot ask questions outright but there are ways and means. But in order to make this work, you must stay concealed at least until we know the lie of the land.'

'But then what?' Toby asked. 'In the end, if all we do is sneak back to the galley under cover of darkness, then one wonders why we came at all.'

'Tobias', Mehmet's mouth flattened. 'I am sorry it has come to this. When I invited you both to accompany me, I had hoped Fate would not place such difficulties in our path. But the reality is another matter entirely. I would ask you what is the common denominator in each of the attacks since we left Venezia.'

Toby thought. An attack is an attack after all, so why would there be a commonality? He sat on a stool with legs extended onto the mattress, tapping the balls of his feet together. 'Oh!' His feet froze. 'I see. *I* am the common detail.'

'Indeed,' Mehmet said. 'And?'

'I am the one who would be recognised and I prejudice anyone with me.'

'Exactly so.'

'So if Tomas was out and about as Julius of Lübeck, he would be safe?'

'No longer. You are both small people and you left Venezia together. Malcontents won't care about any assumed history. They know you partner each other right now, on this journey. It's just another link in a chain that some clever person has forged to bind us into inaction.'

'Inaction over the purple.' Tomas said.

'There is nothing else *but* the purple, Tomas. Whoever knows we seek the dye will try to stop us, make no mistake, so let us not make it any easier for them. Stay here until we return. I hope we will have the information we need to complete our task and leave before we are placed in any more danger. I take it you are in no hurry for food?'

The twins shook their heads.

'Then I shall bid you adieu.' The curtain swished down behind his vanishing robes and Tomas said,

'If I had an inkling that there was a single Komemnoi somewhere in this city who could help Zoë, purple or no, I would be out of that gate and after them faster than Saladin's mounted archers at Arsuf.'

'Would you, Tomas? How do you know that in all the time she has been a slave, the Komemnoi may not have compromised themselves with the Angelids?'

'Well, either way she could be returned to her family, and if they have become part of the accepted nobility again, all the better surely. Besides, it would be easy enough to find out. Ask at the markets. The common man always has the truth of things.'

'You'd get yourself recognised in the process. The imperial family in Byzantium lacks a certain chivalric code, Tomas. Remember that. You would not be treated kindly. What use to Zoë then?'

'Damn you,' Tomas slammed his fist against a pillow. 'What do we do for the rest of the day then? I am filled with agitation.'

'I can play you at chess. Use your energies to beat me. You haven't beaten me since we lived in Genova. Oh!' He clicked his fingers. 'I saw a lute. Play me your new melody.'

Tomas brightened and for his brother, it was as if the sun came out and he let his tense shoulders drop.

'You know,' Tomas said. ' I doubt Peire Vidal could sing a better song. Or even de Nesle. I suspect that when I join King Richard again, this will be a favourite amongst the courtiers. You will agree when you hear it, I'm sure.' He began to pull on his tunic. 'Is there anything like a bath here do you think?'

There was however, more than just a hogshead filled with water. In the cloister that edged a paved square, there was an old *laver* filled with clear water that trickled from a fountain. Further on and behind a wooden door, they found a small Roman *balineum* with a square pool heated by piped water from a smoking furnace at the far corner of the garden. From the *balineum*, the brothers could look toward a loggia and across the city to the watery sheen of the Propontis as they bathed, relishing the warm water on their aches and pains. For so long they had lived salt-encrusted lives and to soak the blisters, splinters, cuts and bruises seemed like a gift from God.

'Methinks Anwar must be a highly respected physician. Either that or he has fingers in many other pies,' said Tomas as he pulled towels from the shelves and passed one to Toby and then dried himself and knotted the towel around his hips.

Both brothers were well built for their size – stocky with barrel chests and muscled backs. There were scars too; many a jab from blades of all kinds had tattooed stories across their bodies.

'Tomas, you need more hair-dye,' Toby said. 'You are showing your true colours.'

'Mehmet has the dye. I am not concerned,' Tomas rubbed his legs with another square of linen, wincing as he massaged his calf muscles. 'Those steps last night! Dear God but I have bunches of grapes at the back of my legs. I need to find some fitness again if I am to remain unscathed as I help Zoë.'

'You think?' Toby was tired of Tomas' obsession with the noblewoman but said nothing. 'Then perhaps we leave the lute in the corner and the chessboard in its box and do a little dancing. Nothing like leaping around a blade point. What say you?'

The truth was that Tobias too felt unfit from his long journey on *Durrah*, and this despite his mental acuity being honed to knife-edged sharpness. Yes, he needed to address his level of fitness because he was the one after all, who had been forced far too often to caper over an edge on this journey.

They dressed and collected their weapons – favoured daggers and the smaller, lightweight swords with narrower hafts that had been wrought especially for the brothers' size. In truth though, they relished the dagger – its insidiousness, the close quarter fighting that it enabled. Being smaller of stature gave them the swift edge – they could run in under a sword, strike deep and leave before an opponent took a breath. The twins like to call it the Dance of Death. Obviously, they joked when talking about it, they always lacked partners. One wonders why, they would ask with a sly grin.

As they headed toward the garden, Anwar's factotum and last night's gatekeeper called to them, indicating there was a visitor to see the mistress. When he had indicated the lady had gone to the markets, the woman, for it *was* a woman, asked to speak with the physician or his brother.

'But…' Toby was surprised. 'Who would know Mehmet was here or that he was the physician's brother?'

'I thought the same, sir. This woman is adamant she needs to talk to one or the other. I do not wish to send her away because the mistress uses her services often…'

'Who is she?' Tomas asked.

'Her name is Dana; she is the embroiderer.'

Tobias and Tomas looked at each other and asked Abdul to show her to the garden immediately. 'And perhaps bring some Syrup of Lemon and some fruit?' added Toby.

Abdul hurried off, his robes flying around him, his belt with keys hanging off, crashing against the doorframe.

'Did this woman not know Sophia was visiting her today?' Tomas asked.

Toby shrugged and walked forward as Abdul ushered a young woman into the garden and backed away again.

'Good day to you, lady. I am Tobias of Venezia and this is … Julius of Lübeck. I am sorry that you appear to have had a wasted morning.'

'Good day to you, Master Tobias,' she said with an accent that came far from the land of the Byzantines. 'And to you, Master Julius. I assume if you are in this house that you are familiar with the physician, Mehmet al Din?'

'Yes,' Toby acknowledged with some caution.

'Then you are here with him on trading business?'

'He is a firm friend and our travelling companion. The three of us have worked for the same nobleman in Venezia for a number of years.'

Tomas scrutinised the woman. 'How do *you* know Mehmet al Din, madame?'

'I am aware of all who might work for our friend in Venezia.'

Tomas looked startled and before Toby could stop him, he asked, 'Are *you* involved with the House of Gisborne?'

Abdul returned before Dana could answer the question, hands holding a pewter tray loaded with a pitcher of Syrup of Lemon and a platter of plump dates, everything rattling as he laid it upon a low seat under a pomegranate tree. 'Do you need anything further, sir?'

'No thank you, Abdul. We shall call if we need you.'

He bowed and backed away, closing the door to the garden behind him.

'A drink of lemon, Mistress Dana?'

'Please…'

She was as tall as Ysabel of Gisborne and although her head was covered, tendrils of brown hair escaped and curled round her face. Her skin was the colour of smooth cream and she had a natural sparkle in her very alert eyes. She took the drink from Toby with long, slim fingers, the nails short and functional. Toby could imagine a needle in them, pulling silk thread carefully through fine fabrics.

She sipped the lemon and then lowered the cup, 'Refreshing. It is a goodly walk up the hills from the Harbour of Prosphorion.'

'Um, two things, Mistress Dana. Firstly, why did you come here when Sophia and Mehmet are on their way to *you* as we speak. Did they not send a message? And in the second instance – you are not from here I think. I would swear I can hear a Lyonnaise accent.'

She smiled, a brief softening of a serious countenance, and replied, 'I did not know they were to visit me today. I received no message or I would not have come. In answer to your other question, I am from Lyon. You do not need to know anything more about me…'

Perhaps I don't, but by God's toenails, I would love to.

'I think I must impart the news to *you* then, if Mehmet al Din is not here. I must trust my instincts and this is so very important.' She frowned and then took a breath. 'Does the colour purple mean anything to you?'

The brothers shared another look.

'Ah,' she leaned forward and lowered her voice. 'I see it does. I have a message from Michael Sarapion. He hides in the crypt of Saint Theodora's near Prosphorion.'

'He is alive?'

'Yes, but he is in danger and injured. I stitched the wound as best I could but I think he needs a physician's care. I could not risk his safety by fetching one.'

'Is this the wound he received some time ago?'

'You know?'

'Letters reached Venezia before we left. Has he been hiding all this time?'

'He left the city after he had been wounded and I helped him find a galley leaving for the Mar Maggior. He is hampered by the way in which the wound is healing and it has opened again after a surprise attack last week. He was making his way from the Golden Horn down to Prosphorion and someone shadowed him.'

'Huh, being shadowed does not surprise me,' Toby said and Dana studied him carefully. 'Has he the purple with him?'

'No, he has hidden it for safety, but what makes you unsurprised that he was followed? He had been here little more than a sennight and presumed after such an absence, that he would be safe.'

'Someone from Venezia or points north knows we are come to collect the purple and they track our every move.'

'Who?' Dana's voice rose a notch. 'And how would they know of Michael?'

'I can't imagine how they know of Master Sarapion, except that he is perhaps known for being a trader with the north. In any case, it matters little. He is marked. Sadly we believe we all are. It seems my lord Gisborne's young son may have let slip about the purple at the market in Venezia before we left.'

Tomas sat back, stunned. 'Really? William? Christ's teeth but he can be a little loudmouth...'

'Enough, Tomas,' snapped Toby. 'We are unsure.'

'This is very bad news, Master Tobias. If it is true, Michael needs to leave here and soonest. The purple is not worth his life. And trust me, if he is captured and tried by the imperial courts, he will beg for death. The Angelids have no compassion for thieves. Especially thieves of the godly and protected purple.'

Toby blew out a long breath, wondering how long it would take Ahmed and Mehmet to find out that their morning's business was futile. He chafed to run after them or perhaps he should send Abdul. But no, attention must not be drawn. They would return and he and Tomas could tell them then...

'But he is safe for the moment?'

'I believe so ... I hope so.'

'Then we must thank you, Mistress Dana, for the role you have played. Let us ask you this. Are *you* safe?'

'For the moment...'

By the stars and heavens above, she was collected and calm. Toby warmed to her. She had the fighting spirit that he loved in a woman. The kind of spirit Ysabel of Gisborne possessed.

'If you can procure me a cloak, a robe, anything of Mistress Sophia's, I can leave as if I came to collect goods...'

'Of course. Tomas, will you take care of our guest?' Toby jumped up and hurried inside, seeking the factotum. He found the man polishing a brass table by a window. 'Abdul, the embroiderer says she has come for a cloak of the mistress's that is to be mended. Do you know which one that might be?'

'No, but I can ask my wife to check. She is an oft-times companion to the mistress.'

'You have been with the household for a long time, I think.'

'My wife has been with the mistress for many years, sir. Almost since the master arrived here with his brother. We have much affection for the house of al-Din.'

He disappeared in pursuit of a suitable cloak and Toby returned to the garden, pleased to see Tomas engaging with the embroiderer.

'I've been asking Dana about the Komemnoi, Toby. She says there is no one from the family here. Not that she has heard, anyway…'

'He has told you of Zoë,' Toby said.

Dana nodded.

Of course he has…

Abdul returned with a kermes-dyed woollen cloak. 'This is torn, sir. It is the only one my wife could find that appears to need care…' He passed it to Dana who shook it out to find the tear.

'This is the one she mentioned, thank you. I am sorry to have missed her, Abdul. We seem to have crossed paths. I may see her as I return. I will take my leave, sirs. It has been a pleasure to make your acquaintance. Perhaps we will meet again before you leave for Venezia. You will make sure my news is passed on with speed?'

The brothers nodded and bowed over her hand as if she was a noblewoman.

No, she is not from a noble family but I would bet my nosehairs that she's from a merchant family.

She left without fuss and the twins sat still for a moment, digesting her visit.

'Huh. Bloody little William. Interesting,' Tomas finally mused. 'Should we seek out Mehmet immediately? We can find Michael, get the dye and then concentrate on other things.'

'No. I think they will not be long in returning. Another hour or so won't hurt because everything will go awry if we are spotted.'

In truth he was thrilled they had Michael's location and he could feel the purple within their grasp. Then they could leave, thank the Saints, and not a moment too soon. As for Dana, *she* was impressive. He would *love* to talk more with *her*.

'Let's have some sword practice, Toby. This enterprise gets more fraught with each moment and I intend to be fully ready. Are you game?' Tomas asked.

A neat paved forecourt edged in clipped *rosmarinus* provided their arena and they began with simple stretches accompanied by groans as unused joints clicked and rolled. But in essence they were lithe, their height giving them a lowered and therefore strong centre of balance around which they could swing their bodies with ease. Tomas' speed was hindered by his bowlegs but he made up for it with supple rolls and smooth turns. Both had an exceedingly good eye as well, and it was a rare moment when a target remained unpinned in some way.

Toby thought back to the gentle jibes from the Gisborne guards about his lack of prowess with a sword. Especially Guillaume of Anjou, who claimed Toby's sword was mere costume decoration. But there was no venom in the words and each respected the other's strengths. He found he missed the Angevin's dry irony.

The brothers stood apart from each other, hefting their swords and tossing and rolling the hafts in their palms, feeling the weight, taking it through the wrist, arm and into the shoulder. They began to strike and feint at shadows – poetic motion that the sun cast as dancing patterns across the paving.

'Ready?' asked Tobias as a bead of sweat rolled down his cheek. The early sun reminded one of Outremer and the northwesterly breeze skipped over the top of Anwar's house, affording no succour.

'Are *you?*' replied Tomas and swept his edge within a blade length of his brother, the sword sighing past Toby's middle so that he needed to arch back. His balance skewed and he tottered.

'Tomas!' he growled, disturbed at the speed with which his brother had moved.

'Come now, brother. Our enemy so-called with be half as polite and twice as fast.' As he spoke, his sword returned, this time from left to right and Toby leaped back again. He tightened his grip and took a step forward to bring his sword hard against Tomas' return stroke, the swords ringing round the square and putting up a pair of turtledoves who clacked their wings with fury and fear. As the blades vibrated with the crash, Toby caught his brother's eye. Tomas looked at him, daring him, and for one moment, Toby wondered if this was what he had been like on the edges of the killing fields of Arsuf.

He attacked again and with every stroke, Toby caught it on an edge, the screech drilling right into his heart. Left, right, uppercut, downward slash, thrust, sparks filling the air and as quickly dying as the sun drowned them in its luminescence. With the speed of one far more professional than Toby had guessed, Tomas caught Toby off-guard and dove in, sword pulled back for a death-stroke.

'Tomas, stop!' Toby's grip slipped and he leaped over a fledgling *rosmarinus,* scattering green spikes and releasing a heady fragrance. He tumbled to the ground, his hand flying out to support himself, sword clanging as it fell impotent to the pavers. But still Tomas came on after him and he scuttled backward on his backside. 'Tomas,' he yelled. 'Cease this!'

But Tomas lifted his sword as if to bring it down upon his brother.

'Tommaso!' Mehmet burst into the garden, running behind Tomas and grabbing his sword arm, yanking it back, twisting so that the sword crashed to the ground. He grabbed Tomas' shoulders and shook him so hard that his head rattled back and forth. 'What do you do?'

'What? We are practising. 'Tis all we do. You fuss overmuch, Mehmet.' He turned round to see Tobias puffing, levering himself to his feet, brushing the *rosmarinus* away, shaking the hand on which he had fallen, and his eyes widened a little. 'Toby, you think I would kill you?'

But Tobias just glared, bending to pick up his sword before stalking to the *balineum,* ignoring his brother. He sat on the bench, peeling his tunic away from the sweat that ran down his chest, catching in the fine dark hairs that spread between chest and belly.

Tomas! Mary Mother! He had such force. What in the name of Christ?

He bent forward, elbows on knees and buried his face in damp hands. Footsteps sounded on the paving stones and Mehmet and Ahmed swept into the *balineum* but he didn't bother looking up.

'I sent him to the loggia to cool off, 'Mehmet said. 'You are not injured?'

'Define injury, Mehmet.' Tobias replied. '*That* was my brother, not some attacker in the dark. I felt completely put upon by my own brother.'

'Battle lust,' said Ahmed. 'I have seen it before.'

'This was no battle,' Toby snapped. 'It was sword practice for Christ's sake.'

'Huh. A weapon equals a battle in the mind of a madman.'

'My brother is *not* mad…'

'Enough,' ordered Mehmet. 'No, Tomas is not mad. But he has lack of control and a certain arrogance, Tobias. Surely you can see that.'

Toby grunted.

'You should go to him. When you are ready, bring him to us. We have news for you both.'

'News? By the hems of Mary's robes we have news to tell *you*. But it must wait, I think,' said Tobias, pulling on his damp tunic and heading to the door.

'Go to your brother, Tobias. As you say, it must wait.'

As he left, he heard Ahmed's lowered voice.

'You trust Tomas to continue with us? Allah protect us!'

'Tomas is a good man,' Mehmet replied. 'He has proved himself time and again for the Gisborne house and for King Richard. We just need to put our faith in him and pray to Allah to give him light and strength.'

'And sense,' huffed Ahmed.

Toby could hardly accept what had happened. He'd seen Tomas like that in tavern brawls but to be the butt of such physical aggression from his own brother…

God but I wish I was back in Venezia…

He walked along the path to a small loggia set in the middle of the garden. Vines cloaked the timber spans and birds filled the air with a chorus that calmed the atmosphere. Through the end of the loggia, the Harbour of Theodosius glistened in the blue distance, the sun glittering in jostling discs on the water. A seabird flew up from the harbour, gliding toward the slopes, up and over the roof of Anwar's house and reminding Tobias that *Durrah* would have begun to move by now. The sea chains would have been been lowered and the galley would have cast its moorings, the crew laying out the oars and rowing without causing any interest at all - as subtle as a transparent puff of a sea breeze. Just one more galley amongst many heading into the Harbour of Prosphorion in the Golden Horn, a belly full of whatever cargo Ahmed had purchased and with Zoë carefully disguised as part of Julius of Lübeck's act.

Zoë…

Much as Tobias was beholden to her for his creative reawakening, he began to wish she had never crossed their path. From somewhere, his intuition floated close and tapped his shoulder, reminding him of that dreadful moment when he had heard three words whispered to him.

Death stalks him…

Chapter Eight

✕

Tomas sat at a trestle table, his jaw cushioned on his hand, an expression of perturbation crisscrossing his face.

Toby's voice cracked as he spoke. 'Tomas?'

Tomas looked up, his hand falling away to the table. 'I am…'

'No matter,' Toby walked to him and laid a hand on his shoulder. 'Shall we not talk of it again?'

'But you will never trust me now, Toby, will you? This has buried it.'

'Only in *your* mind, Tomas.' He pushed in next to his brother and sat down. 'I was taken by surprise, Tomas. You are far stronger, more battle-groomed than *I* even knew. It scared me.'

'Sometimes I think I'm like a pot of oil waiting for the flame. I could have killed you.'

Toby's magnanimity toward his brother stretched tight but he said, 'Tomas, let us not speak of it again, please. You are my brother and in my heart I know you would never hurt me. In your head you know this to be true. Now clean yourself up because we have news to deliver to Mehmet and equally he has news for us.' He stood, turned and then hesitated. Returning to the trestle where his brother still sat with clenched fists, he said, 'As God, Mary and Jesus are my witnesses, I swear that I want none other but you by my side and at my back. If you can do this for me as we collect the purple, then I will help return Zoë to her family.'

Tomas said nothing in reply and Toby was unsurprised, so he left him to gather himself and change.

When he re-entered the house, he found once again that he had been holding his breath and he held his arms out wide on either side, stretching his barrel chest and taking the deepest breath he could and another, letting it out with a giant puff. Did he mean anything at all that he said to Tomas or was it mere palliative wordage? He decided he did, but some traitorous finger pointed at him, emphasizing the fact that he had claimed to be tired of being his brother's keeper.

Mehmet looked up from his cup of Syrup of Lemon when Toby walked into the room. Nothing was said, but the physician gave an infinitesimal nod as if he approved of what Tobias had done. Ahmed was nowhere in evidence and Mehmet broke the silence.

'He has gone to confirm our papers were returned to *Durrah* by the harbour official and to check that the galley is on its way safely to the Prosphorion.

'Does he anticipate trouble?' Toby walked to a window and gazed out through glass – a finer quality than that he had seen throughout the churches and courts in the north. He laid his palm flat on the surface and it was cool beneath his fingers, facing into the garden and away from the sun. But the room was bright with whitewashed walls and furnished with thickly woven rugs from the eastern traders, and with fret-worked divans covered in heavily embroidered cushions. When Mehmet replied, Toby noticed the faintest hesitation in his voice.

'Perhaps,' the physician said carefully. 'At this point it is wise to keep our eyes wide open. Besides, he cherishes his cargo.'

Toby thought to ask just what the cargo was, but he took another tack instead, designed to take his own thoughts and emotions far from the moment. 'Your brother is successful, I think.'

'Imperial patronage paves his way, yes.'

'But that must have its precarious moments, surely. I understand that every second emperor blinded his predecessor or poisoned them. Not a happy lot, are they?'

'True, but no different to rulers worldwide. Jealousies and insecurities are rife wherever there is power. The ruling families of Byzantium have always behaved in a rather typical fashion. The emperor is believed to be a representative of God on Earth and therefore he must be perfect. The Byzantine logic is that if a man is imperfect, for example blind, then he is not fit to rule. Thereby making the path quite unobstructed for one who is fortunate to possess all his faculties still and who can then don the purple.'

'Christ Jesus! And they claim to be Christians.' Tobias had always held the Byzantine culture in such high esteem and now it appeared to have feet of clay. 'And Anwar doctors the blind, I suppose.'

'No. He is a physician to lesser nobles, for which I thank Allah. I would live in fear for him otherwise.'

'The courts do not mind Arab doctors within their midst?'

'Not at all. As you know, medicine has its roots in my culture and Arabs are the best doctors. The Byzantines have always valued the best.'

Tomas entered the room as Mehmet finished speaking. He had washed and slicked back his hair, but his eyes looked down to the floor as he walked to the furthest divan. Tension had carved lines from nose to mouth and he sat hunched forward, his hands playing with anything within reach.

Tobias sat beside him, leaning forward and laying his own hand calmly over the restless fingers. 'Michael is in the city,' he said and proceeded to describe Dana's visit, telling of Michael's injury, of his need to pass the purple on and make haste away from the city before his life made haste from him.

Voices sounded from beyond the chamber, Sophia's throaty chuckle sending unwanted but delightful shivers down Toby's spine. 'You missed Dana by a hair's breadth, Mehmet, and she is sorry for it. She is a remarkably game woman who seems filled with energy and fire and she is one I would expect to work for Gisborne. I suspect she craves excitement, else she would not do what she does. Were you aware she comes from Lyon?'

He shook his head but seemed unsurprised, commenting that now they had the location for Michael, he wished Ahmed would hurry because time was of the essence.

'Could we leave without him?' But in so saying, Toby knew they could not, because Ahmed's leadership and *Durrah* were implicit in their escape from Constantinople.

Escape…

That one thought implied so much.

'And what of your morning? Was it as unremarkable as ours has been remarkable?' Toby asked as he glanced at his brother, praying that those earlier bonds had not been severed by sword-strokes.

'Ah,' Mehmet sat back. 'We left with Sophia, her maidservant, and three of Anwar's guards. Sophia was dressed in a simple robe and *qaba,* designed to attract no interest, and Ahmed stayed behind us initially. We decided this as a precaution. He would allow us time to walk along Water Street to the steps and down towards the Mese. He would retain two of the guards with him. By the way, the house had two guards left to protect you. We made sure.'

'Why would you do that?' Toby was surprised at the overt care used in this small operation.

'Protect you?' Mehmet sighed. 'Toby, we have been through this…'

'No. I mean plan as if we stormed the walls of the Great Palace.'

'Obviously you *still* do not accept that we are in danger. Tobias, I really need you to understand this and to accept that we are playing with lives. *All* our lives.'

'I do, I do. But…'

'No buts, my friend. Listen to what I will tell you. We did what we did to see if we were shadowed.'

'And were you?'

'Yes.' Ahmed walked into the chamber chewing a date, then wiping his hands on a silk square which he tucked back into a small leather pouch at his belt. 'It was as we thought…'

Between Mehmet midway down the steps and Ahmed at the top, two men followed quietly. They were clad in hooded cloaks which seemed oppressive on a balmy morning. Ahmed whistled loudly, his fingers in his mouth, and Mehmet turned and raised a hand as he and the women and their guard reached the walls of the Basilica of Saint Basil.

'Wait for us,' Ahmed called out in Arabic. Leaving one of the guards concealed at the top of the steps, he and the other hastened down. They were an impressive sight – Ahmed tall and with a bald head and gleaming dark eyes and the guard taller still, with neatly trimmed hair, a grey robe and a murderous janbiya *tucked into a leather belt.*

They proceeded with soft footsteps and if Ahmed had not whistled, the cloaked men could easily have been taken by surprise. As he and the guard hurried past, he glanced at them, calling blithely, 'Allah has blessed this day, good sirs. May

He reached Mehmet, bowed to Sophia and they turned left along the Mese, their guards behind.

'We did not turn back to see if the cloaked men followed. The guard we had left at the top of the steps was there for that reason, to track them and see what they did. He followed them from a discrete distance and they turned left, exactly on our own pathway, and tracked us almost the entire way to the embroiderer's house.'

'But they left you then? Why?'

'I have no idea. They spoke together in a huddle and then just hurried away in the direction from which they had come.'

'Perhaps it was all coincidence…' Tobias hoped so. All this cloak and dagger business was more than he wanted today. 'Anyway, it matters little because of the news we have from Dana.'

'Ah, minstrel-man, don't you think it's important that you know your enemy?'

'*My* enemy?'

'Yours, mine, Mehmet's, your brother's…'

For as much as Tomas' name was mentioned, he had played no part at all in the conversation, so much so that one wondered if he had heard a thing. But Toby guessed he had been listening. Ahmed began to describe the cloaked men but it meant little to Tobias. He wanted to know what they sounded like.

'Did they speak? What language?'

Ahmed said the guard that followed them thought it was Latin but it could have been a provincial dialect anywhere north of Sicily.

Venezia?

But Toby would not countenance enemies from his home. They surely had to be from somewhere else. He wished they could be someone he had offended through the years – revenge for a petty *canso* sung in high spirits – that would be understandable, perhaps. But he knew he played with a fantasy and that in truth, this was a dark and far more insidious enemy.

There! I admit it, Conscience. Are you happy?

'Then we will plan now that you are here…' Toby began.

'No!' Tomas said forcefully. 'Is Anwar returned? Does he have news from the palace? I need to know.'

'He is returned,' said Ahmed, his eyes closing to slits at Tomas' flushed expression.

'And?' Tomas stood, impatience beginning to burn the wick shorter. 'Call him!'

Anwar came immediately, ordering Abdul to fetch food to the loggia. Tomas stomped outside, beating a singular path to his former seat and leaving Tobias to look anywhere but at Ahmed's 'what did I tell you' face. Mehmet paced alongside his brother, discussing Michael's physical state and whether it could be too late for any treatment he required.

'You do not know Dana, Mehmet. I trust her to do as much as she could. She will have re-stitched the wound and kept it clean,' Anwar said as all five men sat down with a platter of bread and a spiced and sweetened paste of carrots and parsnips in which to dip the torn bread.

The sprawling vines created laced patterns upon the food and upon their hands. The vine stems were thick and woody, grown since Roman times, whereas the soft leaves had begun to unfurl here and there, mocking the aged wood with newborn beauty.

'What is your news, Anwar?' Tomas pushed his platter away roughly after eating only a finch's mouthful.

'I will tell if you eat something. You do yourself and others no service by starving, Tomas.'

Tomas pulled his platter back, tore off some bread and dipped it in the paste, chewing with ill humour and raising his eyebrows impatiently at Anwar.

The story began to unfold. One of the palace nobles, one of the lesser ones Anwar claimed, was a patient with itchy, red skin – a condition in the folds of her arms and legs that caused her great distress. Anwar cleaned the lesions and commented on the pomegranate skin cream he used.

'I sourced the pomegranates from Trapezus last autumn. They were particularly rubescent fruit. Always a good sign, I think. The skins dried and then ground down beautifully. Odd, isn't it, how softly green the ointment becomes when the skins are so pink?'

The noblewoman flicked her eyes over the ointment and began to talk.

'Trapezus is an attractive place, although not so beloved of those in this palace,'

she said snidely, finger beside her nose. 'I remember they had a beauty there, her name was Zoë and she had no claim to fame beyond a gentle nature, a divine face and a marriage to John Komemnos, cousin once removed from the governor at the time — I remember him because he was a polite man, very popular.'

Anwar let her reminisce as he rubbed the cream into the ugly sore. She was a loquacious old thing who welcomed chatter and it was easy to let her run on.

'John Komemnos was of petty rank being once removed from power. Perhaps that was just as well one thinks, for all his family, the Komemnoi clan, were not best loved by our Angelid house.'

Anwar moved to check behind the woman's knees — lesions had appeared there often. Her maidservant sat at the door busily sewing and all was seemly. 'Madame, continue your story whilst I work,' he reached for a new jar of the pomegranate lotion. 'It is a most interesting history you relate.'

'Well, our emperor, Isaac II Angelos, had a furious dislike of the Komemnoi and I am sure you know,' she lowered her voice to a whisper, 'how he came to power after a popular uprising against that family…'

Anwar nodded, reaching for her other leg. 'Ah, Madame, you have another outbreak behind this knee and I think we shall have to watch that it doesn't ulcerate…'

'It is a penalty of age, my dear doctor. One ends up with more folds than a courtesan's robe and nothing as pretty or enticing, although I was once, you know. Pretty…' She tapped Anwar's arm almost as if she flirted, but then returned to her flagrantly honest self. 'I sweat, so I get sores. Make me better; it is your job.'

'Then I shall do so if you continue with your story…'

'What did I say? Ah, yes, the Komemnoi. Well, needless to say all the Komemnoi within shouting distance of Constantinople beat a retreat to the far-off Balkans, John and Zoë and their children included. They took a galley across the sea from Trapezus and in so doing were attacked by pirates. The wife and children were seized and placed on one galley, the father supposedly on another and the family was sold at a slave market. But the truth as I understand it is that John Komemnos was put to death to prevent any further uprisings from the family against the Emperor. As to the wife and children, it's very sad…'

'You say? It gets worse?'

'Lovely Zoë, for she had that reputation, was lost. No doubt sold to whore around the Mar Maggior seaboard, but Emperor Isaac was distraught at the children's fate and sent officials to seek them out in the slave markets. They were

discovered a year later – the son had been castrated – he had a blessing of a voice and whomever had bought him sought to keep him as a castrato. *The daughter was a menial slave in a kitchen of the same merchant's house. The two were brought back here to the Grand Palace but the son died not long after – apparently he had Tertian Fever. And I say 'apparently' with a certain irony. But the daughter lives here still.'*

'You say? Madame, this is like a ballad!'

'Even more so when you hear she can't speak.'

'Allah protect her! How old is she?'

'Ten, twelve, I don't know. Pretty. But mute.'

'She could be cured, then. I would venture to say it is trauma from her experiences…'

'Not at all. Her tongue was cut out somewhere between Trapezus and the Great Palace. Apparently.' There was the same harsh tone as she uttered that last word before continuing. 'It is perhaps why she is tolerated here. She is no threat to the Angelids, being as imperfect as she is. Now – are we finished? I find I am tired, my dear doctor, and in need of my rest.'

'Oh indeed, Madame. You must rest – but do so in a loggia where you can have fresh air and filtered sunlight and hear the birds. You must look after all parts of your body and your mind.'

'At my age, doctor, all those parts are becoming redundant. I thank you and I shall see you very soon, I am sure. Leave the cream with my maidservant.'

'So there is a daughter,' Anwar finished almost apologetically. 'Your friend has a daughter.'

Tomas' face was no surprise to Toby, probably to no one at that table. He was lit by the glow of fervour. Not unlike a zealot, thought Toby, and we know what happens to *them.*

'I knew it!' Tomas thumped the table with his fist. 'I knew there would be someone somewhere. I have to tell her…' He jumped up, knocking his platter and the air crackled.

Ahmed reached out and grasped Tomas' arm, holding firm. 'Not now you don't. No.'

Tomas looked at the galley master's hand and then his gaze shifted with no undue malevolence to Ahmed's face. 'Unhand me!' He tried to shake the man off.

'No,' Ahmed replied through gritted teeth. 'Sit, little man. Sit down and listen.' He pushed Tomas and the small man fell back onto his seat.

Tobias held his breath. Ahmed had insulted Tomas on two counts – he had disparaged his height with none of the gentle mockery of other times and then he had manhandled him. Others had been attacked with fury for less.

'What do you think? That Zoë can rush to the Emperor with you as her supporter and say *"I am the child's long lost Komemnoi mother returned. Give her to me."* Allah protect you if that's the case. You would both be snapped up by the Varangians and locked in some cage in small pieces that would feed ravens.'

Tomas growled.

'Don't speak unless your God has suddenly given you wisdom,' Ahmed snapped. 'In case you have not noticed, it is also daylight. See?' His arm pointed beyond the loggia. 'Sunshine? Birdsong? Should you leave here now, you would be recognised within moments. I would venture to say that your chance of even *reaching* the Prosphorion without your enemy grabbing you would be nil. The enemy, by the way, who is also *our* enemy.'

'Whether 'tis day or night, our height makes us stand out like tits on a bull anyway,' Toby broke in.

'My point exactly. If not quite so colourful,' Ahmed agreed.

'Then how do you propose we ever return to the galley,' Toby asked. 'Zoë not withstanding.'

'It must be in the dead of night…' Mehmet went to speak but Tomas raged over him.

He hit his fist on the table once again. 'Christ Almighty, I couldn't give a shit in a bucket if it's day or night. You do nothing but sit here proposing one thing after another and doing nothing! All I want to do is get to the galley and tell a mother she has a living child.'

Which to Toby's ears sounded reasonable beyond doubt and as he turned his head to observe another seabird glide on a wind draught up and over the house, he knew he had the answer. 'That,' he said pointing, 'is the solution. Providing we do it at night, we can be on board the galley in an hour, maybe two, without anyone knowing we have gone.'

Four heads swung toward the roof of the house.

'That?' Ahmed's eyebrows rose for the heavens. 'You propose to climb the aqueduct and walk it in the dark?'

'Yes,' Toby grinned, feeling enlivened at the thought of what he was suggesting. 'We would finish near the Forum, I believe. Theodosius's Forum? Well is it not just a quick run across to the Second Hill and then down to the Harbour of Prosphorion?'

'Go on,' said Mehmet. 'You are speaking some sense I think.'

'Ah well, that's a change, isn't it?' said Tobias, maybe not so lightly. 'How many of the enemy are close by?'

'Two. They lurk in Water Street as we speak.'

'Ahmed, if I have read you wrong you have my profound apologies, but I think there is a touch of the *peirate* in you. If you can't create a diversion, then you are not the man I took you for. Whilst that is happening, Tomas and I can easily climb the aqueduct without anyone being aware.'

'But Tobias,' Anwar said. 'It is a huge structure that you must climb, with barely a foothold. And *if* you reach the top, the surface will be wretchedly uneven and you could stumble in the dark and fall to your deaths.'

'We are nimble and lithe, Anwar. It is part of our trade and I have no doubt we can scale the aqueduct easily. *My* only concern is that the enemy may be guarding the galley when we reach the harbour.'

'Ah, you are sharp, my little music-man,' said Ahmed. 'They have indeed done that. At this very moment, there are two men watching every move made by my men aboard the galley. Whomever wants the purple is very keen.'

'Tobias has conceived a good plan and I suspect that Allah willing, this will work. But timing will be everything…' Mehmet said.

'Timing,' scoffed Tomas. 'You worry about men we have never seen and all for the purple, whilst onboard *Durrah* sits a mother who was forced to spend years as a prostitute. A woman who hopes her family is still alive and that she can be reunited with them. You sicken me. You place money before life. Because that is all the dye represents. Money!'

Toby sat back.

Yes, his brother obsessed over Zoë but his words held such an honest truth that he could not help patting him on the back. So many things about Tomas frustrated him, that to hear such concern ring forth – it reassured at a time of high anxiety. Checking Ahmed's expression would be a waste of time and sure enough, the *peirate* followed hard on Tomas' heels, his voice as sour as a lemon.

'Money and life! Little Tomas, in this world, the world of trade, the two are linked tighter than the best-forged anchor chain. And it is because of it, that we will indeed take heed of Mehmet who has never, I believe, made a wrong decision in his life. Timing will indeed be everything. Michael will be transferred to the galley in secret this night. Diversions will be organized, and you'd better be damned good at running along the aqueduct because your job is to get out of here and to the galley without attracting one tiny bit of notice. If *you* fail, we all fail. Do you understand? In which case, Zoë's life will be worth nothing, because the authorities will merely see her as part of a plan to steal from the empire. So,' the smile Ahmed cast upon Tomas was sharper than a *kilij*, 'money and life. You see, little man?'

'How dare you…' Tomas jumped up.

'But I do dare,' roared Ahmed '*That* is how it shall be. Do we understand one another?'

Tomas glared at Ahmed, and Toby knew all respect for the two had collapsed and died at that very moment. They would stand in the same room, but their backs would be turned.

No kindred spirits there…

As if Tobias needed to be told.

Ahmed and Anwar left to seek Michael. It had been considered too dangerous for Mehmet to leave and as it was, Ahmed would continue to the docks to supervise the last of the lading and to pay his harbour dues. He would in fact be seen to do all that a galley master must do, at the same time organising the much-needed diversions. His very own plan to be seen as an active galley master with no concern for his former passengers was part of the diversion.

'What cargoes does he carry?' asked Toby. 'He has never divulged…'

Mehmet had been sorting herbs that Anwar had laid on the table. 'He has offloaded a supply of the best Cretan wines and delivered bales of wool which Saul bought in Lyon. The wool came originally from England, I believe. In return, he has taken aboard exceptional silks and fine spices for the Venetian market and will be expecting frankincense for which he signed a contract with a papal representative before he left Venezia. His cargo is worth a fortune.'

Something about that struck a chord with Toby but he couldn't recall the detail, so he suggested to Tomas they formulate their plan because darkness would pull its curtain soon enough.

'You stood up to Ahmed,' Toby ventured as they sat in their alcove.

'He doesn't like me. The feeling is mutual.' Tomas rubbed at his sword edge with a wad of lambswool.

'Perhaps you take too strong a line there, Tomas. I think it is more a question of trust. Seafarers rely heavily on the trust they have in each other. Lives depend upon it. Think on your own experience with King Richard most recently and you will see I am right.'

Tomas merely grunted and so Tobias changed the subject to the imminent ascension of the Valens Aqueduct. He was wondering if the idea would work because what had seemed feasible at Sext, now seemed flawed at None.

'Of course it will work,' said Tomas. 'Remember Paris?'

Oh yes, Toby remembered Paris well.

After settling into the priory that was their home as they studied within the College of Minstrels, a curfew had worried them little. They were so overawed with the size, the wealth, the intellect and the creativity that swirled around them, they would fall into their cots in the *dorter* and sleep as if felled by Death.

But in time, and as they became familiar with others within the College, they began to hear things. The city that had once been as elegant as a noblewoman now became a whore overnight. She beckoned to the twins, offering earthly delights the like of which they could only dream.

Thus they would let themselves down over the priory walls and enjoy nights of freedom and abandon, even the loss of virginity before climbing back up the walls in the dark and so very nearly dawn.

The first night of this errant behaviour had induced a heightened level of anticipation – one that caused mild hysteria within the *frater*. Brother Francis glared at them before standing at the lectern to read lessons for their edification as they and the monks chewed their way through the remains of the day's wastel along with a watery but herb-laced pottage. The lesson was punctuated with slurps as the pottage was sucked through rotted teeth and occasionally, as Brother Francis paused for breath, an auditory and less than fragrant expulsion of air might rumble from beneath the coarse woollen robes of the monks. It was such heady moments that oft reduced the minstrels to helpless laughter. In the *dorter* later, they would recall the tonal variations expressed through the meal and endeavour to put them to music or lyrics. Such levity filled them with high spirits, and on the first night of escape, they considered themselves invincible.

They retrieved stolen rope from under the hay within the barn and with great care, with boots stuffed beneath their belts and cloaks tied to their backs, they crept from the *dorter*, venturing into the cloister and around the corner of the *frater* where an old hogshead stood against the wall of the communal eating space.

The moon shone with ivory brilliance, not a wisp of cloud trailing anywhere.

'If Brother Francis doesn't catch us, the moon will certainly try.' Toby looked across at Tomas. 'Hey ho, leg up!'

Within moments, they stood looking down upon the small garden of the priory, thanking the Lord it was tiles beneath their feet and not the timber and thatch of the barn. The roof of the *frater* extended upward toward the roof of the chapel and it was to this they climbed, the weatherbeaten tiles providing odd footholds through which a toe could grasp at a timber frame. Not so very different from the many times they had climbed the pockmarked rock walls of Pigna as children.

'Ouch,' Tomas growled, 'the broken tiles are sharp. I've sliced my fingers.'

'Then your *vielle* shall have a day's rest. Be quiet, Tomas.'

The chapel's ridgeline was neatly rounded with a smooth capping and the twins sat astride for a moment, absorbing Paris spread out around them. The priory, along with others, sat comfortably on the Ile de la Cité. Ahead they caught a glimpse of the Capetian palace of King Phillip and the stark, soaring beauty of Notre Dame begun twenty or more years before. Not far away on this bank were the colleges that made up the pulsing heart of cultural Paris. The twins' egos shone that much brighter as they realised their own College of Minstrels was a part of something truly great. Flame and candlelight flickered like the starlit heavens above and smoke ascended on this still night as if it were delicate wisps of fog. Winding around was the aroma of roasted pig and poultry and the ever-present stench of decay. The bell of the chapel sounded Compline and the twins slammed their hands against their ears until it had stopped and until the vibrations beneath their bodies had stilled.

Then music drifted upward – a mélange of *carole* and chant. *Carole* from the taverns and chant from beneath them as the monks began to honour God at this dark hour.

'Do you think Brother Francis will miss us?' Tomas asked.

'We barely ever attend Compline so he will assume we are asleep … I hope.' Tobias stood and brushed his hands together. 'Come on, it'll be dawn and we'll have seen nothing. Are you ready?'

This was the part they had both looked forward to least – a swift descent to the priory wall and a true possibility of injury or worse.

'Go slowly,' added Toby, always cautious.

But Tomas lay down and turned over. Stomach pressed against the tiles, he began to move.

'Tomas!' Toby's heart leaped into his mouth as his brother started to descend. He imagined smashed limbs, brains dashed on stone blocks…

'It's safe. Come on,' his brother had the gall to grin widely.

Below them, the monks chanted on and the belfry sat sentinel, missing nothing. The twins slid down the tiles to the top of the wall, bracing with their feet, arms flailing as they grabbed at anything to slow their flight over the top and into the Seine.

'Jesus, God and Mary,' hissed Tomas as his feet finally connected with a hard edge.

But Tobias shot past and Tomas thrust out his arms, grabbing at the cloak tied to his brother's back, halting him as legs dangled into nothingness. Stone fragments fell and hit the water with a splash.

'Thank the lord,' puffed Toby as Tomas yanked him back. Cold sweat pumped across his body as he pulled his legs up and sat for a moment, gathering wits and sense and breath.

'I think not,' said Tomas. 'Better thank me. Let's go.'

They levered themselves to their feet and hurried along the narrow wall with deft steps, never missing a mark, as sure-footed as cats in the dark. The wall angled away from the river along a dark alley and here they tied the end of the rope to a protruding block of stone on the top of the wall, a convenience they felt sure was placed just so for them to use. Tobias shimmied down, huffing on his hands a little as the hemp burned into his skin. Tomas followed but jumped off halfway, landing on the ground and tumbling in a perfect somersault.

'The cut from the tiles hurts – it's bleeding again.'

He pulled a square of linen from his purse and wound it round and then they both turned to stare at the end of the alley – gateway to the pleasures of the world. Light from a tawdry inn beckoned with a lascivious lick of flame and they needed no second invitation.

Paris became theirs for the taking and the route across the roof became so easy they mused they could walk it in their sleep. Tomas, who had discovered a predilection for copious amounts of wine, would make the return journey blind drunk more often than not, but then drunks had such profound and ungodly balance. Along with no fear and no sense.

Ah, yes, Tobias remembered Paris well…

'The wind strengthens from the northwest.' Tobias watched the alcove curtain shift in a draft. Outside, twigs rolled along the paths and a sharp dash of rain hit the roof with a clatter and then stopped – as if God had turned the faucet. 'And rain threatens.'

'So?' Tomas slipped one of his two daggers into the sheath in his boot. 'It's to our advantage. A good cover, no moonlight…'

'Slippery stones, darkness…' Tobias muttered.

'I can hear you, Toby. Don't forget this was your idea. Can we rely on Anwar and Mehmet to get our swords to the galley?'

'Yes, of course we can. And, Tomas, don't forget we do this so as you can get back to Zoë. For myself, I would have preferred to see Michael, get the purple and then make a run for the galley and Zoë.'

'Oh yes,' Tomas sniffed. 'Let's not forget the damned purple. Why did you not suggest such a plan earlier, then?'

'I… I don't know. I think I agreed with you over the need for Zoë to know of her child as soon as possible and the purple came second to that thought. Now I am not so sure. I wonder if we are making this whole exercise so much more convoluted than it need be.'

'Too late now,' said Tomas, giving his second dagger one more wipe with the lambswool and then sheathing it at his belt. 'And I for one care not one scrap if we have to leave without the confounded dye. But I would care to the Heavens and back if Zoë had not found out about her daughter or worse, had not been given the chance to reunite with her.'

Tobias said nothing, leaning already armed against the wall, and chewing his thumbnail. Privately he knew Tomas was right and yet the thought of Saul and of Gisborne losing their family fortunes and the havoc that would wreak upon two families and those who depended on the families was almost as great a dilemma in his very loyal and loving mind. And just for one moment, the hairs once again stood on his neck and he wondered why.

The brothers had eschewed their cloaks for ease of action, and were clad in the travel-stained clothes of their sea voyage, all the better to blend with shadow. Tomas had pulled a dark caplet down over his fresh barley-tinted hair and had shaved his dark Ligurian stubble. As he ran a hand over the smooth skin, Tobias noticed a gleam.

'Wait,' he said and ran outside, returning moments later with a hand full of damp soil. 'Rub it on your face. You glisten like the moon.' As they waited, so Tobias' heartbeat began to pick up pace. It reminded him of the time in Cyprus when he playacted as Di Dia, the Spanish troubadour – singer of songs not only for Richard's court but for the bastard Templar knight, Halsham. Every moment with the Templar, his throat would close as he imagined his disguise wearing thin. Every moment, he was stunned when glib words and entrancing song emerged from the selfsame stranglehold. It was truly astonishing what one could do under duress.

And tonight is no different…

Mehmet pulled the curtain aside. 'We begin,' he said. 'They have been lured to the steps and whilst they are engaged you must go.'

'And Michael?' Toby asked as they hurried through the yard to the gate.

'Anwar has pronounced him able to make the journey to the galley. It is a nasty wound upon his leg, a hair's breadth closer and he would have bled to death. On the battlefield he might have lost the leg, but Dana stitched it and doctored it well.'

'And the dye?'

'He has not said. We have to trust him. Now go. Insha'Allah.'

'Stay safe, Mehmet…' Tobias grasped his friend, praying to God and Jesus and anyone who would listen to protect the gentle physician and guide him with care, back to the galley and to Venezia. Then he and Tomas were in Water Street, the gate locked behind them and a fracas occurring in the eastern distance near the steps.

They moved quickly in the dark, across the street to the massive structure that loomed above.

'Hey ho,' Tomas said. 'Leg up.' He put his foot into Toby's cupped hands, and onto his shoulders, Toby reeling a little. It was some time since they had played this game.

'Hurry,' he hissed.

'Got one,' Tomas said, 'and another,' as he felt for footholds. 'I'm away.'

Toby looked up and sure enough, Tomas made swift speed to the rows of evenly spaced arches. A skein of rope snaked down and Toby grabbed it and began to walk his way up the viaduct wall to where Tomas sat waiting. The ease of that first climb gave them both confidence and he quickly coiled the rope back over his shoulder.

'Upwards?' he asked.

Tobias looked up. The arch bloomed well above their heads, a graceful parabola, and he wondered how they would move on. Running his hand over the cut stone blocks and the regularly inset rows of brick, they seemed smooth, not marked enough with wear and tear for footholds. He ripped off his boots and folded them under his belt, felt along the wall and up until he found a chink and stretched his foot, placing toes in the gap. But he needed another and then one again at head height.

'Christ, the Romans built things well, Tomas. There's barely a fingerhold…'

'Here,' whispered Tomas from next to him. 'I found a crumbled brick and more above it. I think we can go this way…'

A shout further down, and then running footsteps back toward their position.

'Quick, go!' Tobias pushed his brother and they began to climb, barely stopping for breath, damp stone under their toes and fingers, even moss, hearing the wind as it pulled at hair and tunic. It burrowed beneath the wool to Toby's skin, dragging cold fingers across and he shivered. Tomas was well ahead of Toby as a figure came running through the ground level arch, another behind him. 'Keep going,' whispered Toby. 'Don't look down.'

They hauled themselves over the top of the viaduct and lay there as a knife fight broke out below them. They tried to guess which was one of their own but had no clue. A cloak-clad man dove in low with a *janbiyah,* drawing it upward with a grunt. His opponent screamed and hunched over. It needed no light to illuminate the murder that had been committed. The wounded man sobbed, falling to his knees and as his attacker reached for his throat, Tobias signalled to Tomas to move on.

They crept away and began to walk as swiftly as they could in an easterly direction.

'Christ…' said Tomas.

'Hope he was one of ours,' Toby replied. Neither was unused to death but he worried at the effect such violence would now have upon his brother. 'We need to increase our pace, Tomas. Speed and invisibility are our only allies.'

They began a careful jog but the distance beyond their sight was dark and the wind blustery, the surface, although flat was quite moist and thus care was vital.

'Listen…' Toby stopped for a moment and Tomas drew up next to him, the two just able to stand side by side, the width of the aqueduct as Anwar had said – a man's shoulder width and a half wide. 'There…'

The grumble of volumes of water ran beneath their feet, fresh from the forests of Belgrade and rushing fiercely toward the cisterns of the Great Palace. Even in the gusting wind, the vibration growled around their unshod feet.

'A pity we aren't able to crawl inside and float down un-noticed by anyone,' Toby said as the wind ruffled his hair.

'Like I said,' Tomas muttered. 'Too florid an imagination. Let's go.'

But Tobias held him back. 'Get our bearings, Tomas. It's as dark as an unlit crypt ahead. And feel the surface. It's getting slippery.'

'But we've walked a hundred times in the dark.'

'In Paris we were lit by flambeaus and braziers. We are yards above the ground, enough to smash our brains from our skulls should we fall. We might as well be blind as we go.'

'Then tie ourselves together. If one falls the other can pull him back.'

Tobias wondered at the value of this, but soon he and Tomas were strung together like twins in a womb. They set off again, arms outspread for balance, looking straight ahead.

The wind snorted around them, unpleasant and bullying, and as they passed above the steps to Water Street, the rain began to fall, lashing their left sides.

'God's bloody chest hairs…' Tomas shook his head in raging disgust and Toby cursed God's humour.

Below them, two men fought hand to hand, punches flying. They looked for the survivor of the attack further west and could see no one in the rain. The men below slipped and grunted – uppercut, left jab, right jab, and another upper cut, the thinner man reeling and falling to his knees, the bigger man running behind him to lift both fists and bring them crashing down on the man's skull so he fell to the ground whereupon his attacker kicked out.

'Come on,' said Toby, aware of the outcome and eager to keep Tomas moving. 'Zoë's waiting.' He pushed his brother and Tomas began to jog, Toby following. But his foot slipped and he sucked in a breath as his knee hit the stone of the aqueduct. The pain echoed through the bone like a cry for help in the mountains. As he landed, he thrust his hands out for balance, a cat on all fours, and a fragment of brick went flying through the wet night, falling down to the road below with a clatter that defied the noise of the wind.

No…

'Run, Tomas!' he whispered urgently.

His knee screamed with pain but he pushed up and on, convinced they must be more than halfway. He strained to hear if someone followed below but it was as impossible as trying to look behind without tumbling over the precipitate edge. One could only look forward and hope. Often, Tomas would get further ahead and the rope would yank tight and he would quicken his pace until it hung more easily between the two.

Some vague feeling of success bubbled as the rain stopped as swiftly as it had begun and the wind eased up a notch.

'Thank Christ,' huffed Tomas. 'Watch out – scaffolding.'

Parts of the aqueduct were worn and the city officials had rigged timber scaffolding and for one moment one could feel safe with a handrail at waist height. Tomas slowed to a walk and dislodged a piece of brick which went tumbling through the scaffolding, banging as it fell. Tobias hoped the Saints had kept any likely walkers away from underneath, praying that all the citizens observed curfew and were in their beds sleeping the sleep of the good and the just. He began to step carefully past the scaffolding.

'More care, Tomas. Don't dislodge any more. *Jesus…*'

A hand reached up from below and grabbed his ankle, tugging, pulling him off balance so that he fell on his hip, the rope to Tomas tightening. Both had the prescience not to speak and by the way the rope tightened even more, he knew his brother had looped the coil around something unyielding and was able to take the strain. As the hand yanked again, almost separating leg from hip socket, he pulled his dagger free from the sheath and struck out.

'Satan's seed!' a voice snarled in a Ligurian dialect.

Ligurian? Genova?

He struck again in the dark, aiming for eye or neck but the other hand grasped his wrist and pulled and he felt torn apart as the rope tightened further.

'Tomas! Help me!'

But the mouth that growled began to gurgle and the tension on his body eased, the attacker collapsing upon the scaffold before being tipped over.

'Well, little minstrel-man, I seem destined to save your life once too often.'

'Ahmed!'

The galley master's teeth glistened but his voice held no warmth as he wiped a knife on a piece of torn fabric caught on the scaffolding. 'Your brother?'

Toby's rope jerked and he was reeled heavenward. 'Up here,' he grinned.

Ahmed followed behind as Toby half-climbed and was half-pulled onto the top of the aqueduct.

'Well played, Master Tomas. You saved your brother. It would have been his throat cut perhaps and not the attacker's.'

Tomas had looped the rope twice round a piece of the scaffolding, holding and bracing against the strain. Lucky then that he and Toby were small, for the scaffolding would not have held the strain of fully-sized men.

'Presumably they would have tried to get the location of the dye first, think you?' said Tomas with barbs aplenty. 'As you can see, Ahmed, I am capable some of the time.'

'Tomas, he killed my attacker. Leave it be.'

Tomas grunted as he bent to untie the rope from Toby's waist to loop it over his shoulder.

'I admire your prowess, my friends,' said Ahmed. 'You are not far from the Forum now and will have to climb down before the viaduct enters the cisterns. There is a right angled wall…'

'Were you a part of the diversion?' Toby asked.

'Yes, but they were far more proficient than we imagined. Have no doubt;

they are trained killers. We lost one of Anwar's guards, Allah welcome his soul to Paradise. After I removed one of the opponents near to Anwar's gate, I hurried back to the steps, arriving just as the enemy delivered a final kick to Anwar's guard, killing him. The felon stood there for a moment and was rewarded with a glancing blow from a piece of falling masonry. He looked up and whom did he see, do you think? And thus he began to track you and *I* followed him. Fatally for him as it turned out.'

'Expeditiously for us,' acknowledged Toby. 'My thanks, Ahmed.'

'Enough I think. It is my job,' the galley master brushed the effusion aside. 'We must get on.'

'*We?*' Tomas bridled.

'I will come with you now that I am here so be done with it, Tomas. I can show you the speedy way down the Second Hill and with luck, we will reach the docks just as the next diversion begins.'

Tomas' sigh of umbrage was noticed.

'When we begin our return voyage, little Tomas, I shall allow you to breathe your disgust of me into my sail and we shall reach Venezia with great speed.'

Tobias couldn't help laughing but Tomas remained sour.

They hurried along the remaining length of the aqueduct, treading on more sturdy masonry, able to notice more of the city spread out below.

'The heavens are clearing. Not good for any of us until we are aboard.' Ahmed heaved his own sigh.

Above them, the black cloud of a stormy night had thinned, ragged wisps trailing away to leave a softer, shadowy, almost iron-coloured sky, and here and there the occasional star. A shaving of moon glimmered weakly. It could have been a poet's sky, thought Toby, but not now...

'There it is,' said the galley master. 'Straight down there,' he pointed slightly to the left over Tobias' shoulder, 'the harbour and our diversion. Prepare yourself, my little minstrel...'

CHAPTER NINE

×

To Toby it meant nothing.

One dark shape on top of another dark shape.

He had wanted so badly to wander the streets, to observe the beauty, to walk the walls of the city that had so much history. He wanted to stand above the quaint cupolas of the churches and marvel at the construction, to sigh over the icons within. He wanted to hear the music, to bargain for a *lyra*. Instead he ran from killers in the night and would likely only ever see Constantinople from the wale of a galley as they sailed away.

'And here – here is the wall of the forum abutting the aqueduct.' Ahmed pulled at his arm. 'This is where you must climb down. Can you do it?'

An enormous colonnaded square, perfect in its symmetry, stretched before Toby, shining with subtle beauty as the wafer thin moon cast a wan light across the building. Water fell from fountains and gathered in a vast pool, the cistern to which Ahmed had referred. In the centre of a paved open space, a column rose heavenward and the moon settled on it – a marker perhaps.

'Truly, galley master,' sneered Tomas. 'You have neither sense nor sight. Look again.'

Ahmed stepped close to the edge, looking at the forum walls as they veered away.

'Do you see anything to which we can attach a rope? Or perhaps you think we are like spiders and able to crawl up and down the vertical.'

'Then what do you suggest, my friends?' Ahmed asked. 'You must have thought of what might happen when you reached the end of the aqueduct.'

'To be truthful, no,' Toby shrugged. 'But something will reveal itself, it always does. We've never been truly stuck anywhere, have we, Tomas? Besides, Ahmed, are we not always here to tell the tale? Have faith! Now, tell me – is this forum a public space or sealed by closed gates?'

'Public. It is the marketplace. As to gates, I'm unaware. I have never been here.'

'Jesus...' Tomas swore.

'Well, let's see...' Tobias jumped from the aqueduct to the roof of the colonnade that surrounded the vast square. 'It's like a cloister, yes? These colonnades go right round the perimeter so let's follow them. They may lead to a gate, a statue, something to which we might tie rope and scale down.' He plunged on, grateful to be off the narrow walkway of the aqueduct and atop a wide, flat and well-tiled roof. The enormous space echoed with the sound of running water as it trailed away into the cistern that supplied the Great Palace.

'What's that?' Tomas pointed to a triple-arched structure ahead. 'Ahmed, give us the benefit of your extensive knowledge.'

Ahmed gritted his teeth, a fist lifting as if he wished to slam Tomas' disrespect back down his throat. 'I'm...'

'You know nothing,' Tomas interrupted, brushing past Ahmed and moving toward the structure.

'I am a sea captain. Ask me what are the various harbours in this city and the names of sea-gates set within the walls and the churches along the waterfronts and I could name every one *and* draw a map. This high up away from the water means nothing to me. But I will hazard a guess, *little* man, and say this is the Arch of Theodosius. The columns are supposed to be carved like the bark upon trees.'

Toby had reached the end of the colonnade and was hoisting himself onto the archway above the first of the three arches, deliberately ignoring the sparring between the galley master and his brother. 'Ha! We now have something to which we can easily tie a rope.' He lay on his belly and examined the supports. 'And I think we have found some footholds. The sculptors have carved folds in the stone, just like bark as you say. Tomas, pass me the rope. I'll go first.'

Moments later, after climbing down the marble folds and using the rope as insurance, all three stood on the even paving beneath the triumphal arch. They moved beneath the grand centre span, higher than the two that flanked it. Tobias allowed himself one brief moment to admire the fluid nature of the arches and the grand design of the triumphal gate, but it was indeed a brief pause as Ahmed, having checked that no one was beyond the gate, chivvied them to move. They ran in bare feet, as quiet as shades, boots tucked into belts, down amongst winding little streets that led between houses of timber, brick and mortared stone. They stopped briefly to slip on their boots and check weapons and then continued on past closed shutters, barred gates and unlit doorways.

So odd, thought Tobias. Surely there should be a drunkard, the fragrantly poor, outcasts of society lying in the gutter. At their feet, surely there should be scavenging dogs. Indeed, not even one cat had crossed their path. But then perhaps that was good luck.

The houses were large, the doors and window-frames neat and with little weather-wear and somewhere they heard a man cough and then the sound of a babe crying.

So, the houses are inhabited. Perhaps it's the merchants' quarter...

Tobias had heard the merchants from Venezia had created a large settlement with the agreement of Emperor Basil II almost three hundred years before. It sat southwest of the Golden Horn and represented power on a substantial scale. They had their own church, the basilica of Saint Akyntos, and the church's priests were the merchants' notaries and surely trustworthy because of it.

But during the rule of the Komemnoi, the Genovese and Pisans expressed concern at the ever-expanding power of their Venetian competition and riots broke out which lasted for many years. It was Emperor Isaac II Angelus, the man who might have had Zoë Komemna's husband killed, her son emasculated and her daughter made mute, who conferred trading rights and privileges back to the Venetians at the expense of the Genovese. It was never forgotten and Tobias had memories of men spitting on Venetian names when he lived within the Gisborne house in Genova. At the time, he and the Gisborne family straddled the dislike heaped upon the Venetians easily. Indeed, Gisborne had no thoughts of settling in Venezia...

No – that came later. After a wife ran off to find her husband and a child was kidnapped…

'Toby!' Tomas dragged his brother to a stop. 'Ahmed said we must wait here and watch.'

Ahmed looked round at Toby. 'Methinks you were dreaming, music-man. If you want to keep your head connected to your body, now is not the time. Understand me?'

Toby nodded. They had halted in a tiny alley, space compressed so that timbers of warehouses leaned against them and even the heavens could not be seen. It smelled of piss – cat or human – and ordure squelched under their boots. It could have been typical of any city in which Tobias had lived and he sniffed, his lip curling with wry disgust.

Ah, familiarity at last…

'What are we waiting for?' he whispered to Ahmed and the sea captain answered, his voice satin smooth in the dark of night. Something about his base rumble always sent shivers through Toby, as if the galley master was just *waiting* to have a *canso* sung about him – a grand song, words to describe his magnificence:

He, who in you *puts his trust*
Needs no other for defence,
Such that if the world were lost,
He will not be carried hence…

Ah yes, thought Toby, the *'you'* in that verse was definitely the *peirate*, Ahmed.

'We wait for the diversion and for my crew to play act. When it happens, I want you both to run for your lives to the docks. See the barrels stacked there? Get behind them. You must then work out how to get aboard *Durrah* without raising interest. My men will do all they can but should you fail, we will deny any knowledge of your activities. Do you understand? You will be completely alone until you are aboard my ship.'

Tobias knew it was an unwritten law in the dark world of secrets, that one always denied another. If not, it had the capacity to bring about the destruction of that whole intricate web of deceit. He noticed Tomas studying the barrels and the distance to the galley and concentrated his own mind to the task. Oh, indeed he knew what his brother had surmised and he knew the deep-seated fear it would engender.

Damn it to hell and back…

In the vague distance, he heard voices, shouts, a crack of laughter, the hum of relaxed men – perhaps too relaxed, and Ahmed's brow tightened. The men came into view from a street to their left, joking, pushing each other and making more noise than a tavern full of inebriates in Paris or Genova.

Above Toby's head a shutter slammed open, a cracked voice yelled, 'Quiet, you bastards! Quiet!' The shutters were slammed closed again, dust and timber shards falling on top of the threesome below.

A cue perhaps, because walking onto the harbour square from the right, past the barrels without pausing, buckles and weapons ringing in the occasional breaks between raucous laughter from the drunkards, were four Varangian guards. And in their midst, an expensively robed and cloaked man in the verdant shades of Byzantine officialdom.

'You must go,' hissed Ahmed.

The square was large enough for cargo to be piled for loading and unloading but currently it was bereft of goods except for the neatly stacked barrels and rolls of fishnet reeking of old catch and rotting weed. The docks were filled with a row of moored galleys, but all in darkness, although the various crews had woken and were standing watching the noise in the square, excited at the appearance of the Varangians, a low burble beginning to fill the night air.

The outer edges of the square shifted and changed in dancing shadow whilst the middle was lit with flaming *torchères* and along the edge of the docks, tired braziers dozed with the last of the coals. The Varangians moved forward in a loping, long-limbed manner, their trousers ballooning in rippling folds before being mercilessly imprisoned under leather leg-guards and boots. The wrists of their sand coloured tunics ended in broad bands of leather and it would seem they had a fancy for the stuff, because belts of it criss-crossed their chests and backs. Amongst such bondage, they had thrust leather-hafted axes and daggers and the blades were honed to devilish brightness, flashing in the light of the flames as they moved.

Even a mild blow would sever a body part and Toby needed no more evidence of the need for subtlety, the group radiating uncomfortable power. The official could well have been the one so engrossed in Tomas' papers; Toby thought he recognised the man's nose – a hooked thing that hung over a fat set of lips. Not the handsomest man but then he had no need to be with axes, daggers and the famous strength of the Varangians behind him. The fellow wore the green with a swagger, both tunic and cloak in harmonising shades from the forest and at his shoulder, the cloak corner was again pinned back with a flashy fibula – a badge of rank and office.

The drunken seamen lurched across the square, oblivious to the approach of the law, engrossed in a mocking tale told by a tallish crewman with part of his dark hair pulled back tightly from his forehead.

'By the hems of Mary's robes!' Toby could not help himself, the words coming out in a breathless rush. 'It's Mehmet, look! I'm sure. He's dyed his hair…'

Another fellow whacked Mehmet on the shoulder as he delivered the conclusion to his tale and the crew brayed like a herd of asses. One fell over the nets occasioning a further asinine burst at which the harbour official ordered the Varangians to advance and encircle.

'Leave!' Ahmed spat. 'In Allah's name. I am about to begin Act Two and you must use the time wisely. Go.' He pushed past Toby and swept down into the square, robes billowing around him, the torchlight flaring upon his gleaming head, his hand closed over the hilt of his *kilij*, the carrying rings jingling as the weapon swung from his belt. He was as impressive in his theatrical stride as the Varangians and he roared in Arabic, demanding to know what in the Prophet's name was happening.

This was the twins' chance and whilst noise and argument raged from the other side of the square, they ran, boots once again tucked under belts, until they had reached the pool of shadow behind the barrels.

Ahmed's voice rang across the square and Toby muttered, 'He's giving everyone a lashing, but mostly Faisal and now he's rubbing salt in. Listen…' He leaned to the edge of the barrels and peeked out. 'Ha, seems Faisal should not have allowed the crew ashore. A good bluff…'

Oblivious to his brother's commentary, Tomas stared at the seemingly depthless water. 'We have to swim. We have to get into the water, swim to the starboard wale and climb aboard.'

The despair in his brother's voice pierced Tobias' fascination with events in the square and as he reached for a dangling mooring line to shimmy down the seawall, he said. 'I will be with you, Tomas. Just beware the other vessels. The harbour is more crowded than a whore's chemise.'

Indeed, every mooring was utilised and the risk of discovery was high. Their only good fortune lay in the way *Durrah* was moored – along the pier with the larboard wale against the structure. Their own entry to the ship faced out into the harbour and was patterned in darkness and with luck, they could feasibly climb aboard unseen.

'Tomas, come on…'

But as Tomas went to move, a hand slipped over his mouth and fought to drag him away. Tomas, quicker than lightning, grabbed the dagger from his belt and drove it backward, jerking it up. The hands fell away and even before the felon could utter a cry, Toby had let go the line, rushed forward as the man fell to his knees, slit the throat and rolled the expiring body into the water.

'Two,' he said. 'They said there were two on watch here. Come on…' They scanned as far as they dared and seeing no one and begging God to protect them, they followed each other down the rope, avoiding the body that floated in a sanguine stain near the harbour wall. Across the water, the official had begun laying charges in ringing tones and Ahmed begged to pay any fines so that his boat might leave on the midday tide.

The water bit at every part of them. The year might be moving well beyond Easter and galloping into the arms of summer but the water had the frozen chill of mountain streams. They took a breath each, looking toward the square and measuring the distance to *Durrah*. The crew shambled along the wharf and Toby would swear Mehmet looked for them, examining the harbour space between the hogsheads and *Durrah* because he stopped and drew the crew into an untidy but effective huddle, blocking any view the official might have of the water beyond. They stood as if waiting for Ahmed, befuddled and disorganised as only the most drunk of inebriates can do.

Tomas gasped as the water covered his shoulders and immediately he sank below the surface. Toby ducked under and grabbed him, trying to shake sense into him, hoping to God he wouldn't flail and shout in his panic. As he hauled him to the surface, he punched him hard in the arm and glared at him, then pushed him in front, following close on his stroke.

They swam across the dock, barely disturbing the surface. At one point, someone yelled from one of the moored vessels and the brothers ducked under the surface, holding hands until lungs almost burst. They broke the surface as gently as they were able, sucking air like bellows and grateful for the row between Ahmed and the official. But Tomas' breath continued soughing in and out and there was a shout.

'Oi, there's somethin' out there. I saw somethin'!' Fellow crew joined the seaman and stared and Tomas and Tobias sank below the surface again, swimming underwater and praying they swam toward *Durrah* in the murk. At last the planks of her hull lay beneath their palms and they were able to grab the rope that hung over the side with the ubiquitous wooden pail knotted on the end. They grasped it like a lifeline until their breathing had evened out.

'We have to climb it, watchers or no. There is no other choice. Keep praying, brother.' Toby pushed Tomas forward and the twin pulled on the knotted hemp, hands clasping as tightly as crabs' claws. In a moment he had flopped over the side, and Toby hauled himself up behind, water running off his sodden body, his boots God be thanked, still hanging through his belt. He and Tomas slithered into the shelter of stacked bales, Tomas shivering violently with much more than cold.

Ahmed's outrage raised a gurgle from *Durrah*'s dockside crew. Haggling continued and then Ahmed could be heard jingling coins in his purse and then slapping them down on the timber lid of a hogshead.

'*Hyperpyrons.*' The official's voice rose by degrees. 'Then you are a successful merchant, are you not?'

'It is money to pay for the arrival of tomorrow's frankincense. If Your Honour leaves me any…'

The official counted the coinage into his own purse and looked up. 'This will suffice. And how you pay for your frankincense is a problem that only you can solve. But before you go, galley master…' The Varangians moved a little closer as he tightened the drawstring on his purse and stood. 'Tell me, what do you know of Tyrian purple?'

Durrah's crew hushed and one could almost feel the vessel itself floating above the surface of the harbour in suspenseful expectation. Ahmed, consummate *peirate,* did not miss a beat.

'The dye? Only that it is an imperial possession. How odd that you should ask. It is the second time in the immediate past that I have had the question put to me.'

The official's head tilted to the side and he murmured, 'Go on…'

The tone sent shivers through Tobias, almost as if the Varangians already had their axes poised.

'Everyone who trades has longed to have access to the dye. The northern nobility crave its usage, marvel at the magic nature of the colour to define power. A goodly price would be paid to anyone who could carry it back to sell.'

'Even you?'

'Allah protect me from unwise choices!'

Still so smooth and so very believable. So it seemed to Tobias as he prayed with cold hands clasped tight. He realised he hadn't talked to God so much since they searched for William of Gisborne at the Toulon Commanderie. When Tomas had gone missing with King Richard as they played cat and mouse around the Adriatico, his soul knew immediately that Tomas was still alive. But with little William, and much as he might have wished that blood connection, at no point could he determine if the child was alive. He had only hope and God – just like now.

'I would never risk my boat nor my life,' Ahmed continued. 'Not for the ink of a shellfish.' He closed his own purse and let it hang emptily at his side. 'But others might.'

'Go on…' the official purred.

'It was a trader. He wanted to know if I knew where to seek it. I told him if he valued his hands, even his head, it would be better to trade in spices than shellfish.'

'Where was this trader from? What was his name?'

Ahmed shrugged. 'I suspect north of Sicily. He knew the waters of the Middle Sea well. As to his name, I did not ask. He was young and brash, 'tis all I know.'

A vision flitted forth from Toby's memory – of a young Genovese called Pietro. Tobias wondered if there actually had been a chance meeting between Ahmed and Pietro and if the topic of conversation that ensued had indeed involved the purple. Could it be he? He did after all covet much the same cargo as Ahmed and had filled his ship with quality goods. But it was the very fact that he seemed so loyal to his family's business, so intent on building a good and trustworthy name with it. Toby dismissed the Genovese as being too honourable to do anything as underhand as…

As what? Stealing a prized commodity as the Gisborne house intends to do?

He shook his head and drew his attention back to the square. How easily Ahmed had covered himself. The words had flowed like a tidal current, without deflection. *It is the second time in the immediate past that I have had the question put to me…'*

Toby longed to see the expression on the official's face, to see behind his eyes and know without doubt that he had believed Ahmed. If he did, if he had taken the bait so blithely offered, they were safe.

If not…

'I suggest you prepare your ship for a swift departure, galley master. You and your crew have outstayed your welcome in the city of Constantinople.'

'But Honourable Sir, I have a cargo of frankincense arriving this day. In a few hours it will be here. I have a contract with Pope Celestine – Coelestinus Tertius himself. I have the signed papers from his representative who met me in Venezia. Surely you would not prevent the transfer of goods for the Holy Father.'

'For the Byzantines, we honour diplomacy across the world. In your case, I cannot imagine that a papal contract would mean anything to *you*, an Arab, beyond money. From whom do you buy the frankincense?'

'A Byzantine. Michael Sarapion. He is a spice merchant, but I am sure you are aware of that…'

Michael…

'I do not know the name, there are many spice merchants that come and go through our gates. If he is legitimate, and be sure I shall check the rolls, then there is no more to be said. If he is not, you will be held accountable. If all is well, load your frankincense when it arrives, we shall have guards here to see that all is as it is purported to be, and then leave at midday. Leniency has worn thin. Goodnight.'

The Byzantine turned and the Varangians swallowed him in their midst, the avaricious official almost hidden by the broad men from the north. Ahmed watched them leave, face livid, fingers flexing on the hilt of his *kilij* and then he yelled, 'Faisal!'

With that, the crew hastened on board, all signs of inebriation gone. Toby grasped the physician's hand as he passed. 'Mehmet, what happened? Where's Michael? What did you…'

But Mehmet put a finger to his lips and whispered. 'Later. All is well.

Keep out of sight for the moment.'

'Still?'

'If anyone watches, they need to think the old physician and the little men are still ashore.'

Tobias nodded, the grim feeling that had sat in his belly renewing its pressure again. He twisted round to discuss this latest with Tomas but the space beside him was empty – wet marks heading toward the stern-castle.

He crawled aft, making himself even smaller, feeling like a snail, life's burdens on his back and a slimy wet trail behind. Pulling open the draping folds that acted as a door, he shuffled in, relieved to see his brother and Zoë, water pooling around him as he stood and smiled at the slave woman. She passed him a cloth with which to towel his face and hair and tears marked her cheeks, her eyes sparkling with yet more. But they were wretched sparks of grief, any fool could see that, and she turned quickly from the brothers.

'She knows?' Tobias mouthed to Tomas and Tomas nodded.

'There are some clothes for you. Faisal prepared for your return as we sailed from the Harbour of Theodosius.' Her voice cracked. 'I will leave you to change.' She wrapped her cloak tight about, pulling up the hood and hurrying past the door hanging.

'Zoë,' Tomas called after her.

'Leave her, Tomas. She must digest what she has heard. In a very brief time, she has found her family, only to have them murdered, castrated and mutilated. It is more than any mother should bear.'

'But her daughter…'

'Her daughter being alive makes this even harder. If her daughter were dead, we could take her with us to Venezia where she might be safe. Now – God knows.'

'You know the daughter is not yet twelve?' Tomas asked.

'I did not. What is her name?'

'Candida. Candida Komemna…'

'A bright and glowing light – what a name for a child so damaged.'

Tomas pulled off his wet tunic and hose, chemise and braies. 'My bones are bloody frozen.'

But Tobias suspected it was his heart that was chilled. Tomas' affection for this Byzantine woman was a very real thing. 'Then rub yourself down hard and get dressed. The last thing you need is a return of your bad chest. There are cloaks as well, so wrap yourself tight, and see? They've even left us unwatered wine,' Toby sniffed a small carafe. 'They expect us to survive this night, no question.'

Warmly dressed and drinking the wine, letting the alcohol heat their bellies, Tomas spoke.

'I don't know how I might help her, Toby.'

'I'm not sure that you can,' Toby poured another wine and welcomed the glow that came with drinking on an empty stomach. 'It may require someone of Anwar's standing to make the necessary contact. By the Saints, he will have to be cautious.'

'But a mother and her daughter should be together…'

'Tomas, you have existed enough amongst dynasties, indeed you have written songs about them, to know that nobility is a two-faced thing. On the one hand, it is compassionate and kind and on the other, rampant with insecurity and jealousy. This Angelid dynasty is just so.'

Tomas did not reply as the curtain was hooked aside and Ahmed walked in, followed by the physician carrying with a tray of food. Two steps behind as any servant would do.

'Do you do this as a physician or a seaman, Mehmet?' Toby indicated the tray of breads and hot dumpling broth.

Mehmet laid the tray down upon the stacked bales that had filled the stern-castle whilst they were ashore. 'To you, I am Mehmet. To any who watch, I am a crewman.'

'You look younger…'

'And yet I crave my own face and hair. I have no wish to visit youth and its impetuosity again. It is filled with self-doubt.'

This may have been directed at Tomas, thought Toby, as both twins dragged flatbread through the steaming juices. On top of the wine, warmth crept outward and with the clean, dry clothes and cloaks and the thought that they had escaped from the city, Tobias basked in a temporary glow.

'Well,' said Toby to all in the closeted space. 'We did it. Did we not?'

'Define *did*, little man,' said Ahmed. 'There were casualties. My crew were set upon by two watchers. Trained to kill, I would say, with their subtle tracking and their skill with knives. I lost a crew member, a young Sicilian, but my men wiped the ground with one of the felons, dragged him through his own blood apparently…'

Mehmet coughed and Ahmed looked at him, 'Forgive me. I am distraught at the loss of Sasso. At any rate, the other killer got away…'

'Sasso. Dear God, a loss for sure. He was a personable young man. But, Ahmed, he has been avenged. The other killer did not escape,' Toby said as he offered the last meatball to Tomas, who shook his head. 'Even now, he kneels contrite before Saint Peter, confessing the error of his misbegotten ways.'

'You say?' Mehmet gathered up the tray and the carafe.

Tomas spoke, his voice harder than Tobias had expected. 'He surprised me and I got in a lucky backwards swipe. Toby finished him off before he could cry out and we rolled his body into the harbour. My only concern is that there will be blood – quite a trail of it.'

'It will be dealt with before dawn,' Ahmed said. 'May Allah bless you with a long life, little Tomas. I salute you.' He touched his forehead and bowed.

'You needn't. It was my life or his. As it turned out, *we* won the day. Or night. So what?' Tomas drank off the last of the wine in his mug and Toby guessed that belligerence might follow if he wasn't sensitively handled.

'But what of Michael? Surely this is why we are here,' he said.

'It worked out well,' Mehmet replied. 'Michael made his way to the tavern where we had gathered. Dana had forewarned him and we simply absorbed him into our midst, as was the plan. He was to all intents one of us and acted so.'

'He is here?'

'Indeed.'

The rest of course, they knew, although the appearance of the official and the Varangians was unexpected and perhaps a little too much like a coincidence. It seemed that before the watchers met their Fate, they had spread the word. But to whom was the issue – to their master, the trader who wanted the dye? Or perhaps directly to the Byzantine official.

'This gets more convoluted by the moment. I for one will be glad when we leave. Midday, the official said.' Toby arched the tension from his neck.

'Yes…' Ahmed sucked a breath through his teeth.

'Oh come now, why do you hesitate? We have Michael and presumably the purple. Why do you shrink from my words like that, Ahmed?'

'The purple is not here.'

'Not...' Toby spluttered.

'Yet.'

'What do you mean... *yet?*' Tomas said, his manner tightly reefed.

'It comes with the frankincense resins which are packed in clay jars. One hopes it will be well hidden. If Allah smiles upon us, by midday our oars will be pulling us through the harbour exit. Moments after that and may Allah give us a strong following wind, our sail will be raised.'

Tomas stood. 'Jesus wept! All of you appear, in your self-congratulatory way, to have forgotten Zoë. Christ damn you all to the bottom of the ocean.' He stormed out into the dark, oblivious of the need for concealment, leaving air pregnant with fury.

'Not forgotten,' said Ahmed. 'But the truth is we cannot afford to dally longer than it takes to load the jars. Once the purple and the frankincense is aboard, we need to be gone from here as if we had never been.'

'I had not forgotten her,' Mehmet said. 'Toby, please go after Tomas and bring him back. I need to tell him that Anwar will go to the palace tomorrow and carefully talk about Zoë with the elderly noblewoman he treats. One hopes that there can be some sort of rapprochement.'

'But Mehmet, we will be gone. What of Zoë? She can't linger alone around the docks.'

'Dana will collect her from the dock as the frankincense is loaded. It will be crowded on the wharves and very much to her advantage. She will take her to Anwar and Sophia where she will be safe until she can see her daughter. It is all arranged.'

'Then you have been busy and Tomas should be grateful. But what if Zoë is unable to see her daughter? God forbid, what if they take her...'

'It is not something we can countenance, Tobias. We must leave with Michael and the dye at midday and we must leave *her* to whatever Anwar can contrive.'

'Do you not worry for your brother's safety in this, Mehmet? He conceals a Komemnoi after all.'

'I do worry. But he is also a skilled diplomat and respected by the palace. I have faith in his reputation and his manner.'

Toby kept his thoughts to himself as Mehmet prepared to leave the stern-castle. That Ahmed had only cursory respect for Tomas was obvious to a blind man and even then only because he had killed this night. Toby would not betray his brother to Ahmed, no matter how much he himself might want to kick his twin to Kingdom Come sometimes.

As for Mehmet – Mehmet held a degree of hope for Tomas. Why destroy that? A degree was better than nothing.

But the bald truth was this – if *Durrah* sailed on the tide with the purple and Zoë's situation not resolved, there was no doubt Tomas would stay behind. The dilemma for Toby was whether he should stand by his brother.

Why would you do that? You are not your brother's keeper... You say so often.

No, Toby thought, not his keeper, just his brother, and in this place perhaps the only friend he might possess. The sad lyrics of Guillaume de Poitiers, the first troubadour, grandfather of Eleanor of Aquitaine and great grandfather of Tomas' hero, Richard of England, flooded his mind.

If neither good nor worth he knows,
When I'm gone from, suppose
They'll quickly cause his overthrow
Knowing him young...

He shook his head, disturbed at the pathos of the words.

Ah, it is you *I think of, my brother. God forbid...*

'Tobias?' Mehmet's voice broke through the irony of the song. 'Are you listening?'

'I'm sorry. What say you?'

'I said go to Tomas and bring him to me. I would speak with him. And please, my friend, take care you are not seen.'

'Yes. Yes, of course.'

He pushed beyond the door drape, noting a faintly lighter sky presaging the dawn. Seabirds stood one-legged on the dock, the occasional gull stretching wings to either side and flapping – testing muscles, feeling the still air all around. Somewhere a rooster crowed, reminding Toby of their own clutch of chickens in Venezia. William would search, lifting the feather-encrusted and speckled eggs to place them tenderly in his little reed-woven basket.

For one brief moment, Toby allowed a wave of nostalgia to spread through him, but then he took a breath, filling his chest with the spiced air of a strange city. Pepper, nutmeg, cinnamon and cloves; even the precious frankincense so beloved by the Pope and Ahmed. And what was that? The fragrance of fresh-pressed olive oil? Maybe camel dung as well. Lord, but it could excite one's blood. There was even the smell of more sinister goods, the pharmacopeia of escape. Toby turned away and searched the decks for his brother and Zoë because it did not pay to wonder too much on what he was missing ashore.

He ducked down, keeping below the wale, passing Faisal in the semi-dark as he and others greased the rowlocks and oars, ready for silence should they need it.

'Have you seen Tomas?' he asked.

'For'ard. A while back.' Faisal's paucity was an artform to be wondered at.

Toby climbed the slope toward the bow but there was no sign of Tomas nor the Komemna.

Of course, there isn't. You should surely have known...

His heart sank and he closed his eyes, sliding to sit on the planked deck. Tomas was so predictable. He supposed in all honesty he was never surprised by his brother's actions. The cord of life had held fast all their lives, after all. Tomas would be speeding Zoë to a place of concealment whereupon he would plan the next move.

But he lacks rationality, Toby thought, and is never free from emotion. It is why I watch out for him. Have always watched out for him.

To your detriment, do you think?

'Mary Mother!' Toby hissed. There was only one moment when he had misread Tomas in the past. Even though some native instinct had caused him to lie about the presence of the icon in the hermit's cave, he remained shocked and disappointed when he discovered the piece wrapped in Tomas' cloak. *That* he hadn't intuited.

What to do now, damn it? Tell Mehmet?

He snorted. That meant informing Ahmed.

The dawn light shone its gold and apricot tint across the Harbour of Prosphorion. Perhaps some Divine artist had taken a sheaf of goldleaf and brushed it on every mast, every spar, every rope, bowsprit and banner. The water too – no longer depthless ebony but sheeted gold, as if one could walk upon it. No wonder they talked of the Golden Horn, or that this city sat upon a foundation of gems and precious metals. It was breathtaking to behold and Tobias hated every glittering corner of it.

'Toby?'

'*Sard!* Tomas!' Toby grabbed his brother and pulled him down to the space beside him. 'I thought you'd left…'

'Not yet.'

But soon my brother? By Sext tomorrow will you be gone?

'Where is Zoë?' Toby asked.

'Under the canopy at the masthead. She is very distraught.'

'I couldn't find you.'

''Tis because Ahmed has loaded the vessel to the very wales with cargo. There are tight spaces that can conceal one readily. Why did you want me?'

To make sure you hadn't left.

Toby relayed Mehmet's command and Tomas seemed content to go to the physician. He had calmed. Almost, Toby thought, like the idealist who can see nothing but the best way forward.

Dangerous…

His brother crawled away, edging around bales and crates to gather up Zoë and make their way to the stern-castle. Toby thanked God for Ahmed's avarice. If indeed all this cargo was for his benefit. Perhaps some of it was Saul's. Or maybe even Gisborne's. So much cargo, so much money and so many places to hide.

He followed Tomas and Zoë whilst the light grew ever stronger and the dockside began to quicken like a heartbeat that had flagged. It reminded Toby of a sleepy giant who had wakened, yawned, stretched and flexed as the new day was welcomed.

'I would like you all to meet someone,' Mehmet said after speaking quietly with Zoë whose eyes sparkled with unshed pain. Keeping his arm around as if to fortify her, he gave Ahmed a signal and the galley master pulled back the door covering. A tall man ducked under the folds, almost as tall as Mehmet and well built with it. He had olive skin and dark eyes. 'This is Michael,' the physician said, drawing him into their circle.

The man had a curious expression – a mask atop the real man.

'Michael Sarapion,' he said of himself as he bowed. His voice had a bass timbre not unlike Gisborne's. Tobias liked it, anything to remind him of home.

'Purple Michael,' said Tomas, little concerned with the man in their midst. There was no doubt that his interests would always be focused on the lovely Zoë. What an unconscious hold she had on him, Toby thought. Like a bee to a honey pot.

And were you no different with Lady Ysabel?

'I have been called worse, Master Tomas.'

Oh more than just the timbre, thought Toby. You are as smouldering and cool as my lord Gisborne has ever been. I *like* you!

'I'll bet you have. And we are to have the presence of the infamous stain at any moment?'

'Apparently so,' Michael replied, unmoved by Tomas' vinegar.

'Indeed. Any moment,' Ahmed added. 'And you can be sure, the Varangians will be back to check that all is as it should be. Please excuse me whilst I see it aboard and try to get our papers signed so that we may leave.' He pushed through the door folds and Tomas' mouth set into a truculent line.

Oh God…

Michael was dressed like the rest of the crew – men of little substance. Worn tunics, discoloured chemises, most often bare-foot except when onshore. Then they might wear soft leather boots purchased from a shoemaker somewhere in the Middle Sea. Or perhaps they might wear leather sandals bought at a market in Limnos or Crete.

Michael's boots were stained and creased and his hair, one presumed, might be black. Or brown when it grew back. But right now, his skull resembled nothing as much as pig's bristle. His beard was so understated as to be stubble. In fact, thought Toby, if he hadn't had such even features, or a chin of the kind women would want to caress, then he might just be pig's bristle everywhere. Not hirsute, Toby thought. Just bristly.

By nature?

God's toenails, but if he was, he must surely be from the Gisborne family, Toby thought and turned away with a wry grin on his face.

When Michael was introduced to Zoë, he was polite, respectful, man to woman. Toby wondered if he knew Zoë was of the Komemnoi – he guessed Mehmet or Anwar may have told him. Thus he found Michael's deferential manners acceptable and warmed even more to the man.

'The purple is hidden in small bags underneath the blocks of frankincense resin. I suspect we must just hold our breath that it is not found,' Michael said, so sanguine with the explanation. As if they had no need to be stretched to the limits because at any moment the Varangians would leap aboard the galley, take everyone prisoner, march them to gaol, to trial, and then watch as their hands were struck off in the Square of Theodosius by an executioner. Before they were ultimately beheaded for crimes against the Empire.

Toby shuddered.

'Are you cold, brother?' Tomas whispered.

'No. Just concerned…'

'This was not what we expected, was it?' Tomas glanced at Zoë, her face breaking the hearts of the brothers.

Tobias didn't answer. There was nothing to say. *Lyras*, curiosity and music had been his motivation for coming on this adventure. That and the need to shepherd his brother. But the need for adventure pure and simple had been Tomas' motivation.

Well, Tomas got his wish. Whereas I…

''Twas well-conceived, Master Sarapion, to conceal the powder amongst the resin.'

'Time will tell, Master Tobias. And please, call me Michael.' The spice merchant grimaced as he shifted his weight from one leg to the other, Mehmet noticing and asking him if his wound pained him.

'A little. It bleeds since the attack of a sennight past.'

'Then I must examine it…'

'Your brother has re-stitched it, sir, and it's clean, but I fear some permanent damage will have been done in the attack. In any case, let us see the dye aboard first and us well away from the city. Time enough for doctoring then.'

There was noise ashore, the sound of hooves. Toby hoped to God it was the wagon pulling the frankincense, and not mounted law-enforcers from the Great Palace.

'It's here,' said Mehmet. 'We must help load it as we are crewmen after all. Can you manage, Michael?'

'Better I am seen to manage,' Michael said. 'I will do whatever it takes to deceive the guard. Have you weapons aboard?'

'Yes. Brothers, your weapons are behind the crates here. Michael, there are also two extra swords – if you need one, take whichever suits. The rest of the crew are armed discretely. It would not do to present a picture of a crew at war.'

'I have a knife in my boot, it will suffice.' Michael walked to the door-folds and pushed on through.

'Don't move from here,' Mehmet said to the twins. 'It is best you stay hidden until this is all over. Zoë, when Dana is on the dock I will come for you. Tomas, it may be as well for you to say your farewells to Zoë whilst the resin is being loaded.'

With that pronouncement, words like salt on an open wound for Tomas, Mehmet hurried after the spice merchant. Tobias glanced at Zoë – she stood mute, eyes bright with unshed tears. He wondered how long over the last ten years she had held herself aloof from the pain of grief. Knowing now that her daughter was in the same city, in any one of the palaces that could be seen from the harbour of Prosphorion, perhaps it was the key in the lock of her heart.

Perhaps too, she wished to weep because she would be losing her advocate, Tomas. How long had it been since she had a man speaking out for her and protecting her? Too long indeed.

And perhaps she might weep for fear of the unknown – the possibility that she might never see Candida, or that in trying to do so, she herself might be imprisoned or worse by the Angelids.

Tobias touched her arm and then laid his palm against her cheek. Perhaps not the way one should behave with a noblewoman but she did not draw back.

'Lady Zoë, it has been such a God-given thing to have met you. You probably have very little idea how your manner and your calm beauty in the face of unbearable odds has inspired Tomas and I to write again, to make words about life and love, to create music and give the poetry wings.' He smiled and continued. 'I am going to leave you and Tomas alone because he is your dearest friend and supporter. He showed such foresight in buying your freedom. It is my own wish that in so doing, he will precipitate the righting of a great wrong and that you and Candida can be reunited. My lady…' he bent over her hand and kissed it.

She covered his hand with her own and then as he backed away, whispered 'Thank you, Tobias.'

He turned and left quickly, knowing that Tomas would have things to say to Zoë and as the folds of the door-covering fell behind him, he saw the crew lining up between wale and cart and the resin being hoisted hand over hand until each crate was stacked neatly aboard. He stooped low and hastened between some bales of far eastern silk, moving until he had a view of the wharf and thanking God that he was small. It had advantages.

The Varangians were once again in evidence along with other guards who were taking the odd jar from the crates and smashing it on the ground. It was an expensive way of checking what lay inside and Ahmed made his feelings known, shouting at the obnoxious official who had once again swaggered onto the docks to make his presence felt. The docks had begun to heave, men of all shapes moving here and there, some loaded with panniers of goods, others with full purses. Toby could imagine every man licking lips – the wealthy with anticipation and avarice, the poor with hunger and desperation. Many of the docks Toby had seen were mere reflections of one another – men, horses, whores, dogs, children, hawkers and the occasional and usually very bad *jongleur*. But Prosphorion broke the mould – highly organised with officials checking the variously moored galleys. No children ran between folk, no dogs threatened to tip up overloaded dockers. And whilst booths had set up to sell food and cordials, there were no minstrels in evidence. Trading was the lifeblood of this city that straddled east and west like a perfumed courtesan, and was treated with a professionalism that bordered on adoration.

Cargo arrived on carts, pulled by both horses and by men. Bills of sales were signed off. There were notaries – most often men of the cloth, but there were some who were not and Tobias had a gut feeling he would rather trust those than men of God. He crossed himself swiftly, but didn't disabuse himself of the thought. Dressed in black gowns, perhaps a black cap on the head, if asked they could say they had studied the *trivium* at Oxford, Paris or Bologna.

Durrah rocked gently, as the twenty-four crates were loaded. Minus twenty-four individual jars, thought Toby. Watching the guard reach for one jar and then another was like watching games of chance. Although instead of money being the prize, it was that resin, *olibanum*, so prized by Jew and Gentile alike. Then again, Tobias supposed, it's all money.

He held his breath as the last boxes were unloaded from the cart – that last row sitting there mocking the official and the guards, whom Toby thought were sure of finding Tyrian purple amongst the consignment.

How have they missed it? It has to be in those last jars. What sleight of hand has Master Sarapion employed? Or is God smiling upon us just this once.

Ahmed was now discussing, no, disputing the damaged blocks that lay around the trestle at which the official sat.

'Get your crew to collect the resin pieces and you can take them, I do not see the issue,' said officialdom. 'You have paid for them, they are rightly yours and we are fair, galley master. Although Pope Celestine may be concerned when he sees the cracked blocks. But then, that is not our problem. We merely protect our own possession – the dye, you understand.'

'And as you can see, I have no dye. If I could sue for damages, I would.'

The official twisted his lips in what could pass for a sneer. 'You could try I suppose, but then the Pope would have to wait for his shipment. Galley master, I suggest you load your remaining resin and depart. Do you not think that is an excellent idea?'

Toby could see the veins on Ahmed's arms as very fibre of his body vibrated with the desire to slam a fist into the pernicious jaw. Instead, he roared to poor, scapegoat Faisal, ordering him to the dock immediately with two men.

Faisal grabbed Mehmet and Michael, shoving them toward the wale.

Christ's fingernails, thought Toby. Why *them?*

Michael showed no sign of a damaged leg as he jumped ashore. Tobias knew what such an action would have cost him and admired his resilience as he and Mehmet unrolled an oiled cloth and began to pile the fragments of *olibanum* into it. Toby could almost smell it from where he watched, wedged between the bales.

He swivelled slightly and noticed a small chest being carried along the wharf by two crewmen. It was heavily tooled, its black lock solid and unyielding.

'What is inside that?'

'Pearls and gems. Do you not believe me?' snapped Ahmed.

'I believe no one. Open it.'

Ahmed stormed to the chest, used a key on his girdle and unlocked it, whereupon the official thrust his hands amongst the pearls and semi-precious gems. 'You stand to make a lot of money when you return to Venezia, galley master. It is as well we have such a solid treaty with the Doge, allowing you more freedom than we would otherwise give.' He rolled a pearl in his hand, a beautiful ivory drop that sat like a tear from the Virgin in his palm. 'You are done, I think. As well, because it is almost midday.'

He pocketed the pearl, handed *Durrah's* papers over and then he and the guards turned and walked away, heading toward the Great Palace.

He stole the pearl. Brazen theft.

The official looked back at Ahmed, tipped his head to the side and then kept walking.

Graft, pure and simple…

Toby let his breath go in a rush but then sucked it in again when he noticed Dana walking along the dock, casual and unconcerned, stopping to watch the activity and chewing on a handful of dates.

Toby slid from between the bales, meeting Mehmet at the door folds of the sterncastle. 'You saw her?' he asked Mehmet.

'Yes, I will get Zoë and escort her ashore. It will be done discretely.'

'I am unhappy with this, Mehmet. I cannot see that a Komemnoi will be welcomed by Isaac Angelus.'

'Allah protect her,' said Mehmet, his young-old face serious with concern. 'And you must pray to your God.'

He pulled the folds aside and together they walked in.

But the space was as empty as a pauper's pocket and as quiet as a tomb.

CHAPTER TEN

✗

'You are not surprised, I think.' Mehmet went behind the bales and retrieved Toby's sword. As he passed it over hilt first, he said. 'His is gone.'

'No, not surprised, Mehmet,' he said, tiredly. 'Are you?'

'No. I had hoped that I would be wrong, that he would not be precipitate, but he is reverting to a form we have seen in the past.'

Toby shook out the straps of his sword belt, busying himself whilst his mind jumped back and forth. Tomas was like a thunderstorm. There was nothing to divert the roiling mass once its direction was set. Perhaps it made him the more fascinating of the two brothers.

But what is fascination when one has to rescue it from self-harm every second moment of its life?

Tobias had seen this predicament racing toward him from when they cast off in Venezia. Some part of him knew that at some point he would be unbelievably frightened for his brother. Far more so than when Tomas had accompanied King Richard on that fated voyage. Because this time, there were three words that accompanied Tomas and they chilled Toby to the bone.

Death stalks him...

As he buckled his sword, every sound resonated – the rattle of metal against metal, the slide of leather on leather, the jingle of buckles. Each movement took a lifetime to complete – as if the world had slowed but his mind galloped far ahead. Beyond the stern-castle, the starboard oars were pushed out, the boat rocking as the starboard crew took their seats. Ahmed called for fore and aft lines to be released.

'Tobias, I've watched you playact with success in the field of your work for Gisborne. You can fool anyone. But at home, I beat you at chess for one reason alone. You drop your guard amongst friends and it reads upon your face like a map of intent.'

Tobias grabbed his cloak and swung it about his shoulders, fastening it with a fibula of three barbed arrows.

'You need to hurry, my friend,' said the physician. 'Get ashore and go with Dana.'

'I am that easy to read? God knows I shall have to smarten my game, then…' The irony of the comment fell to the floor as Mehmet left to ask Ahmed to slow the departure enough that Tobias could jump ashore.

As he climbed the wale, he said, 'My respect to my lord Gisborne, and my love to William, my honour to the Lady Ysabel. Take care, my dear friend. And you, Ahmed…'

'Music-man, just go. You talk too much,' Ahmed swung away to call orders and Toby jumped to the dock where Dana stood behind a group of pilgrims walking past.

One of them stopped and grasped Toby's arm and he went to prise it off but the man spoke, cheerfully acknowledging Toby whom he remembered from only two nights before as they walked together along the Mese. Toby cringed at the unwelcome attention garnered not two steps from the galley.

'Do you leave this day, my young friend?' asked the French pilgrim.

'No. I have business for one more day…'

'Ah, glory be to God, we leave for Marseille today. A long voyage to be sure but by the end of summer we will be at home in Paris, God willing…'

Paris – in the name of Christ I wish I could accompany you. To listen to music and be free from guilt and responsibility…

'A pity you cannot travel with us. We would welcome your companionship.'

Toby thanked the pilgrim and wished he and his friends a safe and uneventful journey, sidling closer to Dana as the group began to walk along the dock toward a large galley.

No smile greeted him as he joined her, so he leaned against a pile of crates and watched *Durrah,* her starboard oars feathering. When the boat had clearance, the larboard oars rattled out and the men pulled evenly, edging their way with consummate skill through the waterborne traffic toward the seawalls where the Bosphorus awaited. He wanted to watch until they had turned right and hoisted the sail, heading into the Propontis and thence toward the Adriatico. He wanted to gallop to the point of land where the sea met the Hellespont and watch *Durrah* sail safely away with the dye on board.

He wanted to know that all this pain hadn't been for nothing.

'Zoë?' asked Dana.

'Tomas and she left the ship earlier unbeknownst.'

'I see. And you are here why?'

'To find my brother. In so doing, I might find Zoë.'

'And if you do?'

'I… I'm not sure.'

'So brotherly affection drives you away from *Durrah* and the chance to leave a city that might be rife with trouble for you?'

Toby cocked his head in answer. What could he say?

Dana sighed. 'Well, then, you had best come to my house and we shall plan what to do.'

She busied herself in the small space, setting a tray with syrup of pomegranate and with flatbreads and paste. Beyond her, a curtain hung and he could see a cot with a bedroll, and a chest against a wall. Above her head as she worked, a small icon, nothing grand, bestowed its grace upon the place.

'I'd kill for wine,' said Toby. 'Hogsheads full of it.'

'I have no quality wine, but I have *konditon*…'

'*Konditon*, good wine, bad wine – I care not. I just want wine,' Toby snapped.

Dana slapped a jug of *konditon* down in front of him, her bright eyes sparking. 'Listen little man, I am helping you, so show some respect. If you will.'

The vibrant snap in her tone, the way she glared at him, the way she was unafraid to call him *'little man'* – it caught at his sensibility.

'I am sorry. I was rude…'

'Only a *little* rude, *little* man,' she said and turned away. She wore a long Byzantine tunic with a shawl over one shoulder knotted at the diagonal hip. The material was nondescript and with no embellishment.

'I am not at all defined by my unfortunate stature, Dana…' he said.

She lifted a glass of *konditon* to her lips and assessed him but he cared little, meeting her glance for glance.

'No. You are not. I can see that. Gisborne picks well.' She sat down on the other side of her table, pushing neatly folded piles of clothing to one side. The materials ranged from velvets and silks to common linen. In baskets along the walls, hanks of threads were twisted in like colours and one basket contained metallic threads.

A highly organised space for a systematic woman...

'He will have gone to Anwar's house in Water Street. Anwar will have news for them,' he said.

'Whether the Angelids will allow Zoë Komemna to see her daughter?'

'Yes.'

'And where does your brother fit within this?'

'He has appointed himself Zoë's protector.'

Dana snorted. 'No offence to you or your brother, but does he think he can protect Zoë against the vast array of men, weapons and … techniques that the Emperor has at his disposal?'

'He does and I admire him for it.'

Even though I think he is a fool.

She fetched another carafe, this time filled with syrup of pomegranate. 'And that is why Gisborne picked you both. Stalwart...'

They decided that she should deliver the mended cloak to Sophia. Tobias should stay until she returned as there were still those who had tracked him and he should remain concerned. She left immediately and Toby listened to the silence of the thick-walled little house. He stood with his back pressed against the heavy door, the internal beam across it to seal it from unwanted intruders. The sun shone through a high barred window leaving a bright band across a floor that Dana had softened with a muted rug. Again, nothing grand, nothing to alter the suggestion that she was merely an artisan embroiderer living on her clients' generosity.

He yawned. He'd not slept for a day and a night. She'd be a while yet and the house was secure. God knows she'd made sure of that – the price one paid for spying. He wandered to her bedroll and thought she wouldn't mind. He needed to be fresh for whatever news she retrieved. As he pulled off his boots, he wondered where Tomas was and what he did.

*Tell me, Tomas. We have always understood each other and I knew you were
not dead when King Richard's boat sank off Aquileia. Let me know what you
plan. Please…*

Moments after laying out the roll, and with the faint sound of doves outside,
and as he waited for some sign from his brother, he fell into a deep sleep.

The door rattled and a heavy knocking pierced his heavy dreamless state.
He jumped up, wishing he could see through the high window, wanting to
ascertain friend or foe.

God's nosehairs…

'Music-man!'

Ahmed?

He thrust the bar from the door and pulled it open.

'Ahmed!'

The Arab pushed him aside and walked in, slamming the door shut.

'Christ in all His Glory. What the hell…'

'My talkative friend, how could I leave you to sort this business out yourself?'

'But the Byzantines have you in their sights…'

Ahmed's mouth turned down and he shrugged. 'No more than someone has
you in theirs. It seems we are equal,' he placed his arm across Toby's shoulders.

'But *Durrah*…'

'Praise be to Allah, one would think you didn't want my help. If you are
worried about *Durrah*, she makes headway down through the Strait of Saint
George to the Propontis. There is a good breeze and so far all aboard are safe.
Faisal will sail to Gallipolis and he will wait for us…'

'Wait? For how long?'

'Three days in Gallipolis. After that, they sail onward. So we have little
time to find your brother, make sure the slave-woman is safe and make our
way to Gallipolis. With Dana who wishes to leave.'

'So short a time!'

'Three days too long, my friend. I want my *Durrah* to be beyond the
wrath of this city. Once she is in the Adriatico, she will be safe. Surely Tomas
and the woman are at Anwar's. It is what Mehmet thought.'

'Dana has gone to find out.' Toby's head was reeling with Ahmed's
presence because in truth he was glad to have the Arab at his back. He had

been at such a loss – unsure of direction, confused and now he had someone who knew him, knew Tomas. But… 'Ahmed, you are not a favourite here. You risk your life.'

'They will not find me, rest assured.'

Toby sat at the table and poured the remains of the syrup into a mug and downed it.

That's what I like about the man – the God-given confidence.

'Why does Dana want to leave?' he asked.

'She feels that her time here is done. That she has nothing more to offer Gisborne. The Byzantine Empire is withdrawing into this city, the emperors come and go with great rapidity. Perhaps she may be of more use elsewhere.'

'Perhaps she is sick for her home.' Toby had an intuition.

Again that expression from Ahmed – bottom lip curved down and a shrug of the shoulders. He reached for a piece of bread and wiped it through the remains of the vegetable paste as the door opened and Dana walked in, garments folded in her arms.

She cast a look at Ahmed and said without preamble. 'They have been and gone.'

Toby hit the table with the palm of his hand. An empty mug toppled to the floor with a clatter and a clay jar with a branch of rose-tinted blossom from the Judas tree wobbled. Dana thrust the clothes on the table and reached to steady the jar.

'It's called *kerkis*,' she said. 'It is a Greek word for shuttle because the seed-pods resemble a weaver's tool. I've always thought it was my good-luck tree. Weaving and embroidery are closely bound. This is the last of the spring blossom.'

'And yet, they say Judas hanged himself from exactly this tree. Does that not bode for ill?' Toby said. 'Ill indeed if my brother has already left the safety of Anwar's house.'

'And Heaven help them, that is what he and the woman did. Found out what they needed to know and whilst Anwar was gone from the room, they left. In broad daylight.'

'To do what?' Toby asked.

'I can't begin to guess,' Ahmed growled, beginning to prowl around the small space. 'Tell me, Tobias, why are you and your brother so very different. Methinks you would have shown much more caution.'

Methinks I would have stayed on Durrah. *Therein lies the difference. He is bold and I am a coward…*

'Dana, what did Anwar tell them that has prompted them to move so swiftly?' Toby asked.

Dana pulled off her veil and laid it on top of the clothes. Her nutmeg hair curled in wanton ribbons around her face and at any other time, Toby might have been charmed by her beauty. He had often been fatally charmed in his life – it had been a fault. Sometimes the fatality was heavenly, but sometimes, only occasionally, the fatality had been like a ganching.

Fatality…

'It seems Anwar went to the palace to doctor his patient and in the doing, they talked of Zoë…'

'Madam, I left here last time with all that you had told me going round and round in my head,' Anwar said. 'It was a tragedy of huge proportions.' He sponged her lesions gently, rinsing the soft linen cloth in salted warm water and then patting them dry.

'And what was that? The story of Zoë Komemna?' The old woman closed her eyes as the salt stung a little. 'Careful how you go, physician. That hurts.'

She was a remarkable old lady – wrinkled and drawn to be sure, but there were hints of an admirable bone structure and her hair was folded and pleated and a veil embroidered with a wide silver strip had been laid by her side with an ivory comb atop.

'But my lady, you know we must cleanse the lesions and dry them before we anoint them and dress them again. It must be done, even though I do not like to inflict pain on you, indeed on anyone.'

'Unlike our Emperor…'

'Those words come from your mouth, my lady. Not mine.'

'Ah yes, but let us be honest. If he had been even a little bit charitable, then those whom I mentioned last time would not have had such terrible outcomes.'

'Too true, lady, too true. Which prompted a thought. You mentioned that Zoë Komemna had been sold into slavery and had disappeared, presumed dead. What do you think would happen if she were not dead. If she came to the city and tried to see her daughter?'

The old woman shrugged and then sat thinking. As he rubbed in the first application of pomegranate cream, she said, 'You speak in hypotheticals, of course. But let us assume she is indeed alive and has somehow made her way to Constantinople. Let us also assume she knows her daughter is alive and within the Great Palace. She has many hurdles.'

Anwar began to wash and pat dry the lesions that lay in the elbow creases of the elderly woman. 'If you were she, what would you do?'

'By Saint Athanasia the Wonder Worker! Me? Hah!' She sat back and stared hard at Anwar who plied the cream with great care. 'Fine. I will pretend I am the Komemna. Ah, that I could be that young again, because if I remember, she really was a charming thing. But, be that as it may, I would endeavour to meet with Patriarch George II Xiphilinos and plead my case. I would swear before God and every Saint that even though I am a Komemnoi and even then only by marriage, that I want only to see my daughter and hold her.'

'And then what? You are a mother. That would surely not be enough.'

'True. And I am indeed a mother, even a grandmother thrice over. Thus I would ask the Patriarch if he thought the Emperor might allow the girl, Candida I believe she is called, to leave the palace and accompany me far from the Byzantine Empire. To the south, west or north – whatever is decreed by the Emperor.'

'Do you think the Emperor would allow that to happen?'

The elderly noblewoman pushed back a strand of thinning white hair with her free hand. 'It depends. If I am true to my word, I have no interest in being a Komemnoi. Patriarch George would have to convince the imperial court that I am to be trusted and that I only want to be reunited with my flesh and blood and then leave. That I have no interest in dynastic power play.'

'But might the Emperor not think that hate is a good motivator? That you might be lying. That you might want to create a Komemnoi uprising because of what he did to your husband and your children?'

The old woman huffed out her breath, shrugged and then continued, 'He might. It is where I must rely on the Holy Father to protect my interests. Now, enough of this game.' She tapped Anwar's hand with the ivory comb. 'Have you finished? I find I am becoming tired. My mind is not used to imagining itself in other people's heads...'

'And so it seems he found out nothing and yet in its own way, it is quite something from a woman who scrutinises the court with sharp eyes and has a wisdom made of years of surviving both Komemnoi and Angelid rule. I believe she is right. I can't see any other way Zoë might see Candida – this may be the right way, the way of God and His representative. Other than that, there is only to break into the Palace and risk death.'

'To do it the old woman's way makes a deal of sense,' said Ahmed. 'The problem would be your reactive little brother. What think you, Tobias?'

'I think that he is impulsive and brave enough to break into the Palace … no, hear me out Ahmed, before you cast stones. I think his affection and respect for Zoë will preclude that and even now they will be trying to have an audience with the Holy Father.'

'Then we must go.' Ahmed stood and settled his *kilij* by his side.

'And do what?' asked Dana. 'Barge in to the Patriarchal Palace and do what exactly?'

'Ah, the dulcet tones of reason,' muttered Toby.

'We need to know that what we have to offer Tomas and Zoë is better than what they think they can achieve themselves,' Dana said.

Ahmed sighed and looked directly at Toby.

'Ah, I see,' Toby said. 'You want me to offer the solution. Then you will not like what I say because I don't think we have anything to offer them other than moral support. We can't stand against the Varangians or anyone else within the Great Palace. I think we have to let Zoë do what she must, and hope that both of them will be treated with respect if they come with the Patriarch's blessing.'

'Then tell me again why you are here?' Ahmed asked.

'To protect my brother's back should he need it. Why are you here?'

'Ha. Well-played, little music-man – a neat turn of hand. I am here to protect yours, and as you and Tomas seem to be indivisible by your calculations, I think it must mean I protect his as well…'

They ate quickly, a *moussake* that Dana had cooked early in the morning. Its taste was probably fine with ground goats' meat and grains and some goats' cheese and spices. But to Toby it was ashes in his mouth and cold coals in his belly because he couldn't shake the sadness that had grabbed hold of him the minute he knew Tomas had gone. Tomas had left nothing for his brother but memories and those from the voyage were so tarnished.

Toby thought on that.

True. When Tomas met Zoë, he did indeed soften. But he was still impulsive and seemed to care little beyond his own immediate interests. Any loyalty to Tobias seemed very much a thing of the past; that was where the pain lay because they were twins, they were brothers. There should have been a lifelong blood fellowship…

In ballads maybe, in stories of heroism and bravery, but in real life?

Tobias followed Ahmed and Dana into the narrow street on which her unassuming home sat with fifty others, marching up the hill from the Golden Horn. As they climbed the zigzag steps, Tobias' legs ached and he sucked in a deep breath every now and then. Ahmed turned.

'Do we walk too fast?'

Toby shook his head but took the moment to glance back over the city, down to the Horn where vessels moved about, onto the Strait of Saint George where even more vessels headed toward the Mar Maggior and then he glanced south, where craft moved to and from the Propontis – busier ever than Venezia or Genova, or any of the coastal towns along the Middle Sea.

They reached the top of the hill and below them to the south was the Great Palace and the Hippodrome, monuments to the grandeur of Rome. But then that church, the one that had observed every single move that Tobias and Tomas had made – Sancta Sophia. The gloriously domed building sat like a dove in a nest, overseeing the peace of her city. Her cupolas glistened in the afternoon sun and Toby's heart raced that little bit faster as he thought that Tomas and Zoë would be somewhere close by.

You hope…

Dana set a steady pace, up and down little alleys until they had almost reached the top of the Second Hill and the Basilica Cistern.

Ahmed looked over his shoulder and muttered, quickening his pace. Dana too, lengthened her stride. Toby began to jog, his sword rattling at his side, almost falling as Ahmed turned sharply to the left into a dark alley and then reached out and yanked Toby's arm.

'Wha…'

'Hush. Listen…'

There is no sound, Toby thought. Noth…

Exactly. Nothing.

No people, no donkeys, not even birds. A dead silence…

'This way,' Dana said. 'And run. There is a square…' she took off, fleet of foot despite her long tunic. In her hand, she carried a *misericorde*.

Ah, how she reminds me of my lady, Ysabel…

The three pulled around a corner into a small blank square surrounded by the backs of buildings and with an arch on the far side, an escape to another alley. There was no sign of the heights of Sancta Sophia and Toby felt smothered by tawdry, dark-shadowed brick and stone. And still no one around.

'Where are we?'

'Behind Sancta Sophia and near the end of the Mese. Someone follows us.'

'They do? I did not see…'

'No, your mind as ever was elsewhere,' said Ahmed. 'But we heard their feet. There are three of them and big men at that.'

'Who…'

'Not from the imperial guard I think,' Dana said, pressing herself hard against the wall and looking over her left shoulder.

'Your friends, Tobias,' hissed Ahmed. 'Those who have played with you since we left Venezia. Guard yourself.'

Toby's hand curled on the hilt of his sword and he moved along the wall to the other side of the alley entrance. He withdrew the sword with care, no sound, and held it double handed, bracing his legs, trying not to hold his breath. He'd been taught to breathe steadily and from deep in his belly when he had been learning the troubadour's art. But fear was another thing entirely.

Surely you do not intend to let some arse kill you before you even get to your brother…

And the fire of anger began to flood through him. He closed his eyes with a kind of relieved ecstasy. Yes, it made it easier, the anger. Anger at God, life, Tomas…

He flexed his hands and as the first of the followers sidled through the entrance to the square, he swung hard and fast and caught the miscreant in the thigh, blood spurting out in a stream and the fellow collapsing as Toby tried to pull his blade free. Air rushed over his head and he ducked lower as Ahmed jumped across him, *kilij* swooping in that cruel close-hand uppercut that so sickened Tobias. It was the stroke that so many veterans of the Crusades had talked of – the one that almost split a body apart. But Toby found the anger didn't allow the thought to dwell, especially when Dana's fierce cry pierced the bloodlust as he finally shook his sword edge free.

Her back was still against the wall and the third man had her pinned there, dagger to her throat with one hand whilst the other held the hand that grasped the *misericorde*. Her veil was on the ground and her tunic had ripped, her hair had fallen from its Byzantine twist and she snarled expletives at the man, her Lyonnaise accent filled with loathing. Toby stepped over the man he had killed, his boot sole slipping in the blood that had pumped more furiously than a Roman faucet, regaining his footing, hurrying to defend Dana.

But Ahmed was there at the same time, his *kilij* working close, the man screaming. So much noise and no one came to their aid. Was it the way all citizens across the world kept themselves safe? Never becoming involved? Never risking a life? Two men had yelled to the houses all around as their lives left them to go to Purgatory. One felon was so surprised at the ferocity of a man, a woman and an evil little Devil spawn, that when Toby's sword cut through the life-giving vessel in his leg, he died within minutes as he whimpered and tried to plunge hands into the wound to stop the blood.

Toby looked around. He had seen this so often in his work for Gisborne and there was some tiny *armarie* in his mind where all the horror was shelved and then locked and chained and never thought of again. Till the next time. He bent to wipe his sword on the cloak that had darkened with blood as the man died from Ahmed's *kilij*.

Sliding the weapon into the scabbard he found he didn't want to speak to anyone and he walked away toward the arch and through which, beyond the next alley, he could see the walls of the basilica surrounded by smaller cupolas – like hatchlings in the dove's nest. Here and there, the top of a cypress tree or the verdant crowns of ancient walnut trees softened the vast structure.

'Tobias!' Ahmed called.

He turned and waited as the Arab walked up to him, Dana close behind, looking down at his own clothes, at his boots and saying, 'How can we seek an audience in the palace of the Holy Father looking as if we have been in a massacre?'

Ahmed looked down at his robes and at Dana's tunic. 'It is your problem,

I think. As an Arab, I will not be welcome so I will wait outside.'

Dana sighed. 'We'll find a fountain in the next square, there are many through here that empty from the cisterns filling from the Valens Aqueduct. Ahmed, I think we should have been a little less aggressive and more judicious and kept at least one man alive to question. I could have handled my attacker and he would have had voice enough to answer, before you despatched him.'

Ahmed placed his hand against his chest and bowed. 'I am sorry I defended you, lady.'

'I need no defence. Better that we find out exactly who tracks Tobias, do you not think? This may have an adverse result on anything we do later.'

'Then we will deal with it when it happens,' Ahmed said smoothly, not at all put out. 'Where is this water? I find I want to move from here and clean myself.' He looked back. 'May your God welcome them to Paradise...'

Toby shook his head and walked on. He could see why Dana was a Gisborne employee. She was tough – he had thought to say as tough as leather but she was more like a diamond. It seemed nothing could break her. He wished he had half of her strength. Christ's sweet breath but he was tired. He wanted so much to just find Tomas and...

And what?

God knows, just find him and see him sent safely on to where he might find Plantagent supporters somewhere. He snorted. If Gisborne could see how disorganised were Toby's plans, how erratic was his thinking, he suspected he would disengage him immediately.

No different from Tomas, then...

He bent and picked up a broken brick, a rising howl streaming from him as he hurled the fragment against a wall.

'Better now?' Ahmed asked.

'Cease!' Toby shouted. 'Just cease!' And he stormed down the steep alley toward the peace of a fountain and a church.

The afternoon light flooded down upon the square. The water spat and chattered and provided merry music at startling counterpoint to what Toby had left behind moments before. Women sat in the sun, jars beside them, some walking away, their tunic folds swinging round their feet, their hair plaited and rolled. They walked with a magnetic sensuality as they carried water jars on their hips or even on their heads and Toby's eyes followed them.

So perfect, a memory to be cherished, but no time...

They waited till the square had emptied before walking to the fountain. It would not do to be seen bloody, let alone washing their hands and faces in the city water supply. But they had to wash and there was no option.

Dana dipped her veil under the fountain's watery fall, using the wash to clean her hands and face and dabbing at the worst stains of her tunic. Toby stood beside her, a linen square moistened, before rubbing at the stain on the sleeve of his chemise, the water spreading and the bloody mark diluting, but he wished he had his old *gambeson*. It may have been tired and worn but it had a gravitas that might have been acceptable to the church hierarchy. Instead, it hung on a hook behind the bedchamber door in Venezia, waiting for his imminent return.

If...

Ahmed washed his hands and face, looking at the spray mark that arched across the chest of his robes. It was a huge painterly slash and he grimaced. Instead, he pulled at his cloak, drawing the edges across so that they fell down over his breastbone and covered the signs of fighting and worse. 'We need to make haste,' he said. 'The day is starting to close its eyes. See how the sun sinks to the far side of the sky?'

The sun had moved well past its apogee and the shadows of the fountain crept across the square, the sunlight filtering through the spray and casting a rainbow light that spoke of hope and possibilities.

They filed behind each other, down to a wide walkway that had a chiselled sign indicating the way to the Augusteion and the Patriarchate. More people stepped along – all with purpose. Monks in black, their arms loaded with sheaves of papers and crosses glowing in the remaindered sunlight, made haste in and out of the Patriarchal Palace gates, passing guards in leather-plated *klivanion,* neat *basinets* on their heads with cloth neck coverings, their green hose reminiscent of the harbour official. *Spathion* swords hung by their sides and they stood to attention with narrow spears clasped in their left hands. Their presence was expected – again, the normality of their stance suggested nothing of concern and Toby took a relieved breath.

Cypress, walnut and Judas trees provided landscaped shade and some elderly monks sat under the last of the blossom, rose-coloured petals falling around them. They had their eyes closed and were presumably meditating on God, if not asleep. Guards in imperial colours walked in groups of fours and sixes, relaxed but in formation…

A litter passed, carried by two brawny slaves in knee-length carmine tunics and hose. The curtain was drawn but a languid white hand hung through the folds, a gold chain and enamelled cross in a delicate clasp, blue veins lacing across the top of the noble hand, amethyst and emerald rings decorating the fingers. Toby longed to see the face that was secreted away but the litter moved onward and presently he and Dana, with Ahmed behind, had passed through a discreet garden filled with trees, falling water and the singing chatter of small swifts, the plaintive coo of doves and the demanding cry of the ever present seabirds of the Propontis. They had worked their way round to the south gate and Dana waved her arm, saying 'There…'

Tobias glanced up.

The biggest church in Christendom stood above him, the staircase could have been the one that led to Heaven for all he knew, so beautiful, so perfectly cut from marble, the basilica walls stuccoed and the colour of faded Judas blossom, windows underlying the gold leafed cupola like an imperial diadem. It sat almost in silhouette as the late afternoon sun sought to bed behind it.

Notre Dame had a Norman grace about it but it was fledgling, a quarter built compared to this. San Marco? Tobias shrugged. Nothing like *this*.

This sang.

He was right about the dove and her hatchlings – Sancta Sophia was like a plump dove crowded by other smaller structures that supported, that hugged, that skirted around her, touching her. As if the touch of wall against wall was a Divine blessing from the Theotokos.

'Who in their wisdom built this?' he muttered.

Dana stepped down to stand next to him, looking at the vast cupola. 'A number of far-sighted men back in Justinian's day but they chose the site badly. The view of course, is sweeping and makes a statement but it sits on a weak piece of the hill. The structure shakes and quakes every time the earth trembles.

'It could fall down?' Toby's aesthetic sense was scandalised. 'But that would be a tragedy…'

'It has done so periodically but such is the Empire's desire to make an impression and claim to be closer to God, that they keep rebuilding it and buttressing it against the next earth tremor. Toby, why do you think Tomas will be here?'

He huffed at the suddenness of her question. He had thought of nothing but this since the news of Tomas' departure from Water Street. If Tomas and Zoë had approached the Patriarchal Palace, he had no doubt they would have been rebuffed immediately. A woman entering the Most Holy's gates? Unless she was a nun, he doubted it would be permitted. But if they came to Sancta Sophia, humbly sought an audience with one of the senior priests, maybe a bishop, then Zoë could press her case, begging to speak to the Patriarch. Humility of course, was the key. With what was at stake, he had no doubt that Zoë would be more humble than most.

And Tomas? When has he ever been humble?

Indeed. When? But then he answered his conscience with relief.

In the face of Zoë, he is more humble than he has ever been in his life!

As he enunciated his thoughts to Dana, something about it seemed natural, as if he *did* know what Tomas was thinking. If Dana noticed that he gave an infinitesimal nod to himself, she said nothing. Instead,

'Then we must find the most senior priest in the basilica. That can't be beyond our capabilities.'

Ahmed had been leaning against a marble balustrade, arms crossed and looking southwest over the Great Palace and the Hippodrome to the Harbour of Sophia and on to the Propontis. 'Then if it is not so hard, please accomplish it swiftly. My ship,' he nodded toward the sea, 'is out there without me and I pine for her.'

'You will wait here?' Dana asked.

'It is a pleasant enough view…'

'Then let's be gone, Tobias. I hope you are right about this.' She unfastened her dirty veil and laid it upon roughly tidied hair. Toby watched the light fabric – saw the setting sun silhouetted through it, catching on the weave. It fluttered slowly, to settle on Dana's soft hair like a leaf falling from a tree, a graceful motion. He pocketed the image for another time and place as she brushed at her tunic – the stains somewhat faded, the water dried. It looked as if the wearer had travelled a long distance.

No evident bloodstains…

Not really – more like rust, he thought as he centred his belt buckle and ran fingers through black hair that had grown to his shoulders. Dana had begun to climb the steps to the thick iron doors and he ran after her, following in her footsteps like the retainer he thought to be. He glanced behind at Ahmed who watched them go with an intense expression on his face – as if he calculated risk for outcome. Toby preferred not to think on that. Best to focus on achieving his goal. He had often found that believing in things happening for the best made it so.

Please, Mary Mother…

They stopped at the top of the stair. Behind them, the world opened out, tantalising in its vast opportunity. Promising so much, Toby thought. In some monastery chapel close by, men's voices drifted on the air in a chant, just the one word – *Alleluleia,* a single voice and then choral responses in tonal rises and falls. Had he come to Constantinople for this? For Divine music and inspirational words? Or for excitement and lust?

But all he could think of as he turned back to the massive doors that made him feel like an ant was, *No, I came to buy a* lyra.

Dana walked through the south gates and along the *narthex,* avoiding the imperial gates. He followed like a child, skirting the *omphalos,* his eyes drifting up to the dome that hung weightless it seemed, above them. Light streamed in through the windows and to anyone who thought God didn't exist, this sight above all others must change their minds. Toby crossed himself as he spun slowly in a circle, eyes fixed on that sight.

How in Heaven's name had they created arches strong enough to hold the dome in place?

His eyes drifted further and what he had thought were smaller buildings, clustered around the skirt of the basilica, were in fact supportive smaller domes. It was a wonder of construction … coloured marbles that reminded him of Dana's *kerkis* trees and golden mosaics, a richness that made one question if one was now in Heaven. He stared at the huge silver iconostasis in the distance, but then his glance caught on the most perfect icon – the Pantocrator's face, placid, wise, all-knowing. He crossed himself again.

'Tobias,' hissed Dana. 'Tobias, pay attention. I have found a priest who can help us…' She grabbed Toby's arm and yanked him behind her toward a tall man whose hair flowed luxuriantly and whose beard intermingled with his hair. On his head, a small cloth *skoufos* balanced precariously and he wore a plain but richly golden pectoral cross. 'Tobias, this is Father Symeon. He has been within the Church all day and had an enquiry from a small person … did you not, Father?'

'Indeed. He was … not unlike yourself,' he nodded at Tobias, a hand reaching for the prayer rope at his wrist and fingering the knots.

He is afraid of me…

'Except that his hair colour was different.'

'Father, would you know if he asked to see the Patriarch?' Toby spoke clear and unambiguous Greek, anxious not to disturb this priest any further.

The priest looked to Dana.

'My retainer forgets himself, Father Symeon,' she said with modesty. 'But he is right – The woman with him is my cousin Zoë, and in travelling to Constantinople, we lost each other in an attack in the Belgrade Forest. We sought to plead a case with the Patriarch and ask for his help in finding her. I had thought my lovely Zoë might be dead, but when I walked into the basilica, I had an obscure feeling that she may have been here. It was almost as if God told me that all would be well.' Dana's eyes had filled. 'Her parents looked after me as a child when my own died. I want nothing but the best for her…' She crossed herself as a single and cleverly expressed tear rolled down her cheek. 'In God's name…'

'Ah there, child,' Father Symeon said. 'I can see she means much to you. So yes, your cousin did indeed ask to speak with the Patriarch. But it is a difficult thing. He only sees the most worthy of cases, so they must first talk to one of the bishops to see if the case merits the Holy Father's intervention.'

'Oh.' Dana seemed genuinely crestfallen. 'But they must return here?' She brightened with hope. 'I have a chance to see her?'

'You may see her now, my child. They wait for the bishop who even now, is making his way here.'

'Truly?' She turned and gave Toby a look of delirious happiness, one that could be interpreted in many ways.

At least that is not feigned…

'May I ask where they wait?' she continued. 'I would thank the Virgin Mother a thousand times if I could see my cousin and know she is alive.' Dana's eyes sparkled with an almost holy zeal.

'Of course you must see her. Come, she and her little servant man wait in the Atrium gardens.'

Father Symeon turned away, a thin and ascetic column of a man, his unique black robes accentuating his height and dimension. They followed him, both hurrying to keep up with the man's stride. Toby thought he heard other steps nearby but decided it was the cavernous space of the basilica that took their own steps and magnified them.

'Father Symeon, Father Symeon,' a voice called from near the imperial gates. Toby heard it above the sound of booted tramping and the priest stopped, impatience twisting his mouth.

'The novices. They don't understand the need for respect and peace. I regret you must excuse me. Follow the line of pillars and you will come to a door that takes you along a passage that opens into a peri-style. The garden atrium is there, a meditative place where your cousin awaits.'

He placed his hand over his pectoral cross and bowed slightly, backing away before turning and hurrying through the candlelit lanes of pillars toward the *narthex*.

Dana pulled Toby behind a great porphyry pillar and shook her head.

'What?' he asked.

'I don't know. Something…'

The porphyry chilled Toby's back as he leaned hard against it. 'Did you hear the sound of boots as well?'

Dana nodded.

'Not novices then. Jesu wept!' His heartbeat began to bolt and his hand leaped for his sword hilt, but Dana grabbed his arm, shook her head and held a finger to her lips. The sun had almost disappeared from the west facing windows below the cupola and the many mosaics were now lit gold upon gold by flame. The smell of burning candles, a thousand upon a thousand, blended with the smell of *olibanum* from the ornate gold *thymiateria*.

Perhaps the emperor was to grace the basilica and that was why the priests were anxious that all be peaceful and respectful. Tobias leaned out and examined the galleries but they were empty of candlelight and dark with shadow.

'Toby, keep back!' Dana hissed.

'Why?'

But before she could answer, he heard a cry, a woman's cry, funnelling along the passage from the atrium.

'It's Zoë!' He leaped forward. 'Tomas is…'

But Dana grabbed the back of his tunic, hauling him back, holding his arm in a grip tighter than a wild boar's bite. 'No. Do not, Toby. We have to get out of here.'

Toby tried to shake her off.

'Listen, you fool,' she whispered in his ear. 'Something has gone very wrong and we can be of no help if we are taken as well. Understand?'

Of course he understood but it infuriated him. The noise of booted feet echoed amongst the porphyry forest and he and Dana moved swiftly from one pillar to the next in the unlit shadows, moving toward the south end of the *narthex*. The whole place reminded Toby of a cave – dark on the edges, echoing, speaking of mystery and danger, and icy cold despite the warmth of a late spring dusk outside.

He sidled round the pillar and gasped as six guards marched along the *narthex* with Tomas bound and gagged between them. Worshippers gathered in whispering clusters and one close to Dana growled, 'A thief is what he is. Stole a saintly icon.'

Toby cast an anguished look at Dana.

'Heed me,' she whispered. 'Is that Zoë?'

A woman with the face of the Theotokos walked out between four guards – upright, graceful but pale as the driven snow, fear rich in her eyes. Toby could bear it no longer and with thoughts in his head of a vulnerable English knight so long ago, he shouted into the reverend space, moving to keep out of sight. 'Sanctuary, Zoë!' he called in Greek. 'Cry sanctuary!'

The guards almost left her to seek out the voice, spinning around, hands with drawn weapons. But Toby moved on quickly toward the south gates, mixing in with worshippers who were being shepherded away. As he moved, he saw Zoë turn and for one brief moment, there was relief in her face and she cried out, 'In the name of God, I cry sanctuary within the confines of Sancta Sophia!' She dropped to her knees, repeating 'Sanctuary,' as the guards hauled at her. The noise of the guards, of Zoë and of the excited worshippers brought yet more monks and priests and no one took any notice of Dana and Tobias crossing the crowded *narthex* to the other side of the basilica, sliding toward the south gates.

Looking back briefly, Toby saw Father Symeon speaking to the guards whereupon they backed away from Zoë Komemna. She in turn stayed kneeling, head bowed. All Toby could do was hope the Patriarch, informed swiftly of a penitent seeking sanctuary, would make haste to his church and that she could plead her cause.

Ahead, the six guards prodded Tomas and he tripped. They moved toward the Great Palace confines, through the Augusteion where the giant column of Justinian watched over the people, those same people whose faith had been shaken by someone stealing an icon.

Tobias began to run toward his brother. Would the Byzantines try him? What had they been told about him? And what of Pietro? Had they already dealt with him summarily for purchasing the stolen icon?

Jesu and Mary, Tomas, God help you!

He had gained on the guards and just as he went to push at one of those in the rear, he was caught in a smothering grasp, a voice cutting through his anger and fear.

'One to deal with is enough. Two would test my patience.' Ahmed held him fast. Tomorrow Toby's arm would be blue and yellow.

'A pig's turd on your patience, Ahmed. It's my brother!'

'Indeed, and your God no doubt expects you to love your brother and forgive his misdemeanours.'

'Keep your irony to yourself and let me go! I have to rescue him…'

'Do you think the guards will just step aside and let you sweep him away? Allah have mercy upon you, little Tobias. You have no brain.'

Toby pulled fruitlessly, watching the guard move on. 'No!' he cried. Tomas heard him and struggled but was thumped in the shoulder blades and pushed on.

'My friend, you must let him go for the moment,' Ahmed said. 'We must hope for help in other directions. Ouch! Don't you dare bite me or I'll twist your head off!' He tightened his grip so that Tobias had to cease moving. But it was perhaps more from defeat as Tomas disappeared from sight and he sagged.

'If I let you go,' said Ahmed, 'will you stay here quietly?'

Tobias nodded as Dana hurried down the steps.

'They take him to the cells at the Great Palace,' she said. 'He will have a closed trial because they have first-hand evidence that he is guilty. The trial will be short and a sentence passed swiftly.'

Toby threw back his head, crying out, 'And you call yourself our Father and Protector? 'Tis nothing but bulls' balls!'

'Tobias, hush!' Dana said. 'We are in the basilica grounds. Show some respect and beware heresy.'

'*Sard!* Respect?' His laugh was as hollow as an empty carafe. 'You think my life can get any worse? Or my brother's?'

'Yes.' She did not expand and Toby wanted no explanation. Ahmed asked her how she had come upon the information on Tomas and she said one of the priests had been forthcoming.

'Damn the priests to Hell,' Toby growled. 'If they cared for souls, they would see that Tomas saved Zoë from a terrible fate by the sale of that icon – stolen or not. Who will plead for him on that count?'

'If Zoë is the noblewoman I think her to be, she will plead Tomas' case with the Patriarch.' But Dana's tone lacked any confidence that might have anchored Toby and he began to pace back and forth along the step between Ahmed and the embroiderer.

'But we can't wait…'

Turn…

'We need to break him free…'

Turn…

'We must do it this night. He will be a victim of lies, don't you see?'

Turn…

'We need to go now! Come on!'

But Ahmed stood in his way and Dana slid her arm kindly along his shoulder.

'Tobias, we are three people against the guards of the Empire. Our heads would lie on the floor before we even got close. In ballads, three people could storm somewhere like the Great Palace, free their brother in arms, and leaving a sea of blood behind, be on their way before anyone so much as blinked. But that is in ballads told in great halls, not in life.'

'Then what do you suggest? That I hide myself away whilst my brother is condemned and then mutilated? Because that is what they will do, let us not be coy. They will cut off his hands and probably blind him. Maybe even cut out his tongue. He is a minstrel – no hands, no eyes and no tongue. They might as well behead him outright! So tell me – what should I do? What should *we* do?'

'Tobias…' Dana struggled to find something to ease Toby's pain.

No, thought Toby. They have no idea of how to help Tomas. And their plain truths had been right. They were three against many. He knew they protected him against himself so that he might be there for his brother, but…

'I must go back into the basilica and seek an audience with the Patriarch.'

'Tobias…' Dana broke in.

'I must. Don't you see? Ahmed, do *you* understand?'

Strangely, the galley master nodded and his response quite knocked Toby back on his heels. 'It is your only option, I think, and it irks me to say so. Within the church, you can claim sanctuary if you must but at least it protects you and allows you to argue a case…'

The long pause pricked Toby's awareness.

Ah yes, slim case though it is, Ahmed. Is that what you would say?

He knew timing was everything and that if the wheels of ecclesiastical law turned slowly, Tomas would be tried and punished by civil law and dealt with summarily before the Patriarch had made the short journey from his own palace to the Great Palace in order to intercede.

If he chose to intercede…

'Go to your house, Dana, and will you attend her, Ahmed? I may be some time.' He began to climb toward the south gates to enter Sancta Sophia again.

'Father Symeon, you must believe me…'

He had been as honest as he could with the priest, had told him about Zoë Komemna and about Tomas taking the icon. Here, he had re-ordered the history slightly, saying Tomas, in truth the minstrel Julius of Lübeck, had thought it was an old painting lost in a cave – forgotten and of no interest to anyone. Which made his act of selling it to buy Zoë and release her from servitude quite selfless. The minstrel had no idea the icon was so valuable or that it should have remained hidden where it was. Was it not an act of compassion to use it to free a woman from such a terrible existence?

'Well, yes, Master Tobias, but why did he buy her in the first place? The sale of an icon for the services of a whore could not be born…' The tall priest shook his head, although the flowing locks barely moved.

'No, no, Father. He had plans to include a female voice as part of his act

and she had a pleasing sound. It was later he found that she had been forced to
be a whore. Later still that he found she was a noblewoman and a Komemnoi.'

The discussion ran back and forth with the priest shaking his head
frequently. Time galloped and Toby wanted to pull it back and tie it down
as tomorrow approached with sadistic and confronting rapidity.

'Father, he does not deserve to be punished. Surely our Father in Heaven
would see the freeing of an exploited woman as an act of unsullied kindness,
not a crime.' Tobias' voice shook.

'*I* may agree with you,' Father Symeon said cautiously, his pectoral cross
swaying and swinging as he paced back and forth. 'And the Holy Father may
find that he thinks the same way, but the civil court is another thing entirely.'

Exactly what Ahmed and Dana think…

But Tobias would not give in. 'Then please Father, I beg of you in God's
holy name, take me to the Patriarch.'

'I cannot, Master Tobias. But I shall inform His Holiness of all that you
have said. No, do not be concerned. It is part of the story of the woman
who seeks sanctuary so he *must* know and it shall be done immediately. But
I must warn you, if he decides the theft of the icon is unforgiveable, then
he will agree with the civil court and will accept whatever punishment the
Emperor decrees.'

Tobias nodded. He had done all he could. Almost…

'Father, may I see Zoë Komemna please?'

'My dear Master Tobias, you ask a lot…'

'Please. We have travelled far together and she has been a kind companion.'

Father Symeon looked pained, as if he thought Tobias meant something
else entirely.

'Father, she is anything but a whore. She has the grace and bearing of a
noblewoman.'

The priest bit his lip and then, 'Very well. You may speak with her briefly.
She has already been questioned by one of the bishops and he is even now
with Patriarch George II Xiphilinos.'

So soon?

'I thank you, Father Symeon.' He took the priest's hand and kissed it but
the priest pulled it away and began feeling for the prayer rope round his wrist
as he led the way toward the ornate iconostasis once again. It seemed gross

and overpowering to Toby's sensibilities and as the priest fingered his prayer rope furiously, it annoyed Toby whose flame burned strong. 'Do I disturb you, Father Symeon? You seem discommoded when you are with me.'

The priest's hands froze. 'No…'

'Father Symeon,' Toby said with a large sigh. 'I can assure you – I am as ordinary as any of your worshippers. I was born of normal, kind parents who loved me all the more for my … stature. So did the village in which I was born. God saw fit to grace me with the gift of a singing voice and the ability to write music and verse and to play the *vielle* exceptionally well. I studied in Paris and have sung and played for kings and queens. My God is your God and the Virgin protects me and I give thanks daily. You need not feel threatened.'

Father Symeon had the grace to confront Toby with a shamed expression during this homily and his fingers ceased their agitated coursing around the prayer rope. 'I have wronged you. It is my own lack that does so. Forgive me…'

''Tis no matter,' Toby began to walk and Father Symeon quickly took the lead.

'Have you been to the basilica before?'

'No, today has been my first time.'

'And what do you think?' The priest asked the question with some pride for which Toby felt God would not have been impressed. Humility was surely a requirement for the priesthood.

'A wonder. I have seen many large cathedrals but they do not compare. And I will say, the mosaics are the things I appreciate the most. The Pantocrater is truly the image of our Lord – compassionate and forgiving.' He stressed the words and left them dangling in the *olibanum*-scented air. 'And the Theotokos – ah, such grace…' He lapsed into a puffing silence as he hurried to keep up with the priest's long stride.

'But?'

Toby halted. 'I beg your pardon, Father?'

Father Symeon explained that he believed there had been hesitation in Toby's voice and Toby chafed that they had stopped to discuss aesthetics. He wanted to roar at the priest to move his arse! For God's sake!

'It is very simple,' he said trying not to grind teeth together or grimace like a rabid dog. 'The Limnos icon was truthfully the most beautiful image of the Virgin I have ever seen. Nothing compares, I am sorry.'

They began walking again and Father Symeon seemed more mellow as he responded. 'There is no need for an apology but perhaps now, you can see its value. Even more so when I tell you that tears have been seen to run from the Theotokos' eyes. In fact, the hermit's cave has been a place of miracles for a long time and Father Giorgios grieves mightily for the icon's loss.'

Toby had nothing to say in return. He just cleared his throat and looked awkwardly around the candlelit shadows, feeling Tomas' life drifting away. They reached a small ante-chamber at the back of the basilica, where a nun sat embroidering gold work into a cloth. The priest spoke and she laid her precious work down to move to the door. Father Symeon beckoned to Toby and he sidled past the rotund nun.

'Leave the door open while you talk and all will be well. I shall send word to the Bishop and wait for you in the basilica *narthex.*'

Zoë sat by a window staring out at a sky that drifted toward darkest night. It promised an end to troubles; a night to salve wounds and awake refreshed. Her hands lay crossed over each other in her lap and her hair looped in a braided roll in an old-fashioned Roman style. She still wore the serviceable gown that had seen so many meals aboard *Durrah* but the hands were what tore at Toby. They alternately clenched and then rolled over each other and occasionally she would wring them together like a woman who has lost something of immense value.

'Zoë,' he said gently.

Her head flung round and for a moment the relief on her face was palpable. But then it faded.

'Tobias. I thought you… I…'

'You thought I was Tomas.'

She nodded. 'I owe him so much and they have taken him away on a charge, they say.'

He said nothing as she continued. 'But I told the Bishop what he had done for me and how he had protected me and how he had looked after my interests.'

Toby's heart sank. Looking after Zoë's interests could be assumed by the Emperor to be building support for the Komemnoi. 'You are kind, Zoë. I came to see how you fare and to ask for you to plead Tomas' case. I should have known it was something you would do anyway.'

She gave a small, mirthless laugh. 'The difficulty is, who cares what a Komemnoi has to say? They are hated with a passion by the Angelids, the Bishop was kind enough to underline it for me as if I wasn't already aware, having lost my son, my husband and had a daughter mutilated.' Her hands twisted and her speech quickened. 'They see me as a threat and a reminder and with that in mind, I told him I am not a political animal. That all I want is to be reunited with a daughter I have loved and lost and have found again. The Bishop suggested in all seriousness that my daughter and I become nuns, and Tobias, I'm not repelled by the idea. It means peace for us both to come to terms with life. I told the Bishop that and added that I would be serving our Saviour in the doing.' Her voice slowed down and she finished, 'I meant it…'

It was the most loquacious Zoë had been and Tobias found he was not adverse to the idea of she and her daughter taking holy orders either. Within the right place and protected from the world, it was a kind and gentle solution.

And what a song it would make, what a ballad…

'You must do what you feel is right, Zoë.'

'Tobias, I shall argue more for Tomas, have no fear. And I shall pray for him. I wish I could do more. As it is, I feel utterly futile.'

'As do I, Zoë, but I spoke to Father Symeon and he is going to tell the Bishop what I have said. And as you say, prayer is all we have left.'

He approached her, took her hand and kissed it. 'Thank you for what you have done for us, Zoë. For me.'

'Done for you? Dear God, I have done nothing…'

'You gave me my soul back, gave *us* our souls back. It is immeasurable.'

The nun coughed at the door and beckoned to Toby, so he kissed Zoë's hand again, clasping it between his own. Her fingers were cold and tense and he said, 'Go with God's grace, my lady.'

He turned swiftly before she could see how distraught he had become.

Because of a sudden, he could feel Tomas' fear as the heavy cell door was locked behind him and he could feel the pain where they had jerked his brother's arm and dislocated the shoulder joint. He could hear a prayer that his brother whispered:

'At the hour of my death, care for my miserable soul and drive the dark visions of evil spirits far from it. On the awesome day of judgement save me from eternal

punishment and make me an inheritor of the ineffable glory of your Son, our God.'

That prayer above all else terrified him because Tomas had never been God-fearing, nor was he ever heard to beg for God's help in times of need.

He wanted to sob but instead he muttered, 'Turds and the raging wrath of Hell upon Emperor Isaac II Angelos. May you and your empire be erased from the face of the earth!'

CHAPTER ELEVEN

✗

He seemed to have done nothing but chase people.

Or else he had spent too long avoiding people like those who attacked from the shadows. So much time when time meant the difference between life and…

Say it!

The difference between living and life, he thought.

He ran through the basilica, his soft boots pattering on the glossed floors. Reflected rivers of gold candle flame flowed around him and wavered as he ran past. Monks turned, whispering fiercely, hands skimming chests and sketching crosses, their prayer and meditation disturbed by an imp who had the gall to enter their church and race through it.

There were no public worshippers, curfew having sounded. No crowds, so Tobias had nowhere to hide. He skirted the *omphalos* and hurried toward the *narthex* with barely an idea of what to do but he ran anyway. Trying to gain his bearings and searching for the south gates as his breath huffed in and out, he skidded to a halt and a young novice called him by name, saying Father Symeon wished him to be guided from the basilica.

'Where is Father Symeon?'

'He has not returned from the Holy Father's presence. Come this way, please.'

The south gates slammed behind him as bells rang – he assumed for Compline.

Oh Mary mother! When *will Tomas' punishment occur? And* where?

He slammed his knuckles hard against his temples.

Help me! What do I do?

The night was dark, no stars nor moon – merely black velvet sky meeting ebony silk water. A few torches lit the way to the Augusteion and he thought to find his way to the Great Palace and despite that curfew had come, he would risk breaking it to save his brother, to *see* his brother…

'Master Tobias, Master Tobias!'

He looked back to see the elongated shape of Father Symeon speeding down toward him from the south gates, grasping his cross with one hand and his *skoufos* with the other. 'Master Tobias, I'm sorry I did not get back in time but the Bishop and His Holiness had much to tell me…'

'Father Symeon, I *have* no time…'

'But this is to do with your friend. The man who stole the icon.'

'You say?' Toby found he had no definable heartbeat and that held his breath like a man diving leagues deep in the ocean.

'They have tried him and found him guilty. He will be punished at dawn.'

I know it. I felt it…

Toby closed his eyes in utter defeat. 'Where?' His voice croaked as if the weight of the world pressed on his throat.

'Sit, my son.' Father Symeon took Toby by the arm, and Tobias was glad the man had overcome superstition because he so badly needed a kind word at this moment. 'By the light of the flame I can see you are distraught.'

Toby decided that nothing mattered now. No hiding of truths. Absolutely nothing. Sitting, hands closed to tight fists lying like dead weights upon his knees, he said, 'Father Symeon, Julius of Lübeck is a disguise. The man is Tommaso, my brother. I love him and I am filled with despair for what has happened.'

'I see.' Father Symeon sat back, a dark icon-like shape in the golden mosaic illumination of the torch behind him. 'I will not ask why he disguises himself and I am glad you decided on truths at this hard time. I am bound to honour your confession to me and besides, it will make little difference now to your brother. Do you wish to hear of what transpired?'

Toby nodded. 'It makes no difference, but yes, because he is my brother…'

If someone had driven a knife into his shoulder and twisted it, the pain could have been no worse as they pushed him to his knees in front of a grand noble of the

Byzantine Court. The man sat in a carved chair, his dark blue silk tunic belted with a jewelled girdle and with gold and silver work around the neck, wrists and hems. Tomas wondered that he could walk with the heavy metal thread. Maybe that's why he sat, he thought.

'You speak Greek?' he was asked by a green-clad court toad, mercifully not the harbour official whom he had grown to dislike in the time it took to pick one's nose.

'Yes,' sneered Tomas. 'And Latin, French, Occitan, Ligurian and even a smattering of words from the Russias and the land of the Danes.'

A guard cuffed his ear so that it rang in counterpoint to the high-pitched notes of pain from his shoulder.

The melody has promise...

It was the only way to survive this — to lift himself out of his mind and body and be someone else entirely. Christ knows if anyone could do it he could.

And Toby...

So he would indeed be anyone but *Tommaso Celho, in honour of his brother and his mother and father.*

'Your name?' The nobleman uttered the question with a thick layer of boredom dusted over the top.

'Julius of Lübeck.'

'Place of birth?'

'Lübeck. I just said so.'

Another cuff...

The melody plays louder...

'Where do you live?'

'I had thought to live *here in Constantinople but apparently not...'*

A further cuff to the ear and this time he spun round, hissing at the pain from the dislocated bone and glad because it made him sound like some malevolent offspring from Hell. He glared at the guard with as evil and mad an eye as he could.

'Touch me again, and my Devil spawn family will seek you out, cut off your balls and stuff them up your nostrils in little pieces.' He bared his teeth in a ghastly rictus and the guard, a brawny Varangian with heavy bracelets, reached for an amulet at his neck and took a step back.

Turning round to face his richly-clad interlocutor, Tomas said,

'My home was in Lübeck from my birth until I began to travel to earn money for my singing. Most lately I have been singing in Venezia, but money was less

*than I had thought it would be. I had heard of this great city and took passage on
a trading vessel that was sailing here. I thought the city would have possibilities
for me to entertain folk and make money with it. I have been oft told my voice
is pleasing.'*

*'We have many musicians in the city. An ill-thought choice to come here,
Master Julius,' said the bored nobleman.*

'So it would seem, my lord. But then you haven't heard me sing.'

*Tomas had fallen easily back into the bravado of old. It was a pleasing armour
that fit well and if he needed it to protect him in this latest skirmish, then so be it.*

*'On your voyage, did you make landfall at Myrina Harbour on Limnos?' The
nobleman who had dripped with boredom had now sharpened his attack, his eyes
widening slightly.*

And so we come to the pointed questions.

*'As it happens, yes. There was a storm whilst we were ashore and my fellow
musician and I took shelter in a cave on the way to a chapel on the hill where we
had hoped to secure a night's lodging.'*

*The nobleman sat a little straighter and the official picked up a document,
reading the words contained therein, sliding his finger along the parchment, line
after line. He looked up and Tomas smiled brightly at him.*

*'Did you take anything from the cave?' the official asked, angling the document
to the candlelight.*

*'Apart from a chill, do you mean? Well, if the document says so, then presumably
I did. I took an old painting. It was lying in the back of a cave, it was dirty and
seemed forgotten. It looked quite lovely beneath the dusty grime and I thought that
if I cleaned it and then sold it, it might be my security for a roof over my head in
the city. Does your document say that?'*

*The official appeared uncomfortable and the nobleman merely replied, 'The
document says all we need it to say, Master Julius. We are merely checking your
words against the words of your…'*

*'My accuser? And who might he or she be? Does someone who looks as if he
might be condemned have the right to know such things according to the laws of
the Byzantine Empire?'*

'Such knowledge is immaterial. We are corroborating facts. You took it?'

*'The icon? Indeed. Clearly the cave was empty of life and had been for many
years, it seemed. Why not take it?'*

'Our facts tell us the cave is quite well looked after by the villagers because they have great respect for the monks who choose to retreat there.' The nobleman tapped his fingers on the arm of his chair. 'Did it occur to you that the icon might belong there, that the place was of religious significance?'

'Why would it? I am neither Greek nor of the Eastern Christian faith. I am a Latin Christian and besides, there is the chapel that sits on the hill above Myrina Harbour and looks across to Mount Athos. It is in fact being built under the aegis of Mount Athos. Why then would I assume the cave meant anything at all beyond a refuge from the weather?'

The official leaned over and whispered in the nobleman's ear and he nodded. The Varangians had been cast in stone so little had they moved. For one moment, Tomas thought to try their reflexes but then his shoulder reminded him he was beyond tumbling.

'We are agreed you have a point,' said the official.

''Tis nobly done, I thank you.' Tomas bent from the waist in his best and most painful courtly style.

'But sadly, Master Julius, what you did was a crime against the people of Limnos and most properly a crime against our great Church, against the Theotokos and against God. You stole to make a personal gain and with an icon that is deemed to be miraculous.'

'Then why am I not being tried by the Patriarch and an ecclesiastical court?'

'The charge laid against you came from a civilian…'

'And of course, it's immaterial that I believe a complaint over an important religious artifact should be dealt with by the Patriarch. Anyway,' he said in a light voice, 'what miracles do you talk of?'

'The Virgin's image has been seen to cry real tears. Those who have seen it have been so favoured by the Theotokos that they have been cured of any malady they may have suffered.'

And they believe this?

Tomas might have claimed to be a Latin Christian, but his faith was on weak foundations and he could never believe that relics, paintings and mad fits from strange people could cure maladies.

'What sort of maladies?' He decided it was amusing to keep his judge and jury talking through the night, particularly as the nobleman's face was tightening by the moment and he was such an unlikeable man.

'Blindness, leprosy, possession…'

'Ah, the usuals then,' Tomas commented sagely and tried not to grimace as his shoulder ached. If only they had tied his hands in front rather behind…

Theotokos, if You are watching and feel sadness for Your most humble and apologetic servant, could You just take a little of the pain away?

A frown flashed across the nobleman's face. 'I hear mockery when there should be none!'

'Not at all,' said Tomas. 'In the north, we have our share of miracle givers. In fact I have oft thought to visit one and ask to be stretched to a normal height. It would make my life much simpler.'

'Like I said, Master Julius,' the nobleman almost snarled, his expression cooling to winter-ice. 'You mock and that is displeasing. Would you have stolen the icon if you had understood its value?'

'There is a point of semantics here. You say stolen, I say taken. But in any case, I was raised to have respect for the Faith, my lord, so no.' He crossed his fingers behind his back. 'Most probably I would not have taken it. But that said; I find it hard to believe that so valuable a commodity should be dumped at the back of a cave. It should have been kept clean, perhaps wrapped in linen. You say I show disrespect, but what of those who have been the keepers of the icon? It was not safe. Clearly.'

'But it was safe, Master Julius. Until you landed at Myrina.'

'As you say, my lord.' Tomas refused to drop his eyes in deference to the nobleman. 'May I ask a question?'

'If you must. And be quick. The night passes.'

'Why isn't His Holiness present and judging the … thief of the icon?'

The official glanced quickly at the nobleman and a tacit message passed between the two.

'His Holiness requested that you be tried by Emperor Isaac II Angelus, and I was designated trial judge by the Emperor. On the receipt of your evidence, I am to pass judgement.'

'But if the icon is miraculous, then surely it is the Patriarch's duty…'

'You seek to admonish His Holiness now?' The nobleman's voice froze the winter-ice, anger and fury in abundance.

'Not at all, but the Patriarch is a fair man, fairer and more honest and trustworthy perhaps than our own Pope. I am surprised that he is not here. That is all.'

'We have his thoughts on your crime, Master Julius. To be honest, I think he would have been vastly disappointed by your hubris, by your mockery, by your lack of remorse. With that in mind, we have heard all we need to hear and I find I am ready to pass judgement on your crime. And it was *a crime. You stole something of great religious value and sold it.'*

'To buy a noblewoman's freedom. Do your notes tell you that?' Tomas wished they would hurry to the end-game as this was becoming tedious. He knew he had no hope of a reprieve and just wanted it done.

'It tells us you bought a slave woman who was a whore. We do not need to hear anything more from you, Master Julius. You are to be punished at dawn on the morrow. You will have your hands struck off for the crime of theft and because you have mocked the Faith of the Byzantine Empire and looked upon the image of the Theotokos with no respect, you will be blinded. May God protect you.'

Tomas found he had no definable heartbeat and that held he his breath like a man diving leagues deep in the ocean. And yet he knew this would be the outcome and had done everything to make it worse rather than defending himself. And for one crystal clear moment, he wondered why.

Because you have been living on the edge for too long and just want it done…

'And so, my son, your brother effectively wrote his own punishment. The saddest thing is that the Patriarch felt he should be freed because he had Zoë Komemna's best interests in his heart. The Patriarch believes that this is something of which God and the Virgin Mother would approve.' Father Symeon's hand reached out and touched Tobias', patted it very gently, and then the monk sat quietly whilst Toby took breath after breath.

'Thank you, Father.' His hands twisted upon themselves. 'Did my brother say anything else?'

'In fact yes. As they took him away, he prayed. Loud enough for all to hear.'

Toby knew the prayer – had heard it himself only an hour before.

'At the hour of my death, care for my miserable soul and drive the dark visions of evil spirits far from it. On the awesome day of judgement save me from eternal punishment and make me an inheritor of the ineffable glory of your Son, our God.'

'Father Symeon, can I see my brother before his punishment?'

'No. They will not let anyone near him.'

God…

Toby thought of his brother, thought of him bleeding, of him blind, of him never being able to play a *vielle* again…

'Father, why did His Holiness not try my brother? Why did he request the imperial court to take charge?'

'He made no such request, my son. They asked him to step aside. It is the belief of the Patriarch that your brother is being punished for returning the Komemna to Constantinople. But you have not heard this from me, I beg of you.'

'It is a given, Father. Thank you. I just can't accept that my brother did what he thought was right, what he thought was the Christian thing to do and now…' Toby's heart hurt. It sat in his chest and ached so deeply he thought it might grind to a halt. That it had come to this. That Tomas would possibly die on the morrow and if he lived, would want to die anyway.

There has to be a way. Ah Mehmet, how I wish you were here…

That small wish flickered into a bright light.

'Can he have a physician visit?'

'I do not know.'

'Father, please. If his Holiness was prepared to declare my brother innocent of the charges, then I beg of you, please ask him to arrange for my brother to be tended by the physician, Anwar. He can help him in his moment of need. My brother is not a well man.'

'Perhaps your brother needs a priest in his hour of need, my son, more than a physician. Nevertheless I will ask. But it is late. Perhaps too late…'

'I beg of you.' Toby grabbed Father Symeon's hand and kissed it and thanking him, he ran then, faster than he had ever run in his life.

He ran to Dana's house.

Rapped the door as hard as he could, bashed it till his knuckles bled and until Ahmed pulled it ajar and he fell in. He could barely speak and they had to sit patiently whilst the breath roared in and out of his chest, waited whilst he drank one mug after another of Dana's inexorable *konditon*.

He told them the unambiguous news. He felt empty and dry, cracked and mazed.

He told them he had asked for Anwar to visit Tomas, to help him. Ahmed left immediately to go to Anwar, to arrange things. Toby had no doubt the physician would make himself available. The man's compassion was a twin to that of Mehmet, in the same way that Tobias and Tommaso were linked in brotherhood.

He found he was leaning against a wall and he slid down, the cold, whitewashed wall grabbing at his clothes as he slid. When he reached the floor, he drew his legs in and rested his elbows upon them and then sank his head down upon the bloody knuckles. Dana left him with a candle light, left him to sit quietly, thank the Lord.

But his head was empty of thought, it was just his heart that hurt. He wished the pain would go away but it sat with him, just as Tomas had done so often.

Light shone in a stream through the high window and onto the floor as Tobias stretched. One calf cramped with the effort, the muscle knotting under and over and he leaped from the cot to try and stretch it out whilst beyond the house walls, the doves cooed and bells began to ring for Sext. Ushering in the afternoon, he thought as the muscle loosened and his mind returned to its curdled state, almost as if he had left his thinking on the cot.

After noon… it is afternoon!

He spun round. He was in Dana's sleeping alcove, a curtain separating it from the rest of the one-roomed house. He shot through the drape, batting it aside, and yelling, 'No! No!'

But strong arms grabbed him as they had so many times before.

'Ahmed, please, no! Let me go…' he sobbed. But Ahmed held him tight and he noticed the *peirate's* expression, so far removed from its mercenary machinations and filled with something else…

Compassion?

'Christ Jesus,' he whispered. 'It's done.' Ahmed's hands fell away from him and he backed away. 'I should have been there…' He leaned against the wall again and slid down to the self-same spot of yesternight, holding his head in his hands. And then, 'I knew, didn't I? I knew, and Dana, you held me, and then gave me something…'

Dana sat beside him, the fabric in her robes whispering as the folds settled round her. 'Yes, I think you did know. And yes, I gave you *konditon* with some poppy in it.'

'But that's what they gave Tomas…'

'Perhaps,' said Dana.

'I remember.'

Toby had fallen asleep on Dana's mat with such thoughts of the times that he and Tomas had through the years. Of crawling across the rooftops of Paris, of singing for kings and queens and pretending to love the most beautiful *and* the ugliest women in Christendom, of singing love ballads and being adored by nobles everywhere, of venturing to Spain, France and Italy for Gisborne, and of Cyprus, of Outremer, of the Third Crusade. Good times, inexorable times.

Sleep claimed him and he dreamed.

Sleep claimed Tomas too…

Tomas leaned against the cold walls of the Great Palace cells. The moisture dripped with determined syncopation and the shit bucket hadn't been emptied for an age. Rats glared at him and he glared back. He wouldn't be eaten by rats. Not yet…

His shoulder roared with white hot heat and his hip ached as it was prone to do when he had been forced to move at pace with no rest. At least they had untied his hands and shackled him to a longish chain on the wall and he was able to support the right arm with the left. He wished he had a knife and he would have cut a slit in the breast of his tunic and slipped the damaged arm into the slot to rest it. But they had stripped him of his knives, pulling the boots off and leaving him bare-foot on the rotten straw.

He barely noticed anything beyond the flame of pain. But concern for Tobias pierced his state of mind as he wondered how his brother did. For he was his brother after all. And then concern for Zoë loomed large and his heart softened with the image of her tragic face.

Ironic really.

He suspected his punishment had more to do with her being a Komemnoi than with his theft. Someone, probably the Emperor damn him to Hell and back, was taking their angst out against him rather than Zoë and that must surely be because she had the Church's protection and he was glad. He knew it was Tobias who had shouted to her to claim sanctuary and he loved his brother because of it. Besides, if he was to be punished because of Zoë, he thought it was honourable to meet death as a martyr.

The cell was lit with one limp and sad cresset. So limp that he was afraid to breathe in its direction in case he blew it out. It was still dark outside, but he guessed dawn approached with a rapacious rapidity and he shivered. He was brave, but not quite that brave…

He heard voices and then a key in the heavy door and it was pushed open and the priest from Sancta Sophia came in.

'Give us two stools, if you will, my son,' Father Symeon said to the guard. 'Tomas, I am here to sit with you until dawn. We shall talk and pray.'

It had been almost too much for Tomas' sensibilities. That he should have to share his last hours with a monk! He began to berate the priest but then he recalled it was Father Symeon who had fetched the Bishop and Father Symeon who even now, cared for Zoë.

Perhaps it is he who betrayed Zoë and myself…

The guard shoved two stools through the door, growled and left. But he stood on guard outside – his feet were not heard clipping away.

Ready to take me at dawn…

'The Lady Zoë?' he asked of the priest.

'She is comfortable.'

'She remains in the Church?'

'She does. She is under the protection of the Patriarch. He and his bishops have done all they can to make sure she and her daughter are reunited. And it has been suggested that they both join a religious house. Patriarch George feels that if Zoë Komemna really wishes to show she is no threat to our Emperor, that she will take her daughter and retire to a nunnery. And I must tell you, she is compliant with the suggestion. She believes it will keep she and her daughter safe and allow them to repair with God's good graces.'

Tomas digested this. Despise the Church's hypocrisy as he did, he knew little of the eastern Christian faith and must hope that this was indeed the best solution for Zoë. To a point he was relieved.

'I am at ease, then, Father. And I thank you for your care of her.'

'It was God's will, Master Tomas. May I ask, are you afraid?'

Tomas sat back and looked at the priest, at his black eyes and compassionate expression. The flickering cresset drew shadowy lines down the monk's face but there was nothing fearsome about him.

'You know that I am not Julius of Lübeck? Ha! You have been speaking to my brother, have you not?'

The priest nodded.

'I am glad because he will take all this very much to heart. He's softer than I. But you ask if I am afraid? Not of dying. I have already faced death and been cowed by it once so that it made my life a living hell. If I am afraid of anything, it is the pain. I've never been good with pain. What they will do to me will probably kill me.'

'That is their plan, yes.'

Tomas nodded. 'Yes, I thought so. Someone is afraid of me and of the Komemnoi and I am a convenient scapegoat. It is a message to many, I think.'

'I should not say, but I think you are right.'

'I cannot escape what is coming.'

Father Symeon touched Tomas' shoulder. 'No.'

'Ah, I would love to wipe myself out with some good wine. How much easier it must be to die when one is deep to drowning in one's cups. And I have nearly drowned, Father, so I know what I am talking about.'

Father Symeon dragged at a purse at his waist and pulled out a small stoppered flask. 'This comes from the physician, Anwar. He said it is what you might know as deuil *and that it is up to you whether you wish to use it. For myself, my son, I cannot condone it but then I am not in your position.'*

Ah yes, Tomas knew of deuil or dwale – that mixture that some surgeons used on the battlefield to send their patients into a sleep where they would feel no pain as their limbs were removed or their innards sewn back into their stomachs. Boars' bile, hemlock, bryony, opium, henbane and garden herbs all mixed with wine. Tomas had always thought hemlock, henbane and the poppy would knock anyone into death sleep. Forget about the garden herbs. He reached out and took the cold little flask from the priest and unstoppered it, smelling the liquid therein.

'Ugh,' his nose wrinkled. 'None too sweet. Would be nice with a good Cretan wine.' He closed his eyes. 'Father, forgive me. I am not courageous, I fear.' He tossed the flask back and drank one or two gulps.

'Pig's piss,' he said and his eyes slitted as the bitter taste sat on his tongue for a beat too long. He held the flask in his hand, leaving the stopper hanging on its little chain.

'I will not judge you, my son,' said Father Symeon. 'His Holiness believes you

to be a kind man who sought to rescue a fine woman, a mother who had been wronged. He knows that such sentiment as he has will not leave this chamber and is happy for me to tell you.'

Tomas' head had become quite coddled and he blinked, enunciating the words carefully. 'Besides, I am to die. I take secrets with me.' He shook his head slightly as if to reposition thoughts that were drifting like clouds. 'Father, I do believe I have been good with secrets in my life. Do you think God will forgive me for drinking rather than praying at this time of my impending death?'

Where had that question come from?

'God forgives everyone, Tomas. And will welcome you with the arms of a loving father.'

Tomas' shoulder had lost its fiery breath and the cold in the cell no longer rankled. Warmth crept from his toes and his slumbering poet's soul said it was a kind of peace which lulled him. He tipped his head back, bought the flask to his lips and drank again, shuddering as the bitterness hit his tongue. 'Gets no better,' he muttered. 'Y'know, I've a loving father, somewhere.' He shook his head again, trying to pluck a memory from the ever-thickening fog. 'Pig... Pigna...'

Father Symeon reached to grab him as he fell sideways but Tomas was not done. 'Father, there's words written somewhere. In a purse... Find it. For Toby. An' say a prayer, an' I'll... I'll...' He managed to lift his good arm once more as the dueil blanketed him in a feeling of loving kindness.

Such a mellow feeling, worth remembering.

He sucked up the last of the flask and then fell forward.

Father Symeon grabbed him, took the flask and replaced the stopper, shoving it in his purse and yelling for the guard.

From some distant hallway, Tomas heard the priest say the prisoner was ill, had some sort of fit. The guard, accompanied by another, said it was no matter, because dawn had come.

If they dragged him he felt nothing and presently he was trussed at a block with his arms laid in front of him. In that far off hallway, he found he had no definable heartbeat and that his breath had stopped like a man sinking leagues deep in the ocean and this time there was no Lionheart to pluck him from the deep. Only a father's arms waiting and he was glad. If they took his hands from him, he did not know, nor his eyes, because the hallway was gently bright and welcoming and a man called him as he said calmly and quietly to whomever was listening,

'At the hour of my death, care for my miserable soul and drive the dark visions of evil spirits far from it. On the awesome day of judgement save me from eternal punishment and make me an inheritor of the ineffable glory of your Son, our God.'

'And even though my brother was almost dead and felt nothing of his punishment I felt both his pain and his ecstasy and I screamed, didn't I? And you gave me wine with poppy. And I slept and slept.'

Until he had looked up from the cot and had seen the light streaming down to the floor. He had often called streams of such light as God's Light but how wrong that had been. If God had shone his light on the city, Tomas would still be alive.

'Anwar helped Tomas?'

'Yes. Father Symeon aided him as well.'

'Then the monk is a good man and like to be condemned by his church.'

But in truth, Toby cared not a wit for the priest. He knew he should – for the man's kindness, but he needed to hate right now and anyone would do –even Ahmed who sat down next to he and Dana.

'His church may never know just how kind he *has* been. My little music-man, you are my very good friend. What can I do to help you?'

Ahmed's patience with Toby's grief surprised him and he knew that one day he would thank the Arab.

Just not today.

'Where *is* Tomas?' he asked, knowing that in every civilisation throughout his world, felons were dumped in unmarked graves. His heart ached mercilessly.

'Father Symeon has arranged for Tomas to be removed and buried in the graveyard of St. Akyntos in the Venetian quarter. It was considered expeditious and diplomatic by the Byzantines to have Tomas returned to the Venetians from whence he had most lately come.'

'Hypocrites!' Toby spat and just sat in a dark silence as the afternoon passed through its varying colours. Outside, it had become warm, and it seemed that Tomas' passing had marked a change from spring to summer. Doves still cooed and somewhere a dog barked. It was a friendly bark as if the dog had seen its master and wished to welcome him home.

Dana moved around her little house – folding and sorting. Ahmed disappeared outside and Toby just sat on until he heard a tinder strike and noticed shadows had formed and that a kind of dusk had spread through the close space even though the sky was still blue in the high window. Dana lit candles and Toby stirred.

'Dusk is falling,' she said and moved to a small travelling chest to place things inside.

'You are going somewhere?'

'We all are, Tobias. You, Ahmed and myself. We leave for Gallipolis at dawn if we are to meet with *Durrah* and travel on to Venezia.'

But no. That was wrong and he said so. 'I can't leave. My brother is here…'

Ahmed pushed the door open allowing a breath of summer warmth and spices to waft in around him. The dusk sky slid through apricot and violet, even Tyrian purple and Toby thought if he so much as saw one block of *olibanum* resin with the dye hidden beneath, he might go berserk.

'I have three good horses. If we keep luggage to a minimum,' he scrutinised Dana's small chest, 'then we can make Gallipolis in time. *Insh'Allah!*'

'I do not go,' Toby said. His anger grew like a hungry flame.

'But of course you do,' Ahmed said, ignoring the belligerence. 'And in the meantime I shall escort you to Sancta Sophia. Father Symeon wishes to speak with you.'

But Toby didn't wish to engage with anyone; least of all a monk to whom he owed so much and to whom he could say nothing but thank you. The image of Tomas from his dream stood beside him but he was mindful enough not to let it enter his head. Not yet. He had dreamt it and he had felt it. It was enough.

In the meantime, anger churned below his skin like an army rattling swords against shields. It battered eardrums and Toby knew if that anger ever charged, it would be a massacre.

As they walked, Ahmed said, 'You serve no one, least of all your brother, by staying here.'

'And what would you know of it?' Toby could not hold the sneer. 'Have you lately lost a brother so that you know what I feel? You think you have the right to tell me what I should be doing?'

'I lost a wife. I lost a child. I know what it is to lose and to grieve. Remember that, my friend.' He didn't expand. 'As to my right to tell what you should do? No, I suppose I have none. So what will you do? Sit at the foot of Tomas' grave and weep until you are old and grey? Somehow I think Tomas would laugh at you and mock you for such foolery.'

And the pity of it was that Ahmed was on the mark. Toby knew this and it galled him. He said nothing as they reached the south gates of Sancta Sophia and rapped hard on the aged wood. The night sky had darkened and stars scattered themselves daintily across the nap, the moon dancing amongst them. A soft breeze wound up the hill from the harbourside and Toby knew that despite all the horror, he would carry the spiced scent of Constantinople with him forever. Whether he could smell *olibanum* or pepper, cumin or nutmeg ever again without wanting to vomit was another thing entirely.

A novice opened one of the gates and Ahmed asked for Father Symeon, saying that Master Tobias had been summoned. The monk opened the gate a little further and Ahmed spoke to Toby.

'I will wait here. It is best.'

Toby squeezed past, noting with distaste that the novice eyed him with something approaching fear. He waited, grinding his teeth as the young monk who must have seen no more than fourteen years slipped a bar across. And then he followed the boy along the *narthex* underneath the massive candelabras. They moved toward the *iconostasis*, still glowing in its cool silver glory, and Father Symeon met them halfway, a kind smile on his face as he greeted Tobias. He expressed his sorrow and dismissed the novice and it gave Toby time.

He became an actor at that moment; acted the role of bereaved rather than bereft. Gracious, receptive, grateful. 'Father, I owe you many thanks for you kindness to my brother. You went above and beyond your calling.'

Father Symeon's brow creased. 'You know?'

'My friends told me.' Toby didn't see any reason to expand on the thread that twined between he and Tomas. How since birth they had been connected by more than family but how it had faded when Tomas had changed, and how not long since, it had returned.

Painfully so.

Imagine what the priest would think – Devil spawn indeed.

'They heard from Anwar.'

'Oh.' There was a kind of relief in Father Symeon's voice and Tobias felt a moment of sorrow for him. He carried a weight, of that there was no doubt.

'Father, what you took to my brother from Anwar was an act of sheer kindness and I know God will see it so. I know it. He will thank you one day.'

'I am glad you think so. It was a heavy weight to carry but your brother deserved it. I have never been in favour of such awful corporal punishment and I doubt God would be either.' He crossed himself and reached down to take a fold of parchment off a chest. 'Master Tobias, your brother had a purse with him, a small leather purse in which there was this roll. He asked me to give it to you.' The parchment crackled in the heavy silence of the church as he passed it over. 'Here too is the purse but it has been damaged by the Varangians. I managed to stop them burning it.' The worn leather had charcoaled stripes across the skin and Tobias reached for it, placing the parchment inside, knowing the purse would never leave his side. He buckled it to his belt as Father Symeon continued. 'He was adamant he wanted you to read the parchment and I hope you get much joy from it, my son.'

Tobias fingered the burnt leather. 'I thank you, Father. I wish I could repay you in some way but I am currently without money. But one day, I shall find a way to pay my debts. Please understand me.'

'I do not expect payment, nor does our Church.' He stood, a willowy black column against the flickering candle flame. 'The Lady Zoë only has one more night in sanctuary and then she and her daughter leave at dawn for a nunnery at the north of the city. Both begin as equals, novices under the protection of God and she wishes to speak with you before she leaves.'

'She does?' Toby was surprised and annoyed. He had wanted to grieve for Tomas in peace but it seemed unlikely. Despite that he owed Zoë much for releasing his muse at one time.

Jesu and the Saints! I owe everyone. My life will be full of debt. I lose one anchor chain and I gain more!

And then he cursed himself for thinking so ill of his dead brother.

What am I become?

'Master Tobias? Will you come to her chamber with me?'

'Yes. Yes of course…'

They walked slowly as if Father Symeon understood Tobias' pain. He offered no platitudes for which Toby was grateful because there were no real words and he was glad when they turned into the chamber.

Zoë sat with a beautiful girl. Her face was even lovelier than the image of the Theotokos and Toby had thought She was the apogee.

'Tobias…' Zoë placed some stitching aside and went to him with tears in her eyes. 'I am bereft…'

Toby said nothing, just took her hand and kissed it as he bowed.

'This is my daughter whom he helped me to find. Candida, this is Master Tobias of Venezia. He and his brother will always be in our hearts, won't they?'

Candida stood, a graceful wraith of a girl in need of care and love and freedom from fear. She gave a ghost of a smile and he bent over her hand but she withdrew it and stood slightly behind her mother.

Zoë took Toby's arm and led him to the window as Father Symeon stood at the doorway. 'Tobias, forgive her. She has been tormented and is coming to terms with meeting me again and with the possibility of a more gentle freedom.'

'There is nothing to forgive, my lady…'

'And forgive me for not being able to save Tomas…' her voice broke. 'I tried and I believe the Patriarch expressed a wish that he go free.'

'So I understand,' Toby acknowledged but then his manner changed to pure fire. 'But the Byzantine state appears so much stronger than the Church.'

'Tobias, I owe you and I owe Tomas and I wish to give you this,' she passed him a small slip of parchment. 'It is from the bishop who questioned me and who is a distant cousin of my own mother, and therefore *not* a Komemnoi. No, don't unfold it until you are gone from Sancta Sophia. But remember that before I took holy orders I was a woman who wished to pay a debt and that,' she touched the parchment, 'is my payment. You have the name of Tomas' accuser in your hand.'

Toby gasped. This was payment beyond his wildest thoughts. 'You say?' He had never understood revenge to any great degree. Oh, he had been part of it to be sure, with Gisborne chasing enemies across Europe but he had always been an accessory, never the perpetrator.

Now his future had real meaning.

'I thank you. Jesu, how I thank you.' He reached for her hand again and crushed it in his own. At the doorway, Father Symeon coughed and beckoned and Tobias stood. 'Go with grace, Lady Zoë. It was a gift knowing you.' He backed away from her and she moved to her daughter's side in the light of soft candles.

He and Father Symeon walked toward the *narthex* and the south gates.

'You feel more sustained now?' the priest asked.

'Oh yes, Father. More than you can possibly believe.'

'I am glad.' They reached the gates and the priest lifted the bar easily despite its size and weight. 'Go with God's grace, my son. And remember that your brother was a brave man and that he found God in the end.'

Toby turned away as the gates closed, the bar thudding down behind and all the while the little scrap of parchment burned a hole in his hand.

Found God. Really?

'All is well, Tobias?' Ahmed moved out of the shadows as Toby unfolded the parchment and angled it to the light of a flame. He didn't answer as the spidery script moved into focus before his eyes.

The name there should have come as a surprise he supposed, but the pieces of a puzzle dropped into place and it was in fact no surprise at all. He turned to Ahmed, folding the scrap and placing it in his own purse, saying, 'Before we go, may I visit Tomas' grave?'

Ahmed scrutinised him. 'The priest has convinced you to leave?'

'In a manner of speaking.'

'Then we shall visit the Venetian quarter before we go. I would pay my own respects to your brother.'

It was dark when they left Dana's house, although cocks were crowing a street away. Her little travelling chest had been strapped to Ahmed's bigger horse but neither Ahmed nor Tobias carried any luggage. Only Ahmed's *kilij* and a purse swung from his belt and from Toby's belt his small sword hung. And two purses – one with charcoaled stripes in its hide.

People had begun to move about, servants running to markets, people carting the tools and produce of their trade. Toby couldn't care. He longed to leave the place. Now that he had a name, he *knew* without doubt that Tomas would understand. Not only that, he knew his brother would *demand* revenge. A pearly light lit the east and Toby's focus was only on reaching the church, of seeing Tomas' grave, of swearing an oath by the side of his brother.

The Prosphorion Harbour came into view and they passed beyond the Pisan quarter. It was busy with men dealing in wealth and commodities, coins being weighed and transferred to purses as they rode by – obvious to all and so bloody venal. Toby cursed them for their avaricious and corrupt ways. He knew what they were like, trusted none of them…

They walked their horses along the edge of the Neorion Harbour, and amongst the buildings of the Venetian quarter he could see the Latin basilica of Saint Akyntos with its carved wooden doors showing the Passion of Christ. They halted and dismounted, paying a young lad to hold the animals and saying they would double the price if the horses were still here and quiet on their return. They made their way to the opened door of the church but the space was empty, two candles smoking on the unadorned altar, Toby swallowing hard against the faint smell of *olibanum* that drifted on the breeze through the doors. He turned away and they followed him along the side of the building, passing between stonewalls to a small green sward at the back. Oaks and elderly spreading cypresses canopied the meditative space and any other time Tobias might have thought what a tranquil resting place it was for those lying interred there. But he was charged with a fervour, probably the selfsame fervour of which he had often accused his brother.

The light wove through the gently shifting leaves of the oaks, spotting the ground with discs of gold, and there was only one freshly filled grave – a small mound the size of a child. Tobias found he had to swallow on a cry – if he had been on his own, he would have turned his head to the heavens and howled like a wolf. But now was not the time. Instead he fed the emotion into another more insidious feeling – a type of battle fever. He had never experienced it as strongly till now and he liked the way his blood flowed harder and faster and how he felt invincible.

The three went toward the grave and Ahmed touched his forehead and chest and bowed in deference to the little man with whom he had quite a few sharp passes. Dana bent and laid a stem of blue flowers, wild chicory, on the mound of dirt.

'Music-man,' Ahmed said. 'I have made arrangements for a headstone. It will have his name and his birthplace. Is that enough?'

'Thank you,' Toby said in husky tones. 'Yes…' Another debt, he thought. 'It is enough.'

'Then we shall leave you for the moment. Join us when you are ready.' Ahmed helped Dana stand and Toby heard their footsteps as they moved away.

'You made the right choice, Tomas,' Toby said. 'You cheated those Byzantine pig shits of their pleasure. You got your excitement too, didn't you?' His eyes prickled but he blinked and took a breath. 'I wish I could say I regret that we had ever come here but you'd hate the weakness of such a thought. I know you would have festered and rotted if we had stayed in Venezia.' He smoothed the dry dirt in a half circle as he knelt. 'Ah, you have given me such seeds for a ballad, Tomas. Such seeds ... a true *chanson de geste.*'

And then he remembered the purse and Tomas' folded parchment and he pulled it out to read. It was a poem about a woman they both knew and he pictured her even then, vowing that he must, one day, find a melody and make the song as famous as any from the Occitan troubadours. He folded the piece and put it away and then opened the tiny scrap from Zoë Komemna. 'I will create the melody for your words one day, and it will become the *canso* about which the whole world talks, Tomas. But listen. First I have a debt to settle.' He waved the scrap above the grave. 'I found the one who betrayed you, Tomas. Well ... no, that isn't quite true. *Zoë* found your betrayer and I have the name and so help me, before winter comes he will lie with his guts spilled around him and we will honour your name!'

CHAPTER TWELVE

✕

Gallipolis had not changed in the few days since they had passed through. And yet Tobias' whole world had shifted, reconfiguring to an unrecognisable degree.

Cicadas buzzed among the olive trees that were set back from the harbour and Gallipolis baked in early summer heat. Tobias however, burned with fury, and wondered if he could burn any hotter; deciding that yes, it would happen when he had his sword positioned for the death stroke.

He had no qualms about killing his brother's accuser. No priest nor gospel, no words from on high would change his mind and he was quite equable about it – it was something that had to be done before he could move on.

Move on to what?

But in truth he didn't care. Accomplish one and the other would take care of itself.

They rode into Gallipolis as a single bell rang for None on the day after Tomas' death. Tobias replied when he was spoken to but otherwise, Dana and Ahmed left him cocooned in peace and talked quietly with each other. Toby might as well have been blindfolded for the notice he took of his surroundings, because his mind plotted, then plotted again. At one point he wondered if he should tell Mehmet what the parchment scrap said but could find no reason why he should. Part of him knew that Mehmet was the voice of reason and he worried that the physician, being his close friend, would convince him that revenge was not the act of a clear-thinking man.

But in his own mind, he would see himself avenging his brother in cold blood. *Cold* blood. Curious that, he thought, I burn with vengeful desire and yet I shall kill rationally and in *cold* blood…

'Tobias! Tobias!' Dana's voice pierced his thoughts, a hand grasping at his reins, his horse throwing up its head. 'Toby, we go *this* way – through the town gates. You will end up in the Hellespont if you follow that road.'

He looked around, saw the stone walls and the timber gates open to the skein of traders, artisans and farmers who looped in and out with sumpter mules and camels, horses and carts, baskets and bags. Animals brayed, neighed and snorted and there was an air of the bazaar. More than Toby had seen in Constantinople.

But then my time in that city was filled with running and hiding…

He followed behind Ahmed through the gates and glanced along the street as they turned toward the water.

'There she is!' Ahmed turned a radiant face to Dana and Tobias. He had the enthusiasm of a lover seeing his woman after a separation. 'Ah, my little *Durrah*. How I have missed her. She looks well. Faisal has cared for her.' He pushed his horse to a trot, driving through the people who walked the street, pushing them to the side, his eyes fixed on the harbour.

'Curious, isn't it,' Dana observed. 'He is a man of such strength and deviousness and yet he melts like ice in the sun in the face of his boat. He may as well be married to it.'

She laughed and it was the first time Toby had heard her be anything but brusque and he found the sound of that throaty chuckle cut through his grief and his hate just for a moment. Just for a mere beat in time he became the Tobias of old and smiled back at her, caught in the belly by her attractive face and dark hair that waved in the wind where she had tied it at the back of her head.

Not for Dana the trappings of Byzantium as she prepared to leave it all behind. She was dressed in hose and tunic and a linen chemise with the sleeves rolled up. She wore short leather boots and she sat comfortably astride her gelding. He reminded her of Lady Ysabel and he felt a pain of longing. Dana's eyes sharpened and he caught the intensity of her gaze as she swept the decks, looking for someone.

Ah, thought the Toby of old, she seeks Michael Sarapion. Perhaps there is a match there.

He quite liked the idea. It warmed him.

But his own eyes looked at *Durrah* and saw Tomas, wretched and leaning over the larboard wale on their voyage to Byzantium and his heart hardened and he kicked his horse on.

They caught up with Ahmed who had dismounted and was yelling for Faisal to report to him as he unbuckled Dana's travel chest and loosened the horse's girths, ordering crew to lead the horses to the nearest stable. 'I shall come shortly to settle any charges the horses will incur. Tell the ostler where to find me if he has a problem.'

And then he had jumped aboard, grasping a stay, his robes flapping in the warm breeze, his shaved head glistening.

The *peirate* had returned.

Toby took his time dismounting, smoothing his horse's neck, loosening the girth – anything to delay the inevitable meeting with Mehmet. He had nothing to say and was hoping that Ahmed would explain it all. In many ways, he felt as mute as the beautiful Candida Komemna. But the crew took the horses, reaching for the reins he still held in his hand and there was nothing between he and the ship's larboard side.

Mehmet stood there as the horse moved away – as still as the statue of Justinian. His white robe blew in soft folds and his black *keffiyeh* lifted off his shoulders and then settled. His face displayed nothing beyond calm. But his eyes? Ah, Toby fell into them. Filled with compassion, with understanding and most definitely with love, like a father for a son. He and Tobias were friends of such longstanding and now the physician was the bridge between dark and light and Toby wasn't sure where he wanted to be.

In darkness he could avenge. In lightness he could remember with a good heart. But still he was mute and Mehmet said nothing to break the silence. As Toby swung aboard and found his sealegs upon the deck planks, Mehmet slid an arm around his shoulders and squeezed. As light as a feather but as strong as an iron anchor chain. There and then gone and Toby was glad. He left Mehmet's side and went to stand in the bow of the ship, looking around to see other merchant vessels anchored off shore or moored against the harbour walls.

He wondered how many sailed back to Europe loaded with the finest goods for the marketplace and how many sailed onward to a city that now claimed his brother as one of its own. Such an inconsequential thought. Such a painful thought. It slashed down his chest like a *kilij* blow.

Ahmed moved to stand beside him. 'There are a few who head to the Italian coast like us, but if we reach Venezia ahead of them and unload our cargo for the merchants to pick over whilst it is new and exciting and before the market becomes saturated, then the more money Saul and my lord Gisborne will make. And the more money I shall make in consequence.'

'*Insha'Allah*,' Toby muttered.

Ahmed stared at him with curiosity and then added, 'As you say, little music-man. *Insha'Allah*.'

'When do we leave?'

'Tomorrow early. We must battle through the heads again and the tide shall be our ally.'

Toby drew in a deep breath. 'I'm going for a walk along the foreshore, Ahmed. I shall see you anon.'

Toby thought he heard Ahmed call after him, but he jumped ashore and began walking, examining the other vessels that sat around the harbour. They were all of a kind – deep-hulled but sitting low with full cargoes, ranks of twelve to sixteen oars, and a sail. Some like *Durrah* had an aft castle. Looking back, he observed Ahmed's galley. He'd never noticed before how dark were the planks of *Durrah*. Oak, he supposed, and almost black with age. She had an air about her, for what better ship for a trader like Ahmed than a black ship?

He continued walking, unsure what he was looking for. A galley? A man? The last tiny piece of the puzzle that might redeem his future?

Ah, all of those...

Or none.

The sun baked the earth and he was glad they departed on the morrow. Whilst Venezia would be baking in its own summer heat and the laguna insects would be driving all to distraction, he longed to sequester himself behind the cool villa walls and allow the lap of the water to lull him.

But of course that was after...

The little purse hung at his waist and the name on the scrap almost jumped out to taunt him. He rubbed at the leather, feeling the burned stripes. They reminded him of bloody whiplashes and he cursed the pig's bladder of a guard who had thrown the purse onto a searing grate. As well Father Symeon came when he did; at least Tomas' *canso* would be a beautiful legacy to offer the world.

'Tobias, Tobias!' A voice called from his right and he was unfamiliar with it, lost in thoughts as he was. Whoever called was concealed by the shade of an arbour and he crinkled his eyes to get a better view – a young man walked toward him with his arm extended. 'My friend! I did not expect to find you here on my journey homeward.'

'Pietro!' Tobias took the Genovese's arm and gripped it, detaching a smile from muscles that had grown stiff with pain.

The swarthy Genovese grinned. 'You are here on business perhaps? I thought you were intent on fleecing the Byzantines of much of their coin.'

Toby's mouth twitched and he took command because the twitch came from anger and impatience and he wanted to wipe the inane grin from the face before him. 'Not at all. If I remember, Pietro, it was *you* who was fixated on fortune hunting, myself not so much. And if I also remember, you tried to teach *me* how to make money. Did you not?'

Pietro shielded his eyes from the sun and it was difficult not to notice the fine silk chemise and the padded silk gambeson.

Sard. Padded silk!

'You are doing well, I think,' Toby said, touching the gambeson, fingering the soft silk, 'and you haven't even sold your goods in Genova. You must have struck gold.'

Pietro shrugged. 'I have been lucky. I gambled on a good hand and won. I looked for you in the city, you know.' He touched Toby's arm, running his hand in an almost feminine sweep. 'I recall you owe me a meal…'

'Then I shall pay my debt. Have a meal with me now.'

The Genovese's lip curved down and he looked at the sky, then shrugged. ''Tis early, but we can share wine and cheese and some olives and bread. And we can talk.'

Jesu, I don't want to talk, you oversilked bastard. Talk is the last thing I want to do as I seek my brother's killer. Words? Christ on the Cross, I am done with words…

But Toby smoothed out his face – letting the muscles loosen, opening his eyes wider with feigned interest. They walked together back to the arbour and sat at a trestle. The vine had robust growth and the stem was thick and throttling the old timber upright to death. The image suited Toby's mood.

Seated and with a flagon and mugs between them, Toby said, 'In answer to your question about my impression of the city, I found it filled with pontificating priests and mealy-mouthed officialdom hiding behind a veneer of silks and prayer.'

Pietro raised his eyebrows. 'Just like home?'

'Worse. I am not at all impressed with the city and found I was treated with disdain and even fear. The northern courts and halls treated me with much respect. Here, I feared for my life…'

'You say?' Pietro placed his mug carefully, his eyes wide.

'Yes. I have never had to fight for my life. This time I did. So I leave whilst I can still play a *vielle*.'

Pietro shifted and then lifted the mug and drank deep. 'Perhaps a wise thing to do…' he managed.

'You don't sound convinced.'

'I have never lived in fear for my life so I cannot imagine, my friend. My life has only ever been geared to building my family's trade. I do what is right for me and you must do what is right for you.' He flicked a dark hair off the snowy silk of his chemise. 'And what of your singing friend. The man from Lübeck…'

'The man from whom you purchased the icon? Do you still have it?'

Pietro smiled and slipped off the gambeson, rolling up the sleeves of his chemise to reveal ropy forearms with course black hair. 'Indeed. I suspect I will make more money than I imagined with it. Your friend should have been more farsighted.'

'He was. In his own way. As to his whereabouts right now, I have no idea. He … disappeared.' Toby could barely speak and had never acted so well in his life. 'It is perhaps as well. We had grown apart and were unlike to continue on together.'

Pietro lifted his mug again and then said, 'Perhaps as well, as you say, if that is the situation between you. Shall we talk of happier things? What ship do you return on?'

'The one on which I sailed here. *Durrah*. You may know of the galley master, Ahmed.'

'I have heard of him. They say he is clever, wily and a trader of whom we should all beware.'

At that Tobias laughed. 'Beware? Shouldn't all traders be cast in the same light? From what I've observed, you would kill your grandmothers to get to a valuable cargo first. I'm stunned and in awe.'

Pietro returned the laugh. 'Perhaps not kill grandmothers… But trade is trade and the strong man wins. What does your galley master carry home?'

Toby's eyes closed to slits. 'Would you tell me what is in your hold?'

Pietro pursed his lips and then grinned. 'Probably not now, not with us all racing home to get the best prices. Inside information is all, my friend and I think you know this.'

'Then I will tell you in all honesty that I have no idea what he carries nor do I care. All that matters is that he carries me back to Venezia from whence I shall journey to Aquitaine and try again to be a troubadour of note.'

'You sound jaded…'

'Do I? Then I am. As sour as old wine. We aged men do that sometimes. For I think you might be much younger than I and have yet to experience true life.'

'I have seen twenty five years…' Pietro seemed put out, almost as if he suspected Toby had patronised him.

'Then you need to see more to catch up.' The wine seethed in Toby's belly and he found he was sick of the ego sitting opposite him. 'Where do you sail from here?'

'The route we sailed to get here, weather pending.'

'Then I wish you well. I must bid you adieu.' Toby stood, staggering a little, and placed some silver *denarii* on the table. He gripped the Genovese's arm. 'We may yet see each other again.' He began to walk away and heard Pietro vaguely as he tried hard to push his foul mood down.

'Thank you for the wine and food. Good luck to you and if we are in port together, we shall eat again perhaps.'

Toby raised an arm and kept walking.

He wished he had not been so moody, wished he'd drawn the fellow out more, anything to divert the anger that burned. But his mood had flooded him from the toes up. He found everyone tiresome and fury and impatience licked his boots. Ahead, as the sun eased its way to the west and the cicadas shrieked, he could see *Durrah*, saw Mehmet seated with Dana under the canopy and like a dog running home to its master, he suddenly wanted to be with familiars under the canopy and in the shade.

He lay on the decks as the violet and peach-coloured sky blurred to an ever-darkening indigo, bunching up his arms behind his head and staring at the heavens as stars began to flicker. The planks were still warm under his back, the shore-side cicadas had ceased trilling and only the occasional barking dog or a chorus of drunken voices could be heard from the taverns.

The ships were lit as if by fireflies along the quayside, and offshore, vessels floated with lanterns illuminating their position on the water, a plethora of small golden pathways all leading to the harbour walls.

Faisal had begun to cook on his brazier, the ever-present bucket of dowsing water close by. The smell of onions and garlic sweating in oil drifted toward Toby and he thought some cumin and pepper must have been added because of the aroma that wound its way through the galley shrouds. He had an image of a spice merchant's in Constantinople down by the Prosphorion harbour. Small hessian sacks had been lined up, one after another and revealing rich yellows, ochres and garnets and with odours that could float one to lands of oliphants and dragons. He turned his head away – Tomas and he had always wanted to see an oliphant.

When grief threatened to consume him, he would open up that *armarie* in his mind and allow vengeful thoughts to pile upon the sadness until he became lost in his plotting again.

He had almost worked it out. Another few nights of sifting through the detail and he thought he may just have something foolproof. His adversary wouldn't know what was coming.

'Tobias, I bought you some spiced fish. You must eat.' Mehmet sat down with two small pieces of unleavened bread oozing spicy paste.

'I'm not hungry, Mehmet, but I thank you.'

'Do you realise you have lost weight?'

'In two days and nights? It's a miracle.'

Mehmet frowned. 'Don't be fatuous, Tobias. Some of us are concerned for you.'

Toby replied that he was comforted by the compassion but that all he needed was time so Mehmet left and even though Toby didn't look at him, he knew Mehmet examined him through to the very heart and soul. It was why he, Toby, had always been such a fickle chess player. So easy to read…

He grabbed the empty sacks he had used previously as bedding and wadded them, lying on top and turning on his side. The smell of flour drifted up his nose and he recalled the sacks had been loaded in Limnos – the island was renowned for the quality of its grain.

Ah, Limnos – the beginning of the end for Tomas.

Limnos – the beginning of the end for another if the Theotokos gave Toby Her blessing.

Durrah departed Gallipolis just before the tide changed the following day – pulling into midstream, shipping oars and hoisting sail, letting the breeze from the north east push them toward the heads. Ahmed rested on his helm, barely adjusting it as the galley moved across a slightly raked sea, the robust sail filling with little jibing or snapping.

Tobias could feel the tide beneath the hull, lifting *Durrah* and speeding her westward, Ahmed laughing with sheer pleasure. Even heavy with cargo, the small galley sat evenly on her keel, so finely tuned that she barely pulled to left or right.

Five other boats had left at the same time – a small flotilla making for the exit into the Adriatico. Ahmed had said only two sailed to Venezia – themselves and one other. Of the other four, one sailed to Sicily and the rest to Marseille with loads of silks to be taken to Lyon. Toby looked for Pietro's galley – he had no idea what it looked like, merely assumed the Genovese would be glaringly obvious in the bright sunshine, his white silk chemise flashing like a signal to the world.

'Look! Here I am, the great Pietro Vigia, building my family's fortunes. We shall become the greatest trading family alive!'

Pig's arse, Toby thought. I guarantee in a hundred years, it won't be *his* family ruling the trade of Europe. Toby had never had any time for misplaced ego, even less since Tomas had died – even though the Genovese had been good company.

And there he was – slightly to the starboard stern. Pietro raised his hand and saluted as their gazes collided. Toby waved back.

'You know him?' Ahmed asked. Toby jumped as the galley master spoke. He hadn't heard him approach.

'Yes. I met him in Chandax. I thought I had told you.'

'Perhaps you did, I do not recall. He is the other trader heading to Venezia. I met him at the spice merchant's house in the city and we haggled over the frankincense. The fellow was determined that he could better me, not knowing that the merchant is an old friend of mine from the past, and that the deal had been done long since. My friend opted to price the stuff at a high level to push the Genovese out. He is nothing if not bold and persistent. But before he gave up, he offered me a deal – that we should become partners, keep back a large portion of the frankincense thereby driving the price up whereupon we could sell the rest to a premium market. I quite liked his idea and his energy…'

Toby had no interest in talking with Ahmed or anyone really, on anything at all. They could all take their merchandise and go to Hell… 'Ahmed!' he snorted with derision. 'He's a young man, younger than myself, filled with egoism, and this is his first foray into the marketplace – he told me so himself. Surely you are wise enough to see that. But then perhaps not!'

Ahmed's eyes slitted and he replied. 'He is cunning and hungry.' But then he laughed. 'He has gall and I admire that.'

And yet you disliked my brother…

'Allah be praised that you should think so,' said Toby with as much sarcasm as he could dredge up. 'Forgive me if I say that I couldn't give a rat's arse for Pietro's qualities. You have your cargo and he presumably has his. I meanwhile have lost my brother. You will excuse me.' He turned and surveyed *Durrah*, finding the canopy deserted and like the aforesaid rat, scurried there and hunkered down. He relished that Mehmet was at the stern, that Ahmed had re-taken the helm, that the crew sat at their benches and that Dana kept to herself. He just wondered if he could stand being immured on the ship for the weeks it would take to reach Venezia.

But, he thought, there is always Limnos…

The island beckoned, because he knew they would lay over for re-provisioning. He knew the flotilla would heave to as well and he wondered if Father Giorgios would stand on his hill and curse them all as thieves and cutthroats.

But more than anything, he asked the Virgin, She whom the Byzantines called Theotokos, to honour him with Her support in his endeavour.

The voyage began smoothly enough, but on the second day, the summer atmosphere had become humid, sticking to their skins like molten wax. The sky had thickened from endless blue to become clotted with grey and from the northwest thunder grumbled.

'A storm,' Ahmed said. 'But it will be done swiftly. Drop the sail,' he ordered, 'and tighten everything!'

The weather hit like a herd of unyoked and angry oxen. The ship listed to larboard in a furious blow, a wave scooping from underneath as Ahmed ordered the starboard oars to pull if they valued their lives.

Tobias clung to the masthead, Dana beside him as lightning illuminated the crew standing at their oars, cords of muscle erupting in their arms and necks. Michael Sarapion had taken the place of the dead Sicilian, Sasso, and he pulled with the rest, as hard on the oar as he was able. Needle slivers of rain pelted the canopy as the fully laden boat began to turn, Faisal and Ahmed leaning their weight on the helm and the Arab's shouts tearing strips off the crew. The larboard oars began to back-paddle and with the extra muscle, the vessel swung more. One errant wave smacked into the starboard bow and Toby lost his footing, falling hard onto his shoulder on the deck but Dana reached and grabbed him, pulling him back to the mast and he shouted his thanks.

By the time he had wiped the rain from his eyes, *Durrah* was facing into the wind, Ahmed holding the helm firm and the rowers on both sides at the ready. But Ahmed was right. The storm blew itself out in a heartbeat. He said it was like a mistress's temper tantrum – flashy, loud and over in the time it took to pass her a gift.

'What gift did you give?' Toby asked.

'A bale of silk – and may the fish choke on it!' the Arab replied sourly. 'What about you? Did you lose anything? Apart from your balance?'

Toby felt at his belt – his sword still hung there, and his purse and…

Tomas' purse was open.

Worse, it was empty.

'No,' he said, furious and frightened at once.

Frightened of what, he thought? And then he saw Mehmet further aft, checking his medicine boxes.

Am I frightened that Mehmet should discover my plans? Why should it matter?

The sky had paled to delicate blue, the breeze shifting to a light easterly, the sea placid and uncomplaining. As the oars dipped and rose, Toby stood at the wale, just staring, and the susurration of the sea along the planks of *Durrah* smoothed his ripples. For one brief moment, he allowed his eyes to fill, he wanted to mourn so much that his heart ached. But then he blinked, realising Mehmet stood beside him, looking toward a landmass to their starboard north.

'Mount Athos. Limnos must be close.'

Toby's heartbeat quickened as Mehmet continued. 'My dearest friend, if what Ahmed says is true, Anwar would have made sure that Tomas did not suffer.'

Toby grimaced. ''Tis true,' he finally admitted. 'He felt nothing.' He knew Mehmet would understand the twin connection. 'But in feeling nothing, he lost his life.'

'Tobias, we have talked many times about possible eventualities with Tomas.'

'But it doesn't make it any easier. He *lost* his life.'

'And you lost your brother.'

'I lost so many things, Mehmet.'

'Then did you perhaps lose this?' Mehmet held out two pieces of parchment, carefully laying them in Toby's palm. The smaller one flipped open revealing spidery writing. 'The name means something perhaps?'

There was no point in lying, no point in keeping secrets…

'Yes.'

'Of importance?'

'Yes.'

'But you will not say.' Mehmet's comment held no umbrage and Toby flushed with guilt.

'Mehmet,' he began. 'My brother was many things of late – a bully, a drunkard, even a thief. But he redeemed himself when he bought Zoë and freed her.'

He told Mehmet that Zoë had taken sanctuary, that she had been reunited with her daughter and that even now, the two were being inducted into the noviate of a Byzantine nunnery, thus under the protection of the

Patriarchate. 'So you see, whatever he was, whatever he did, he saved two women from odious fates. Father Symeon told me Patriarch George felt he had redeemed himself and would be forgiven and should go free. And yet he was punished out of all context.'

They stood in silence then as seabirds dipped and dived in their wake and Toby thought Tomas' soul was likewise as free. Free as the wind or the birds that rode on the wind.

'Someone reported him to the authorities, Mehmet. It is my belief that the same person was encouraged to sign a document of so-called *truths* about Tomas for a hefty price. The imperial court then had a scapegoat they could punish as a sign to the Komemnoi – anyone aiding and abetting the Komemnoi should live in fear of their lives.'

'Why wasn't Zoë killed, then? And Candida?'

'I think because she agreed to join the Church as a nun, with her daughter, and also that her uncle is a respected bishop. The Angelids clearly don't want the Church off-side. Amongst all of that, my brother, Tomas, was so very convenient as a message of power and might.'

'And this person,' Mehmet indicated the parchment scrap. 'Is the person who swore against Tomas?'

'Yes. The bishop told Zoë and she passed the information to me. She said she owed Tomas…'

'And so you plan to take revenge for Tomas' life.'

The look that passed between the two men was long but Toby said nothing.

'You intend to do this alone?'

'I could hardly ask you to assist me, nor would I want to lay that burden upon you. So yes, I will do this alone.'

Mehmet's hands gripped the wale. 'I see. When? Might I know? As your friend?'

'Mehmet…'

'Tobias, I swear by Allah the Beneficent and Merciful that I will not interfere. Nor allow anyone else to.'

Moments passed as Toby weighed his plans from one hand to the other. He knew what Saul felt like as he weighed coins in his little gold scales. He tucked the scrap and Tomas' poem back into the purse and buckled it tight. 'In the next day perhaps…'

'Ah. Limnos.'

'Yes.'

'Such poetic justice,' Mehmet said, reaching for Toby's shoulder. 'My dearest friend, be careful…'

Poetic justice? Swords? Blood spilled? Lives lost?

Yes, poetic justice, Toby thought.

Nothing else was said and day glided into night as smoothly as silks falling off a whore's hips.

The harbour in Limnos had gradually filled with the six vessels beating a path toward the Middle Sea and the small inns were filled to the roof joists with raucous voices. The weather had swung again and wind raged on the sea, ships' masters deciding it was better to have drunken crew ashore than merchandise on the bottom of the ocean.

The gale roared down alleys and waves whipped the rocky foreshore walls, spray arcing into the air and leaving a salty rime on the buildings. Far above Myrina on the headland, Father Giorgios' church stood foursquare to the gale, its bell grabbed by the wind and sending the clapper into a furious ringing rhythm.

Toby like the sound – as if the bell represented an army crashing swords against shields; the kind of sound that sent shivers and belly pains into the enemy. The sound charged his battle fever because his quarry was on the island – he had watched the disembarkation from behind a mouldy hogshead and was ready.

The man walked past, grinning widely at something one of his crew had said. It was all Toby could do to restrain himself. But he waited, then withdrew the dagger from his boot, beginning to follow – tracking discretely, allowing the wind to muffle any movement and slipping from shadow to shadow.

He walked the length of the foreshore, and it was as he turned to follow his quarry up a side alley that he knew he too was being followed. It was one of the possibilities factored into his plan and it confirmed everything. He would be captured, knocked around to a pulp perhaps but alive nonetheless, and then he would be ransomed.

For the purple.

Of course.

His heartbeat ratcheted up a notch and sweat prickled at his armpits. He listened. Three men? No – perhaps two.

Theotokos, make it two. I beg of you, Holy Mother.

His dilemma lay in slipping out of sight and surprising his followers but losing his quarry in the process.

Limnos is a small island – you'll find him again.

The voice was not his conscience voice. It smacked of Tomas' insufferable arrogance and Toby loved it.

He spotted a shadowy alcove ahead and as a handful of loud revellers fell out of a miniscule inn, he slipped through the inevitable confusion and pressed himself hard against the alcove wall, swallowing on his breath. The fusty smell of dust and dogs' droppings slipped up his nose. Christ, he could almost shit himself.

Scared, Toby?

He closed his eyes to block the image of Tomas taunting and then opened them. The drunk crewmen had departed and his followers had stopped close by, speaking in Genovese accents.

That merely confirmed his deductions and he listened as they debated following the revellers. But no, they decided to continue and hurried on.

He prided himself on moving like a shadow, stepping as light as a wisp of river fog. It was a skill learned on the rooftops of Paris and never forgotten. One never knew how strong a roof or wall might be.

This Limnian alley had narrowed to single width as it bent between aged dwellings, and the path to Hades could have been no darker. The howling wind had dropped a little and in the alley's shadow, one could almost forget that the harbour had been whipped to a frenzy. Toby crept close to the man at the back with both daggers drawn, thanking the Saints for single file. Nothing about what he planned would be quiet so it had to be quick. He needed to be on his feet and facing the other man swifter than a sword swing.

He slashed out at the legs in front of him, hamstringing the man instantly and he went down screaming, crashing to the ground. Toby grabbed his hair, jerked the head back and slit the neck. He had never been so swiftly brutal before, closing his mind to the horror, letting the battle fever take charge. The man died quickly and he leaped back behind the body, using it as a barrier over which to face the other.

The man was big and broad, slow on his feet and stupid. He came at Toby in the dark, tripped over his partner's carcass and stumbled forward as Toby used both daggers with a proficiency that was fuelled by battle fervour, because it had come – swirling like a dangerous current and he barely recognised himself.

He ran then, following the alley which turned to the right and then the left. Christ above and Mary Mother, Toby begged. Let me find the bastard.

Ahead was the village square, a paler shade of dark as a pallid moon struggled valiantly against heavy night cloud. The bottom edge opened onto the harbour and the place had the air of a graveyard, empty and windswept, the easing blow still strong enough to toss twigs and leaves and to twist the pliant branches of the olive trees into a knotted mass.

Toby's quarry stood in the middle of the square, his back to Toby, the wind pulling at his clothes and hair and as he turned the moon lit a white chemise and white teeth in a swarthy complexion.

'Tobias! Dear friend! I did not expect to see you here.' Pietro indicated the square with a sweep of his arm.

Toby said nothing, just walked closer – his daggers back in their sheaths, hands sweaty and bloodied.

'At least the wind begins to ease. But it has been such a nuisance,' Pietro continued. 'I sail to a tight schedule.'

'And no doubt, I'm part of your schedule,' Toby finally ground out.

Pietro's eyes grew wide with surprise and then he grinned. 'You know? Oh that is delightful.' He was charm itself. 'When did you work it all out?'

'Possibly when I met you. My skin crawled. But confirmed with my brother's death.' Toby showed no emotion, just a calm deliverance of the facts. 'How much did they pay you, Pietro?'

'A chest of the most perfect sapphires and rubies – almost a king's ransom. It is the making of the Vigia house.'

'On the blood of my brother. As I said, you would kill grandmothers to succeed.'

By now, the two were a sword length from each other.

'And I replied *not grandmothers*, did I not? But your brother? You should be pleased that he was worth so much because I detected a certain aggravation in your manner when talking about … who was it now? Ah, *Julius of Lübeck*.'

Toby held tight to the rage that boiled inside him. He remembered something Mehmet had told him once – guidance from an Arab book of Faith: *The strong man is one who controls himself when he is in a fit of rage.* It was a good philosophy. 'For how long did you know he was my brother?' he asked.

'That took some time to work out. You are clever at disguise, the pair of you. But there was the occasional mannerism from your Julius – not often, mark you. But ultimately it was like watching someone walking with their shadow. In the end, they are inseparable. I am nothing if not observant.'

'Observant enough to know when a young son of the Gisborne house mentions purple in the marketplace, he means something valuable beyond your wildest desires.'

'Ah, Tobias,' Petro sighed. 'I wish we could have been on the same side. I suspect we would have worked brilliantly together. I could have given you anything you wished for.'

The wind had eased to the occasional puff and those words, *anything you wished for*, dropped like boulders between the two men. The moon had finally won its battle and hung in the night sky, holding the clouds at bay, and the weak beams illuminated the heavy but handsome features of the young Genovese. His hair had tangled and continued to lift when the breeze shifted around them.

'Come with me, Toby. We can perhaps reconcile this. You will find you have to come with me anyway so why not come like the civilised and urbane man that you are…'

'I *have* to?' Toby sneered. 'You think? To reconcile the death of my brother? You jest, Pietro.' He turned his back on the merchant and began to walk away. One dagger slipped from the sleeve of his chemise into his left hand and his right hand curled round the hilt of his sword.

Keep walking, listen for his approach…

His heart rattled as he continued on with his back to the enemy. With every beat, he expected to feel a blade slide into his spine. But he kept on walking.

'Don't move away from me, you little Devil-turd,' Pietro's voice chased after him.

But Toby kept on toward a row of ancient olive trees.

'Do you hear, you little piece of shit?' Pietro hastened across the square which was lit by the exhausted and windblown moon. Toby was unsure if he would have preferred the dark and the wind, but he stepped swiftly behind a tree as a sword stroke slammed into the trunk. He swallowed when he realised it was at head height. This was no game.

'Ugly spawn like you should be drowned at birth.' Pietro dragged at his blade, levering it up and down to try and release it

Toby ran to the next tree and the one after that as the moon hid again. Pietro tottered backward as his sword came free, but then he dashed on with speed, his face snarling. Toby yelled, 'Catch me, then, Pietro. Drown me.'

Pietro swung his blade at Toby and Toby ducked, the sword once again lodging in green and hungry wood.

'The Limnians won't thank you for shredding their little square, my friend,' Toby taunted, dashing to the next tree and the next.

'Fight me!' screamed Pietro. 'Coward!'

'But I am a minstrel, not a swordsman, Pietro. We have talked about this. I fight with word and song and sometimes I am,' he somersaulted as he had been taught long ago in Pigna, 'poetry in motion!'

'A coward – a snivelling, shrunken Godforsaken coward!'

'You want to kill me? But how do you barter for the purple then?'

Pietro halted, 'You know?' He seemed genuinely surprised.

'I'm nothing if not clever, my friend. Just like you, God forbid,' Toby said, circling the tree and stepping as if across the Parisian rooftops, coming behind Pietro, slicing his sword through the dark.

Maybe there was a faint shadow, maybe astute Pietro heard the almost indefinable intake of breath as Toby swung, but he turned and with a resounding clash, met edge with edge.

The fight began.

Toby's strength was his sure-footedness, his low centre of balance allowing him to move quickly from one stance to another. But they were matched so unfairly – Pietro's reach was longer and his arms bent easily and moved smoothly. Toby's elbows were almost fused together, the penalty of his build.

Slash, parry, uppercut, block – jarring blows that almost separated Toby's shoulder from his arm. But speed was his friend as he dipped under Pietro's sword length, dragging his own tip down that insultingly white chemise and leaving a decorative red trail behind.

Pietro looked down and with a rising roar, he crashed the pommel of his sword upon Toby's wrist, bones splintering and Toby's sword falling away, impotent.

But Toby turned again across to the other side of the square, his steps as delicate as if he danced a *carole*. Ignoring the sickening pain in his wrist, his left hand twitched a dagger. 'You want more perhaps, Pietro. Come then, I'm waiting…'

Pietro ran toward him. 'I'll kill you…'

'So you say,' sang Toby. 'But to what effect?' And he rolled toward the harbour edge.

Pietro kept coming, blind with anger, spittle on his lips as he swore all manner of curses upon Toby. Indeed blind to the water that lay at the harbour edge, filled with the night's debris – damp and slimy. His foot shot out and he fell hard on his hip, his sword flying forward, hitting the rockwall and tumbling into the splashing waves.

Toby leaped on him like a wild dog, pushing the point of his dagger against the Genovese's neck, feeling no pain as the battle fever raged red and powerful through his body. 'You move,' he said. 'I skewer you.'

But Pietro bucked Toby off like a horse and Toby tumbled and rolled, noticing two familiar figures approaching along the harbour edge. 'Stupid…' Toby muttered, but who to? Himself? His friends? Or perhaps to the Genovese trader who swayed on his knees, hands at his neck trying to staunch the violent flow of blood that pumped from an obscene hole.

Ahmed and Mehmet had halted on the side of the square as Toby called. 'He's dying. It won't take long.' He turned back to Pietro who was the colour of a winding sheet and who had collapsed to the ground. 'You are, you know. Any moment your breath will be your last. And I want you to know that your ship and cargo is forfeit and that the Vigia name and honour, *if* there was any such thing, shall die with you. You discredit your parents. Did they not send you to *build* the house of Vigia? And you destroyed it.' He tutted.

'You little piece of goat dung…' Pietro whispered, 'I curse…'

'No,' Toby said, moving away. 'I think not. You are unable. Adieu, Pietro.'

He had done what he set out to do and didn't want to watch the man die. He pushed between Ahmed and Mehmet and walked away to the waterside where he leaned over and began to vomit, not stopping until he thought he had been turned inside out. Then he fainted, the light closing over him and the world becoming comfortingly dark.

Chapter Thirteen

✕

He hung weightless, upside down but bouncing rhythmically. Opening his eyes, he saw the cobbles beneath him and the harbour to the side.

'He doesn't cope with violence, does he?' Ahmed was saying.

'He has seen plenty in his time, Ahmed,' Mehmet replied. 'This is different. It has been a blood feud…'

'Put me down,' Toby thumped Ahmed in the back. 'Put me down, now!'

He was hoisted off Ahmed's shoulder with no grace and planted on the ground like a sack of flour.

'Thank you, Ahmed,' the galley master said with clear sarcasm. 'Thank you for carrying me to the galley while I was indisposed.'

Toby ignored him. 'I need to see Father Giorgios immediately. I'll be back before you sail.' He ran, holding his smashed wrist, hearing Ahmed and Mehmet calling, aware that his legs felt like delicate barley stalks. Out of the town, along the track they had followed only weeks before, stopping when he reached the steepest point. His wrist ached with sickening pain but he had no time to indulge himself and jogged on, praying to the Blessed Mary for help. He stopped once more, dizziness threatening to engulf him, bending over, spitting out yellow bile.

Toby, for Christ's sake. Get on – do this for me!

Tomas, he thought, I'm trying. Truly I am…

Looking up, he could see the small basilica gleaming in stark simplicity by the light of the moon. He ran the last distance yelling to Father Giorgios, pounding on the plain wooden door.

It was flung open by the priest. 'In God's name, what goes?'

'Father, I must speak… I must…' Toby gasped.

The priest grabbed him as he staggered and guided him inside to a stool to the side of the door. The interior was lit by a myriad of candles, the walls covered in many icons.

'It's my wrist – it's broken…' Toby said. 'But that isn't why I am here. Father, the icon and the men … I killed three men…'

The priest looked at him, frowned, recognising the face. 'You were here when the icon disappeared…' He bent to Toby's wrist and Toby had no doubt what the man thought – that Toby should be consigned to the Devil. 'I shall bind this for you and you can tell me why you killed three men.'

He returned through a door behind the altar – such a plain altar compared to Sancta Sophia, but the walls were alive with faces, with gold leaf, with ruby red and lapis blue. He sat on another stool in front of Toby, taking his right arm gently, laying it on his knee. He placed splints either side and then wound linen round, Toby gritting his teeth as bones ground and moved. But the priest bound it tight and the pain eased a fraction.

Probably used to winding the dead…

'Father, I killed three men. But I was justified. Can you listen without judgement, just for a moment?'

'I will…' he fingered his crucifix.

Toby told him the story that began with an upstart merchant hearing the word "purple" from a child's lips and which ended with the same merchant's death this night. Father Giorgios' face filled with sorrow and anxiety and Toby understood. So many laws of his God had been disregarded – against theft, avarice, dishonesty, murder… The priest ran fingers through his hair.

'Tobias, I am here to spread God's word and what you tell me sickens me.' He moved to the altar, knelt and stayed there for some time. Toby longed for the man to move, to make haste with him to the village. Now…

'I am astonished that your friends should try to steal the purple, but that is a matter for civil law, not for the Church. The Komemnoi? I have no feeling for them at all except to be pleased the woman and her daughter have found God and will be safe. But more than anything, I am desolate about the lives lost.'

'Father…'

'No one has the right to take another's life!' The priest stood his ground. 'My duty is to this island and its people, Master Tobias. Since you were last here, they grieve for the loss of their icon. Of all that you have told me, the fact that you know where the icon is, is the only thing that gladdens by heart.'

'Father, we have no time to debate this. If we don't go down to Myrina now and if you don't tell the Guard that the three who died were intent on removing the icon to Venezia, then as representatives of Byzantine law, they can impound the ship and the icon. Most importantly, unless the Patriarch intercedes on your behalf, it may be some time or even never before it is returned.'

Tobias watched the priest, watched him wrestling with his conscience, deciding then and there that the man was simple and had been sent from Mount Athos because he would cause few ripples … but he splinted bones well.

Jesu, but I am tired. I just want this over…

With a horn lamp swinging in his hand, the priest loped down the track, Toby puffing behind. From the lower slope, they could see torches in the square, raised voices filling the last of the night.

Three guards stood over the body of Pietro Vigia and a crowd of men gathered round them. Everyone clamoured when they saw the priest till he called for quiet. He spoke to the guards so that the populace could hear, telling them that the dead man and two others were thieves, intent on removing the icon of the Theotokos to Venezia and selling it.

'This young man knew and tried to stop them. His wrist was broken in the attack.'

The guards were older than Ahmed and comfortable with their island life, leaning on their spears but the fourth was younger, probably seconded from Constantinople, Toby thought, the fellow's leather spotless and unscarred. He was sharper too and said, 'One of the men in the alley looked to have been killed from behind. Does that not imply that this man,' he indicated Tobias, 'was doing the following?'

Toby bit his cheek but admitted the truth of it. 'I knew they followed me and I hid in the alcove. I attacked while I still had my life. These men have followed me since I was in Limnos last and attacked me because I knew they had the icon on their ship. The galleymaster Ahmed will confirm this.'

Ahmed stood on the edge of the circle and stepped forward. 'It is true. I have seen cuts and bruises on him since we left Limnos.'

'The fact is they accused this man's brother of stealing,' Father Giorgios said. 'He was tried by the court in Constantinople and punished and he died from his wounds. But *this* man is the thief,' he pointed at Pietro's body, 'and the icon…'

'I have it here, Father.' Ahmed held out a dirty linen bundle.

Toby's eyes opened wide but he dared not meet Ahmed's steady gaze.

The priest began to unwrap the linen, the crowd watching, whispering, and then lapsing into silence as the priest held the icon aloft. 'I think we owe this young man and his friend great thanks. We have suffered great distress and now we have our Theotokos returned. May he go?' he asked the guards.

The seasoned guards nodded. 'As you say, Father, we have our Theotokos returned. He may go.'

Toby muttered his thanks and hastened to walk away with Ahmed but the priest called them back and spoke very quietly. 'Master Tobias, you will have noticed I was expeditious with the facts just then…'

Not such a simple priest…

'This holy icon represents a kind of surety for the Limnians and we have suffered a collective demoralisation since it vanished. Things will change now that it is back. I thank you.'

'Father, I don't require gratitude, but my brother…'

'He was forgiven by Patriarch George, was he not?' the priest said.

'Yes, but he needs to be forgiven by the island of Limnos.'

'I see.' The priest turned the bundle over in his hands. 'Then be assured. He is indeed forgiven by the island, by the Patriarch and therefore by God.'

Toby's lips twitched in thanks and he inclined his head and then walked away with the Arab, holding his bound arm against his chest and feeling the ache with each surge of the blood round his body.

You did it for me, Toby. Not just a boring minstrel after all. I'm proud, brother…

But Toby knew his brother's nature. Forgiveness? Maybe. But revenge was all and it left him feeling empty to his soul.

'Ahmed, the icon…' Toby walked as if weighted down by anchor chains.

'We went aboard the ship.'

'How?'

'As one does. Hopped across the wale.'

'Don't patronise me.' Toby's temper began to shorten.

'Mehmet knows you well, little music-man. He knew immediately why you ran to the priest, so we went to Vigia's galley, told the crew their master was dead and the ship like to be impounded. Mehmet waved around some parchment, probably a recipe for poisons, and said that it gave him the authority to search the vessel for a stolen icon that must be returned to Limnos forthwith.'

'And they let you walk all over the galley without so much as a single protest?'

'My men were armed.'

'Christ…'

'By the grace of Allah the Beneficent, we found the icon under Pietro's bedding. Stupid man! We also found a small coffer that Faisal smashed open…'

'Tomas' death price.'

'The gems are yours to keep.'

'Mary Mother! Give them to lepers, to the poor and sick, to someone who needs them. They represent my brother's life.'

As if he could take them, he thought. Every time he handled anything purchased with the sale of those stones, he would see a severed hand, or an eyeless socket. He shivered and his skin prickled.

'As you wish,' Ahmed said as they reached *Durrah*.

'Pietro's cargo?'

'I have taken the ship,' Ahmed said mildly.

'You've what?' Toby grabbed at Ahmed's arm.

'I replaced half his crew with half mine and put Faisal in charge. I filled my own benches with the rest of his crew and have chained all Vigia's, promising them their freedom to stay or go when we reach Chandax. If they behave as I expect them to.'

'All the crew were there when you boarded?'

'Two were missing.' The Arab scrutinised Toby. 'As I am sure you are aware. In any case, it was more important to get the ship and the cargo away from any likely interference from the authorities.'

'But that's piracy!'

'You think? I see it more as spoils of war. Do you forget that war was declared upon us, and especially on you and Tomas when we reached Chandax? Probably even before that?'

Toby had not forgotten that first attack when he had almost become a piece of *tesserae*. 'What will you do with the cargo?' he asked in awe of the speed with which Mehmet and Ahmed had moved. Ah, how Tomas would have loved the theatre of it all.

'Some I will claim by right because my crew sails the galley. I am sure my lord Gisborne will agree. But the rest goes to he and Saul. And the ship? I fancy to begin a fleet, music-man. What do you think of that? With a little modification so that she no longer resembles the Vigia vessel, she will be a fitting companion for my *Durrah*.'

Mehmet greeted them as they jumped aboard the galley. The sky had lightened to dove-grey shot with the soft shades of a peach. Lighter still in the distance where Toby's life had changed irrevocably. Myrina had begun to stretch, shutters and doors being thrown open. He frowned and turned his back on all the east had to offer.

'Cast off!' Ahmed called as the three men stood at the helm. 'Ready the larboard oars.'

Within moments *Durrah* had begun to break through the morning sea. Mehmet pulled Toby toward the stern castle, ordering him to sit whilst he checked the grossly swollen wrist with its blue and violet bruises. He tutted as he re-splinted and bandaged it.

'It may mend awkwardly, Tobias, but I shall watch it. You are otherwise sound?' he asked.

Toby mumbled vaguely. 'No. Not really.'

'I understand…'

'Do you, Mehmet?' Anguish tightened Toby's nerves and muscles. 'Because I'm sure I do not. A sennight ago I would not have cared if Tomas had gone from my life. But now that he is and by the very manner of it, I feel immense sorrow and profound rage.'

'Even though revenge was yours?'

'Even so. We were twins before we were brothers and that is the nub of the issue. It is a soul thing that defies any priest or physician to explain it. We were joined to each other the way one's shadow is joined at the foot.'

'Like I said, Tobias, I understand…'

Toby knew Mehmet would comprehend the raw emotion swirling through his soul more than anyone. He also knew that with Tomas' death, he was dry and wrinkled with no expectation of joy or light.

'Tobias, you and I have been kindred, have we not? For a long time. And I see in you what others may not. I see a heart that is bigger than a giant's and you take so much into that heart. So I say this to you, my friend. *Feel* your pain. Do not run from it but equally do not let it consume you. Eventually there will be a blink of a time when you notice something inherently lovely. Do not reject it, let it enter your spirit. In time, your rage will quench and you will be able to live with your loss.'

Toby said nothing, just sat in the stern castle long after Mehmet had left.

Of course the physician was right. There *were* blinks in time, but mostly the voyage passed with Toby unresponsive to all. Ahmed, perhaps with orders from Mehmet, let him be and he was glad.

Once, Dana sat with him and they talked.

'What shall you do, Tobias, on your return?' she asked. Her hair blew free in the wind and as once before, he was surprised at how beautiful she was. He had caught the glances between she and Michael Sarapion often.

He shrugged, 'And you?'

'I return to Lyon.'

'With Michael?'

'He says so…'

'What shall you do in Lyon?'

'I am an experienced embroiderer with knowledge of textiles. My family will welcome me back…'

'Your story begs interest, Dana.'

'It is for another time, Tobias.'

'Then tell me, why did you leave Lyon?'

'Which brings me back to the story I said was for another time.' She looked up at the mast, and then leaning her head back and closing her eyes, she heaved a sigh. 'I left Lyon to go to Constantinople for two reasons – on business for my cloth-merchant father and also for Sir Guy of Gisborne.'

She opened her eyes and stared at Toby then, daring him to ask anything else but he nodded politely and subsided and she closed her eyes again, effectively locking him out. Something about the Lyonnaise cloth-merchant rang bells with Toby, but he let it slide as the familiar heaviness settled upon him.

In Chandax, a small leper's hostel run by a Knight of Saint John benefited from a casket of gems and Toby whispered to the wind that night, 'More than free, Tomas. Debts paid ten times and more. Go in peace, my brother.'

Venezia was pristine calm in the early morning as they docked one galley behind the other. No one met them and when he heard Ahmed send a messenger to the villa, Toby leaped over the wale and allowed himself to be swallowed by the dockside crowd. He lowered his head, even though folk called surprised and joyful greetings, and just kept doggedly on, responding to no one.

They had been away a three month? Maybe four? He had lost track and cared less but he noticed the cathedral had grace now and that some buildings sat almost at the water's edge. Venezia was a curious place – he never could understand its ancestors building along the canals of this swampy archipelago. Security? Didn't they understand that violence and death would find you anywhere?

He left the town behind, wandering the tracks and flat bridges from islet to islet. He wanted something to stir his heart, to say, 'You are home, Tobias. Welcome back to your heart home.'

He waited for it to happen with a kind of desperation but as he approached the villa, his heart sank because even the sight of those longed-for walls struck no note. He headed for the long stretches of sedge – there was a place he and William had created with stones and old planks and he sat there watching the summer sun dust the water with gold leaf, watched the lacy wings of insects beat the air, listened to the contented honks and squeaks of water fowl.

Once a teal floated by, pausing in front of Toby, its legs hanging down, studying him, waiting, wondering and then bored, it began to paddle and glided on. In the distance he heard the bells ring for Sext and Biddy's voice chiding those within to table.

But still he sat.

'Life has changed, then,' the bass tones of his lord and master sounded behind him. He didn't look round.

'So it seems,' he replied.

'There are no words…' Gisborne began.

'None,' Toby forestalled any condolence.

'Toby…' My God, that voice could melt the blackest heart. Even in men. Toby jumped up.

'My lord, my heart is not here. I need to leave. I must go to Pigna, to my parents.'

'Toby, of course you must go. Take as long as you need.'

'No. I mean that my time with you is done.'

Gisborne folded his tall frame onto the temporary bench seat and Toby noticed the finely carved hands that had accompanied him on the *vielle* of an evening. 'I see,' Gisborne said.

'I am sorry.'

'Why should you apologise? You must do what is right for you and your own life. It would be churlish of me to expect otherwise.'

A vision of Lady Ysabel floated between them as Toby realised how this man's manner and tolerance had been moulded by her love. He had turned toward Toby and it was more than the aesthete in Toby could do not to admire the sharp planes of his face and the straight, uncompromising nose, but especially the clear blue eyes that were never ambiguous.

'Will you let me say one thing?' Gisborne asked.

Toby nodded, picking up a pebble and pitching it into the canal, watching the ripples spread outward to touch the sedge, the bank, then fading.

Like life…

'You are kindred in my house, Tobias. You are my brother, Lady Ysabel's confidante, William's uncle, his best friend. And so it shall ever be. The gates will always be open…'

Toby's eyes prickled. 'Where is Guillaume?'

'In Lyon. He escorted Ariella and Lady Ysabel there not long after you left. Jehan de Clochard died suddenly and Amé, his wife, wished to sell the business. Instead, Saul and I offered to run it in a partnership with her, and Ariella has gone there to represent us and help the widow until her family returns.'

'And Guillaume?'

'He has a good head for business and where Ariella is, then it seems he shall be also…'

'That is happy news, then. Not for Jehan, of course, but for his wife, and good fortune for all of you, I think.' Toby had a flash then, of Dana.

'Dana is Jehan de Clochard's daughter, isn't she?'

'Indeed,' said Gisborne but not expanding further.

'And William?'

'Inside.'

'He is very quiet.'

'You noticed,' Gisborne said with a smile in his voice. He flipped a pebble after Toby's. 'He has been lost without you. I should not say so but it is true.'

'My lord…'

'Truths hurt, Toby, but life is full of truths.' Gisborne let the words hover. 'Tomas will be missed. He too was a brother and I loved him like my own.'

And there it was.

The defining moment.

This man who orchestrated, arranged and ordered, whose smile was rare, and astonishing for that reason, had said he loved Tomas as a brother. Toby tried to deflect the emotion welling inside before it drowned him. 'You have a good cargo, my lord. The Gisborne and Ben Simon houses should do well.'

'I expected nothing less from Ahmed and Mehmet. But do you remember what I said when you were all about to embark? I said if it looks at all as if sword points await, I would prefer to sell an extra secret than lose my close friends. I stand by that.'

Toby looked away and noticed a cobweb stretched across the sedge and a spider walking delicately from one filament to another. A snowy duck feather lay on the damp ground and in the distance, dogs barked.

'Tristan and Isolde?'

'Oh yes.' The wry response from Gisborne made Toby smile as the knight levered his length up. 'Come in when you are ready.' He left, his feet crunching dried leaves and twigs.

It had been an age since Toby had been mindful of the minutiae of life and he confessed to a kind of muted relief that his soul was not quite dead yet. But he needed to leave and so he walked to the stables, glad of Biddy keeping everyone eating, finding his stocky little mare who nickered as he approached. With difficulty, using one hand and the help of a mare who was seasoned and placid, he saddled and bridled her, finding a purse of coins in his saddlebags and thanking the Saints for Gisborne's kindness. He would buy clean clothes and food at the nearest market.

'Toby?'

God in all Your Glory, please no…

He sighed and turned round at the sound of that childish voice.

'Christs and the Saints, William! You are almost taller than me. Look at you!' He took the boy by a shoulder and looked into the charming face. 'You have learned to be a knight while I have been gone?'

'Yes.'

The lisp had faded, along with babyhood. All gone. So much gone.

'Johannes has been teaching me as Guillaume took Mama and Ariella to Lyon. In three years, Papa said I might go to Mama's cousins in Aquitaine to be a squire.'

'Ah, William, you will like that. Castles and moats, feasts and tourneys…'

'But I don't want to leave. I want to be like Guillaume and Papa and learn to trade.'

Toby's mouth tipped up, remembering Guillaume's dry manner. Still, the boy could do worse than model himself on the half-brothers. 'Then tell your papa, William. It is better to say what you truly feel. There is more to gain with truths.'

William gave Toby one of those looks that reminded him so much of Gisborne – the considering look from clear eyes. It skewered Toby and he reached out and smoothed the young boy's feathery black hair.

'Papa said you are leaving.' The child's voice held a faint tremor. He was so prescient – hadn't asked why Toby hadn't come in to see him, even to say goodbye.

Oh Jesu, my little William…

William walked back to the door of the stable and reached round the corner, revealing something that had been Toby's heart and soul. 'You forgot your *vielle*.'

The instrument glistened in his small grasp. Toby had always likened his *vielle* to a woman – its curves those of a female breast or hips, its strings those of a heart that must be plucked. Lady Ysabel's ribbons danced blithely in the breeze that whispered from the water's edge and Toby wished it still leaned against the corner of his chamber.

'I had thought to leave it behind, William. I don't feel much like singing these days.'

'Oh,' William laid the *vielle* on a heap of oaten hay and it chastened Toby, flirting with his sensibilities.

Jesu, he could even feel his hand twitch. Perhaps one last stroke of its curves? *No!*

He stepped back as if stung and William took the opportunity to touch his arm. 'You have a splint like Mama had a long time ago.'

'Yes. I broke my wrist.'

'But it will get better. Mama's did and she can do anything now.'

'Well I hope so. I need both arms.'

'Toby?'

'Yes?'

'If I must be honest with my Papa, may I be honest with you?'

'Lord, William! What have you done? Stolen the Doge's rings?'

'Of course not! But I cannot sing without you and I have no one to play tables with. Please don't go, Toby. You are my best friend.'

Best friend…

Toby remembered another best friend that William had lost.

'I lose all my best friends. I lost Ulric and now I am losing you. Maybe I will lose Triss and Iss and Mama and Papa.'

'Stop, William, stop,' Toby knelt by the little boy. 'Listen, let me put The Maid in her stall and we shall go to our place by the river and talk, yes?'

They walked together as they had so often and anyone watching would have just smiled and said history repeats – a boy and his friend.

They sat on the bench so lately vacated by Sir Guy, the canal at their toes. Toby longed to thrust bare feet into the water, but this was not the time.

'William, life is full of change. We cannot expect it never to alter. Every day is a new day…' Momentarily, Toby wondered whether he spoke to his own frailties, rather than William's. 'Things can't stay the same.'

'Why not? If we are happy, why can't things stay the same?'

God only knows…

'Because sometimes God has a purpose for us all, Wills, even you. And you do Him no credit by thinking otherwise.'

'But Toby, aren't you happy here? Haven't you liked being my best friend?'

'Of course. You have been the light shining in my darkness.'

William's dark eyebrows drew together for a moment and he opened his mouth as if to speak but then subsided, expelling a sigh that Toby felt drift over his hand and he wanted to catch it and take it with him.

'I need to travel to see my mama and papa, William. Something of great significance happened and I need to tell them.'

'About Tomas? You need to tell them he died?'

'You know?'

'Papa said.' Williams' eyes filled with tears. 'I loved Tomas.'

Toby rubbed William's soft head and the child lay against him. He recalled the first time they had sung together, that tense time in front of the fallen Templar, Robert Halsham. William looked up at him as Toby delivered his instructions for the song and he had never really recovered from the deep sea blue of that moment. There was intensity, bound with admiration and it took the wind out of Toby's sails. From that moment he loved the child as if William had sprung from his own loins.

Then why do you seek to leave forever?

Goddamn, thought Toby. I need no conscience voice now…

'Toby, please come back.'

'I shall make a deal with you. When my mama and papa are feeling stronger after the news of Tomas, then I will think about returning. In the meantime, you must live your life to the full. Can you do that?'

'If you say…'

'I do. Life is not for wasting.'

Make sure you listen to yourself, Toby…

The two sat together, Toby feeling the warmth of the child leaning close.

'Toby?'

'Yes?'

'Can we sing together now?' William's voice thickened and he crushed his face into Toby's tunic, the tears soaking through to Toby's skin.

'Of course,' Toby said lightly. 'But how do we sing if you weep? Stop now and join me.'

Thus Toby, who had not sung a note since leaving for the east, cleared his throat and began to sing the first voice:

'Somer is y-comen in,
loudë sing, cuckóu!'

And as he sang the chorus, William joined him. At first they both sang quietly and even the waterfowl would have been lucky to hear but the singing voices began to lift across the space. The sky was the delicate blue of veins in a lady's breast and the water had calmed to a reflective pool, each note falling seamlessly – no splash nor ripple to despoil.

The voices soared – two friends, one young, one older, looking at each other and it was as if an invisible and unbreakable cord wound around, binding them together, and Toby knew he would return.

The song finished and Toby placed his thumb under the child's eyes, wiping away the tears. 'Can you take my *vielle* and place it in my chamber, William? I do not want to risk dropping it.'

'Are you coming with me?'

Toby sighed. William was nothing if not persistent. 'No. I leave to visit my parents, as I said I must.'

'But you *will* come home?'

Toby didn't answer immediately, just grabbed William, scruffed him and tussled and then they walked back to the stables hand in hand. Kneeling, he hugged the boy and said, 'I have missed you so much, my little William, now get you gone with my *vielle*.'

He watched William pick up the instrument with great tenderness and walk out the door. 'And be careful!' he called after him. 'Don't let those dogs touch it!'

William's chortle floated back and when enough time had passed, he mounted the horse and he and The Maid picked their way over the bridge from the islet. He looked back just once and Gisborne stood at the gates of the villa. Toby lifted his bandaged arm and waved and Sir Guy saluted back.

It was enough.

He felt the purses at his waist, the burned one filled with the folds of a song.

One day, Tomas, he thought, one day I shall sing about Zoë.

But in the meantime I have a great *chanson de geste* I must sing…

T H E   E N D

ACKNOWLEDGEMENTS

First and foremost, to Jenovesia and Jax Porteo from www.dwarfaware.com who were so helpful when I knew nothing.

As always, thank you to John Hudspith, my editor, without whom I am unable to exist. His expertise, his wise words and his humour have lit many a dark moment as Tobias moved forward.

Thank you too, to Pat and Jane for their beta-reading and their willingness to tell it like it is.

To Simon for being the most generous writing friend one could have. Our friendship goes back to the inception of our independent careers and I owe him much.

To Jane V for her unstinting research in Istanbul. She took time from her own daily commitments to walk Tobias's steps and to find the unfindable.

To my intuitive cover designer and typesetter – Clare Batten.

To my e-formatter, Daniel Gillan, for swift and professional delivery.

To Tim Carrington, sea captain and rogue, for the coast, wind and tide information of the Aegean and Adriatic Seas.

To writers and readers online for their continued companionship and solidarity.

To my little muses – the JRT's who have sat patiently sometimes, and not so patiently most times, whilst I wrote. But especially to T, the littlest one of all who found life was just too hard in old age…

And finally to my husband who is my agent, my publisher and so much more – quite simply, thank you.